"Don't look now, but Paradise Beach's biggest gossip is watching us."

"Maybe we ought to give her something to talk about," Jillie said, a mischievous sparkle coming into her eyes. "Wanna arrest me?"

"I'd rather do something much more exciting." Without another word, he swept her close, bent her back over his arm, and proceeded to kiss her with thorough wickedness."

Jillie was stunned. She hadn't been in any way prepared for his kiss. Not that that would have made much difference. Something about being wrapped in Blaise Corrigan's arms with his hot mouth pressed to hers was enough to blow nearly every circuit in her brain.

Never had she imagined that a kiss could be this dangerous. It was like taking an unexpected roller-coaster ride in the dark, with no idea what curves and dips lay ahead.

Her heart slammed into high gear and an exhilaration not far from fear gripped her. *No!* shouted some rational voice in her mind. *No!* She couldn't afford this. Not now. Not with her life overflowing with problems.

Other Avon Books by
Sue Civil-Brown

CARRIED AWAY

Coming Soon

CHASING RAINBOW

SUE CIVIL-BROWN

Letting Loose

AVON BOOKS ◆ NEW YORK

AVON BOOKS, INC.
1350 Avenue of the Americas
New York, New York 10019

Copyright © 1998 by Susan Civil-Brown
Inside cover author photograph by David Ewart Photography
Published by arrangement with the author
Library of Congress Catalog Card Number: 97-94076
ISBN: 0-380-72775-7
www.avonbooks.com/romance

First Avon Books Printing: February 1998

AVON TRADEMARK REG. U.S. PAT. OFF. AND IN OTHER COUNTRIES, MARCA REGISTRADA, HECHO EN U.S.A.

Printed in the U.S.A.

WCD 10 9 8 7 6 5 4 3

Letting Loose

One

Just as Jillie McAllister turned into her driveway, a
huge dog leaped out of a shrub right in front of her.
Instead of continuing its dash, it froze, looking
straight at her, pinned by the glare of her headlights.

Instinctively, she braked and wrenched the wheel
to avoid hitting the dog, then heard a sickening thud
and clang as she struck her neighbor's mailbox.

"Oh, hell," she swore as her car jolted to a halt. Just
what she needed, another bill.

The cause of it all stared at her for a few moments,
as if defying her, and calmly lifted its leg to relieve
itself on her front tire. Tossing one last look in Jillie's
direction, the dog then darted off into the night.

"You stupid animal," she shouted after him, feeling
mortally insulted, "if you'd just kept running to begin
with, I wouldn't be in this mess! Did you have to pee
on my car, too?"

"Who are you talking to?"

Startled by the deep male voice that seemed to be coming from nowhere, Jillie turned and found herself looking at one of the most intimidating figures she had ever seen. Worse, he was a cop.

"Oh, shit," she muttered under her breath. "Oh, shit."

He stepped closer, into the beam of her headlights, giving her the full force and impact of his size and uniform. He loomed over her, his uniform as crisply starched and pressed as if he had just stepped off a recruiting poster.

And he didn't look happy at all. In fact, he appeared to be in a very bad mood.

"Who are you talking to?" he repeated, an edge of impatience in his voice.

"The dog."

"What dog?"

Jillie leaned out her window and waved in the general direction the dog had taken. "He just ran away."

"Turn off your engine and lights, please. I'll need to see your operator's license, vehicle registration, and proof of insurance."

Oh, wonderful! As if life hadn't dealt her enough bad turns lately, now she was in trouble with the law. Scowling, she did as she was told. Arguing would only cause more trouble. She switched off her lights and ignition.

He had a flashlight, one of those really big ones, and he pointed it in at her, watching as she nervously fumbled in her purse for her license and insurance card. Of course, because she was nervous, her fingers didn't seem to work right, and her wallet kept slipping out of her hands. Finally she managed to find both items and give them to him.

"Registration?" he repeated impatiently.

That was in the glove box, only her glove box was

full of gasoline receipts, repair receipts, store receipts, and candy wrappers . . . and the compartment light was out. Piece by piece she pulled papers out of the compartment, peering at them in the near dark, trying to read them. Rapidly a pile of scraps began to build on the floorboards.

"I can't see," she finally said in a burst of utter frustration. "I know it's here, but I can't see." She waved a handful of small papers at him. "I couldn't tell the registration from a credit card receipt!"

"I can see why."

She wanted to cringe.

Obligingly enough, however, he came around to the far side of her car, opened the door, and pointed the flashlight right at her glove compartment, revealing the extent of the mess.

"I guess I need to clean this out," she said on a nervous laugh. He didn't say a word, making her even more uneasy.

Finally she found it. Somehow the registration, which was only a few months old, had sifted to the bottom of all the other papers, some of which were three and four years old. God, it was embarrassing. Mutely she handed it to him.

He brought his flashlight to bear on her license and registration, then pointed it at her again. Behind it he was an almost invisible, looming shadow.

"Please step out of the vehicle and keep your hands in plain view."

Oh, God! Was she going to be arrested? For knocking over a mailbox? "Look," she began to babble nervously, "I didn't mean to hit the mailbox. I'll pay for it, I promise. It's just that this dog was sitting right in the driveway and I swerved to avoid it . . ." She put her hands up helplessly as she stepped out and faced him. "I know I shouldn't have done that. I've heard a million times how you shouldn't swerve to avoid an animal because you could get yourself or someone else killed, but... it's been a long night. I've been working since four, it's nearly two, and I'm just so tired, I'm not sure I can even see straight..."

Jillie trailed off, suddenly realizing that might not be the best thing to admit under the circumstances. Could you be arrested for driving when you were too tired?

He pointed his flashlight right at her eyes, making her blink rapidly. "Have you had anything to drink tonight?"

"Of course not!" And then, with a creeping sense of horror, she remembered that a customer had spilled a beer on her not one hour ago, just before closing time. God, she smelled like a brewery!

Then she really started to babble. "The beer smell, you mean? Oh, really, I'm working as a waitress and someone spilled a beer on me a little while ago..."

The night was unseasonably cold for this part of Florida, and she began to shiver as she stood on her paved driveway wearing only her skimpy waitressing uniform.

The cop tucked her license, registration, and insurance card under the wiper blade of her car and brought his flashlight to bear on her again.

"How long have you been working as a waitress here, Ms. McAllister?"

"What difference does it make? Do you mean do I come home reeking of beer every night?"

His voice took on a hard edge. "Just answer the question. How long have you been working as a waitress here?"

"Just two weeks."

"The law gives you ten days after taking employment in the state to get a Florida operator's license and vehicle registration. You are outside that window, Ms. McAllister."

"I didn't know that! Honestly! In Massachusetts it's thirty days!"

"Ignorance of the law is no excuse."

"Why, you—" she bit the words off sharply, catching herself before she made her situation worse.

Behind the light, his silhouette became very still. "You were about to say?"

"Something so stupid that I think I'll shut my mouth."

"That might be a good idea. Now step over here. I'm going to ask you to perform some tests to determine whether your driving ability is impaired. These tests aren't required, but if you refuse to take them, your refusal can be used against you in a court of law."

Horror rooted her to the spot. "Against me? In a court of law? You can't possibly be serious! I haven't had anything to drink!"

He ignored her. "I also need to tell you that if you don't comply, I'll have to make a decision based upon what I've seen so far, and that decision will be to arrest you for DUI."

"DUI?" She felt as if she'd slipped into a nightmare of Kafkaesque proportions. "But I haven't had anything to drink!"

He was implacable. "In that case, the test won't give you any difficulties. Please step around the car and come over here."

She did as he bid, standing on the level part of her concrete driveway. "I can't see a thing," she complained. "Your flashlight blinded me."

He solved the problem by reaching into her car and turning on the headlights once again. The beams spotlighted her.

"You'll wear out my battery."

"This will only take a couple of minutes. Now, I want you to listen very carefully to my directions. I will explain each test carefully, but don't begin before I tell you to. Do you understand?"

God, this was maddening. He was treating her like a child . . . or a drunk. "Of course, I understand," she snapped. And when she got done here she was going to drive her car back and forth over that mailbox until it was smashed totally flat. "Look, Officer, this is my driveway. I'm not going anywhere. Good heavens, it's two in the morning! You don't need to see if I'm safe to drive because I'm not going to drive anywhere."

"I have no way of knowing that's true, Ms. McAllister. Now listen to my directions."

He approached, standing only a foot in front of her, reminding her again of his impressive size. *Cops!* she thought disgustedly. They all knew how to stand, how to talk, how to intimidate. This guy was a master of the technique. Only she wasn't intimidated.

"My dad was a cop," she said suddenly. Now, why had she blurted that out?

He ignored her, lifting his flashlight so that it illuminated her eyes from the side. Then he held up a pen in front of her. "Follow the tip of my pen with your eyes, please."

Back and forth, checking whether her eyes could track. That was easy enough. She began to feel cocky.

Adrenaline notwithstanding, she was exhausted. Her feet hurt, her back hurt—waitressing was a tough job, tougher than most people realized. When he asked her to do the heel-toe walk, her legs screamed mightily, and a blister on her heel caused her to stagger to one side. Immediately she turned to him.

"I have a blister," she told him. "It hurts. I can't step down on it."

"You were stepping on it a minute ago."

"But I think it just broke!" Jeez, didn't this guy believe a word she said? That was another thing she'd always hated about cops, the way they never seemed to believe anything . . .

"Try it again," he said.

She did, wincing each time she put her left foot down, but she took the nine requisite steps, then turned around and took nine steps back.

"You didn't turn correctly," he told her. "I showed you, remember? Keep your weight on one foot and turn yourself around with the other, like this." He demonstrated again.

"You're kidding, right? It's two in the morning and you just want to make this go on forever, right? I'm tired, my feet hurt, my back aches, and it was just a dumb mailbox! I told you I'd pay for it!"

Silence greeted her words and she stood there feeling more like a jerk with each passing second. *Why* couldn't she keep her mouth shut? Why? All she had to do was let this tin despot have his way for a few minutes and then she'd be able to go inside and get into bed and forget the whole damn thing had ever happened. All she had to do was pretend to be a sweet, obliging, *helpless* female long enough to get this guy out of her hair.

She was nuts.

He waited, as if wanting to be sure she was through. Then he said, "I want you to stand on one foot. Keeping your hands at your sides, hold your other foot out in front of you like this." He demonstrated. "At the same time, count to thirty."

She looked at him standing there on one foot as if it were a perfectly normal thing to do. Yes, this had to be a nightmare, and if she didn't wake up soon she was going to scream. Closing her eyes a moment, she strained for calm. "You want me to stand on one foot and count to thirty?"

"Yes, ma'am, just like this."

"You can't be serious."

"I'm perfectly serious, ma'am. Now, just do what I'm doing—"

"I told you, I haven't had a drink."

He put his foot down on the ground and his hands settled on his hips. "Are you refusing to complete the test, Ms. McAllister?"

He was going to be an ass about it, she realized. Well, she could be every bit as stubborn. Setting her chin, she folded her arms across her breasts. "I offered to pay for the mailbox. I explained how I hit it in the first place. I even explained why I smell like a brewery. You have chosen to disbelieve every word I've said. I'm not going to play out this farce any further."

Two minutes later she was sitting in the back of a police cruiser with her wrists cuffed behind her and his words still ringing in her head.

"You have the right to remain silent . . ."

Maybe, she thought glumly, it's time to ask for a lawyer.

"Christ, Blaise, she sure knocked the mailbox for a loop." It lay on the ground, its supporting pole bent at a ninety-degree angle.

Blaise Corrigan looked at the woman sitting in the back of his cruiser, then at Peter LeClerc. The younger cop was looking at the mailbox, shaking his head. "Take pictures of it, will you, Peter?"

"Sure. Want me to move the car?"

"At least so it's all the way out of the road. This is her driveway, so you don't have to move it far."

"Will do." The younger man scanned the license plate on the car. "Damn tourists. Don't know what makes 'em think they can come down to our neck of the woods and drive drunk."

"They probably do the same thing at home, Pete."

Pete shook his head. "Nah. At home they'd expect to go to jail. Here they expect us to give 'em a slap on the wrist and let 'em go because they're almighty tourists and our economy depends on 'em."

Blaise privately agreed with him. He'd sure seen enough of that attitude. On the other hand, he was fair enough to realize that those people represented only a small number of the tourists who flooded Paradise Beach. "Don't let the merchants hear you talking that way, Pete. They'll have my hide, and it's nailed to enough barn walls as it is."

"Bad time with the city council tonight, huh?" Pete asked sympathetically.

"You could say they were loaded for bear. Look, I'm taking the lady down to the station for a breath test. Just leave her car parked here in her driveway and bring the keys on down to the station."

"She's fried, huh?"

"She says she hasn't had a thing to drink, that somebody spilled a beer on her."

"Ha! That's what they all say."

Almost in spite of himself, Blaise felt a grin stretch his mouth. "You're forgetting that guy who crashed into the guard rail last year down on Waterfront. The one who climbed out of his car wailing that he was drunk and we might as well just take him away."

Pete laughed. "Okay. So one in a million is honest about it."

Jillian McAllister maintained a frosty silence when Blaise climbed into the front seat, turned over the ignition, and headed them toward the Paradise Beach police station. That was fine with Blaise. He'd heard about all he wanted to of her excuses. There she was, running down mailboxes, talking to dogs that weren't there, unable even to follow simple directions on the heel-toe walk, all the while reeking of beer. Did she really expect him to believe she hadn't been drinking?

He glanced into the rearview mirror and took a look at her. She appeared mad enough to spit. Well, that was just too damn bad. Fool woman ought to be giving thanks she hadn't killed somebody, driving around in that condition.

"You're making a mistake," she told him suddenly.

"I'll take that chance."

"I'm going to sue you for false arrest."

"You won't get too far."

Her scowl deepened; he could see it in the mirror. "You had no right to arrest me."

"Lady, under the law I had no other choice."

She subsided, sinking back into the seat and wondering where her life had gone so wrong. First there had been the divorce and the loss of everything except the clothes on her back, the old Toyota, and a small cash settlement. Then she had decided to move all the way down here from Massachussetts because she got tired of being cold all the time, and tired of people who were sure that the divorce had been all her fault and not Fielding's. Well, of course they'd feel that way, since Fielding's family had roots in the town stretching back to the *Mayflower*, while she was an interloper from Waukegan. Talk about insular!

So she'd come down here for warmth and sunshine and a place where you didn't have to have roots back to the Crusades in order to be accepted. After she'd had a chance to get to know the area and the opportunities, she was planning to take her settlement from the divorce and open a small bookstore.

If she didn't get herself convicted of DUI. God, she couldn't believe this. It wasn't as if she *had* to work in that damn lounge. No, she had just felt it would be a good way to keep busy and get to know the kind of people who vacationed here. The people who were eventually going to be her customers, she hoped. Instead, some jerk couldn't keep his hands off her posterior, and when she whirled around to tell him to cut it out, she'd bumped his arm and wound up wearing a beer. Worse, the management had insisted *she* pay to have the guy's suit cleaned.

Now Supercop here was taking her in for drunk driving when she hadn't even had the damn beer. If she had to be arrested for something, it ought to at least be for something she had *done*!

When they got to the station and he'd escorted her into the building, Jillie wished she could crawl under a rock. It was humiliating to be treated this way. At least, since it was the middle of the night, there was hardly anyone around to see. But damn it, she was going to get even for this if it took the rest of her life.

Once inside she was turned over to another officer, a much older man with gray hair and a paunch. The name on his badge said he was R. Witt. Officer Witt took her back to a small room without windows that had a video camera perched up near the ceiling.

"I'll be back in twenty minutes to take you for your breath test," he said.

"But . . ." Looking around, she felt dismayed. Not only was she being confined in a large closet; there was no place to sit. "Can't we just go do it now?"

"No, ma'am. We have to be sure you haven't had anything to eat or drink for twenty minutes before the test."

"Well, of course I haven't. I was arguing with that other policeman at least that long!"

Witt smiled slightly. "Gave him a good cap to his evening, did you? Sorry, ma'am. Rules is rules."

"Well, it's a stupid rule."

He frowned, looking genuinely concerned. "No, ma'am, really it's not. In the first place, it's the law. In the second, the state can do an awful lot of bad things to you if they prove you've been driving drunk. A lot of that proof is going to be in this here breath test. You sure wouldn't want to score over the max because you took some cough syrup, or was chewing some weird kind of gum."

Jillie had the grace to feel ashamed. "I know, you're right. It's just that I'm so tired! I've been working since four—"

"Me, too."

"Then you must be exhausted, too." She didn't figure she was going to get much sympathy here, but at least she could protest her innocence once again. "But truthfully, Officer, I haven't had anything to drink! Not even a sip of beer!"

"Then that's what the breath test will say."

Jillie rolled her eyes as the man closed the door on her. "That's what that damn cop said about those tests he gave me!"

But no one was listening. After ten or fifteen seconds, she gave up and sank to the floor, leaning her aching back against the wall. She was going to quit that job. Absolutely. Definitely. Very first thing when she got out of this place, she was going to tell the Seaside Lounge to take its job and shove it off the pier. She'd sell newspapers at stoplights before she'd take any more of the crap she had taken tonight.

Her feet and back sure wouldn't hurt any worse.

Police Chief Blaise Corrigan glanced at the black-and-white TV monitor and felt a twinge of unwanted sympathy for Jillian McAllister. Sitting there against the wall with her eyes closed, she looked lost, forlorn, and exhausted . . . as if she needed someone to take care of her.

Scowling at himself, he turned away. Regardless of how she looked, she was a drunk driver, a menace to the honest, law-abiding citizens of this community.

Maybe.

Well, the breath test would settle it, but she sure as hell hadn't been acting like a sober person. Sober people in her position generally didn't argue and threaten. Most people didn't want to piss off a cop. Then, not being able to do the heel-toe walk correctly, and refusing to do any more of the tests—it was classic combative drunk behavior.

Sitting at his desk, he shuffled through some papers, waiting only to get the results of McAllister's alcohol test. God, he was going to feel like a whipped dog come morning. He should have been in bed hours ago.

And might have been, except for the damn city council. Those jerks couldn't make up their minds whether to shrink his police force or simply erase it entirely and turn law enforcement over to the county sheriff. Both, naturally, were being promoted as cost-cutting measures.

Twits. More concerned with making a few bucks than with the safety of their own community. And Mayor Burgess—Dan Burgess, restaurant owner, bar owner, nightclub owner—was angry that the police were strictly enforcing the DUI laws, the public intoxication laws, and the open container laws.

"We have to make allowances!" he'd told Blaise this very evening. "These people come from places where the law is different! Many of them come from other countries. They don't know they're not allowed to do these things!"

Blaise seriously doubted it. He didn't know of one

country in the world where public drunkenness was permissible. "I have to protect the public," he'd replied. "The rest of the people. Particularly the *tourists* who might get run over by one of these drunks."

That didn't penetrate, but Dan was a really thick-headed guy when he had his mind fixed on something. "Look," the mayor had finally shouted, leaning over the desk, his face turning choleric, "these people are going to go home and tell everybody what a terrible time they had in Paradise Beach!"

At last, the real problem here. Not that Blaise hadn't already figured it out. "Some people go home and tell their friends the same thing because they found a cockroach in their motel room." That was a direct slam at Councilman Hegel's rent-by-the-week cottages. "Or because they got spoiled fish at a restaurant." That referred to an incident just three weeks ago at one of Dan Burgess's restaurants. The customer had wanted to cut the chef's heart out with a fileting knife, but the timely intervention of the Paradise Beach police—those useless, too-expensive cops—had prevented bloodshed. Dan hadn't been talking about going easy on tourists that night.

The mayor had turned an even darker shade of purple when that came up, nearly matching the dominant color in his tie. He'd spluttered.

Blaise hadn't given him a chance to respond. "Look, what I'm saying, gentlemen, is that you're getting better police protection for your money with my department. If you go over to the sheriff's protection, you won't get the same kind of coverage. And"—he had almost smiled as he'd played his trump card—"you *sure* won't be able to call the sheriff on the carpet and tell him to go easy on tourists, the way you're doing to me. He won't listen at all. And the damn drunks'll just keep right on getting arrested."

Cretins, Blaise thought now, rocking back in his chair and closing his weary eyes. From there it had all gone downhill. They hadn't liked having their bluff called. They also hadn't liked the fact that a group of concerned citizens had decided to show up to defend the police force.

First and foremost among the citizens' group was Mary Todd, doyenne of Paradise Beach society, an aging relic with a peppery temperament who happened to own most of the land on which the city councilmen's businesses were being operated. This naturally gave Mary an unnatural clout with the council. Blaise had long had the good sense to pay a call on Mary at least once a week and keep her informed of all the good his department was doing.

Tonight that had paid off.

"I don't care about the sensibilities of a bunch of tourists," Mary Todd had said bluntly, tapping her cane on the floor for emphasis. "When in Rome, do as the Romans. That's the rule, and hereabouts we don't tolerate drunk driving. Hell's bells, Danny, I don't want to get run over when I'm hobbling my way across the damn street, and neither does anyone else! Where's your common sense, boy?"

"Miss Todd—"

"Don't you *Miss Todd* me! Furthermore, I like having our local boys in law enforcement. I like the way I know all of them and they know me. Every one of us knows these boys—and gal, sorry, at my age a policewoman takes some getting used to—and we know we can call on them at any time. They know who the troublemakers are and where to look for 'em. No, sir, I don't want any county mountie down here driving around in his fancy patrol car, not knowing the good citizens from the bad, hiding out behind his fancy sunglasses and talking to us all like we're worms under his shiny boot!"

Blaise had felt like applauding but had wisely refrained. Sitting wearily at his desk now, he still felt like applauding. Damn if that old woman wasn't a firebrand. She'd turned the meeting topsy-turvy and had left most of the city council wondering if their leases would be canceled if they kept pursuing this matter.

Which didn't mean this was the end of it. No, give them a week or two and they'd find another reason to bring up the subject. They didn't like Blaise because he wouldn't bend on the subject of the law, and they couldn't fire him because he had a wonderful and very expensive golden parachute built into his contract—hell, this wasn't the first small town he'd chiefed in. He knew the kind of politics that went on, so he'd protected himself, like any sensible man. Getting rid of the entire police force would just about buy him out, so the council had decided to get rid of the force.

He doubted they were going to succeed—his cops were too popular with the good folks of Paradise Beach—but he was sure going to get some serious heartburn along the way.

"Chief?" Rob Witt leaned into his office. "I'm going to take the McAllister woman for the breath test now."

"I'll come along."

Jillian McAllister seemed to have fallen asleep against the wall in the holding room. She looked at them both from puffy, reddened eyes, and her expression was just about as querulous as a tired two-year-old's.

"Last step, ma'am," Rob told her cheerfully. "Just come blow in a tube for me a couple of times and we'll get this settled."

A pleasant way of putting it, Blaise thought. She might well find herself settled into a cell for the night. Of course, as sleepy as she was, she might not even notice, as long as she had someplace to lie down. Damned if he wasn't getting to that point himself.

In a nearby room Rob seated her in a chair and handed her a tube. "Now, take a deep breath and blow into this tube until you hear the beep. Easy enough, right?"

But Jillie looked suspiciously at the tube. "Do you clean this thing with something?"

"Fresh mouthpiece for every poor slob who comes in here, ma'am."

She still looked suspicious, but when he told her to take a breath and blow, she did so. Her face had nearly turned red by the time the machine beeped.

Blaise looked over Rob's shoulder at the digital readout and wanted to groan. .02. Cripes, she could have gotten that much alcohol in her system just by absorbing that spilled beer through her skin. It was *well* below Florida's legal limit of .08, well below what she would read from even a single beer.

"Now one more time, ma'am," Rob told her. "We need two readings for accuracy."

She blew another .02, and while the machine happily kicked out a card with the results, Blaise wondered how he was going to apologize.

"Well?" she asked impatiently. "I'm not drunk, am I."

Rob Witt looked at his boss.

"No, Ms. McAllister," Blaise said heavily, "you're not drunk."

She looked triumphant. "I *told* you. You should have believed me."

"That was a little hard to do, under the circumstances." He frowned sternly at her. "In future, don't be so combative with a police officer. It doesn't help your case."

She had the sense not to argue any further, although she seriously would have liked to pull out his tongue and wrap it around his head. "My attorney will be contacting you about this." Some evil genius had gotten hold of her tongue, she thought, wishing wildly that she could snatch back those words. What was she trying to do? Get herself arrested again?

But Blaise stunned her with her response. "Have him contact my attorney. We need to settle how you're going to pay for my mailbox."

Two

The mailbox was still lying forlornly on its side when Chief Corrigan pulled into her driveway. "I'll walk you to your door, ma'am."

This time she was sitting beside him in the front seat, a passenger instead of a prisoner. For some reason it didn't feel a whole lot better. "That's not necessary, Chief."

He looked at her. "Yes, ma'am, it is. I'll see you safely to your door."

He probably thought she'd sue him if she twisted her ankle or something. As she calmed down, she was beginning to feel more embarrassed by her behavior, and she really didn't want to leave things this way. She didn't want to be on the wrong side of the chief of police, nor did she want to be feuding with her next door neighbor. Either one would be wholly counterproductive, especially since Blaise Corrigan was one and the same. God, why did she have to live next door to the chief of police?

"Look," she said, as he switched off the ignition and reached for the door handle. Between them, locked upright to the dash, was a wicked looking shotgun. She tried to ignore it although it gave her the willies. "I'm really sorry about how I behaved. I was tired and very angry because of something that happened at work tonight, and I shouldn't have taken it out on you."

He didn't say anything, just waited for her to finish.

"I'm not really going to call my lawyer. I know you were just doing your job."

He nodded an acknowledgment, but said nothing.

"Anyway, send me the bill for having your mailbox fixed. I'm really sorry I ran it over, but honestly, there was this big gray dog—sort of an Airedale, but the wrong color—"

He suddenly sat forward. "That's Cal Lepkin's dog. Dammit, he's supposed to keep that animal chained. We have a leash law here."

"Well, whoever's dog it was, he wasn't chained tonight, and I didn't want to hit him, but he sat right in the middle of the driveway. I guess my headlights hypnotized him or something."

"No, that damn dog is evil incarnate. I swear he's got as much brain as the whole city council put together, and he's always up to some trick or other. You wouldn't believe how many complaints we get about him. No, he sat right there just to make you swerve. I'd bet my badge on it." He shook his head. "Of course, he's just a dog being a dog."

She was about to bet her night's tips that Blaise Corrigan was seriously lacking a screw or two. He clearly spent too much time gauging this dog's smarts. What kind of hick backwater town had she moved to?

"Well, I'll talk to Cal about his damn dog in the morning," Blaise said, as he climbed out of the car. "And forget about the mailbox. I can fix it easily enough. I was just ... angry." That was a major admission, and he didn't feel real good about it. "I don't like drunk drivers."

"Neither do I."

They walked up to the house together and he waited while she unlocked her door and turned on the lights.

"Good night, Ms. McAllister," he said formally. "And get your Florida license and registration tomorrow. Next time I'll ticket you."

She barely resisted slamming the door in his face.

By the light of midday, Blaise thought, Jillian McAllister was a menace to society. When he came home for a late lunch, she was standing out in her driveway, looking at his ruined mailbox. That wasn't the problem. The problem was those white shorts she was wearing, barely big enough to cover her decently, and exposing a pair of downright awesome legs to the sun.

Stupid Yankee, he told himself grumpily. She was close enough to the tropics here that she shouldn't be showing that much skin to the sun. That honeyed tone could become lobster red real quick.

It was only seventy-five degrees ... sweater weather to a local like him. Only tourists would be dressing like that today, and she'd said she wasn't a tourist.

And he was being absurd because he didn't want to admit how damn pretty she was. Long reddish-gold hair. Last night he hadn't noticed it because she'd had it pinned up on her head. Today it was traffic-stopping.

He caught himself just as he was about to pass his driveway and plow into a parked car. Yep, that woman was a hazard.

He swung his cruiser into his driveway and climbed out, looking over at her. "Something wrong?"

She gave him a tentative smile. "Just wondering what I can do about your mailbox."

"I told you I'd take care of it. Won't take but a few minutes. I'll just dig a new hole, sink a new post, and put the box back in place. No big deal."

As he spoke, the mail truck pulled up out in front. Jim Knapp looked down at the box. "What happened, Blaise?" he called out.

"Just a little accident. I'll have it fixed by tomorrow."

The small, wiry man climbed out of his truck with a handful of mail and looked sternly at Blaise. "All the 'snow, sleet, and rain' stuff is a thing of the past. That mailbox doesn't meet regulations and I'm not required to deliver the mail to it."

"I know that, Jim. Just give it to me."

"Can't do that." The mailman stalked up the drive with the mail, right past Blaise, to the front door.

"Why not?" Blaise asked.

"It's against regulations. I have to deliver it to either the box or the residence."

"But you know who I am."

"Doesn't make any difference. I gotta follow regulations. Now, you get up here and go on inside so I can give you your mail."

Keeping a straight face with difficulty, Blaise walked up to his own door, unlocked it and stepped inside. Only then did Jim Knapp hand him the mail. "Thanks, Jim. I appreciate you going out of your way."

"Just this once. You get it fixed by tomorrow, hear?" As he passed by it, Knapp slapped a warning notice on the outside of the mailbox, then climbed back into his truck. He gave a friendly wave, then drove the ten feet to Jillie's box, where he leaned over and slipped in a single white envelope.

When the mailman had driven far enough down the street that he couldn't hear them, Jillie looked at Blaise. "I can't believe him."

"Jim Knapp? He's harmless—just a stickler for rules; they give him a sense of power."

Like a certain policeman? she wondered.

"Did you go take care of your license?" he asked suddenly.

"No." She started to move her chin forward truculently, but caught herself. She absolutely *was not* going to fight with this man, not when she had to live next door to him. "Do you know how hard it is to do these things? I went to get my license but they told me I couldn't do that until I'd registered my car. So I went to the tax assessor's office to register my car, but they told me they wouldn't do that until I'd had an emissions test. So I went to the emissions place, but it's closed because the computer is broken. Not only that, I got lost three times." She threw up her hands. "What am I supposed to do, wave a magic wand?"

"Didn't the tax assessor give you a map?"

"For the emissions place? Sure, but it's on the mainland. But I just moved here, Chief. I barely know my way around Paradise Beach and the island. I'm totally lost when I go to the mainland."

"Well, I imagine you know your way around a little better now."

She'd have liked to throttle him. Really. But then it struck her that the only reason he irritated her so much was that he was failing to live up to her expectations.

Expectations? What expectations? Then it hit her: he looked like he ought to be somebody's fantasy lover. He had a wonderful craggy, weathered face. He was big, broad shouldered, hard looking. He had light brown wavy hair and a pair of electric blue eyes that could rivet steel when they were angry.

Yep, he was a dreamboat. Only he wasn't acting like a fantasy lover. Not at all.

Ridiculous. Absolutely ridiculous. God, no one would ever guess she was thirty and coming off a bad marriage. Jeez. Dream lovers. Ha!

Blaise's voice penetrated her thoughts. "Is something wrong?"

She blinked, calling herself back from self-castigation. "Oh, sorry. I was just thinking. I guess I do know my way around better, but there are easier ways to learn. Anyhow, *that's* why I don't have my license and registration. Are you going to ticket me?"

He pursed his lips, then shook his head. "No. What I'm going to do is take some time off tomorrow and help you get this stuff taken care of."

He couldn't believe he'd said that. As soon as the words passed his lips, Blaise wondered if he was losing his mind. No, actually he was thinking with his gonads. Christ! She wasn't a kid. She didn't need a father figure to step in and help her deal with something this easy. He wouldn't do this for anyone on the face of the planet, except possibly his mother or Mary Todd. Why was he doing this for Jillian McAllister? Because she had a pair of legs that wouldn't quit and hair the color of sunshine on new-minted copper? Or maybe it was those moss-green eyes of hers, looking so soft and warm, as if you could just cuddle up in them.

But whatever it was, it had pushed him over the edge. And now it was too late to snatch back the words. He'd made the offer and would stand by it.

Jillie looked startled. She glanced shyly up at him, as if uncertain how to take all this. Finally she said, "Thanks—that's very kind of you. But really, I'll manage myself. You don't need to take time off just to help me."

If he'd been using half the brain he'd been born with, he'd have backed out gracefully right then. Instead, he said, "It's no problem. Glad to do it." He smiled and touched the brim of his hat. "Just a little neighborliness for a newcomer."

Then, before he could make more of an ass of himself, he hotfooted it into his house. Jeez! He'd believed he was well past the age to fall sucker to long legs and seductive eyes!

Trouble. The woman was distilled trouble.

"I want you to come back, Jillian."

Jillie listened to her ex-husband's voice and wondered if she'd slipped through some kind of reality warp. She had left him because of his philandering, and he had sworn he would never forgive her for humiliating him. Now he wanted her back? "You're joking, Fielding."

"I'm *not* joking."

"You must be. You swore you'd never speak to me again, remember? You got a restraining order so I couldn't even buy coffee in the shop we used to frequent together. You don't want me back."

"That order expired months ago. It doesn't matter, anyway."

She gaped at the phone. "Doesn't matter? Fielding, have you banged your head on something? Thanks to that stupid order of yours, I had to drive clear around the edge of town to get from one side to another because I'd have violated the order if I'd driven down Main Street. I had to start grocery shopping in the next town. I even had to change auto mechanics! *Of course* it mattered."

"Well . . . I apologize," he said. "It was wrong of me to make the order so sweeping. I just didn't want to see you after you called me a spoiled little boy who couldn't keep his fingers out of the cookie jar. Really, Jillian, that wasn't fair."

"Oh, it was perfectly fair. How many Little Miss Wiggles did you drool over during our marriage? I personally know of four, and I'm sure there were others I never learned about. Would you have preferred me to say you were a spoiled brat who couldn't keep his—"

"Okay, okay," he interrupted swiftly, knowing what was coming. Jillian was famous for her blunt pronouncements. "Look, I'm sorry. There, I said it. I'm sorry. I'm a worm. I'm the lowest form of life, lower even than a caterpillar. I swear I'll never be unfaithful again. Just come back to me, Jillian."

"Your sleaze is showing, Fielding. The answer is no."

"But—but *darling*! You know I've never loved anyone the way I love you."

Jillian sniffed. "That's entirely possible. That doesn't necessarily make it a good thing. Far from it, in fact. For the sake of the rest of the women on this planet, I hope you never again love anyone the way you loved me. Goodbye, Fielding."

She heard him squawk a protest as she hung up the phone, but she never hesitated. She'd had quite enough of Fielding Wainwright during the five years of their marriage, and she'd be perfectly content never to see him again—or hear from him. In fact, she'd be delighted if she could totally forget his existence.

Hell, he'd even cost her her mechanic! Ed had been *her* mechanic long before she'd met Fielding, but that s.o.b. had to fix it so she couldn't even take her car there anymore. And Ed had nearly died laughing when he'd learned he was a point of dispute in their divorce.

It was ridiculous. But life with Fielding had always had a quality of the absurd that was . . . well, *laughable*. Maybe she should have moved even farther away. Maybe 2500 miles wasn't enough.

But even as she had the thought, she found herself remembering that she hadn't always felt this way. There'd been a time when she'd loved Fielding Wainwright, and when she'd truly believed he loved her.

He had been so charming. She'd been drawn to his boyishness, to his freshness. Unlike so many men, Fielding wasn't afraid to feel, or afraid of expressing his feelings. Unfortunately, with time, she had come to realize that expression was more the result of being spoiled than courage or character.

But at first—ah, at first! He had been so intense, so focused on her, leaving her breathless. He had lavished gifts on her until she was dizzy from his adoration. Only later did she realize that Fielding spent money to avoid spending himself. But at the time . . . at the time it had been exhilarating. No one had ever wanted to buy her extravagant gifts before, and it had gone to her head.

But even more than his extravagance, she had fallen in love with his family. It hadn't even bothered her that some of them had seemed to resent her or consider her beneath them. That was part of the charm of having a family, she had believed. No family was perfect, and she didn't expect Fielding's to fit a particular mold. She had believed she would win them

over with time—and some of them she had. But as an
orphan, she had been dazzled as much by his possession of parents, aunts, uncles, and cousins as she had
been by his extravagance. She had wanted to be part
of a big extended family and was ready to prove her
worthiness by overlooking their flaws. After all, that's
what families did for each other.

In short, she decided, she had been a romantic little
twit who'd been blinded by her illusions. By the time
she had seen past her own notions to the truth, Fielding was already in the arms of another woman.

But enough! She had to stop thinking this way!

Before she could turn her attention to something
else, the phone rang again. Fearing it was Fielding,
she almost didn't answer—what was the point in arguing? She wasn't going back to him, ever. Not if he
begged on his knees and promised eternal fidelity.
Not that he'd be able to keep that promise.

She finally reached for the phone, deciding they
might as well have it out once and for all.

"Jillie? This is Harv, down at the lounge."

"Oh, hi. What's up, Harv?" Something inside her
cringed at the likelihood that he wanted her to come
in tonight, even though it was her day off. God, she
hated that job.

"Dan Burgess wanted me to call you and tell you
you're fired."

Jillie felt as if she'd been slapped. Never in her life
had she been fired. "Uh . . . can I ask why?"

"Dan thinks you don't interact with the customers
too great."

"I see." Anger filled her in a sudden hot rush.
"Let's see if I have this straight. If I want to work at
the lounge, I have to let my backside be pawed by
drunks from Detroit. Is that about it, Harv?"

"I didn't say that, Jillie."

"No, of course you didn't." Of course not. If he did, she could give him and Dan Burgess hell. "Well, I'm glad you called, because I was getting ready to quit anyway. You see, my ass is worth a whole hell of a lot more than two-fifty an hour." She slammed the phone down hard and battled an impulse to hurl it across the room. She had to get out of this house *now*!

One of the most charming aspects of Paradise Beach, from Jillie's point of view, was the way everything was mixed up with everything else. That owed partly to the narrowness of the barrier island, meaning that one could stroll the width of it from side to side in ten minutes. It also was because the town had grown haphazardly over the years before anyone had thought of zoning things. By the time the beachfront high-rise hotels and condos had started being built along the barrier islands, a rather haphazard mix of businesses and residences already existed.

Her own house, which she was renting, was a concrete block bungalow amid a wide assortment of other dwellings only a block from the Intracoastal Waterway. Blaise Corrigan's house, in contrast, was a moderately large wood structure painted a silvery gray and elevated on huge stone pilings. All the newer houses here were built on stilts, to protect them from the storm surges that could accompany hurricanes. The concrete block houses scattered among them were likely to last through even the worst winds, though.

There was a sharp contrast house-to-house in size and value, too. It was common to see a huge, beautiful home sprawling on a large landscaped yard right next to a tiny, somewhat dilapidated bungalow.

And it all managed somehow to come together charmingly.

Because of the haphazard way Paradise Beach had

grown, Jillie could get to just about anything she might want to do by strolling a mere block or two. Today she decided to stop at the Palmetto Cafe on the waterway for an early dinner. Maybe the view of the sailboats and cigarette boats cruising the channel would ease some of her irritation.

In the three weeks since she had moved to this town, she had grown very fond of this little cafe with its concrete terraces right on the edge of the waterway. Because it was away from the Gulf beaches, the tourists rarely found it. The locals patronized it heavily, however, and the atmosphere was almost homey, with all the regulars chatting away with one another.

Denise, the hostess, put Jillie at a table on the upper terrace, giving her an unobstructed view of the sailboats wending their way up the channel.

"Try the grouper sandwich," she recommended. "Fresh catch."

Jillian shook her head. "I'm really not a fan of grouper."

"Trust me, you'll like this. Seasoned with lemon pepper, sauteed to flakiness in butter, and served on a homemade roll. Well . . ." She winked. "The roll was actually made in the bakery around the corner, but that's almost homemade. C'mon, if you don't like it, I won't charge you and you can order something else."

Jillie couldn't repress a grin. "You're that sure?"

"Absolutely." She laid her hand over her heart. "Would I lie to you? It's wonderful!"

"Okay, I'll try it."

"How about an ice-cold draft to go with it?" Denise smacked her lips as if she could taste it already.

The thought of beer nearly made Jillie want to gag after last night. "I think I'll stick with iced tea."

"Isn't the sun far enough over the yardarm yet?"

"It's not that. Last night one of my customers spilled a beer on me. Oh . . . you'd never believe it."

Ignoring her other customers—there were only two, since it was already mid afternoon—Denise pulled out a chair and straddled it. Her working uniform was denim shorts and a black apron—a lot more sensible, Jillie thought, than that ridiculous skimpy black nylon outfit the Seaside Lounge had put *her* into. "Try me," Denise said cordially.

"Actually," Jillie said, "I don't think you'd believe the last twenty-four hours I've had."

"If you wait a few minutes for your lunch, I'm all ears."

"Okay then, listen to this. Last night this guy at the lounge got fresh. I don't just mean a pat to the bottom—hell, I get those all the time from customers. I don't like it but what are you going to do?"

"If you ever figure it out, let me know," Denise said. "That's why I work here. The tips aren't as good, but at least everyone knows everyone else and I don't have to put up with the mauling."

"Sounds good to me. Anyway, last night a guy pinched me really hard. It startled me, and when I swung around I knocked the beer out of his hand. Needless to say, it was all my fault."

"Of course." The older woman nodded sagely.

"And I had to pay to have his suit cleaned, if you can believe it. Anyway, I went home smelling like a brewery. Just as I was turning into my driveway, a gray dog leaped out in front of me—"

"What did the dog look like?" Denise wanted to know.

"A sort of grayish Airedale."

"Cal Lepkin's dog. That animal is possessed, I swear. I love dogs, but that Rover is a demon in disguise."

"That seems to be the general opinion." And hearing it for the second time today somehow made it more acceptable.

Denise waved a hand. "Most everybody around here has had a run-in with that dog. So he jumped in front of your car?"

"And then just sat there, smack in the middle of the driveway. So I had to swerve to avoid him, naturally."

"If that isn't just like that dog!" Denise clucked and shook her head.

"Well, in the process of avoiding the dog, I ran over my neighbor's mailbox. My neighbor, the chief of police."

Denise shrugged. "Blaise is a nice guy. Don't worry, he'll fix it himself and it won't cost you a dime."

"The mailbox was only part of the problem. The problem is that I smelled like beer, remember?"

Denise's eyes widened and she clapped a hand to her mouth. "Oh, for—don't tell me he arrested you!"

"Yes, he did."

"Of course he did," said a tart voice from the next table. Both women turned to see an elderly woman with a halo of snow-white hair. She wore a flamingo pink slacks set. Her left hand gripped the top of an ebony cane, and her eyes were as dark and alert as a hawk's. "That's what we pay the police for—to arrest drunk drivers."

"I wasn't drunk," Jillie protested.

"Of course not. I heard the rest of your story, gal, but how was Chief Corrigan supposed to know that when you ran down his mailbox and smelled like a beer keg?"

"I kept telling him—"

"You think he doesn't hear that a dozen times a day

from drunks?" The woman tapped her cane for emphasis. "Anyway, I collect you got off?"

"Well, yes. The breath test established I wasn't drunk."

The old woman hooted. "Must have irritated that boy no end. Does him good once in a while to be wrong. A little humility never hurt anyone. Denise! Introduce me to this gal."

"Miss Mary Todd, this is Jillie McAllister. Jillie just moved here."

Miss Todd narrowed her piercing eyes and studied Jillie intently. "Planning to stay?"

"Yes. Definitely. I really like it here."

The elderly woman nodded. "Come over here and sit at my table so I can get to know you."

Jillie hesitated, reluctant to obey such an imperious order from a total stranger, but Denise was already moving her water glass, napkin, and flatware over. Apparently you were supposed to do as Miss Todd commanded. Oh, well, it would be nice to meet another of her neighbors.

"Much better," Miss Todd decreed, when Jillie was seated across from her. "Now I won't have to eavesdrop to hear your story. Eavesdropping is such a nasty but essential habit, don't you think?"

Jillie spluttered a laugh at the unexpected frankness of the woman, and found those dark eyes laughing back at her.

"I knew you'd agree," Miss Todd said. "Where's your husband?"

"I don't have a husband. What makes you think I do?"

Miss Todd looked pointedly at her ring finger. "I can see the distinctive mark of a wedding band."

"We're divorced."

"In my day divorce was unheard of. A woman had

to stay with the jerk until one of them died. Ridiculous." She tilted her head to one side. "That's why I never married, you know. I just couldn't see signing on for a life sentence."

Jillie laughed then, totally forgetting her annoyance at the imperial summons she had received in response to the strength of her instant liking for this woman.

"Well," Mary continued, "you're probably wondering who I am, so I'll save you the trouble of questioning Denise later."

"That's very kind of you." Another laugh trembled in her voice.

"I've lived here all my life. My family was one of the very first to settle on this island, and I still own a pretty good chunk of it. Developers keep wanting me to sell it so they can build more hotels and condos, but I'll be damned if I'll let 'em."

"I imagine they've offered you quite a bit of money."

The elderly woman waved a frail hand dismissingly. "Money. As long as you have enough for the necessities, what do you need any more for? I can't imagine how a few million dollars is supposed to make me happy when I can't see the beach from the boulevard anymore. This place gets crowded enough when it starts to snow up north. Why do we need another thousand or two hotel rooms all stacked up in those ugly towers?"

"I can't imagine."

"It's not that I mind the people who come to spend the winter here. Lots of them own houses, or rent them here, and they add a really nice quality to the community when they come stay with us. But some of those people who stay in the hotels—*particularly* Andrew Hegel's cottages—oh, my dear, have you seen the place? It's a veritable *pit*. I can't imagine why *anyone* would want to stay there, let alone pay for the privilege. Now *that's* an embarrassment to the community, and I'm still trying to find a way to get it shut down."

Jillie nodded encouragingly, unsure exactly how to respond.

"But that's neither here nor there," Miss Todd decided. "Every community has its warts. If those cottages were the only ones, we'd be doing well, indeed."

"You certainly would."

Mary smiled. "Poor gal, you don't know what to make of me, do you? Well, don't worry about it. No one else does, either. Except possibly Chief Corrigan. Something about that boy..." She trailed off and shook her head.

Chief Corrigan, Jillie thought, was about the farthest thing from a boy she could imagine. She wondered how he liked being referred to that way and felt a strange little tingle when she thought of him. Good God, was she actually looking forward to spending time with Corrigan? The thought was appalling.

"Well," the other woman continued a few moments later, "I can tell you, if I were forty years younger, I'd give that young man a run for his money."

"I'm sure you would."

"Don't humor me, gal."

"I'm not!" Jillie shook her head emphatically. "As you'll soon learn, Miss Todd, I'm famous for being tactless."

"As far as I can see, you've got a long sight more tact than *I* ever had." She cackled. "Well, to get back to the subject, which was me, I believe..." She arched an enquiring brow.

"Definitely. We were definitely discussing you. Or

rather, you were holding forth and I was listening."

"Ha! You *do* have a tongue on you, gal! *Holding forth*. Nobody's every accused me of that before. I like it."

Just then Denise brought the grouper sandwich and set it in front of Jillie with a flourish. "Go on, take a bite and let me know."

"I never could abide grouper," Miss Todd announced. "Ate enough when I was a child to last me ten lifetimes."

"Cut it out, Miss Todd," Denise said sternly. "Let her at least decide for herself."

Jillie regarded the sandwich doubtfully. "I've never been a fan of grouper myself. The bread looks great, though." And it did. It had been a long time since she'd seen a roll with a shiny, crisp crust. Well, she told herself, it was only fish. Picking up half the sandwich, she took a bite.

It was good. In fact, she could hardly tell there was any grouper in it at all, thanks to the spicy lemon pepper. With her mouth full, she could only give Denise an "okay" sign with her hand. The waitress beamed. "I'll tell Doug. He'll be pleased."

Miss Todd watched Denise waltz away, then lifted a brow at Jillie. "It's really good?"

"Mmm."

"Well, maybe I'll break down and try it one of these days. What kind of mood was Chief Corrigan in last night?"

Jillie blinked, startled by the change of topic, and swallowed. She took a moment to dab at her mouth with a napkin before answering. "I got the feeling he was in a *terrible* mood. But maybe that's how he treats everyone he thinks is drunk."

"Well, it could be, I suppose, although he's an advocate for courtesy among police officers. He feels an aggressive attitude is inflammatory."

"Well, he was certainly inflammatory last night. I nearly got into an argument with him." Her cheeks reddened a little as she added honestly, "Of course, some of his mood may have had to do with me. I wasn't exactly being cooperative."

Mary Todd chuckled. "Why should you be? You were being unjustly accused. There's little that'll fire up the emotions the way that does."

"Well, it sure got me annoyed. But why did you ask about his mood?"

"Oh, he had a terrible time at the city council meeting last night. Damn fools are talking about getting rid of the police force and asking the sheriff to take over."

"Why?"

"They say it's to save money, but that's not it at all. Truth is, they think Chief Corrigan's too hard on the tourists. They want a different set of laws for the visitors, something gentler, as Dan Burgess put it."

"*Gentler*?" Jillie repeated the word incredulously. "Why should they be treated any differently from anybody else?"

"Because they'll never come again if they aren't."

"That's ridiculous! Why would anyone want them to come again if they're going to break the law?"

Mary smiled. "Exactly my question. Why indeed. But Burgess and Hegel and a few of the others think with their cash registers."

"Well, I can't say it surprises me about Dan Burgess." Jillie swiftly recounted her firing.

The older woman nodded. "That's about what I'd expect from that man. What's horrifying is that anyone could think tolerating that kind of behavior could possibly be good for tourism. Regardless of what Mr.

Burgess believes, it's been my experience that *most* people aren't comfortable with it. If we become some kind of bohemian paradise, we'll lose all the good solid folks we'd much rather have visit us. And we'll lose all our snowbirds, too. That would be a terrible shame!"

Jillie hardly knew how to answer that, since part of what had drawn her here was the feeling it was a bohemian paradise. Oh, she knew there were plenty of those solid folks Mary Todd referred to, mostly retirees who liked to winter here, but there were plenty of the other kind, too, as evidenced in the out-of-the-way shops that sold handcrafted jewelry and the work of local painters. There were shell shops and craft shops, and an underfunded theater group that staged its plays in a building on the verge of collapse.

Something about all this didn't quite jibe with the middle-class heaven Mary Todd was describing. Of course, Mary Todd didn't exactly jibe with that image herself. The woman surely must have been a bohemian in her own day. She was too damn independent to have been anything else. After all, wasn't refusing to marry unheard of for a woman of her generation?

"Well," Mary waved a dismissing hand, "they won't succeed. I'll see to it. Paradise Beach needs its own police, and Blaise Corrigan is the finest man we've ever had in the position of chief."

Jillie didn't particularly want to join in the singing of Corrigan's praises, especially since she was still annoyed with him. "What I don't understand is why they think the sheriff will do the job any differently."

"It's a matter of funding. There won't be as many county mounties available, so the coverage won't be as good. Hence they won't harass as many drunks."

"Oh."

Mary chuckled. "Amazing, isn't it? Sometimes I wonder if those jerks have enough brains to operate their own cash registers." Then, without warning, she changed topics. "What are you planning to do with yourself? Find another waitressing job?"

"No, I don't think so. It was only temporary, anyway, until I could decide where to open my own business."

"Ah!" Dark eyes peered intently at her. "What kind of business? Just tell me it isn't topless dancing."

Jillie spluttered, laughing. "Of course not!"

"Well, it's always best to ask. Leaping to conclusions is a risky business. And I'll tell you right off, we don't need any more miniature golf, or T-shirt shops, or bars."

"I didn't have any of those in mind."

"Good. And forget flower shops, we've got two of those and one is in serious trouble."

"I wasn't thinking of that."

"And two of my friends are already in the junk business—well, they call 'em antiques, but it looks mostly like junk to me." She *tsked* and shook her head. "Stuff my grandma would have thrown out for shame."

"My ex-husband's house was full of antiques. What a misery to clean. No, I'm not thinking of that, either."

"Then exactly what *are* you thinking about?"

Jillie bit her lip, reluctant to share her plan until she had at least taken some concrete steps. What better time, though, then now that she had been fired?

"Come on, gal, spit it out!"

"A bookstore."

"A bookstore?"

"A bookstore. Both new and used books, with tables for people to read at if they like."

A wide smile spread slowly across Mary Todd's

face. "We don't have a bookstore. The nearest one is on the mainland."

"I noticed."

"Gal, you may be a certifiable genius!"

Three

"Ready to go?"

Jillie was still half asleep when she opened her front door to find Blaise Corrigan standing there in the bright morning sunlight. Working as a cocktail waitress had disrupted her internal clock, turning her into a nightowl who had trouble getting up before late morning. "Ready for what?"

"To take care of your license and registration, remember?"

"I remember. We didn't set a time." She smothered a yawn.

"We didn't? Well, sorry, but it has to be this morning. I have a one o'clock meeting. How soon can you be ready?"

Sleepy though she was, she wasn't immune to the impression he made this morning. Instead of looking like a police officer—the only way she had seen him—he was wearing a royal blue polo shirt and white tennis shorts with topsiders, and he looked almost too good to be true. It was the only thing that kept her from closing the door in his face.

"I need a few minutes," she said groggily.

"Just a few?"

Something in the amused way he said that caused her to look down at herself. What she saw made her gasp in horror and start to slam the door.

He caught it and held it open a few inches. "How soon will you be ready?"

"Twenty minutes," she said desperately. "Twenty minutes!"

He let go and she slammed the door and locked it. Oh, God, where had her mind been? How could she have answered the door wearing an old gray sleep shirt with a huge pink bunny on it? Oh, Jeez, look at her hair standing up in spikes . . .

She dove into the shower before the water was even warm.

She needed more than twenty minutes to make herself presentable, but Blaise didn't seem to mind. When she emerged, he was leaning against the side of his white pickup truck, smoking a cigarette. He didn't even glance at his watch.

"Ready?" he asked again.

"Yes. Thank you." She felt properly armored in the gauzy folds of a patterned broomstick skirt and turquoise top. Looking good, she had learned long ago, was a form of protection. "You shouldn't smoke. It'll kill you."

"I know. It's none of your damned business."

"As long as I don't have to breathe it."

He looked at her for a long moment, then tossed the butt aside. "Anyone ever tell you you talk too much?"

"All the time." She gave him her sweetest smile as she handed him the keys to her car. He helped her in on the passenger side, and she somehow felt as if she had evened matters between them by pointing out that he wasn't perfect.

"Do you have all your papers?" he asked, as he folded himself behind the wheel.

"Title, proof of insurance, and my old driver's license, right?"

"Right."

"Will I have to take a written test or a road test to get a new license?"

"Nope."

"Great." That meant they ought to be done reasonably quickly. "Does the emissions test take long?"

"Not usually more than fifteen minutes."

"What if I don't pass?"

"You will, if you've been taking reasonable care of your car."

Jillie sighed. "I used to have a really great mechanic."

"What happened to him?"

"My husband got him in the divorce."

Blaise gave her a sidelong look, as if doubting what he'd heard.

"I know, I know," she said irritably. "He got the coffee shop, too, and most of the damn town. It's all hysterically funny. But I don't want to talk about all that."

"Sure," he said agreeably enough. "What *do* you want to talk about?"

"Miss Mary Todd."

"Ah, you've met the *crème de la crème* of Paradise Beach society."

"Does Paradise Beach *have* a society?"

"Several of them. The Society for Endangered Waterfowl, the Society for—"

She laughed, interrupting him. "Okay, okay. I get the picture. I just meant . . . this place doesn't look like it would have high society."

He glanced at her again. "You mean we look as if we have only *low* society?"

She darted him an uncertain look, saw that he was teasing, and let herself laugh again. "Okay, you win the pun wars—but only because I'm not fully awake yet."

"I've always been one to take advantage of a sleepy woman."

It was as if she'd been punched in the solar plexus. All of a sudden, Jillie couldn't breathe as her mind was swamped in forbidden images. Oh, Lordy, no! She never again wanted to be attracted to a man. Never, never, never! Males were the lowest pond scum. The slimiest creeps. The slugs of the world. Well, that was unfair, she thought. No need to insult slugs.

And this one had already arrested her! Closing her eyes, she forced herself to remember the cold feeling of the handcuffs as he'd snapped them on her wrists, wanting the harsh humiliation of that moment to banish her attraction to this man. Instead, her quisling mind suggested it might be fun to be entirely at his mercy . . .

Somebody had drained all the air off the planet. Some alien ship had landed somewhere and opened a humongous vacuum cleaner to suck up all the oxygen and that was why she couldn't breathe . . .

"Look, I'm sorry," Blaise said. "I couldn't resist the opening. Another of my failings. I always take an opening."

The aliens must have sprung a leak in their vacuum

cleaner bag, because the air was seeping back. Her lungs, no longer paralyzed, finally drew in one great big gulp. "Sorry," she said finally. "Sorry. I swallowed wrong . . ." Lying. Why was she lying? Because she couldn't tell him that she was losing her mind? Yes, that was a good enough reason to lie.

The emissions inspection was as swift and easy as he had promised. Fifteen minutes after they'd arrived and pulled into line, they were driving away with a computerized printout. Jillie scanned it interestedly, wondering if it would tell her anything.

"Hey," she said, "guess what? This car is so clean it doesn't make any carbon monoxide at all."

"None?"

"None. Jeez, what a rip. Do you realize this vehicle is useless as a suicide machine?"

He turned his head to look at her, clearly astonished, then burst into a laugh.

Getting the car titled and registered took longer, but even that wasn't as bad as she had expected. And getting her driver's license was an absolute snap that involved paying a few dollars, getting her picture taken, and then waiting about fifteen minutes for her license.

"That was too easy," she remarked to Blaise, when they were back on the road heading home.

"Did you mind?"

"That it was easy? You bet. I'm a dyed-in-the-wool member of the Harder Is Better Society."

"Oh, one of those 'no pain, no gain' types, huh?"

"You got it."

"Well, we could go back and I could tell them I arrested you for DUI."

"We will not!" Horrified, she glared at him. "I never want to think of that again. That was the most humiliating, frustrating, horrifying . . ." She trailed off. "Well, maybe not the most humiliating and horrifying. It was worse when I found out about my ex's girlfriend. The first one. I'm sorry. I shouldn't have said that."

"Shouldn't have said what? Why not?"

"I shouldn't have mentioned my ex because I don't want to talk about him, and you sure don't want to hear about him."

Blaise didn't say anything until they'd crossed the drawbridge and were back on the island. "You keep mentioning him because you want to talk about him."

"I do not!"

He shrugged. "Suit yourself, lady."

Traffic was inching along the boulevard as tourists moved from one entertainment to another. Once they got past the big hotels, restaurants and shops, however, traffic lightened considerably. The south end of Paradise Beach was still "quaint," lacking the highrise and neon dazzle of the north end of the island, so fewer tourists wandered into the quieter streets. Mary Todd must not have owned much of the north end.

"No, she didn't," Blaise said when Jillie asked. "Most of the land up there was owned by a couple of families who sold it off about twenty years ago, and it's been booming ever since. I don't know what's going to happen down here when Miss Mary passes on. I know she's got a couple of nieces and nephews who think she ought to sell to the big developers."

"That'll be a shame. Maybe I shouldn't plan on staying here permanently, then. I don't want to open a business only to have this town turn into someplace I'd rather not live."

"You're opening a business? What kind?"

"A bookstore."

Before she could volunteer anything else, he was

jamming on the brakes and pulling over to the side of the boulevard. Ahead of them in the middle of the intersection two cars had collided. From the looks of it, no one was hurt, but traffic was blocked in four directions, and people were standing in the middle of the road gesticulating angrily and shouting.

"Stay here," Blaise said. "I need to go straighten this out. It shouldn't take long."

She climbed out of the car, too, watching as he strode toward the arguing crowd. The accident must have just happened, because only a few cars were backed up, but others were beginning to pull up behind them.

Jeez, he looked good, she thought, as she watched Blaise wade into the middle of the crowd. Nicely tanned, the kind of tan you got just from being out and about in this climate, not the heavily dark one of the sunbather. She'd never much cared for that look. Shoulders that were broad without assistance, arms that looked like they belonged to a tennis player, legs that were powerful with compact muscle, as if he ran a lot . . .

Catching herself mooning, she gave herself a mental shake. No. Absolutely not. He could be the most perfect man on the face of the planet, but she wasn't ever, ever, going to get involved with a man again.

She saw Blaise wave a black wallet at the people around and they settled down quickly. Must be his badge, she thought, and absently moved closer to hear what was going on.

"You have to get the cars out of the intersection," he was saying. "We can discuss who did what when the street is clear."

"No!" said one man, waving his arms. "If I do that no one can see what happened. He hit me!"

"Will you shut up?" shrieked a very thin woman

with hair the color of a cherry. "These cops are all violent. Didn't you see that man they beat up on TV?"

"Nobody's going to beat anyone up," Blaise said with admirable calm. "Please, we need to clear the intersection."

"I'm not moving," the man said, folding his arms. "Someone has to take a report. There's no way I'm paying for this when *he* caused the accident."

"I did not," said a small, wiry man, who until now had been quiet. "You ran a red light."

"Red? *Red?* It wasn't red! *You* had the red light!"

"He did not," someone in the crowd called out. "That guy's lying!"

"I don't lie!"

"You stupid tourists are all alike—"

"That will be enough!" Blaise bellowed. Much to Jillie's surprise, everyone shut up. "That's better," he said, when all the mouths were closed. "Now, we're going to move these vehicles . . ."

The plump man started to open his mouth again, but a look from Blaise locked his tongue.

"We are going to move these vehicles," he repeated. "Then—and *only* then—we'll discuss what happened." He glanced around at the crowd. "Anyone who saw the accident please stay a few minutes so I can get your statement."

Heads nodded agreeably. Only the plump man seemed annoyed.

Blaise turned to one of the men on the sidewalk. "Herm? Will you call the station and have them send a couple of cruisers out here so we can get this sorted out faster?"

"Sure." Herm spat tobacco juice on the sidewalk. "Got a quarter? I ain't making no official calls on *my* dime."

"And I'm going to ticket you if you spit on the sidewalk again. Damn it, Herm, if I've told you once I've told you a million times—"

"Okay, okay, I'll pay you for the damned call."

But Blaise was already tossing him a quarter. "Don't let me catch you spitting again."

"Jesus, some cops get so full of theyselves . . ." Muttering, Herm walked away.

Meanwhile, traffic was getting backed up to the point that horns were starting to honk. Blaise glanced over at Jillie. "Sorry," he mouthed.

She shrugged and smiled almost in spite of herself. "It's okay," she mouthed back. Actually, she was kind of enjoying this, and she didn't have anything important waiting for her.

Blaise turned to the plump man. "Move your car over there."

"No."

"What?"

"I said no! It's broken. I'm not moving it."

"Oh, for God's sake," said the woman with the cherry-red hair. "Stanley, he's going to hit you with a billy club if you don't start doing what he says."

"Let him. Just let him! My lawyers will be all over him—"

The woman's voice grew shrill. "What difference is that going to make if you get a broken jaw and my vacation is ruined?"

A man in the crowd near Jillie spoke to the man beside him. "Where do you suppose those two come from?"

"Another planet," was the answer. Somebody else began to hum the *Twilight Zone* theme.

By now Blaise's patience was wearing just a trifle thin, and he was pointing a finger at the man and telling him to move the car now or be arrested for impeding traffic. The man was unimpressed, and to prove it, he turned his back on Blaise.

And as he turned, Jillie recognized him as the man who had pawed her in the restaurant and had ended up costing her her job. While the job didn't really matter to her, the insult did. Before she knew what she was doing, she had charged through the crowd and was confronting the man.

"You toad!" she told him, jabbing her finger at his chest. "You slimy creep!"

"What the hell—?"

She poked him with her finger, hard. *"You got me fired!"*

"I never saw you before in my life!"

"Why, you lying scum! You saw me well enough to grab my bottom at the Seaside Lounge two nights ago!"

The red-haired woman shrieked angrily. "What were you doing grabbing another woman?"

"Cherry, I never touched her!"

"Hold on here," Blaise said loudly. "Get to the side of the road now! All of you."

"You see what I mean?" demanded an all-too-familiar voice. Recognizing it, Jillie spun around and glared at Dan Burgess, her former boss. He was a small, pudgy man, of less than average height. "What have I been saying?" Dan cried even louder. "This is why I want to get rid of the police department! One small accident and they can't even take care of it. It's turning into a damn riot."

"Bullshit," Blaise said flatly. "Step aside and get out of the way."

"Out of the way of what?"

"Out of the way of the police, you stupid lout," Jillie said, turning her ire on him. "What kind of man are you, anyway, firing me because I wouldn't put up

with being manhandled by your disgusting customers!"

"I never—" Burgess began to back up, looking uneasy.

"You did! I got the call yesterday. What are you,
some kind of pimp?"

"Go for it, Jillie," yelled a woman from the side-
lines. Glancing her way, Jillie recognized another
waitress from the lounge.

"How dare you?" demanded Burgess, plainly
aghast. "How dare you use that word with me?"

"I don't know what *you* call it when you make letting yourself be mauled by the customers a condition
of employment!"

"Yeah!" yelled the other waitress.

"Wait a minute," said the plump motorist. "I never
mauled anybody!"

"You sure as hell mauled me, and when I was so
startled I knocked the beer from your hand, you had
the nerve to demand that I pay to have your suit
cleaned."

"Well, of course he did," said Cherry, putting her
carefully manicured hands on her hips. "You had no
business spilling beer on him!"

"He had no business grabbing my ass!"

"Yeah," yelled some of the women in the crowd.

"Hey," a man on the sidewalk shouted. "What's
wrong with youse women! It's gettin' so a guy can't
get a little feel . . ."

He was drowned out by a roar of disapproval from
the crowd.

Horns were honking from every direction. Way at
the end of the street, Blaise could see his two cruisers,
lights flashing, totally unable to get through the
crowd and the traffic jam to help out. The throng that
had gathered was getting into a spirited discussion

about whether cocktail waitresses ought to expect to be manhandled.

Burgess had dropped the issue of getting rid of the police and was trying to slink away, but someone collared him and started shouting in his face about the evil he was foisting on society by running a bar in the first place. For some reason that got Burgess all wound up again about the police department.

Blaise would have settled back to watch the show, except that the crowds were unpredictable and there was no telling at what point someone in this group might decide to throw a punch.

He turned to the pudgy tourist, who was now arguing hotly with Cherry about something, but he couldn't hear what they were saying over the noise being generated by some three hundred gabbing, yelling people and thirty or forty impatiently honking auto horns.

Clearly the situation was getting out of control.

"Oh, shut up, Burgess," somebody yelled. "You just want to get rid of the cops because they're doing a good job."

"Like hell," someone else shouted back. "What's so good about this? They can't even clear up a lousy accident. Dan is right."

"Chief?"

Blaise turned to find that four of his cops had joined him.

"Sorry. We couldn't get the cars through."

"I couldn't either." He shook his head at the mess. "Okay, let's clear the intersection. Once the traffic starts moving, the crowd will disperse. Gary, you take the Buick and shove it over into the Pick-It-Quick lot. Buck, you push the Chevy. Wes, Andrew, you keep folks out of the way if you have to move them bodily to do it."

He waited just long enough to see his men start doing as he'd directed, then he went to Jillie, lifted her with an arm around her waist, and walked her to the side of the street.

"What do you think you're doing?"

"Keeping you from ending up in the middle of a public brawl. I told you to stay put."

She glared at him. "You damn men. You're all alike, pushing us around because we're smaller and weaker."

"You may be smaller, but you sure as hell aren't weaker. Don't give me that crap. I'm not buying it."

"Do you know what that man did to me?"

"I heard. So did most of Paradise Beach." He set her on her feet in the parking lot and looked down at her, trying to be annoyed but unable to muster the feeling. "Did Burgess really fire you for not putting up with it?"

"The exact description was that I don't interact with the customers too great."

Blaise's expression darkened. "Because you got upset with that jerk?"

"Must have been, because nothing else happened."

"I'm sorry."

"For what?"

He shook his head. "That you were treated that way. Nobody should be treated that way."

"I couldn't agree more." But she wondered if he even heard her because he was already wading back into the crowd.

Blaise found the pudgy tourist now toe-to-toe with one of his cops as he tried to prevent Gary from pushing the car off the street.

"My car! My car! Thief! I'll sue you! I swear you'll be sorry you ever touched my property—"

"Oh, for God's sake," said Cherry impatiently. "It's

a damn rental car. Will you quit carrying on? You're giving me a headache, Stan!"

Stan didn't listen, but just continued to glare at Wes Tamlin as if he wanted to rip out his heart. "You can't do this."

"I'm sorry, sir, but I can. You're impeding traffic." Wes was polite. Too polite. Blaise grinned.

"Hey, Wes."

"Yes, Chief?"

"Please escort Mr. . . . Mr. . . ."

"Potter," spluttered the pudgy man. "Stan Potter. And you'll sure as hell have reason to rue the day we met. My lawyer—"

"Please escort Mr. Potter to the parking lot . . . by whatever means are necessary."

Wes grinned. "Sure thing, Chief." He looked down at the pudgy man. "This way."

But Potter set his lips mulishly, ignoring Cherry's warnings that he was going to get clubbed over the head. So Wes Tamlin bent over, grabbed the guy under the shoulders, picked him up, and carried him toward the parking lot. Cherry followed, excoriating Potter loudly, while the wiry little man who had been in the other car trotted along behind, grinning.

The crowd cheered.

"Okay, folks," Blaise called out, "let's clear the street so traffic can move. Back onto the sidewalks!"

Much to his relief, they complied, swiftly clearing the streets.

Except for Dan Burgess, who followed him back to the parking lot, loudly criticizing his handling of events. Finally Blaise turned on him.

"You know, Dan, I think we did okay. Nobody had to use a nightstick or a gun. But," he paused for emphasis, "that could change at any moment."

Dan's eyes widened, then he drew himself up

haughtily to his full height. "Are you threatening me?"

"Not yet." Blaise paused significantly. "I suggest you move on like everyone else and let the police deal with this matter. That's what we're getting paid to do."

"As the mayor of this town—"

Blaise felt his face freeze. From long experience, he knew that his expression right now was terrifying and no amount of effort on his part was going to change it. Christ, this wasn't going to help matters at all, but the simple truth was, he was fed up to the gills with this crap. "As the mayor, you shouldn't be interfering with police work."

Dan Burgess apparently decided it was the better part of valor not to argue further at this time. Particularly since Miss Mary Todd had arrived on the scene, waving her cane like a sword.

"Let the boy do his job, Danny," she said sternly. "I don't want to have to take you over my knee the way I used to when I caught you stealing my cookies off the windowsill."

Dan Burgess turned a bright red, embarrassment swamping him at having a juvenile misdeed recounted in front of so many people. Blaise nearly chuckled out loud.

"Miss Todd!" Dan protested.

"Oh, I know it was a long time ago and I shouldn't embarrass you with such an old tale, but I always felt the boy becomes the man . . ."

Dan fled. Literally. For fear that Miss Todd would publicly dissect his character, he turned and hurried away as fast as his legs would take him.

Miss Todd shook her head and *tsked*. "That boy's character certainly hasn't improved any."

Then she turned a basilisk eye on Stan Potter, who

was threatening all kinds of legal retaliation against Wes Tamlin, Blaise Corrigan, and the Paradise Beach police department.

"You, sir," she said, in a voice that would have withered the leaves on a live oak, "need to learn manners, sense, and decorum."

Stan was so astonished he simply gaped. Cherry scowled at Miss Todd but wisely kept silent.

"I saw the entire accident, Blaise," Miss Todd told him. "This man," she pointed at Potter, "ran the red light."

"She's lying!" Potter shouted.

"I don't think so," Blaise said flatly. "I'd already figured that out from the position of the vehicles."

Potter gaped. "How could you know what color the light was? You weren't here."

"But I could tell which way the traffic was stopped when the collision occurred. North-south traffic was halted behind the stop line in both directions. East-west traffic was in the intersection behind the other man's car, and coming from the opposite direction." He looked Potter dead in the eye. "You ran the light."

A dull red suffused Potter's face, and Cherry punched his arm. "I told you, you idiot!" She hit him again. "I oughtta break your neck, you jerk."

With the swiftness of a pouncing cat, Blaise moved behind the woman and drew her arms behind her. "You're under arrest for battery. Gary, come cuff her."

"Battery! Battery? What the hell are you talking about?"

"You hit Mr. Potter. Twice. You have the right to remain silent. Anything you say—"

"Stan! Stan, tell this gorilla to let me go! I didn't do anything to you . . ."

But Stan was suddenly grinning with delight. "I'm

not going to tell him anything, Cherry. I told you you shouldn't hit me!" He did a little dance.

"I can't go to jail! Stan, you get me out of jail or I'll ...I'll..." The words trailed off as the handcuffs snapped around her wrists. Suddenly she looked lost and plaintive. "Stan?"

Stan looked triumphant. "You shouldn't have hit me, Cherry."

"I'm sorry. Really. I'll never do it again. Just don't let these cops take me away. They'll beat me bloody and dump my corpse in the Gulf!"

"Oh, for heaven's sake," Mary Todd said disgustedly. "Quit whining, girl. If this fool man really wants you back, he'll be able to bail you out in a few hours. In the meantime, you should think about how you're behaving!"

But as Gary led her away, Cherry reverted to type, spewing invectives at Stan Potter, whose grin grew wider with every step the woman took. "Take her away!" he crowed. "Send her up the river! I've had enough of her nastiness!"

But after she was gone, he looked frightened. "I shouldn't have done that," he said to no one in particular. "She's going to be so mad at me ..." He apparently didn't like that idea at all.

"You can go down to the jail and bail her out later this afternoon. If you want to. Now, about the accident. ..."

All of a sudden, Potter was his blustery, obnoxious self again. "I'm telling you, that redneck idiot ran the light, not me, and I'll be damned if I'm paying for this stupid rental car because some stupid cracker can't tell red from green!"

"Let me see your rental agreement, Mr. Potter."

Jillie turned away, tired of the pudgy man and all his complaints. Traffic was moving along the boulevard again, and the crowd of onlookers had almost entirely dissipated. Across the street, between two older cottages, she could see the white dunes crowned with sea oats. Maybe she'd just run across and walk on the beach. Maybe she'd just go home. Blaise could always walk, or get a ride with one of his cops.

But part of her was reluctant to leave Blaise Corrigan any sooner than she had to, so she stayed where she was, hearing the muffled roar of the surf, listening to the raucous calls of the gulls, while Blaise dealt with the accident. With her back to the confusion and her eyes toward the sea, it was nearly possible to forget that anyone else existed.

"Sorry about that." Blaise was suddenly beside her, touching her arm, gently urging her back toward her vehicle. They waited for the light to change, then crossed the street. "I shouldn't have asked you to wait."

"I'm kind of glad you did. It gave me an opportunity to tell Potter and Burgess what I think of them."

He shook his head, fighting a smile. "You sure did that."

"Well, it didn't do any good, but I got to let off steam."

He helped her into the car then before he closed the door, leaned down and looked at her. "Can I take you out for dinner tonight? To make amends?"

She should have said no. She should have backed away from this pitfall as fast as she could move.

"Yes," she said instead. "I'd like that."

And those, she thought, were the stupidest four words that had ever come out of her mouth.

Four

When the bell rang, she flung the door wide open with a welcoming smile, then froze in horror. Instead of Blaise Corrigan on her porch, she found her ex-husband. Fielding Wainwright gave her an ingratiating smile.

"Hello, Jillian," he said.

Her survival instinct finally forced her to draw a deep gulp of air. "What the hell are you doing here?"

He shook his head. "You *do* have a way with words, darling."

"I am *not* your darling!"

He kept right on smiling. That smile, Jillie believed, had made his life far too easy for his own good. Fielding Wainwright could charm the socks off a cat. "We need to talk, and we can't do that if you keep hanging up on me."

She started to close the door in his face, but he just stepped forward into her house. His dark eyes raked her from head to foot. "Florida becomes you, darling. What a great tan! But you'd better be careful. Redheads can burn to a crisp in no time at all."

Just like that he'd made her feel underdressed. Blaise had suggested the Twin Palms beach bar for dinner, so she had dressed accordingly in white culottes and an emerald green halter. One of the things she liked about this place was that getting dressed up meant putting on a better pair of shorts.

But suddenly she wished she were wearing slacks and a baggy T-shirt so that Fielding couldn't look at her that way, as if she were a morsel he wanted to devour. God! Why hadn't she realized long ago how positively sleazy he was?

"You never dressed like this for me," he remarked.

"It's a lot colder in Massachusetts, Fielding, and we never went to the beach." She pointed past his shoulder to the street. "There's the exit."

He started to shake his head, smiling all the while. Jillie hardly saw him, though, because she was suddenly aware that a gray streak was tearing across the lawn right at them.

"It's that damn dog," she said, recognizing the beast that had caused her to drive over Blaise's mailbox. He was heading straight toward them, and she instinctively began to try to close the door, sure that the dog intended to run inside and wreak havoc.

Fielding, however, caught the door with both hands and resisted her push. "Don't try to shut me out, Jillian. I'll never give up hope of winning you back."

As if in a nightmare, Jillie watched the dog run straight at them. It leaped, and the next thing she knew, Fielding was howling wildly.

"It bit me!" he shrieked. "Get it off me! Get it off me!"

But the dog was already running away in another

direction, and Jillie found herself thinking with be-
musement that the animal showed great discernment.

"Oh, God! I'm bleeding!"

Fielding waved his hand in her face, displaying one
or two small smears of blood, and Jillie reluctantly
opened the door. "Come on in and let me look at it."

He came into her living room, limping ostentatiously and groaning. "It bit me, damn it! What was
it? It ought to be shot!"

Jillie found herself nearly overwhelmed by a totally
inappropriate urge to laugh. Fielding glared at her.
"It's not funny."

"I know . . . I know . . ."

But it *was* funny. Nobody on the whole planet deserved to be bitten on the butt more than Fielding
Wainwright, she figured. "Bend over the table and let
me see," she told him.

Moaning even more loudly, he limped into the dining ell and leaned over the table. The fabric on his
pants was torn, and there were a few bright red
drops. "You'd better pull down your pants, Fielding.
I can't see much this way."

He straightened and gave her a distinctly salacious
look over his shoulder.

"Cut it out," she said sharply. "I thought you were
injured. How can you be thinking lurid thoughts at a
time like this?"

"I'd rather have *you* bite my—"

"Shut up!"

Looking like a wounded little boy, he dropped his
slacks and turned so she could see the mark. The skin
was hardly broken, and the injury looked more like a
scrape than a bite.

"It's not bad," she told him. "I think your slacks
took most of the force of the bite. Your skin is just

scratched. Do you suppose you ought to get rabies shots?"

He straightened as if he'd been struck. "Rabies shots?" he squeaked.

Jillian shrugged. "Well, it seems like the wise thing to do. The dog bit you for no reason, after all."

Clutching his pants up around his waist, he started to sit on the couch.

"No!" Jillie said sharply. "You'll bleed all over it."

He paled. "Am I bleeding that much?"

"Just a few drops. Let me get a towel for you to sit on." It was a white couch, after all, and she felt she owed her ex-husband a whole lot less courtesy than she would give to a stranger on the street, considering how he'd treated her. She found a pink towel in the linen closet and threw it at him.

"Hey," he said, looking at it. "We got that as a wedding present."

"Good. It's perfect for you to bleed on."

He shook his head and looked at her. "Give it up, Jillian. We had a big fight, but now it's time to act like civilized adults."

"Did you ever *know* what it means to be civilized?"

He spread the towel out on the couch, smoothing it meticulously, then sat. "Better than you, apparently. Bring in my suitcase from the car, will you? I need to change my pants, and then I suppose I should find a doctor to look at this."

"I am *not* your servant, Fielding. Get your own suitcase."

"But I'm hurt!"

"No more than a little scrape. You're perfectly capable of getting to your car and back."

"I was injured on *your* property! You have a duty—"

"Oh, for Pete's sake! How could I have ever been

stupid enough to think I was in love with you?"

Something in that remark appeared to strike him forcefully, for he stood up abruptly. "You're right," he said. "I'm being an ass. I'll get the suitcase." He fumbled at his belt, fastening it.

Jillie nearly gaped. In all her experience of him, Fielding Wainwright had never been swift to yield in an argument. He always had to have the last word.

Now he tossed Jillie another of his winning smiles and crossed to the door, flinging it wide open in a dramatic gesture. Probably imagining himself as the hero in some movie, Jillie thought sourly, going off to do battle for home and hearth.

Blaise Corrigan was standing there, hand raised to knock. The two men looked at one another in astonishment. Blaise recovered first. "Is . . . Jillie here?"

"Who the hell are you?" Fielding demanded.

"Fielding!" Jillie remonstrated.

"Well, who is he? Don't tell me you're dating before the ink is even dry on our divorce papers!"

"Our marriage was dead a long time ago, and it's none of your business, anyway!" She looked at Blaise, whose face betrayed nothing. "I'm ready to go. Just let me get my purse."

Fielding howled. "You can't leave me like this! I've been injured! I need a doctor!"

"What happened?" Blaise asked.

The younger man turned to him. "Some damn dog came running out of nowhere and bit me! I'm bleeding."

"It's just a scrape," Jillie said. "The major damage was to his ego."

"Did you see the dog?" Blaise pulled a pen and a small notepad out of his breast pocket and began to write.

Jillie answered. "It was the same dog that I swerved

to avoid the other night. The gray Airedale."

"Cal Lepkin's dog." He slapped the notebook closed. "Damn animal is a menace."

"Yes, it is!" Fielding chimed in readily. "It ought to be put away. I wasn't doing a thing except standing in the doorway talking to Jillie when it lunged out of nowhere and bit me."

Blaise reopened the notebook. "What's your name?"

"Fielding Wainwright. I'm Jillie's husband."

"*Ex*-husband," Jillie interjected. "And just getting ready to leave, right?"

"Jillie, you can't be serious! I've driven two days to get here and now I've been attacked by a dog! You can't possibly mean to throw me out."

"You're certainly not staying with *me*." She shook her head emphatically. "We're divorced, Fielding. Find yourself a hotel room."

"But—"

Blaise stepped back and pointed to the street. "You heard the lady. Leave."

"And just who the *hell* are you?" Fielding demanded.

"He's the chief of police," Jillie said, suddenly feeling like grinning again.

"You've been asked to leave," Blaise said flatly. "Now, either leave, or I'll have to arrest you for trespassing."

Fielding threw up his hands. "I don't believe this. I absolutely don't believe this." He looked at Jillie. "You haven't seen the last of me, darling. I'm going to change your mind about us if it's the last thing I do."

Jillie opened her mouth to tell him that nothing on earth could change her mind about him, but then decided not to prolong the argument any further. She wanted him out of here now so she could go out to dinner with Blaise and explain that she absolutely wasn't harboring any kind feelings for her ex. God! Of all times for Fielding to take a stupid notion!

But Fielding had turned to Blaise and was haranguing him about the dog. "Don't you people have leash laws here? Why is a dangerous animal running around loose? You're going to find it, aren't you? Damn it, if I have to have rabies shots, I'll sue the police department for dereliction of duty, or something!"

Blaise remained calm. "We have leash laws, Mr. Wainwright. That animal is running around loose because it manages to escape frequently and is difficult to catch. I believe a check of the veterinarian's records will show that the animal is up to date on its shots. As for suing the police department—this is a free country and you're welcome to waste your money in any manner you see fit. Now, your car is over there. I suggest you get into it and find a hotel room before it becomes necessary to sleep in your vehicle."

"Well, I never . . . !" Forgetting to limp, Fielding stalked away.

And Jillie laughed. She couldn't help it. Blaise looked at her curiously.

"What's so funny?"

"Fielding. He's used to a lot more deference from public officials. At home he's a rather important person."

Blaise shrugged a shoulder. "Around here he's just another pain-in-the-butt tourist."

"Literally," she giggled. "Let me just get my purse . . ."

But even as she turned, the phone started to ring. She hesitated.

"Go ahead and answer it," he told her with a smile. "I'm not in any rush."

"Well, then, come in and have a seat. It's probably just a salesman . . ."

Instead, it was her former mother-in-law. "I'm at the Tampa airport, Jillian, and I'd appreciate it if you would come and get me right now."

"But . . . Mother . . . Mother Wainwright . . ." Feeling like a fish suddenly yanked out of water, Jillie started stammering, trying to find something intelligent to say. "I was . . . just leaving on a dinner date . . ."

"Then I'm just in time," Harriet Wainwright said emphatically. "Cancel the date and come at once."

Jillie hesitated, looking at Blaise and trying to summon the courage to do something she had never done before: tell Fielding's mother *no*.

"What's wrong?" Blaise asked.

Jillie covered the mouthpiece with her hand. "Fielding's mother is at the Tampa airport and wants me to come get her immediately. Blaise . . ."

He shrugged. "Let's go get her. We can always have dinner tomorrow night."

Jillie stared at him, uncertain whether to be annoyed because he was making it so easy, or to be delighted that he wasn't like Fielding, who'd have acted like a two-year-old at any attempt to change his plans.

"Jillian? Are you still there? Look, dear, I know you've been treated abominably, but I didn't have anything to do with it, other than giving birth to that poor excuse for a man! Now, just come get me and we'll have a nice talk and figure out how to sort this all out."

"There's nothing to sort out, Mother."

"It's all a matter of opinion, my dear, but this is

nothing to be discussed on the phone while I'm twiddling my thumbs in this airport—actually, it's one of the nicest airports I've ever been in, but it's still an airport and I'm exhausted. We'll argue later. Just come get me."

"I'm afraid it'll take nearly an hour to get there."

"That's quite all right, dear. I'm going to have a light supper with a very nice gentleman I met on the flight down. We're in Airside C, at the snack shop."

Jillie hung up and looked at Blaise. "I'm being invaded by Wainwrights."

He cocked his head and smiled faintly. "How come?"

"God knows. Fielding claims he wants a reconciliation."

"Do you?"

She shook her head firmly. "Absolutely not."

"So ignore him. What does his mother want?"

"I haven't the foggiest. Anyway, she's having dinner with some man she met on the flight, so we don't have to hurry."

"I take it Fielding's father is dead?"

"That's the only reason Fielding is a person of any importance," Jillie said sourly. "Without all his inherited wealth everyone would treat him as what he is— a spoiled brat!"

Blaise followed her out of the house, trying to smother a grin. "Why don't you tell me what you *really* think?" he said.

"I'm sorry, I'm probably shocking you." Halfway across the driveway, she turned to face him.

"No, it'd take a lot more than that to shock me."

"Good. I tend to be a shocking person. Damn it, what's going on with Fielding and his mother? I wish I could read their minds. Or maybe I don't. At least, not Fielding's. I think it's drowning in sex hormones."

A crack of laughter escaped Blaise.

"He's awful," Jillie told him seriously. "Terrible. He was chasing other women the whole time we were married. And he had four affairs that I know of."

"That's aw—"

"And what about that darn dog?" Jillie interrupted suddenly. "First it causes me to have a wreck, and then it comes charging across the lawn to bite Fielding for absolutely no reason at all—not that I don't want to do the same thing . . ."

"My men will get the dog tomorrow. It usually goes home in the morning and sleeps, so if we're going to have any chance of catching it, the best time will be then."

"You mean, you track the dog's habits? You know it that well?"

"Hell, yes. That damn animal has given everyone around here a pain in the neck from time to time."

"Then why not get rid of it?"

He shook his head seriously. "Cal Lepkin's heart would break if anything happened to that dog. It's all he has."

"Then maybe he ought to keep it chained."

"Cal's tried everything. Chains. Fences. Enclosed kennels . . . I'm telling you, Jillie, that dog is the devil's spawn. It gets out by means of magic."

"You really don't have to come with me to the airport," she said finally, not knowing quite how to respond to his remark about the dog. "I realize I've made a mess of your evening, and I really don't want to mess it up any more."

His brilliant blue eyes softened, and he said almost gently, "You haven't messed up my evening, Jillie. Let's take my Explorer. There's more passenger room than in your Toyota."

*   *   *

They had no trouble finding Harriet Wainwright. Jillie could hear her former mother-in-law's voice as she and Blaise rode the narrow escalator down to the embarkation level. Harriet was holding forth on the subject of young people's manners these days, and how everyone seemed to have forgotten even the simplest matters of common courtesy.

"That's her," Jillie said to Blaise.

He looked amused. In fact, Jillie thought, he was finding this all too amusing. He ought to be at least a little annoyed that his plans for the evening had been ruined by people he didn't know. He ought to at least be a little put out by Fielding's and Harriet's behavior. *She* certainly was.

Judging by the topic of conversation, Jillie expected to find Harriet·in the company of an elderly gentleman. Instead she appeared to be surrounded by the better part of a college football team. Surprisingly enough, they appeared to be enjoying her discourse.

Harriet Wainwright was a magnificent woman, tall, large bosomed, and white-haired. In her youth she had probably been considered too tall, too large, and otherwise plain, but in her later years she was a commanding presence that invariably caught the eye and attention.

"Jillian, my dear," Harriet called out. "Over here!"

"As if anyone could miss her," Jillie muttered to Blaise. He chuckled, annoying her even further.

Harriet rose to greet her with a kiss on the cheek. "This is my daughter-in-law," she said to the young men, "so I'm safe now and you can all go on your way. Thank you so much for keeping me company."

"No trouble" and "Glad to do it" were among the responses the young men offered as they nodded to Jillie and left in a phalanx.

"When you said you were having dinner with a

gentleman, I pictured something entirely different," Jillie remarked to her former mother-in-law.

Harriet sniffed. "Tsk. I sat next to one of those young men on the flight and we struck up an interesting conversation. He quite agreed with me that young people today are barbarians. At any rate, he asked the rest of his friends to join us when we decided to have a sandwich while I waited for you. They were surprisingly civilized for young people."

She suddenly became aware of Blaise standing patiently to the side and turned her disapproving gaze on him. "And who," she demanded imperiously, "is this?"

Wealth and age had given Harriet the notion she could be as blunt as she wanted to be. Once, Jillie had loved Harriet's "charming candor." Of course, throughout her life, Jillie had tended to be drawn to people who were outspoken to the point of outrageousness. But suddenly she was seeing it differently. She didn't like Harriet treating Blaise this way.

"This," said Blaise, straightening and extending his hand to Harriet, "is Blaise Corrigan, Jillie's date for this evening."

"Date." Harriet sniffed and looked disapprovingly at Jillie. "Dating already."

Jillie suppressed a sigh with difficulty. "The divorce is final, Harriet."

"Mother. You always call me Mother."

"Not any longer." She tried to speak firmly, sensing that if she didn't make her position clear to Harriet quickly, she was going to find herself drowning in a sea of meddling.

"We'll discuss that later," Harriet announced. "When we're *alone*. Why did you bring Mr. Corrigan with you?"

"My car is larger," Blaise said smoothly, "and I offered to drive. Jillie doesn't know her way around very well yet."

Harriet looked at Jillie. "He's a meddler."

"No more than you, Harriet," Jillie replied.

"Jillian!" The word was a gasp of disapproval.

Blaise intervened. "Did you check any baggage, Mrs. Wainwright?"

She looked at him with evident reluctance, her chin lifting sharply. "Yes. Yes, I did."

"Then I suggest we go get it. The airport is closing down for the night."

Harriet wasn't accustomed to being told what to do, and she regarded Blaise with a combination of disbelief and dislike. Apparently she couldn't think up a decent argument, however, because she followed along when he headed for the baggage claim.

"Who does he think he is?" she hissed to Jillian, as they trotted after Blaise.

Jillie, who also believed Blaise was overbearing, found herself defending him. "He's used to being in charge, Harriet. He's the chief of police."

"A policeman? Oh, my dear, I can't believe you're slumming like this. It's such a . . . a . . . *common* job to hold."

And Jillie couldn't believe she had ever found this woman's snobbery amusing. "That's all right, Harriet. I'm shortly going to be nothing myself but a common shopkeeper."

Harriet glanced down at her. "There's nothing wrong with being a shopkeeper. Owning one's own business is the best way to succeed. But . . . Jillian, if you open a shop, you won't be able to come back to Massachusetts."

"I have no intention of returning to Massachusetts. Ever. And by the way, I've been working as a cocktail waitress."

Harriet gasped in horror and was briefly silenced. They were approaching the baggage carousels before she spoke again. "You're just distraught over the divorce, my dear. You're not thinking clearly."

"I *am* thinking clearly," Jillie said firmly. "And if all you're here for is to try to persuade me to go back to Fielding, you're wasting your time and you might as well catch the morning flight back home."

"Well, I never!"

The baggage carousels had been shut down for the night, but unclaimed bags stood stacked against the wall. Harriet had no difficulty picking out her three matched pieces of expensive luggage. Blaise hefted them all, refusing Jillie's offer of assistance.

"They're not that heavy," he assured her, and led the way back to the elevators that ascended to the parking garage.

Jillie, who was beginning to feel pretty frosted at the Wainwrights in general, found herself wondering if Blaise was feeling frosted, too. He was being awfully quiet, and there was something about the set of his jaw that made her wonder if he was angry or if he was trying to suppress a laugh.

Either reaction was suitable, she supposed, and laughter, at least, wouldn't raise the blood pressure.

"So you're a policeman," Harriet said from the back seat, as they pulled away from the airport. Jillie stiffened at her tone, but Blaise seemed not to notice it.

"That's right."

"Aren't you a little old for that?" Harriet demanded. "It's a job for boys who need to sow their wild oats before they settle into adult responsibilities."

"Really?"

Jillie couldn't contain herself. "Don't be insulting, Harriet."

"I'm not trying to be insulting! I merely asked an honest question. Wanting to play cops and robbers should be reserved for children."

"Actually," said Blaise mildly enough, "if that were true, you wouldn't be safe in your bed, ma'am, because there'd be a shortage of police officers to protect you."

"I have never in my life needed a policeman's protection!"

"Exactly."

Harriet fell silent, as if she couldn't quite decide what to make of this man. Jillie settled back against her seat and hoped the silence would continue for the rest of the trip. She had a rather glum feeling that she wasn't going to be able to get rid of either Fielding or Harriet easily. And after an evening like this, Blaise Corrigan would probably be hoping that he'd never see her again. Not that she cared . . . of course she didn't. Her life would be far better without a man to mess it up.

But Harriet had never been silent for long, and tonight was no exception. "Well," she said presently, "I suppose I can see what you mean. No, certainly I wouldn't propose living in a lawless society. But surely a more mature man would follow a more mature pursuit."

Jillie cringed, waiting for an explosion. None came. When Blaise replied, his voice was even . . . perhaps too even. "I'm afraid I don't agree with you, Mrs. Wainwright. Protecting the lives and properties of the citizens of Paradise Beach is *not* a job for someone who is immature. Neither is carrying a gun."

"Well, of course it isn't," Harriet replied, illogical as always. "Good heavens, the thought makes me shudder. Boys with guns!" Before anyone could point out her inconsistency to her, she was plunging ahead into deeper waters. "I can't imagine why my daughter-in-law is dating you," she said bluntly. "You're far too old for her—what are you? Forty-five?"

"Thirty-eight."

"Still, that's far too old for her. She's only thirty. And you have a dangerous occupation."

"It's been fifteen years since a Paradise Beach police officer died in the line of duty, Mrs. Wainwright. Besides, I'm the chief. I do most of my work at a desk."

Except when there's a traffic jam, Jillie thought, remembering events earlier that day. She wondered if strangling Harriet with her scarf would silence her. Probably not. Harriet Wainwright would be directing her own funeral from the grave. The mortician wouldn't even be able to get her to lie down in her own coffin. "Harriet, none of this is any of your business."

"Of course it is! You're married to my son."

"Not any longer."

Harriet shook her head. "You'll get over this."

"I already have gotten over it. It's a closed chapter in my life. *Finis.* I'm building a new life now, and Fielding is absolutely not going to be a part of it."

"But of course he is." Harriet turned to Blaise. "She loves him desperately. Anyone could see it."

"Not any more!"

"She's on the rebound, Mr. Corrigan. Once she gets over her hurt she'll want Fielding back. You wouldn't want to get involved with that, now, would you?"

Blaise rolled his eyes. Jillie wished she had a gun. Even a peashooter. Anything to get this woman's attention and get her to be quiet. "Shut up, Harriet."

Harriet turned to glare over the seat back at her. "Don't talk to me that way."

"Then don't talk *about* me that way. You haven't any idea what you're talking about. None at all!"

"My dear child—"

"I'm not a child, Harriet."

"I saw how very much in love with Fielding you were. And you still are, I'm sure. He's hurt you badly, but you'll get over that when you see he means to mend his ways."

"Fielding will never mend his ways."

"My dear, he swears he'll never be unfaithful again."

"He's already sworn that three times, and broken the vow every time. The really amazing thing is that I believed him more than once. I'm not going to be that stupid again."

"But he's changed!"

With effort, Jillie refused to answer. She couldn't believe they were having this discussion at all, let alone in front of Blaise. She was never again going to be able to look the man in the eye.

When Jillie didn't argue any further, Harriet turned around and faced front again. To Blaise she said, "Jillie has been seriously hurt by my son, and of course she feels she wants nothing more to do with him. That will change."

Blaise then astonished Jillie—and undoubtedly Harriet, as well—by stating bluntly, "She'd be a fool to change her mind."

Harriet gasped. "Whatever do you mean?"

"I mean that forgiving him once for cheating was a kind and generous thing to do. Forgiving him after the fourth time would be the hallmark of an idiot."

That, thank God, left Harriet speechless. After a few minutes of strained silence, Blaise began to talk quite cheerfully about all the sights she should be careful not to miss while she was vacationing on the west coast of Florida.

Jillie slumped in her seat, wondering why she felt as if she'd just gone ten rounds with Muhammad Ali.

When they reached the drawbridge that connected the mainland to the north end of Paradise Beach, the bridge was up. Blaise joined the long line of waiting traffic and put on the emergency brake. "Which hotel are you staying at?" he asked Harriet.

"I'm not staying at a hotel. I'm staying with Jillian, of course."

"You are?" Jillie asked, feeling as if she'd just been hit by a runaway train.

"Well, of course I am! I'm family."

The problem was, Jillie felt the same way. Oh, she had her differences with Harriet, but by and large her relationship with Harriet had been a lot better—especially toward the end—than her relationship with Fielding. And when she came right down to it, she didn't necessarily want to throw out all of Fielding's relatives just because she was throwing out Fielding. But this could get complicated.

"I sent Fielding to a hotel," she told her former mother-in-law.

"Well, of course you did. Don't tell me he expected to stay with you! Good heavens, you're still mad at him. Will that boy never learn?"

A feeling not too far from panic was beginning to settle over Jillie as she wondered how long she was going to have to handle this. Having her former mother-in-law staying with her for any length of time would make it extremely difficult to do anything at all. Harriet was the type to interfere constantly with everything, from her plans to open a bookstore to her desire to build a new life for herself. On the other hand, she didn't want to be unconscionably rude to the woman who had been the only member of the

Wainwright clan to make her feel welcome after her divorce from Fielding.

"You can stay with me," she told Harriet, "but only on one condition: you absolutely *will not* do anything to try to get me back with Fielding. I don't want you even to mention the subject."

The drawbridge was lowering back into place by the time Harriet replied. "Very well."

And that, thought Jillie, settled the entire matter. Now she was sure she could handle it.

Famous last words.

Five

Blaise carried Harriet's bags into the house, said a pleasant good night, and vanished.

And that, thought Jillie glumly, was that. She'd probably never see *him* again except over his summons book. Not that it really made any difference. She was absolutely certain that he had taken her to the DMV today and offered to take her out to dinner only as a way of making amends for arresting her. He probably figured picking Harriet up at the airport canceled any debts.

"Jillian, I need some fresh towels."

Jillie turned from the door to look at Harriet. "Those *are* fresh towels, Harriet. I have only one set, and those were washed this morning."

Harriet looked startled. "One set? Only one?"

"Well, except for a couple of old ones that I basically use as rags." Including the one that was still neatly spread on the sofa where Fielding had been sitting earlier. A few drops of blood now looked like rust stains. Bending, she scooped it up, thinking she might just throw it away.

Harriet shook her head. "How are we each to have our own towels, then?"

"I'll use the old ones. Don't worry about it. I guess I need to wash the sheets, though. I slept on them last night."

"And you don't have a spare set?" Harriet was plainly appalled. "My dear, you should have two sets of everything! And why am I sleeping in *your* bed? Don't you have a guest room?"

"I have one set of everything because I had to buy most of it myself. The spare room is unfurnished because I can't afford a second bed at present and I wasn't planning on having houseguests."

"But where will you sleep?"

"On the sofa." And this time she didn't bother to tell Harriet not to worry about it.

"But what happened to all the things that you and Fielding had in your house?"

"Oh, I'm sure Fielding still has all of it. The house was in his name, remember? And according to what he told his attorney, so was everything in it. I couldn't prove otherwise." Nor had she really wanted to. Yes, there were a lot of wedding gifts and other presents she might rightfully have claimed, and a number of pieces she had bought out of her own salary as an assistant to the dean at a local college, but unfortunately, everything had memories of Fielding attached to it. She might have been left with nothing, but sometimes she felt she'd gotten the better bargain. Besides, all that heavy furniture would look awful here in Florida.

Harriet was still clucking disapprovingly. "Well, I'll

see about getting another bed in here tomorrow. This is ridiculous. And I loathe waterbeds!"

Nevertheless, she didn't offer to sleep on the couch or to stay at a hotel, Jillie noted with an inward smile. Oh, heck, she told herself, there was no sense in being irritated. She loved Harriet and probably always would—warts and all.

When she went to pull the sheets off the waterbed, though, Harriet waved her aside. "Don't bother. I'm sure they're clean enough, dear. Tomorrow we can go shopping for something for the guest room." She paused, shaking her head and frowning. "I really can't believe Fielding treated you that way. He could at least have been honorable in the divorce settlement."

"Fielding was very angry at the time, Harriet. Hardly surprising, since he isn't used to being rejected. Anyway, it's over and done with and I want to leave it that way."

"But—"

"And I really can't go shopping with you tomorrow. Sorry. I have other plans." Stepping out of the room, she closed the door with quiet firmness behind her, hoping that Harriet would take the hint—not that Harriet was any good at taking hints.

God, what a day! Feeling whipped, she dragged herself into the kitchen and tried to decide what she could eat. She hadn't had a bite since mid afternoon and it was now fast approaching eleven o'clock. Where had the time gone?

Although a better question, she thought wryly, as she peered into the refrigerator, would be how she had come to be overrun by Wainwrights. And why. Why this sudden interest in reconciliation fully six months after the divorce had become final?

Her decision to leave Fielding had been the occasion of great bitterness between her and the Wainwright family. More than one cousin or aunt had told her that she ought to simply tough it out, that Fielding would settle down with time, and that she mustn't tarnish the family name. No Wainwright had ever been divorced. Jillie had eventually found herself wondering how many of these women were putting up with, or had put up with, philandering for those very reasons. Regardless, she wasn't going to be one of them.

When she made it clear she was leaving, the entire family, with the exception of Harriet, had turned on her. Oh, not that they had been too vicious; they had simply become cold, letting her know that she was now an outsider.

Which was what she had been when she'd met Fielding to begin with, an orphan from Waukegan, Illinois, without roots or family history, or a claim to be descended from Pilgrims. They had all been dead-set against the marriage and equally dead-set against the divorce. Where was the sense in it?

She heard the bathroom door close and the sound of the shower being turned on. Harriet apparently had decided to get ready for bed. Which was probably a smart choice, and one she should make herself. Instead she closed the fridge, grabbed a banana from the bowl on the counter, and stepped out into her small backyard.

No one had ever tended the yard, as far as she could tell, and patchy grasses grew from the sandy soil, but little else. It would probably cost a lot of money to import good topsoil, more than anyone wanted to spend on a rental property. There were a couple of stubby coastal pines that offered thin shade, but little else of note.

With her head tipped back, she looked up at the

stars and thought about this sudden appearance by both Harriet and Fielding. It seemed suspiciously timed, so many months after the divorce, when neither of them had seemed particularly interested in reconciliation before the split. Oh, Harriet had disapproved of a divorce in the family, but once she had become convinced that Jillie wasn't going to change her mind, she had dropped the subject.

Now even Fielding, who had been so wounded and irate over her decision to leave him, was singing a different tune. Maybe he had just come to his senses, but she doubted it. Something else was going on here, something that had caused both Fielding and his mother to go into overdrive trying to get her back.

She didn't like it. She also didn't know what to do about it. With nothing but a nagging suspicion that things weren't right, she had no place to look for an explanation.

"Hi."

Startled, she whirled around and saw Blaise standing on his back deck looking down from its second-story heights. "Oh! Hi."

"You can see the waterway from up here. Wanna come up?"

"Thanks, but maybe another night. I have to make sure Harriet is settled."

"Sure. She seems like a great old gal."

"A little opinionated."

He chuckled. "If I let that bother me, I'd have quit this damn job a long time ago. Everybody's got an opinion. I prefer knowing what it is to wondering what it might be."

"Sounds sensible to me."

"I'm a sensible man—most of the time. Are we on for dinner tomorrow night?"

She felt a quiver of excitement in the pit of her

stomach. He wanted to see her again! Despite everything, he still wanted to have dinner with her. "Sure,"
she heard herself say, even as part of her argued that
she ought to be avoiding men like the plague.

"Same time, same place," he said. "We're supposed
to have some clouds tomorrow afternoon, so the sunset should be spectacular."

When she went back inside, she assured herself that
she'd accepted only because she wanted to sit at a
beach bar and watch the sunset, and it wasn't something she wanted to do alone. It was as good an excuse as any.

"There you are," Harriet said, as soon as she
stepped into the living room. The older woman was
wearing a surprisingly simple pair of silk pajamas
and had curled up in the armchair. "I wondered what
had become of you."

"I just stepped out back to smell the breeze. It's a
lovely evening." She sat on the couch facing her former mother-in-law and waited, knowing Harriet
hadn't sat up for her just to see that she returned
safely.

"We need to talk about Fielding," Harriet said.

"You promised!"

Harriet waved a hand. "So throw me out in the
morning. In the meantime, we're going to talk. I flew
all the way down here to talk about this, and I won't
be deterred."

Jillie propped her chin on her hand and battered
back a feeling of outright rebellion that threatened to
swamp her. It would have been easy just then to
throw a royal temper tantrum.

"Fielding's behavior was execrable," Harriet said.
"Appalling. It was bad enough that you found out
about one of his affairs, but that you should have
found out about *four* of them is beyond belief!"

"That he should have *had* four affairs is beyond belief," Jillie argued. "It's not as if my finding out about it was the only thing that mattered, Harriet."

"Young men are especially prone to this sort of behavior, dear. They just seem to get overwhelmed by their, er, urges, and all we can do is turn a blind eye. Men will be men, after all."

"Men might be less inclined to be men if women didn't keep turning a blind eye to it," Jillie said tartly.

Harriet looked a little startled, as if she hadn't thought of it like that before.

"I'm serious," Jillie persisted. "We shouldn't indulge them in these shenanigans. Saying men will be men just gives them an excuse to keep acting like spoiled little brats."

"A very solid, feminist point of view, Jillian, but since you aren't the only woman in the world, all men need do is find a woman who *will* indulge them. Which is what Fielding did."

Jillie gasped. "Are you saying *I* was responsible for Fielding's infidelity?"

Harriet looked her straight in the eye. "Can you say with absolute certainty that you weren't?"

That was, frankly, the very thought that had been terrifying Jillie for years now, ever since she learned of Fielding's first paramour. How could a woman not wonder if she were somehow so inadequate that her spouse had turned to another woman. And for so long she had tried to become the perfect wife . . . but that was over. She lifted her chin. "I won't buy that one, Harriet. Fielding roamed because he somehow got the cockeyed notion that he can have everything he wants, regardless of cost. You wouldn't know anything about that, would you?"

Harriet gasped. "You can't be implying—"

"Then don't imply *I* was at fault! Fielding has a

serious personality defect. Of that there's no question."

Harriet was silent for a while, so long that finally Jillian began to wonder if their relationship was ruptured for good. The thought made her feel sad.

"You're right," the older woman finally said. "He does seem to be spoiled. But I think he's outgrowing it, dear. That's why I want you to talk to him."

"It's too late for talking. I told him I'm not interested."

"You've seen him?"

"I threw him out just before you called."

Harriet rose to her feet. "You threw him out? My little baby? You threw him onto the street?"

"Now, wait one minute, Harriet! First of all, he's not a baby, he's thirty-three years old. Second, he's one of the wealthiest men in America. He's certainly capable of finding a hotel room."

Harriet sniffed and turned toward the bedroom. "Your problem is that you're an orphan. You don't have any understanding of how a family should work!"

Nearly reeling with the unexpected cruelty of that remark, Jillian could only watch the other woman stalk away into the bedroom and wonder what she had done to deserve this.

Of course. How could she have forgotten? She had married a Wainwright. No other act of stupidity was necessary.

Without spare sheets, Jillian was resigned to sleeping on the nubbly-textured couch without protection. She managed to find a blanket, but since she didn't feel like knocking on Harriet's door to ask for her nightshirt, she was forced to sleep in her clothes. Maybe, she thought hopefully, Harriet would be so offended that she'd find herself a hotel room tomorrow.

The phone rang just before midnight, just as Jillie was drifting into a troubled sleep.

"It's me," said Fielding. "I thought you'd want to know what the doctor said."

She yawned loudly, but didn't bother to apologize. "You'll live, right?"

"Only if the police catch the damn dog so you can identify it. Unless we can be sure it was that insane dog you were talking about, I have to have rabies shots."

In spite of herself, Jillie felt a twinge of sympathy. "Fielding, I'm sorry. Don't you worry. Blaise's men will catch the dog in the morning and you won't have to have the shots."

"One can hope." He sighed. "Are you sure you didn't train that dog to bite me?"

"No! Of course not!"

"Well, the doctor thought it might be significant that the dog bit me without provocation. He's thinking of rabies, of course."

"Well, I've encountered that dog before. It caused me to have an accident. And everyone around here seems to think it's possessed or something. Apparently it's never behaved normally."

"Maybe after this they'll exterminate the thing."

Jillie didn't bother telling him what Blaise had said about Cal Lepkin. Fielding had always been notably lacking in sympathy for the less fortunate. "By the way, did you know your mother flew in tonight?"

"Mother! What's she doing here?"

"She apparently wants to lend her support to your campaign for reconciliation. I told her she's wasting her time."

"Of course she is! I can't imagine how she can think

she'd be any kind of help at all! If that isn't just like her, always getting in the way."

"She's staying here with me, at least for tonight. Stop by in the morning and say hi. I'll be out taking care of business."

"I'd rather stop by and see *you*, Jillian."

"Forget it, Fielding. Try me again in another lifetime."

That having been said, she felt a whole lot better.

In the morning, before Harriet stirred, Jillie slipped out of the house, determined to start looking for a place to rent for her bookstore. Unfortunately, with Harriet in her bedroom, she hadn't been able to get fresh clothes. She felt like hell, actually, stepping out into the bright morning sunshine wearing clothes she'd slept in. The only alternative, however, was to wait for Harriet to wake—whenever that might be— and risk another confrontation like last night's.

"Good morning."

She found herself looking at Blaise across their two driveways. "Hi."

"Bad night?" he enquired with a lifted brow.

She looked down at herself and winced. "You wouldn't believe it."

"So come have breakfast with me. Nothing fancy, but I've got plenty of orange juice and a box of doughnuts." He bent and picked up the morning newspaper from the pavement and scanned the headlines. "Nothing ever changes," he remarked, then gave her a wide smile. "Come on. You can tell me all about it."

Somehow she found herself following him, telling herself that she had to wait until Harriet woke up anyway. In the bright sunlight her dishevelment looked far worse than she had thought in the dim light of her bathroom five minutes before. No way was she going anywhere looking like this.

Blaise's kitchen was on the second floor, like the rest of his living quarters, and sliding glass doors provided a view over surrounding rooftops and between trees. From here they could see the inland waterway sparkling in the brilliant daylight.

"Nice view, huh?" he said, as he guided her to the table on his deck. "Might as well eat out here."

The morning was cool, just a little above seventy degrees. Maybe too cool for what she was wearing. She felt a few goosebumps prickle along her arms and moved her chair a little so that she sat fully in the sun.

Blaise returned a couple of minutes later with two glasses, a pitcher of orange juice, and the promised doughnuts. "The coffee's brewing and should be ready in just a couple of minutes."

"Great. Coffee sounds really good." The box was huge, and when he opened it, she saw what must have been three dozen doughnuts. "You're kind of fond of these things."

He laughed, his blue eyes as brilliant as the sky overhead. "Actually, I was taking them down to the station for the guys. But you looked like you could use one even more."

She looked up at him, with the inescapable sensation that she had just been cared for. How long had it been since anyone had made her feel that way? Had anyone ever? At this point she wasn't sure that Fielding had ever made her feel this way, not even when they were first dating.

Good heavens! Suddenly her throat was tight and her eyes were prickling with unshed tears. Swiftly she looked away, blinking rapidly, hoping Blaise wouldn't see her distress. Apparently he didn't, because without another word he went back into the house. When he returned, he carried two steaming mugs of coffee. "Sugar or cream?"

"Black is fine for me."

"A woman after my own heart." Sitting across from her, he passed her a napkin, then filled their glasses with orange juice. "You looked like you were trying to escape when you came out of your house."

"I was." She helped herself to a chocolate-covered doughnut. "Harriet and I had a little—oh, I don't know. It wasn't a fight, exactly, but I think we both said some things that were a little harsh. I didn't want to get into it this morning, so I was heading out before she woke up."

She looked down at herself and shook her head. "I didn't realize it was so obvious that I slept in my clothes."

"It's not *that* obvious." He bit into a doughnut and leaned quickly forward when strawberry jelly began to run down his chin. He dabbed it away with a napkin. "It was something about your expression." He tossed her a quick smile. "It reminded me of someone just released from jail."

For some reason that made her laugh. Maybe because it was so absurd to compare her avoiding Harriet to someone finally getting out of jail. "It wasn't that bad. Anyway, I figured I'd start looking for possible locations for my bookstore. Guess I'll wait until she gets up so I can change."

"Why?"

"I don't have a guest room, so she's sleeping in my bed. Stupid me, I never thought about getting my clothes or pajamas out of there." She shrugged and gave him a rueful smile. "Fielding called last night and said he has to have rabies shots unless the dog is caught and I identify it."

"We'll take care of that this morning. That's what one of these doughnuts is for."

She gave a surprised laugh. "For catching a dog?"

"You bet. That mutt'll do anything for a doughnut."

"I'll have to remember that."

"Not chocolate, though," he warned her. "Chocolate'll make him sick. It's poisonous to dogs, you know. His favorite are the jelly ones. In a pinch he'll go for one with sprinkles."

She laughed again, and something inside him seemed to unwind a little. She was looking better, he thought. He hadn't liked that pinched look he'd seen on her face when he'd watched her creeping out of her house a little while ago. Right now a smile was dancing in her green eyes, and he wouldn't have been a man if he hadn't noticed the way the sun glinted on her strawberry blond hair, or the way the breeze kept snatching a strand of it and dragging it across her throat. Damn, he'd like to give her a kiss right there, just a soft little touch that would make her shiver . . .

"Why do I get the feeling you're intimately acquainted with this dog?" she asked him, a teasing smile on her lips.

"I don't know that I'd say we're intimate, but you could say that we're closely acquainted. Rover is a regular miscreant, and I figure I pick him up, oh, say, a half dozen times a year."

"What happens then?"

"Cal always pays the fine to get him out of the shelter. He's crazy about that animal." He shook his head. "I'm afraid Fielding is going to be difficult about this. He won't let it go because he feels sorry for Cal Lepkin."

"What Fielding wants will probably have very little

effect on the outcome. We're going to do this according to the law."

Jillie nodded and drew a deep breath of the fresh morning air. In her mind's eye she saw a quick flash of the dog sitting in the driveway, causing her to swerve to avoid it. "I was so mad at that dog—Rover, you said?"

"Rover. Cal's dogs are always called Rover. He claims it's too much trouble to learn a new name."

"Really?" Jillie thought about that for a moment, and wondered if Paradise Beach had more eccentrics than anywhere else she'd lived, or if she was just noticing it more here because the community was smaller. "Well . . . it sounds like a great way to conserve mental energy."

"Cal doesn't have a whole lot to waste. But you were saying about the dog?"

"Oh, yes. I was so mad at him for causing me to swerve and hit your mailbox. Do you know what he did right after I crashed? He lifted his leg on my tire."

"Sounds like Rover, all right." He was having trouble suppressing a smile.

"There was something so . . . insouciant? No, that's not the right word. But it was just the way he did it that made me so mad at him. And then when he bit Fielding . . . well, my first thought was that the dog was dangerous and needed to be put down. But . . . I really don't want that to happen. He's just a dog, after all."

"It won't happen," Blaise said with certainty. "It takes more than a nip to get a dog put away, believe me."

"Really?"

"Hey," he said, "it's just a dog, right? And dogs have teeth. They bite. We don't kill dogs around here just because they act like dogs."

And that struck Jillie as a very enlightened attitude.

* * *

Blaise went with the animal control officer to pick up Rover. Fact was, the dog seemed to like him and would come to him easier and quicker than to anyone else, Cal included. Blaise couldn't figure out why; after all, most of the time when he came for the dog it was to impound him briefly because of some transgression. 'Course, he was probably the only person in all of Paradise Beach who ever gave the mutt a doughnut.

Cal was standing on his front stoop when they arrived. He lived in a tiny little bungalow with a sagging roof and a dirt yard. Periodically the city commissioners wanted to clean it up, but Cal owned it and private property was still paramount until they could find grounds to condemn it. None of them had the guts to do that because they were political enough to realize that a lot of people would get outraged over them evicting an impoverished old man from his home.

The dog was a similar problem. Rover just acted like a dog, although there was a general consensus that he was a far sight more intelligent than a dog ought to be, and more than one person in Paradise Beach had become convinced that Rover knew exactly what he was doing and actually planned his escapades.

Blaise, like most folks, had come to have a difficult relationship with the dog. Rover made his life uncomfortable by digging up old ladies' flowerbeds, scattering people's trash up and down the length of entire blocks, chasing cats up trees, and other assorted misdeeds that got people angry enough to call the police. They _did_ have a leash law, after all.

Cal tried very hard to keep Rover confined, but couldn't, and that was why the general consensus was that Rover was possessed by a demon, because sure as the sun rose in the east, no dog could be smart enough to figure its way out of every type of confinement Cal had attempted. Somehow, Rover had.

"What's he been up to now?" Cal asked with resignation, as the animal control truck pulled in behind Blaise's cruiser. He was an old man, thin as a twig and bent at the shoulders. What was left of his hair was as white as fresh snow.

Blaise, walking up the sidewalk toward him, said, "He bit a guy last night, Cal. I'm afraid we have to put him in quarantine for ten days."

"Why so damn long? He's had all his shots regular and on time."

Blaise nodded. "I know. But the law says we have to quarantine him anyway. In case the rabies shot didn't work right."

"And I s'pose I gotta pay for all that."

"Probably. That's usually how it works."

Cal snorted. "Yeah. And it ain't like I ain't tried to keep the damn mutt t' home. Hell, I'd build him a ten-foot fence, 'ceptin' them stupid city commissioners went and passed that damn law about they being no fences higher 'n six feet. So I put a roof on the damn thing and he tunnels under. So then I—aw, hell, it don't matter. But he's a good dog, chief. 'Ceptin' for this wanderin', he's a damn good dog."

Cal looked aside. "So he bit somebody? You sure about that? Because that dang animal's just about the gentlest dog I ever did have. He don't bite nobody."

"Well, it could be that the woman who witnessed the attack won't identify Rover as the dog."

Cal looked at him with watery eyes. "Not damn likely. You point to a dog and say, 'That the one?' and most ever'body is gonna say, yep, sure."

Cal had a point, Blaise thought. But he still had a

job to do. "Sorry, Cal. I gotta take him."

The old man nodded. "He's out back snoozin' under the porch like he always is. Damn dog." The last words were spoken in a broken voice, betraying the depth of Cal's attachment to Rover. Turning, he went inside, unable to watch.

Not that it was all that hard. Blaise and Marcia Albright, the animal control officer, went around back and found Rover just where Cal said he would be. Marcia—who never told her name to anyone if she could avoid it because animal control officers were so uniformly hated—stepped back and allowed Blaise to go forward. The two of them had an agreement for how to handle Cal Lepkin's dog.

"Hi, Rover," Blaise said cordially, as he approached the porch. The gray Airedale crossbreed lifted his head and thumped his tail in welcome. Blaise couldn't remember that Rover had ever growled at a soul.

"I don't know what you were doing, biting Fielding Wainwright on the ass last night," Blaise said, squatting about three feet from the porch. "That's just not like you, pooch."

Rover thumped his tale in agreement and let out a noisy, nervous yawn.

"You know what's coming, don't you?" Blaise held out a jelly doughnut. "And I'm sure you know exactly what I'm doing right now."

Apparently he did. Rover emerged from the porch and sat in front of Blaise, looking from the doughnut to the chief of police with soulful eyes that seemed to ask why they had to do this again.

"Sorry, old guy," Blaise told him. "I can understand why you bit the jerk, but we have to follow the law."

Rover whimpered in the back of his throat and took a bite of the jelly doughnut. While he chewed, Marcia slipped the lead over his neck. They waited while the dog finished the other piece of doughnut and then walked him to the truck.

It was there that Rover balked. He backed up and pulled as hard on the lead as he could, trying to escape. Marcia began to talk soothingly to him, drawing him steadily closer to the truck while Blaise went to get another jelly doughnut, which he put in the back of the truck.

"Go on, guy," he told the dog. "Nobody's going to hurt you. We just need to be sure you're not sick— which is why you shouldn't go around biting people."

The dog looked at the doughnut and licked his chops.

"Go on," Blaise said again. "Look, I promise I'll bring you a doughnut every day while you're in the slammer."

Marcia snorted. "I'm not sure that's good for him."

"I'll do it anyway. He deserves to have something his way when he's going to jail for nothing worse than being a dog."

Marcia cracked a big grin. "You're just an old softy, chief."

"Just don't tell anybody."

The dog evidently decided Blaise's promise was good, because he leapt up into the back of the truck and settled down to munch contentedly on the doughnut while Marcia closed and locked the door.

"You know," she told the chief, "you ought to make this dog a cop."

"How come?"

"He likes doughnuts, doesn't he?"

Blaise chuckled all the way to the pound.

Six

After breakfast with Blaise, Jillie went home to wait for Harriet to wake up and was instead astonished to find the older woman already in the kitchen.

Harriet was scrambling eggs, frying bacon, and buttering toast when she walked in. The table was already set for two with the cheap plastic dishes and placemats Jillie had bought after arriving here. The colors were bright pink and turquoise, giving the breakfast table a definite Florida flavor.

"Have a seat," Fielding's mother said brightly. "There was no point in cooking for one."

Jillian opened her mouth to explain that she'd already eaten, then decided that might be a mistake. Peace offerings should always be accepted. "It smells good."

Harriet flashed a bright smile. "I hope it tastes as good. It's been a long time since I cooked a meal."

"That's true. I'd forgotten."

"Cooks, housekeepers, maids . . . I'm really quite spoiled. Perhaps too spoiled." She stirred the eggs in the pan. "I wouldn't dare attempt an omelette, at least, until I get back into practice. I used to make a wonderful one."

"I like scrambled eggs just fine."

"Good." She spooned eggs onto their plates, then set a platter of bacon and toast in the center of the table. "Milk? I couldn't find the coffee . . ."

They sat facing each other over the table and for a minute or two ate in silence. Finally Jillie offered an olive branch. "The eggs are very good, Harriet. Just moist enough."

"Oh, good." She looked up and smiled, but the smile didn't quite reach her eyes. "Why didn't you tell me Fielding had been bitten by a dog?"

Jillie set her fork down, feeling suddenly uncomfortable. "Because I didn't want to alarm you. It was just a scrape, Harriet."

"It was an animal bite!"

"Yes, it was. But it barely broke the skin, and the chief of police assured me the dog will be quarantined so that Fielding won't need shots. Did Fielding call you this morning?"

"Yes, he did. And I was so upset . . . you're sure it's only a scratch?"

"It didn't even need a Band-Aid."

"Oh." She sighed and then smiled almost ruefully. "He had me convinced he'd been mauled. I should have known better. He's always been one to exaggerate. Well, that's good, then. Now I don't feel obliged to go stay at the hotel with him."

Jillian didn't know how to react to that. On the one hand she'd much rather have had her house to herself. On the other, she had a feeling she'd miss Harriet if she left.

"What a relief," Harriet continued. "I know he's my son and I love him dearly, but he's so *tiresome* to be around for any length of time. Probably just the generation gap, but ... well, I'd much rather stay here with you. Which brings me back to what I was saying earlier about being spoiled."

"Spoiled?"

"Yes, spoiled. I'm terribly spoiled, and I was thinking about it this morning as I tried to remember how to scramble eggs. I haven't needed to do anything for myself for so long! When Chad and I first married, we didn't have a dime between us. The family had fallen onto hard times during the depression, you know. But Chad worked so hard, and in almost no time at all he put it all together and we were incredibly wealthy. And he didn't want me to do anything at all except take care of the children. So I didn't. I lived like royalty."

Jillie nodded, wondering where this was going.

"But this morning I realized how spoiled I've become. It never even occurred to me ... I'm so used to having everything just as I want it ... well, I shouldn't have demanded you come out to the airport after me like that, and I shouldn't just have assumed that you'd have the means to put up a houseguest, and I never should have evicted you from your own bed ... Good heavens, Jillian, you hadn't even invited me!"

Jillie found herself inexplicably touched. "That's all right, Harriet. Really."

"No, it's not. I'm so used to having everything done for me that I failed to consider your situation or wishes, and I really had no right to do that. I apologize."

"Apology accepted. As far as I'm concerned,

though, you're family, and family is always welcome."

"Really?" Harriet looked almost as hopeful as a child who'd just received a promise of some wonderful happening.

"Really. Divorcing Fielding doesn't mean I divorced you, too."

"Good. The saddest part of this divorce has been feeling that I was losing you for good." Harriet smiled, but her smile faded rapidly. "It was unforgivable last night, what I said about you . . . about your background."

"About my being an orphan? Well, I was. Not much I can do about that, I'm afraid. I had a pretty good foster home, though. My foster dad was a little too authoritarian, and my foster mom was a wimp, but I don't think any of that had to do with Fielding's straying. It probably had a lot to do with me staying in the marriage about four years too long, though."

Harriet looked as if she was going to argue, then shook her head. "No, I won't say any more. I promised the subject was off-limits, and off-limits it is."

Jillian couldn't eat another bite, but she worried that if she put her plate aside she'd offend Harriet. However, the thought of bringing another forkful of egg to her mouth made her want to gag. "Harriet, I'm sorry, I already had breakfast this morning and I just can't eat another bite. It's delicious, though, and I wish I could."

"Don't worry about it, dear. I'm not all that hungry, either. I just needed to do something after Fielding called." She pushed her own plate to the side. "So you won't come furniture shopping with me today? You really should, since it's going to be put in your guest room."

Jillian hesitated. She really didn't want a bedroom

suite for the spare room. As she figured it, if she needed to move to smaller quarters for financial reasons at some point, the furniture would be a serious problem. On the other hand, she didn't want to have to sleep on the couch for the rest of Harriet's visit—however long that turned out to be. She opened her mouth to ask, then decided to stick to the subject of furniture.

"Well . . . if we can do it quickly," she told the older woman. "I really need to start looking at properties for my bookstore."

"I can help you with that," Harriet volunteered. "I've had a lot of experience judging business sites."

Oh, great, Jillie thought. This was something she definitely wanted to do on her own, so that eventually she could claim full responsibility for her success—or failure. It was important to her to prove that she could stand squarely on her own two feet, without help from anyone.

"Of course," Harriet said tentatively, "I can understand that you might prefer to do this yourself . . ."

This time Jillie didn't back down. "Yes, Mother, I'd really rather do it myself."

"Fine." Harriet gave her an artificial smile and threw up her hands as if to say, It's on *your* head, then. "I suppose it *is* better if you do it all for yourself. Well, then, how soon can we leave to look at furniture?"

"I need to shower and change. Say, thirty minutes?"

The shopping expedition didn't take nearly as long as Jillie had feared, so by noon she was pounding the pavement in Paradise Beach, looking for an available storefront space.

"You might try up the street next to the China Clipper beauty shop," suggested the owner of a surf shop. "I hear that video store is closing down. It's getting killed by a chain store that opened just across the bridge. Bookstore, huh? You're getting into some stiff competition with all the big chains that're moving in on the mainland."

"I doubt any of them will come out here," Jillie told him.

He flashed a grin and showed an impressive set of white caps. "Probably not. Wrong clientele. And maybe you ought to think about that, too."

Maybe she should, Jillie thought, as she continued down the street. Tourists wouldn't provide enough of a market. Would the locals?

"It's a great idea," said Betty Chang, who owned the China Clipper. "I'll be one of your best customers. I could *live* in a bookstore. But you might want to check with Rainbow Moonglow."

"Who?"

"Rainbow Moonglow. She does tarot readings. Hey, this lady is one talented psychic. She doesn't tell you what to do—at least she never did with anyone I know—but she makes the options a whole lot clearer." Betty shrugged and grinned. "Maybe she just knows how to ask the right questions, but I've never regretted the money I've spent. Give her a try."

Jillian felt like an absolute ass as she stood at Rainbow Moonglow's door. The sign announcing tarot readings was a discreet, simple black and white card in a corner of her front window. The little bungalow was surrounded by a riot of tropical blooms, giving it an almost enchanted appearance.

Rainbow Moonglow was a surprise. Jillie had been expecting an older woman, plump, with big earrings and hair. Instead she found a young woman only a few years older than herself with gold studs in her ears, dressed in a tasteful navy blue dress. Her hair was worn in a short, businesslike bob.

"Hi," Rainbow said cheerfully as she opened the door. "Can I help you?"

"I . . . um . . . Betty Chang suggested I come see you. I'm Jillian McAllister."

"Well, come on in."

The inside of the bungalow was just as much of a surprise. It had been decorated to feel large and airy, as if Rainbow loved light and room.

"You're Chief Corrigan's friend, aren't you?" Rainbow asked brightly as she led the way to a glass-topped cast-iron table in the corner near sliding glass doors.

"Uh . . . how did you know?"

Rainbow faced her, smiling almost gently. "That's my job, isn't it? I'd be a fraud if I weren't genuinely psychic. You're here because you're thinking about opening a business . . ." Her voice trailed away and she stared past Jillie as if seeing into space. "Yes, you want to open a bookstore . . . oh, how wonderful! We desperately need a bookstore in Paradise Beach. I get so tired of having to drive over to one of the big cities if I want something that isn't on the supermarket rack. Have a seat. Let me get you some tea? Coffee?"

Jillie felt as if she'd been inexplicably caught up in some kind of whirlwind. Somebody must have talked about her to Rainbow Moonglow, she decided. There was no way the woman had plucked these things out of thin air . . . and neither of the proffered tidbits was a secret. How many people had seen her with Chief Corrigan? And she'd told several people about the bookstore . . .

"Here you are, Jillie," Rainbow said, putting a cup of tea in front of her. "It's so nice to have someone new move to town permanently. We have so many transients. There are only a few of us who are here year-round, at least by comparison."

"So far I'm just thrilled to be here."

Rainbow smiled and spread the tarot cards in front of them with a sweep of her hand. "I'm not going to use the cards to give you a reading," she said. "I don't need them. You're doing the right thing, whatever it is. You can count on Mary Todd and Chief Corrigan, but watch out for . . . Dan. Someone named Dan."

Jillie immediately thought of Mayor Dan Burgess. She wondered if Rainbow had any idea her advice might be late. "I'll keep that in mind."

Rainbow's smile deepened. "You're a skeptic. That's good. I don't like my word to be taken as gospel. All I do is give impressions, and they could all be wrong . . . but you certainly give me strong ones. There's a . . . I see a large field full of dying grass. It has to do with someone you're trying to escape. Are you running from someone?" But Rainbow moved on before Jillie could say anything.

"Someone is pursuing you. No, you don't need to worry about it . . . I see . . . I see a dog. A dog is involved . . . Trust the dog."

"Trust the *dog*?" Jillie had to interrupt at that, finding the thought of trusting Cal Lepkin's dog too absurd. "The dog that caused me to have a car wreck? The dog that bit . . . never mind."

Rainbow looked straight at her and said without a smile, "Because of the wreck you met someone. Because of the bite you'll grow closer."

Jillie felt her cheeks suddenly heat up as Blaise sprang to mind. "I really don't want to get involved with anyone. It's too soon after my divorce. I was more interested in advice about my business."

Rainbow sat back in her chair and folded her hands in her lap. "I don't give advice."

"But . . . didn't you just tell me to trust a dog? Isn't that advice?"

"Certainly not. It's merely information. And as I've repeatedly said, it could all be wrong."

"But Betty Chang said—"

"Betty chooses to interpret my readings for her as advice. But they're not, Jillian. You have to make your own decisions and follow your own path. I merely pick up on bits and pieces of the fabric of your life. Those bits and pieces may give you a different perspective, but they most certainly are not intended to be advice."

"Oh." Jillie reached for her teacup and sipped the warm liquid. "Thanks. How much do I owe you?"

"Not a thing." Rainbow frowned. "You really need to relax. You're worrying about entirely too many things. Just ignore everything except getting your business off the ground."

Well, Jillie thought a few minutes later as she stepped back outside, it would be a lot easier to ignore her problems if they didn't insist on moving into her house.

"Jillian!"

She wanted to sink. Across the boulevard, Fielding stood in the parking lot of the hotel where he had probably stayed. Keeping her eyes straight ahead, she pretended not to hear him.

"Jillian, wait!"

Just then a police cruiser pulled up beside her. The passenger window rolled down. "Wanna ride, lady?"

She leaned over and looked in to see Blaise smiling at her from the driver's seat.

"Assuming you want to escape, hop in," he said.

She glanced up and saw that Fielding was getting

ready to dart into traffic and cross the four lanes. Without another moment's hesitation, she opened the door and slid in beside Blaise. He hit the accelerator before she had even reached for her seat belt.

"Nothing like charging in and rescuing damsels in distress," he said cheerfully. "Where can I deposit milady? Bearing in mind, of course, that I'm answering a call way down the beach. Some property owner wants me to eject a couple of ladies who are drinking coffee on the beach behind his house."

"But isn't the beach public?"

"It certainly is, but beverages and food are prohibited on that stretch of it."

"Why is that?"

"It was an agreement made by the city council with the property owners." He glanced at her. "A few years back a number of the older homes in that area were sold to some wealthier types. After they replaced the old structures with their considerably larger and more beautiful homes, they started squawking about the riffraff on the beach late at night, and the littering. Eventually some ordinances were passed, closing the beaches at sunset to all but residents and hotel guests, and prohibiting food and beverages on that one stretch of sand."

"I guess I can understand that."

"Yeah, until you think about harassing two little old ladies with their coffee cups. Oh, by the way, we quarantined Rover this morning. Your ex is safe from the needle."

"What a shame."

Blaise cracked a laugh at that. "Nobody ever has to wonder what you're thinking, do they?"

"No." She lifted her chin defiantly.

He looked straight at her then, his voice warm. "I like that."

Her toes curled happily in her sandals. Not once in her entire life had anyone ever liked her outspokenness. Usually it was deplored.

He returned his attention to the street, tapping the brake gently to give a cyclist time to get out of their way, waving at some people as he passed. "I need to take you to the shelter to identify the dog. Will you have time to do that after I make this stop?"

"Sure. I have plenty of time. I'm just wandering around trying to find a place to put my store."

"Any luck?"

"I haven't looked all that far yet." She twisted to look at him. "Do you spend a lot of time on routine law enforcement? Shouldn't you be behind a desk?" Wasn't that what he had told Harriet just last night, that he spent most of his time at a desk?

"I fill in when we're shorthanded. A couple of my officers are on vacation this month . . . skiing, if you can believe it. It beats me why anybody would want to leave this beautiful climate at the best time of year and spend weeks in the snow. But it also gives me a chance to get back in the saddle, and that's a good thing. I need to keep in touch."

"So you arrest little old ladies with their coffee cups?"

He chuckled. "You bet." He tapped the break again, and pointed out her side of the car. "There, see the swimsuit shop? Right next to it is an available business space. You might want to check it out. At this end of town the traffic is mostly local people, so it'd be better situated for your purposes."

"Can you let me out here?"

He pulled over at once, nosing into an empty parking space. "I guess you don't want to watch me arrest the little old ladies, huh?"

She started to laugh, then looked straight at him

and shook her head. "No, I guess I don't."

"Actually," he told her, "it's usually young punks who don't pay attention to the signs. If you want, wait out here for me. I should be driving back up this way in about twenty minutes."

"With your backseat full of desperate criminals with gray hair who are armed with dangerous coffee cups?"

Another chuckle escaped him. "Actually, the worst I'll do to them is issue a summons. It's a fifteen-dollar fine."

"Yeah, right. I heard Cherry yesterday. Rubber hoses and blackjacks."

She stared after him as he drove away, liking the way he laughed. If only she felt more like laughing herself. Unleashing a sigh, she turned and headed for the empty storefront. At best she expected only to be able to look in the windows, but her luck had begun to turn. The space was owned by the swimsuit shop next door.

It was quieter at this end of the island. Traffic was moving more slowly, people were strolling the streets lazily, and while many of the parking spaces were full, there was no feeling of congestion as there was further north along this boulevard near the big hotels. Charming her were the cafe tables and chairs scattered along the street in front of some of the businesses, and the spotlessly clean wrought-iron park benches. Some of the businesses even sported windowboxes full of flowers.

There was also an air of greater personal wealth around here. Just from where she stood, she could see three dress boutiques. This, she surmised, was where the wealthier property owners hung out. That would be good for her business, but could she afford the rent?

"Of course you can!" said Belinda Harrison, owner of the building. She was a short, plump woman with wiry red hair and a smile that wouldn't quit. "We'll make sure you can afford it. A bookstore would be the *perfect* thing for that space. And you'll find we have a lot of traffic here. Everyone who lives on the island shops along here, so word of mouth advertising ought to get you up and running in no time at all."

Within five minutes, Jillie was hooked.

Only a couple of minutes after dropping Jillie off, Blaise found himself involved in an unpleasant confrontation between Dan Burgess and two middle-aged schoolteachers who were sipping coffee from china teacups. The women were visitors from Canada, and Blaise had a sneaking suspicion they were never going to want to visit Florida again.

They had parked their small motor home along the street and decided to take their coffee with them on a brief stroll to the water. They had unfortunately ignored the sign forbidding food and beverages on the beach.

"In retrospect," said one of the women, "it seems utterly silly that we overlooked it. I made the mistake of assuming the sign was there to prevent littering. Well, we were hardly going to leave these pretty little teacups on the beach, and coffee, if it should spill in the sand, didn't seem likely to leave a mess or attract flies."

Blaise found her interpretation entirely logical.

"Excuse me," Dan said, his face red, "I don't believe the sign listed any exceptions!"

Both women frowned at him. Blaise had no trouble believing they controlled their respective classrooms with exactly that look.

"Excuse *me*," said the second woman. "We already admitted we were at fault. Need you be so obnoxious?"

"Obnoxious!" Dan fairly frothed. "In the first place, if you dropped one of those pretty little teacups and it shattered, splinters would go everywhere, and someone might well come walking along and cut their foot. Then they'd sue the city—"

"A bit of a slippery slope argument, don't you think?" said the first teacher to the second, who nodded. A slippery slope was a fallacious form of argument.

"But apart from that," Dan said, letting spittle fly, "is what'll happen if we start relaxing the rules! This week a teacup, next week a ten-course picnic for forty-five people, complete with charcoal grills!"

"Definitely a slippery slope," said the second teacher.

"Don't give me any crap about icy mountains," Dan roared. "Get those damn cups off the beach. And *you*," he said, turning to Blaise, "had damn well better arrest them so they get the point."

Blaise couldn't resist. He tried, but there was no way. "You know, Dan, enforcing the law this strictly is hardly going to encourage other tourists to come to Paradise Beach."

Dan froze in mid tirade as Blaise's zinger struck home. For an instant he was rendered speechless, but then he let his anger fly, glaring up at Blaise across the seven-inch difference in their heights. "Always an excuse! One minute you're telling me you have to arrest all those people because it's the law, never mind what it does to the tourist industry, and the next you're telling me you won't because it's bad for tourism! What kind of policeman are you?"

Before Blaise could answer, Dan turned on the women again. "Well, I'm the mayor of this town, and I'm going to arrest you myself!"

Blaise tapped him on the shoulder and Burgess swung around to glare at him. "Sorry, Dan, but you can't do that. In the first place, the mayor doesn't have any arrest powers, and in the second place, they haven't done anything they can be arrested for. Let me take care of it."

"You!"

"Hey, I'm the guy you're trying to fire for being too hard nosed, remember? Just go back to your condo and let me deal with this. It's my job."

They left Dan Burgess behind them, looking utterly frustrated by the whole encounter. The two teachers, still carrying their dainty china cups, walked along obediently, chatting between themselves about the perfection of the day. Overhead, seagulls wheeled, filling the sky with their raucous cries.

"You have a lovely town here, Officer," one of them said to Blaise. "We're really sorry about ignoring the sign. We would have apologized to that man, except that he became so irate and threatening. Is he really the mayor?"

"Yes, he is."

"Well, I suppose I shouldn't say any more about him, then."

Blaise glanced at them. "Help yourselves. I've said plenty about him in my day . . . usually to my reflection in the bathroom mirror."

That sent them into gales of laughter. Blaise suspected the laughter was annoying Burgess all the more and he took a small amount of pleasure in that knowledge, because he sure didn't want to ticket these women. If he'd caught them himself, he'd have let them go with a warning. Strolling the beach with a china cup of coffee was a far cry from the white foam and paper litter the property owners had feared. The problem with Burgess, he thought, was that the man didn't understand the *purpose* of the laws. Instead, he was interested only in how things affected him personally. Which made him a royal pain in the butt to work with.

The teachers accepted their tickets with exceptional good grace. "We shouldn't have ignored the sign," one of them said. "It's our own fault. Now, if we leave our cups in the van, we can go back on the beach, can't we?"

"Of course." He glanced over and saw that Burgess was still standing there, looking like an alligator that had just been deprived of its meal. "If he gives you any more trouble, call 911. It *is* a public beach."

When he pulled up in front of Belinda's Bathingsuit Boutique, Jillie and Belinda were deep in discussion, so he parked and climbed out to join them. He was surprised to learn that they were hammering out the details of a lease.

"So quickly?" he asked Jillian. "You've hardly started looking."

"That's okay. This is exactly what I want."

Belinda was smiling from ear to ear. "She'll be okay with me, Blaise. You know I won't take advantage of her."

"Now," Jillie said when she climbed into the cruiser with Blaise, "I need to find an attorney to represent me. Belinda's going to pay to have the work done on the interior. Isn't that nice?"

"It'll raise the rent," Blaise warned her.

"Of course, but I'd rather have her pay for the improvements. That way if the store doesn't work out, I won't be stuck with all of that."

Blaise looked at her, thinking this woman had a lot more brains than had been his initial impression. And she still had those gorgeous legs... "Do you have time to go by the animal shelter?"

She would have vastly preferred to get moving on other things she needed to do to get her business rolling, but in fairness to Fielding, she needed to settle the dog issue right away. Besides, there was always a possibility they had the wrong dog. "Yeah. Sure."

"Don't sound so enthusiastic."

She glanced at him and found him looking amused. "Oh, it's just that I have so many things I need to do, now that I've found the location for my store. Belinda says all the modifications will be done in a couple of weeks—there really isn't a whole lot to do—and I need to arrange for racks, and tables and chairs, and so many other things..."

Her mind was already whirling with all the details she needed to consider.

The City of Paradise Beach had contracted with a local veterinarian to handle strays and quarantines. Dr. Sean Kilkenny was in his late thirties, and had been practicing in Paradise Beach since he'd graduated from veterinary school. He and Rover went back a long way.

"He's been fully vaccinated," Dr. Kilkenny told Blaise and Jillie, as he led the way back to the quarantine kennels. "The man would be in a lot more trouble if he'd been bitten by a raccoon." He turned a serious gaze on Jillie. "There have been quite a few cases of rabid raccoons in the county. It got so bad that we started a wildlife vaccination program. Seems like it might be working, too."

"How do they vaccinate wild animals?" she asked

"There's an oral vaccine that works pretty well

now. All they have to do is get enough of it out there."

Jillie nodded and dropped back as they reached a narrow doorway. "It sounds like it would be a good preventive measure, too."

Dr. Kilkenny flashed her a smile. "Ah, but you have to consider the cost. It's an expensive program, and hard to justify unless you already have a serious problem."

The quarantine room was small and windowless, built of unpainted cinder block. There were four wire cages, each with a trap door in the wall at its back. Between the cages were steel plates. "So they can't infect one another," Kilkenny explained.

Rover was lying forlornly in one cage, enduring solitary confinement for his misdeeds. When he saw Blaise, he immediately rose to his feet and began to wag his tail excitedly.

"Well, he sure likes *you*," the doctor remarked. "He hasn't been that friendly to any of the rest of us. Of course, this is where he comes for his shots."

"And I usually have a doughnut for him," Blaise said wryly. "But not this time, Rover. I promised one a day and you've already had two today."

Kilkenny frowned. "That's not good for him."

Blaise shrugged. "I made a promise and I'll keep it. It doesn't seem to bother him any unless there's chocolate in it."

"Chocolate!" Kilkenny looked appalled. "That's poisonous for a dog."

"I know Doc." Blaise squatted and stuck his fingers through the wire. Rover licked them frantically. "Poor fella. We'll get you out of here just as soon as we can. Jillie, is this the dog?"

"Absolutely." Gray Airedales were not a dime a dozen, and she'd recognize this particular Airedale anywhere. "I still can't imagine why he came streaking out of the dark and bit Fielding that way."

Blaise looked up at her. "Were you by any chance arguing?"

Jillie hesitated, trying to remember. "I'm not sure. I don't think so, but Fielding was annoyed with me. Our voices may have been raised a little."

"So maybe Rover was trying to protect you from a perceived threat."

Kilkenny stood there nodding. "It's possible. Rover's very protective. When he was a pup I had to put forty-five stitches in him after he stepped in to protect a cat from another dog."

Jillie found herself looking at the animal in an entirely new light. Rover seemed to realize it, because his face suddenly relaxed into a grin, with his pink tongue lolling to one side.

"I'll be back to visit him in the morning," Blaise told Kilkenny. "With a doughnut."

This time Kilkenny shrugged. "As long as it doesn't give him digestive upset, I'll look the other way."

Back in the cruiser on the way to her house, Blaise asked Jillie, "Are we still on for dinner tonight?"

Jillie hesitated. She had a houseguest, and that made it so awkward.

"You didn't invite her," Blaise said, reading her mind. "You don't have any obligation to her."

"Well, I suppose she can have dinner with Fielding. I imagine he'll be relieved to know he doesn't need those rabies shots. You know, maybe I should introduce Harriet to Mary Todd. They'd probably have a lot in common."

"Why on earth would you think that?"

"Well, they're about the same age, and they're both wealthy . . ."

"It takes more than money to give two people something in common."

Jillian looked at him with a sense of rising irritation. "Are you *always* so perfect?"

He was startled and it showed. "What do you mean?"

"You're an unending stream of advice on every subject under the sun. It must get difficult sometimes to know everything about everything."

"Ouch."

Jillie subsided immediately, her irritation turning to mortification. How *could* she have said that? She hardly knew this man! His constant advice was probably the result of his being chief of police. People were probably always asking him what to do about things, and that could get to be a bad habit. Who was she to criticize, anyway? Here she was, always shooting off her mouth and saying things that common civility dictated ought to be left unsaid.

Blaise was silent until they turned onto the street where they lived. Ahead of them Jillie saw the mail van making its stops.

"Mr. Knapp is late today," she remarked.

"Yeah." He slowed down to a crawl. "Look, I'm sorry if I'm always giving you unwanted advice. And I'm far from perfect."

"You could fool me." As soon as the words popped out, she clapped a hand over her mouth. "Oh, my . . . I'm sorry. I'll just shut up. I don't know why things come out like that. I wasn't even thinking . . ."

But now he was laughing heartily, enjoying her reaction. She might have gotten annoyed except that she was so relieved that he wasn't angry with her. Her mouth was always getting her into trouble.

"No, you're right," he said. "I've been a police chief for so long that I'm just used to telling everyone everything. It'd probably be good for me to learn stop doing that." He wheeled the car into his driveway with a crunch of gravel beneath the wheels. "Are we still on for tonight?"

Jillie thought of Harriet, and felt a stab of resentment at the way the woman had just moved in on her. But apart from that, Harriet's arrival had kept her from going out with Blaise last night, so Harriet was just going to have to understand about tonight. "Sure. Let's do it." Harriet and Fielding would probably just want to sit around tonight and commiserate anyway. If she could manage to avoid that, she certainly would.

Just then someone tapped on the glass of the window on Jillie's side. She turned and found herself looking at Jim Knapp, the postman. Quickly she rolled down her window.

"You got a letter here, Ms. McAllister. Looks kinda important. But there's a bird nest in your mailbox and I can't be putting it in there. You'll need to get it cleaned out, hear?"

"Yes, sir." She reached for the letter, but Knapp snapped it back.

"I have to give it to you at the door," he reminded her sternly. "Go in the house and I'll bring it to you. Or maybe you'd rather pick it up tomorrow at the post office."

"Uh, no, I'll just run over to my house, all right?"

Knapp nodded. "What's this about Cal Lepkin's dog?" he asked, looking past her at Blaise.

"The dog bit a tourist so he has to be quarantined. Nothing major."

"Damn dog has the temperament of an ornery rattlesnake. But it'll kill Cal if they have to put that dog down."

"They won't," Blaise assured him. "The bite was

no big deal, and Rover's up on his shots."

"Good." Knapp bent his gaze on Jillie. "Well, hurry it up then, missy."

Jillie gave Blaise a humorous smile and quickly climbed out of the car. Knapp jumped back to give her room.

"Well, hurry," he said again. "You're holding up my entire route. Mrs. Peabody's going to be calling the office wanting to know where her mail is if I'm late."

Jillie opened the door of her house to find her worst fear had come to pass. Both Fielding and his mother were waiting for her in the living room, and when she stepped in the door, they leapt up, both talking at the same time.

Jillie ignored them, turning to take the letter from Jim Knapp, who reminded her once again to clean her mailbox. Then she closed the door gently and turned to face her ex-husband and ex-mother-in-law. "What's going on?" What she really wanted to ask was what made them think they had a right to use her house as if it were their own. In an exercise of extraordinary restraint, she refrained.

Fielding waved his mother to silence. "We've been talking about a reconciliation between you and I, Jillie."

"You and *me*," she corrected him automatically, even as she started to back up toward the door and think of fleeing.

"You and me," he repeated obediently. "Well, it's really quite simple, Jillie. Mother and I are agreed. You have to forgive me."

Seven

Jillie gaped at Fielding, hardly able to believe her ears. "*You* have *decided* that I should forgive you?"

Fielding nodded. "Mother and I are in agreement. We discussed it and realized that I can apologize until I'm blue in the face, but it won't make any difference if you don't forgive me."

"Brilliant deduction, Watson!"

Fielding sighed. "Darling, do you have to be so sarcastic?"

"I'm not your darling!"

"Of course you are. You always will be. Even if you hate me forever."

Jillie closed her eyes, fighting to hang onto her temper. There had been a time, she reminded herself, when Fielding hadn't made her angry with every breath he drew. Maybe she was overreacting? "Fielding, I don't hate you. I'm past that. But I don't love you anymore."

"I think you do, Jillie." He extended his hands. "I think you're very angry and hurt, and you don't want to love me anymore, but it's not that easy to fall out of love. I know. I still love you."

Jillie couldn't bring herself to throw that declaration back in his face. She didn't really believe it, but if he did, she didn't want to be that cruel. Instead she said, "Fine, Fielding. I forgive you. But I can't forget the pain you caused me, and I don't love you anymore. Now, please excuse me. I have a date to get ready for."

Walking past them, she went into the bedroom and closed the door. Now more than ever, she wondered what the hell was going on here.

The sun hung low over the Gulf, a fiery red. Above it, arcs of cirrus clouds glowed a deep pink, and to the east, building thunderheads reflected tangerine and turquoise. The calm waters sparkled midnight blue mixed with a light blue nearly the color of the sky. A red streak cast by the sun ran over the gentle waves and white sand as if the sun reached out toward them.

"I have never seen as many beautiful sunsets as I've seen here," Jillie told Blaise.

They sat together on stools at a small table on the porch of the Paradise Pavilion, sipping soft drinks and nibbling on shrimp and crab appetizers. Behind them, an a capella group was singing old favorites to the customers and to passersby on the beach. This, she thought, was the specialness she had hoped to find here.

"We do seem to have a corner on sunsets," Blaise agreed lazily. "Most of 'em are pretty fantastic."

Movement caught Jillie's eye, and she turned to see a couple in wedding attire stepping onto the beach, followed by a little flower girl in pink organdy. A photographer was with them, carrying his equipment. In a matter of moments, he set up and began snapping pictures of the beaming newlyweds against the sunset, and later, with a flash, of the wedding party against palms and sand.

Blaise watched, too, and when he looked at Jillie again his smile had broadened a shade. "Romantic, isn't it?"

She shrugged. "Blind fools."

"Whoa, there." He looked at her with astonishment.

She shrugged again. "Sorry. I'm soured on marriage, I guess. I look at that girl—and she is just a girl—over there in her white dress with all those hopes and dreams, and all I can think is what a damn fool she is."

"In other words, *you* were a damn fool."

"That's right. And so was nearly everyone I know." Jillie shook her head sharply and looked away from him, toward the sunset. The lower edge of the sun's disc was just touching the water now, and everything seemed to be speeding up. "We all make so many stupid assumptions about other people. We assume that when a guy says 'I love you' he means the same thing women do by it. We assume he feels the same things we do. And we assume he really means it when he promises to forsake all others."

"He probably does mean it when he *says* it," Blaise said gently.

Jillie hesitated. "Maybe," she agreed finally, not really wanting to get into an argument on this beautiful evening. "You wouldn't think it could be so hard to keep such a simple promise, would you?"

"It isn't."

Jillie made a face at him. "What would you know?"

"I was married for eight years and I never once cheated. I keep my promises—which is why I don't make very many."

"Oh." Now she felt like a fool for having made one of those assumptions she had just been complaining about. "What happened?"

"She met a guy she liked better." He shrugged. "Being married to a cop is hard on a woman. At the time, I was on patrol, gone a lot at night. I don't think she was ever able to get over the fear that something would happen to me." He shook his head, his gaze growing distant and a little melancholy.

"But was that a reason to leave you?"

He cocked his head. "I guess it depends on how you look at it. Worry and loneliness are hard to cope with. And I was pretty self-absorbed at the time, very job oriented, trying to be the best damn cop possible. I abandoned her in more ways than one, I guess."

Jillie ached for him. "Maybe you're being too hard on yourself."

He shook his head. "The last thing she said to me was, 'How can I ever have babies when I can't be sure they'll have a father?' "

"Ouch."

He half-smiled. "I'm over it. The main thing, Jill, is to avoid thinking that everyone is like your ex. Take that couple over there, for example. He could mean every word of his vows and be absolutely wild about her. And she could reciprocate. And you might be reading about their fiftieth wedding anniversary in the *Times* some day. It happens."

After her confrontation with Fielding and his mother earlier, it was hard to agree, but in fairness and honesty, she had to. "There are always exceptions," she managed to say.

"Of course. Like a couple who used to live just

down the boulevard from here. They married a week after they met, and when she died they had been married seventy-two years. They were absolutely inseparable."

"The poor man! That must have been awful for him."

"He didn't survive her for very long." Blaise reached out and touched her cheek gently with a fingertip. "What ruined your mood? You were so up earlier after finding the place for your business. Did something happen?"

"Nothing happened, exactly." She looked down at the frosty glass in front of her, watching a trickle of condensation run down its side. "There are times when I wonder if I was crazy. How could I ever have thought the Wainwright arrogance was charming? You know what they told me when I got home?"

He shook his head.

"They had decided that I was going to forgive Fielding."

"They *decided*?"

"Yep. That's what they told me—the *first* thing they told me when I walked in the door. Apparently they had a meeting and decided my course of action. The amazing thing is that they used to do that all the time and I let them." She shook her head and rolled her eyes. "I must have left my spine back in Waukegan."

Blaise couldn't help it; a quiet laugh escaped him. "And of course you told them what they could do with their decision."

She sighed. "Actually, I said I could forgive him, but not forget. Then I locked myself in the bedroom until it was time to leave." She shook her head. "I'm terrible. I've always had a problem with saying things I shouldn't, but at first with Fielding I never said much at all. That was kind of a weird effect for him to have, don't you think?"

"Maybe you felt awed by him."

Jillie cocked her head, thinking about that. "Maybe. He came from a whole different world from what I was used to. All that money and prestige, all that overwhelming family . . . I guess I was intimidated at first."

"Most people probably would have been. At least, until they got to know the Wainwrights."

That caused Jillie to laugh again. "You're right. There's nothing impressive about them up close."

"You two seem to be having a good time."

Mary Todd was walking toward them, leaning on the arm of a distinguished-looking gentleman of her own age, her omnipresent ebony cane in the other hand.

Blaise rose to his feet. "Good evening, Mary. How are you, Ted? Jill, this is Ted Wannamaker, one of our more prominent citizens."

Ted flashed a beautiful smile, his bright blue eyes dancing. "Only because I've been dangling after Miss Mary since high school. I figure if she doesn't agree to marry me soon, I'm going to put myself up for the *Guinness Book of World Records*."

Mary sniffed, but her eyes danced in response. "I told you what I think of life sentences."

"At this point, my dear, a life sentence couldn't be any longer than twenty years. Max."

Mary considered that a moment, then shook her head. "Entirely too long when there's no possibility of parole."

At Blaise and Jillie's invitation, the other couple drew up stools and joined them at the tiny table. The sun was almost gone now, little more than a blinding sliver of brilliant orange above the sparkling water.

Overhead the clouds were still bright with the blaze of sunset.

"When I was a little girl," Mary told them, "this beach was nothing like it is now. The sand was a narrow strip, and the dunes were high and covered with sea oats. Around the old fancy hotels they'd groomed the beaches some, but still, it wasn't the huge, white expanse it is now. It was still beautiful, though."

"Maybe even more beautiful," Jillie said.

Mary shook her head. "I don't know. I'm not one to bewail progress, and there are a lot more people in this world than when I was a child. It would be selfish not to allow them to enjoy paradise, too. On the other hand, a little population control might be in order."

The wry way she said it caused the rest of them to laugh.

"Speaking of population control, I heard some interesting stuff when I was getting my hair done earlier," Miss Todd continued. "There's some tourist at one of the hotels who was apparently bitten on the behind by a stray dog." She cocked an eye at Blaise. "It wouldn't have been Cal Lepkin's dog, would it?"

"Actually, yes. He's in quarantine now."

"Poor critter. I think we ought to give a medal to him for giving a pain in the posterior to a pain in the posterior."

Blaise and Ted both chuckled, but Jillie felt her cheeks warming uncomfortably. Not that she minded Fielding being called a "pain in the posterior." He certainly deserved it. But she *was* associated with him, however reluctantly, and his behavior would reflect on her.

"Anyway," Miss Mary continued, when the laughter had subsided, "this tourist is apparently raising Cain about the dog not having been leashed. He's complained to the hotel management and to the

Chamber of Commerce. And apparently he's wealthy enough that people are listening."

Jillie squirmed uncomfortably and felt Blaise's eyes on her.

"I thought I'd mention it," the elderly woman continued, "so that when the flak hits your desk—as it invariably does—you won't be caught unawares."

"Thanks, Mary," Blaise said to her. "But I'm not worried about it. Cal's dog defies leash laws, and Cal just keeps right on paying fines. There's nothing more that can be done."

"I wouldn't be so sure," Ted volunteered. "There have been rumbles before about passing a law to put away dogs that repeatedly stray."

"They'll never pass it," Blaise said flatly. "The dog lovers in this community far outnumber the dog haters. I guarantee there'd be bloodshed before a law like that is passed."

Miss Todd pursed her lips. "As one of the dog lovers, I quite agree. Dogs will be dogs. No sense punishing them for it!"

"To a point, I agree with you," Blaise said. "But we *do* punish people for being themselves, so we can hardly hold animals exempt."

Mary *tsked* and looked amused. "Don't be so literal, Blaise. You know what I mean. Straying is a relatively harmless thing. In fact, the *dog* is more at risk than the rest of the community. It hardly seems reasonable to put a dog down because it wanders around gleefully sniffing the world."

"I'm certainly not going to argue with you on that score," Blaise agreed.

Mary suddenly turned her gaze on Jill. "You see how blessed we've been here in Paradise Beach? We actually get exercised over straying dogs and coffee on the beach. The biggest annoyance in most people's lives here are the occasional traffic jams."

"Well, we have our catastrophes," Ted said. "Real ones. There was the time most of the business district burned down. What was that? Twenty years ago? And there's the occasional hurricane." He flashed Jillie a smile. "My dad survived one in the top of a palm tree when he was just a kid. The whole island was under water."

"It usually is when there's a hurricane," Miss Todd said drily. "You really ought to get Ted to tell you about that hurricane sometime, Jillian. His father told the most hair-raising stories. In all my life we haven't seen one that bad here."

Blaise leaned forward, adopting a low, spooky voice. "All unaware of the overdue threat looming on the horizon, the people of Paradise Beach continued to enjoy life . . ."

Mary Todd cackled gleefully. "Heck, even when there's one in the Gulf for real I never let it keep me from enjoying anything." She leaned confidentially toward Jillie. "When you get to be my age, you get to be a little fatalistic about these things. It's one of the blessings of age."

Then she turned back to Blaise. "Actually, I want to get back to the subject of the dog. I heard—and I may have heard wrong, so don't put too much stock in this—that the pro-leash law folks are planning to picket the police station."

Blaise was surprised. "Picket? Why? The dog got loose and bit someone, and we picked it up the next morning. Why would anyone want to picket over that?"

"Beats me," Miss Todd said. "The leash law is already strong enough, so they can't hope to achieve anything."

"Except possibly the demise of Cal Lepkin's dog,"

Ted said. "That's what I think is behind this."

"I just don't see it," Mary argued. "Most of the people around here know what that dog means to Cal. I'm sure that's the only reason the poor creature hasn't vanished in the dead of night after dragging someone's garbage the length of the avenue. We haven't gotten so modern or so big around here that we've stopped caring about our neighbors."

"No, we haven't," agreed Ted.

"That's one of the things I like most here," Jillie volunteered. "Everyone is so friendly."

"We're more than friendly," Mary told her. "We get *involved*."

Blaise laughed. "Maybe *too* involved. Well, if I get picketed, I'll just sit back and enjoy it. Nobody's ever wanted to picket me before."

"It might even be good for business," Jillie said mock-seriously. "Think of all the tickets you could write."

"Sure. Disturbing the peace. Loitering. Creating a public nuisance. Parading without a permit. We might collect enough in fines to pay for a new basketball hoop over at the Police Athletic League."

"What happened to the old one?" Mary asked.

"One too many slam dunks, I guess."

"Well, you should have told me. Get yourself one and have the store send me the bill. Good heavens, those children *need* safe activities."

"I couldn't agree more."

Jillie was impressed with Mary's concern for such things. It never would have occurred to her to think that wealthy Mary Todd would give a darn about whether poor children had a basketball hoop. Apparently she did.

A few minutes later, complaining that it was getting near her bedtime, Mary departed with Ted. Feeling suddenly inexplicably shy, Jillie looked out to where the sun had sunk some time ago, and saw something she had never noticed before. It was as if the darkness were rising out of the sea in a curving bowl shape to meet the lighter sky above. She pointed it out to Blaise, who nodded.

"Magnificent, isn't it?" he said. "It's the earth's shadow on the atmosphere as the sun moves around behind the globe."

"I've never noticed it before." She was enthralled, watching the shadow creep higher, as if night rose out of the sea to vanquish day. She'd always thought of darkness approaching from the east, but here it was, approaching from the west . . .

Blaise threw a few bills on the table. "Let's walk on the beach."

There were others on the sand, but not many, now that night had fallen. Jillie took off her sandals and walked in the foam, pausing occasionally to enjoy the feeling as the warm waves lapped over her feet and the sand beneath them dissolved away. The gulls had settled down above the tide line, and only an occasional *caw* reminded the world of their usually raucous presence. The warm breeze whispered gently, while the waves murmured a lullaby.

After a bit, Blaise reached out and took her hand. It truly was paradise.

"I don't care what the law says," Fielding Wainwright told the mayor the next morning. "That dog bit me, and it shouldn't be allowed to get away with it."

"It's not 'getting away with it,'" interjected Felix Crumley, the city attorney. "The animal is in quarantine, and will be for ten days."

"Quarantine isn't good enough! It's a dangerous

dog and it ought to be put down, dammit! It's not as if I did anything to provoke the animal."

Dan Burgess looked at the importunate tourist and weighed his political options. He somehow had the feeling that his constituency wouldn't be too happy if he personally had a hand in the death of a dog. Any dog. People could get a whole lot more riled about the execution of a furry four-footer than they ever would over the execution of a man. Of course, furry little animals weren't usually guilty of homicide and other unsavory things. It took a *man* to get *really* vicious.

He cleared his throat. "We have to follow the law, Mr. Fielding."

"Wainwright. The name's Fielding Wainwright."

"I beg your pardon." Like hell, thought Dan. He wasn't going to seriously beg the pardon of any pain-in-the-ass tourist, least of all one who had two last names.

Wainwright jabbed a finger at him. "You need to change the law. Savage animals shouldn't be allowed to roam free."

"They *aren't* allowed to," said Crumley, trying to sound reasonable despite his rising annoyance. Damn northerners always wanted to tell the south how to do things. Well, in his personal opinion, it took a northerner to know how to mess things up really good. Just look at New York City! Damned if he wasn't going to go home at noon and hang the Confederate flag out front.

"Well . . . they shouldn't have another chance to get free!"

The mayor's office was a large, paneled room full of expensive leather chairs and a desk nearly huge enough to play hockey on. It implied a good deal more power and authority than any mere mayor of a beach community with a population of five thousand residents could properly claim, as Dan well realized. Hell, he'd had a dickens of a time getting the state to help fund beach renourishment projects which replaced sand washed away by storms. And he'd all but had to go to war to convince the legislature to fund improvements to the drawbridge which was Paradise Beach's lifeline.

Admittedly tourism brought money to the state, and people who came to Paradise Beach also spent their money in Tampa and St. Petersburg and Clearwater and all the way over to Orlando or Cape Canaveral. Tourism was important in the state's estimation. But Paradise Beach was only a tiny part of that large picture, a fact Dan Burgess often had to choke down with his morning coffee.

Now this jerk was standing here insisting he get himself crossways with the only five thousand people in the state who mattered to him as mayor. He might not have a whole lot of power, but he liked the big office, and he liked being able to threaten that other jerk, the chief of police. Was it worth risking all of that to make some damn tourist happy?

Besides, he had a dog of his own, and Bitsy sometimes strayed, too.

"The law already addresses these issues, Mr. Fielding."

"Wainwright!"

"Excuse me. Wainwright." Dan drew himself up to his full five-foot-six and tried to look as big and important as the room that was his office. "Owners are fined if dogs stray. Dogs *will* bite. They have teeth for that purpose. We declare a dog dangerous only if he bites severely and without provocation more than once. The dog in question barely scratched you, and

I understand from what you say that he may even have had provocation."

"Provocation? I didn't do a damn thing to the animal."

"But according to you, a few minutes later you had to be asked to leave the premises by the chief of police. Are you trying to tell me that you weren't 'fighting' with your ex-wife?"

"What does that have to do with the fact that I was bitten by a dangerous animal? As for the chief of police—he's hardly impartial! He had a *date* with my wife."

That, thought Dan, put a different complexion on the matter. There had to be some way he could use this knowledge against Corrigan. Maybe he could claim the police were being too lenient with regard to Cal Lepkin's dog. Maybe he could reasonably push for stricter leash laws in the name of tourism. Maybe . . . he turned to Crumley. "We can pass an ordinance that's stricter than the state law, can't we?"

Crumley, looking startled, nodded. "More restrictive is okay, as long as it doesn't violate any state or federal constitutional guarantees."

Dan pursed his lips and gave Fielding Wainwright a long look. "Well. I suppose I can think about it. However, this is an election year . . ."

Wainwright had dealt with politicians before. The hint didn't elude him. "Mayor, I'd be honored if you'd permit me to make out a campaign contribution check right now. And later perhaps I can help defray the expense of television and radio spots . . ."

A stricter law was definitely possible, Dan decided. Of course, it would affect only animals larger than fifteen pounds—his Yorkie was a mere seven pounds and couldn't possibly be considered a danger to anyone, anywhere. Yes, setting the limit to affect only larger dogs made eminent sense. Little dogs were too small to be a problem . . .

He turned to the city attorney. "See what you can draft for me in the way of proposed ordinance, Felix. I think Mr. Fielding has raised an important point for visitor safety.

"Wainwright," Fielding said sharply. "It's Mr. *Wainwright*."

"Of course," said Dan, smiling broadly. "Mr. Wainwright. I may be able to get this ordinance passed at the next council meeting . . . on Thursday next week. Will that be soon enough?"

That evening, a group of friends gathered in Mary Todd's lovely home at the south end of Paradise Beach. The house had been built years before, when Mary's extended family had been large and were frequent visitors to the beach. These days she claimed she rattled around in it like a dried peanut in its husk. The rest of the group, all men, gallantly assured her she was far from dried up.

In some cases, the friendship among those gathered went back even further than the house. The group had jokingly dubbed itself the Hole in the Seawall Gang, and occasionally they acted in concert to promote various little projects. Their most recent cause célèbre had been turning a little patch of ground between two private homes owned by the city into a miniature park with benches and a small gazebo.

The gang was never larger than seven. Today it boasted only six members because George Appleby had passed away a few months ago and they hadn't quite decided who to invite to take his place. Mary was tough on that subject, unwilling to suffer fools. Lately she had been considering asking a woman to join the group. Women these days were more independent and much more to her liking than women of the past. Unfortunately, most of the independent ones were too damn young.

The youngest member of the group was Felix Crumley, the city attorney. Mary had at first been reluctant to offer him membership—he was, after all, only fifty-two, and worse, he was involved in city government. The other members had overborne her objections, and in time Felix had won even Mary around.

They gathered regularly, usually on Sunday afternoons, getting together to drink iced tea and coffee, eat a few pastries, and discuss the state of affairs in Paradise Beach. When they saw something that needed doing, they did it, often anonymously with donations of cash, although occasionally they took a noisy political stand, as they were currently doing over the mayor's attempts to get rid of the police department. Being summoned to an emergency meeting, however, was rare indeed.

"I don't think I can ever recall us having one," Hadley Philpott said to the group at large. Hadley had always had a great deal to say at these gatherings, and as a retired professor of philosophy, he often said it at ponderous length. The others were working on him to achieve brevity. Lately he'd been getting the idea.

"Well, it must be important, or Felix wouldn't have asked for it," said Arthur Archer, another of the group's members. Despite his seventy-three years, he was still active as pastor of the town's largest church.

At ninety-two, Luis Gallegos was as spry as any sixty-year-old, but he enjoyed treating the others as youngsters. They usually forgave him. He spoke now in his usual vein. "It may be just that he's young and impetuous."

"Felix isn't an impetuous man by nature," Mary said, looking at her watch for the third time. "But he's late." She tapped her toe impatiently. Miss Todd forgave her fellows a great many of their foibles, but not tardiness.

Even as she spoke, however, the front door opened and the last two members of the gang entered: Felix Crumley and David Dyer, a retired fisherman with a permanently sunburnt face and a diffident manner. While Felix apologized for his tardiness, David quietly helped himself to a tall glass of iced tea and a butter cookie.

"Well, let's get down to business," Luis said, tapping the arm of his chair impatiently. "It's getting late for some of us." Which was why they usually met in the afternoon.

"Very well," said Felix, taking up a station near the seldom-used fireplace. He thrust one hand deep into his slacks pocket. "Dan Burgess is selling out to some damn Yankee with a lot of money."

"What's he selling?" Hadley asked humorously. "Himself? I wouldn't think he's worth all that much."

Chuckles greeted his sally. Arthur looked as if he might remonstrate—as a minister, after all, he believed every human being was priceless—but he caught himself and let it pass. It was, after all, only a joke.

"Well," said Luis, "if he's selling out to the Yankees, maybe they'll take him north with them. Let him go up there and be a pain in the backside."

"He's not selling out that way," Felix said. "Some damn tourist got bit by Cal Lepkin's dog, and apparently he won't forget about it until he gets even somehow. So he's going to make a huge campaign contribution to Dan in exchange for Dan ramming a stricter dog leash law through the council."

"How much stricter?" Mary wanted to know.

"He wants dogs that stray more than once to be put down."

Arthur looked surprised. "But what about that annoying little Yorkshire terrier of his? The little bugger is in my trash at least three times a week. I thought Dan doted on him."

"He does," Felix said. "The law will exempt any dog smaller than fifteen pounds."

"Talk about a worm!" said Hadley in disgust. "He could at least be fair about it."

"He claims that small dogs aren't a real threat."

"It's my understanding that a dog of any size is equally able to contract rabies!"

"A good point, Hadley," said Mary. "One we'll use in our campaign to discredit this ordinance. When is it to be presented for debate?"

"It's not," Felix told her. "He plans to ram it through the council next Thursday without any public discussion at all."

Hadley and Arthur shook their heads in disgust.

Mary spoke. "Well, we won't allow it. A week gives us ample time to raise the opposition, don't you think?"

Her friends all nodded.

"I think we ought to approach the issue from three angles," Hadley said ponderously. "First, there's the angle of exterminating our little furry friends who've done nothing at all except behave like dogs—which they are. Second, we can attack the blatant unfairness of a law being proposed by a mayor who is taking care to exempt his own pet. And then, to get the cat lovers involved, I suggest we either push for a similar ordinance to affect cats, or we argue that the next step will be an ordinance requiring the leashing of cats."

"The latter," said Luis. "We want the cat lovers with us, not against us."

"True, but either argument will serve to arouse them."

Felix spoke. "We also need to let everyone know what's behind this. People need to know that their mayor is selling out for a campaign contribution."

Silence greeted him, and several seconds ticked by before Mary spoke. "We can't really do that, Felix. You see, the only people who know that are Wainwright, the mayor, and yourself. It could well cost you your job."

"I don't care, Miss Todd. Dan Burgess was elected to serve the voters of this community, not some damn Yankee tourist with deep pockets."

"I couldn't agree more, but there's no need for you to lose your job to make the point. It'll come out some other way. Now, how do we get the public's attention?"

They spent the next twenty minutes outlining various avenues of raising a revolt in just seven days. Given that Paradise Beach was a small community, the task wasn't as difficult as it seemed. Arthur, for example, would thunder about it from the pulpit on Sunday to nearly half the island's denizens. The Paradise Beach newspaper, all four pages of it, would seize on the story. And it wouldn't be hard to get some signs up in store windows.

"There's one other item of business," Mary said, when the group had decided it had said all that was necessary about the dog situation. "What do you all think about taking a stab at playing Cupid?"

The answering grins were all the answer she needed.

Eight

"I can't believe how fast it's happening," Jillie told Belinda just a few days later. Already carpenters had gutted the interior of the space she had rented and were busy building bookshelves and racks. The general contractor had estimated he could build the racks for a lot less that it would cost Belinda to buy them ready made and ship them in, so she had given him the job. In the process, he was repairing damaged drywall, replacing ceiling fixtures, and putting in new restrooms.

"It needed doing," Belinda said, when Jillie commented on the expense. "I was just waiting until I had another tenant."

Jillie could hardly believe her good fortune. Already her dream was taking shape, and in just one short month she should be open for business. If anyone had asked her just a week ago, she would have said it could never happen this fast.

Inside, the smell of sawdust was sharp. From the rear came the whine of a table saw, and the *thunk* as a freshly cut piece of wood fell to the floor. Men were everywhere, building shelves, taping drywall, spackling holes—to Jillie it looked like organized confusion.

Mary Todd stepped through the door, leaning on her ebony cane and looking around with bright, interested eyes. "Going good, eh, girl?"

Jillie nodded with a wide smile. "I can't believe how fast it's happening!"

"Jim there is a good contractor." She shook her head as the table saw started to chew its way through a fresh piece of wood. "Could we step outside? I'd like to talk to you, and it's impossible to hear over that saw."

Jillie went willingly enough, even though she couldn't imagine what the older woman wanted with her. She was coming to the conclusion that Mary Todd was an inveterate busybody, different only from Harriet in the wide reach of her interests.

In front of the swimsuit shop there was a cafe table with two chairs beneath the candy-striped awning. The two women sat there, watching the traffic pass on the boulevard. The sun was high and bright, glaring off white stucco, the sky was unclouded blue, and the air was fresh with the sea. Jillie tilted her head back and let the breeze toss her hair.

Miss Todd smiled. "You like it here, don't you?"

"I love it!" She opened her eyes and smiled broadly at the older woman. "It's so wonderful to be able to sit outside in shorts in January and feel so comfortable. I think I'm addicted."

"Most of us are this time of year. Winters here are perfect, but sometimes summer seems to go on forever. I know a lot of transplants are thoroughly sick of it when it hasn't cooled down any by October."

Jillie shrugged. "No place is perfect, but this is sure close."

Mary laughed approvingly. "That's the spirit. We'll make a Floridian out of you yet."

Jillie settled back in her chair, trying to wait patiently for Mary Todd to announce the purpose of her visit. Actually, being patient in this climate wasn't difficult at all if you were sitting in the sun enjoying the outdoors.

A steady stream of tourists passed by, dressed in every description of play clothes. This near the beach, most everyone was wearing as little as possible. Snatches of German, French, and Spanish floated to her on the breeze, along with English spoken in a variety of accents. Paradise Beach was a cultural crossroads.

Mary spoke, raising her voice a little to be heard over the honking of an impatient taxi. "Are you attached to Fielding Wainwright?"

"Fielding?" Jillie turned to look at her, feeling a creeping sense of horror. Good heavens, she had come here to get away from that jerk! How was it possible even Mary Todd was associating her with the man? She had wanted to leave the whole marriage and divorce behind; instead, they had followed her all the way down here, and now she was being questioned about them by people who hardly knew her.

"Yes, Fielding Wainwright," Mary said, her dark eyes sharp and knowing. "I understand you used to be married to the twit."

"Well . . . yes." She was reluctant but truthful. Lying didn't come easily to her.

"Well, are you attached to him?"

"We're divorced!"

"That could mean a great many things, gal," Mary

said with a sharp rap of her cane on the pavement.
"You could be divorced and never want to see him
again. You could be divorced and on the verge of reconciliation—or just divorced and hoping he'll come
to his senses. Which is it?"

"Why do you want to know?"

"Difficult little cuss, aren't you?" Mary shook her
head, unsuccessfully trying to hide a smile. "Just answer me and then I'll tell you. I don't want you ad-
justing your answer to fit my purposes."

Jillie suddenly found herself wondering why she
was being so ridiculously coy. "The truth is, I'm not
attached to him at all. I just wish he'd go away!" The
words were heartfelt, coming as they did after days
of Fielding and Harriet. The two of them seemed
bound and determined to make her fall in love with
Fielding again, but instead they were giving her a
stronger case of aversion. Maybe even hives.

Mary nodded and settled back. "Good, then. I
wasn't going to take him on if you wanted him to
hang around, but since you don't care, he's fair
game."

Jillie looked at her with growing curiosity. "Take
him on? Over what? What's he done now?"

Miss Todd chuckled. "My goodness, gal, you have
some opinion of that jackass. Aren't you even the least
bit surprised that I'd want to get in a tussle with
him?"

"Everybody wants to get into a tussle with Fielding.
I'm still trying to figure out why I ever thought I
loved him. What did he do?"

"Tried to buy the mayor."

"What?" Jillie was astonished. "The mayor? Dan
Burgess? What in the world would Fielding want
with him?"

"What Fielding wants is the passage of an ordinance that would require the execution of all dogs who stray more than once."

Understanding dawned. "Specifically Rover. Why, that son of a . . . gun!" She still didn't feel comfortable enough around Mary to use the stronger version.

"My feelings exactly." Miss Todd nodded emphatically. "Dan—oh, how ashamed of that boy I am! Can you believe I used to think he was just mischievous? I honestly thought that his habit of stealing cookies from my windowsill was something he would outgrow."

"He *has* outgrown it," Jillie said drily. "Apparently he's moved on to bigger things."

"Apparently so. He promised Fielding that he would get the new dog ordinance rammed through the city council next Thursday without any public debate."

"What did Fielding offer him?"

"A generous campaign contribution."

Jillie shook her head. "That sounds like him, all right. At home he owns mayors, a senator, and two congressmen—or so he likes to think."

"Well, now he can add the mayor of Paradise Beach to his list. And what makes it even more offensive is that the ordinance is supposed to affect only dogs larger than fifteen pounds . . . so it won't affect Dan's dog."

"The worm."

Mary smiled faintly. "He should at least be fair about it when he sells out. Anyway, I just wanted to know how attached you were to that damn Yankee, because some of my friends and I are thinking about making the remainder of his stay here extremely uncomfortable."

"Be my guest! The sooner he gets out of here, the happier I'll be. After the way he treated me when we

were married, I just can't imagine why he thinks he
wants me back now."

"There's no explaining some people, gal. Maybe
he's just one of those who doesn't want something
until it gets away."

But that didn't sound like the Fielding Jillie had
known. Of course, as time had passed, it had become
increasingly clear that she hadn't really known Fielding at all. "What are you going to do to him?"

"I don't know yet, but I'll think of something!" Her
gaze sharpened as she looked at Jillie. "What do you
think of our chief of police?"

"I have mixed feelings." That much was true. She
hadn't seen him since their date at the Paradise Pavilion three days ago, and she wanted to strangle him
for not having called. On the other hand, if he asked
her for another date right now, she'd probably jump
all over the opportunity. Part of her was dying to see
him again, and part of her was hoping he'd vanish
from the face of the earth. He left her feeling so . . .
confused. "I didn't like him very much when he arrested me."

"Hardly surprising. Nobody likes a cop when he's
arresting them. But you went out with him."

"And that was a mistake," Jillie said, making up
her mind in a sudden rush. "I don't have time to get
involved with a man right now!"

"That's always good to know," said an all-too-
familiar voice from behind them.

Miss Todd jumped. Jillie turned swiftly and wanted
to sink right through the pavement into some dark
place in the bowels of the earth. Blaise Corrigan stood
there looking at her. He was smiling, but the expression didn't quite reach his blue eyes. Oh, Lord,
thought Jillie, they should have cut out her tongue at
birth.

"Nice day, ladies," he said pleasantly enough. "Isn't Jill refreshing, Mary? You don't have to wonder where you stand with her, do you?"

Mary looked almost as distraught as Jillie felt, but she recovered more quickly. "Nothing a young woman says to a nosy old busybody should be taken seriously, Blaise."

He waved a hand, as if the whole thing were too insignificant to deserve discussion. Somehow that made Jillian feel even worse.

Blaise looked straight at her, but not in the way he had looked at her before. This time it was as if he had never seen her before. "I came to ask you if you know where I can find Fielding Wainwright. He's not at his hotel."

"Fielding? Has he done something wrong?"

"No. I just need to talk to him."

"You certainly do," Mary barked sharply. "Do you know what that man has done? He's offered the mayor a huge campaign contribution in exchange for ramming through an ordinance to kill any poor dog that happens to stray more than once!"

"Where did you hear that?" Blaise asked.

"From someone who could lose his job if this gets around too much, so be careful who you tell. Dan is planning to address the city council on Thursday evening."

"He'll get himself run out of office," Blaise said flatly. "Nearly everybody who lives here owns a dog."

"I don't think it'll go that far," Mary said with a sharp rap of her cane on the pavement. "I assure you, there *will* be public debate."

Blaise nodded. "Good. Now, what about Wainwright? Where can I find him?"

"Probably at my house," Jillie told him glumly. "He

and his mother seem to have taken up permanent residence. I'm thinking about moving out."

For a moment it looked as if Blaise hovered on the brink of saying something, but then he appeared to reconsider. "All right. I'll look for him there."

"Has something happened?"

Again he hesitated, then said, "Somebody freed Cal Lepkin's dog from quarantine last night."

"How do you know somebody did it?"

"Because he left a note."

A leash is like being on a chain gang! Why are all dogs sentenced to chain gangs at birth? Free Rover!

The note left in Rover's kennel was soon echoed by posters up and down the streets of Paradise Beach. On colorful poster board and flimsy photocopied handbills, the citizens were exhorted to show their solidarity with Rover. They were implored to appear at the city council meeting on Thursday to prevent the passage of a criminal law that would cause the "slaughter of our innocent, furry little friends."

By the time Jillie headed home that very afternoon, the posters and handbills were everywhere. Along the boulevard near City Hall, pickets with large signs were encouraging passing motorists to honk in support of Rover. The cacophony was almost deafening.

Fielding's car was parked out in front of Jillie's house, and she felt a surge of annoyance. He used his mother as an excuse to spend the better part of every day at Jillian's, and Jillie was getting sick to death of coming home to find her ex-husband waiting to pounce. Swearing under her breath, she parked the car in the driveway, then stomped her irritated way to the mailbox.

Hanging from the handle was a narrow green nylon dog collar with a tag attached: *Wear this for Rover!*

Amused in spite of herself, she strapped the collar around her left wrist. The idea that it might annoy Fielding tickled her.

Mail in hand, she made her way up toward the house. As she feared, Fielding was standing in the open doorway, ready to pounce.

"What are you doing here?" she asked sourly.

"Visiting Mother." He stepped aside to let her enter, giving her a smarmy smile. "Can't you at least be polite?"

"Polite about what? You've taken over my house without so much as a by-your-leave! I can't even have five minutes to myself when I come home at the end of the day!"

"Jillie . . ." He adopted a wounded expression. "You can't expect me not to visit my mother."

"You live with her all the time up north. Why didn't you just stay there?"

Fielding closed the door behind her and followed her into the living room, where Harriet was sitting, reading a woman's magazine.

"Visiting, my foot," Jillie said impatiently. "Harriet's reading a magazine. Is that how you visit?"

"All right," said Fielding, as if he were reluctantly making a huge confession. "I didn't come over here to see Mother. I came to see *you*."

"And I suppose I'm supposed to feel honored, touched, and grateful?"

He grinned. "That's the general idea."

"Well, you can forget it. I want the two of you out of here now!"

She stormed off to her bedroom, trying not to notice how her house had changed in these few brief days. Harriet had decided to decorate, and there were pictures on the walls, new chairs in the living room, new dishes in the kitchen . . . she was ready to scream.

Oh, God, she thought as she stalked into her bedroom and leaned back against the closed door, now Harriet had attacked her bedroom. There were new curtains and a matching comforter for her waterbed. Where before she had been content with white miniblinds and a royal blue comforter, now she was afflicted with a riotous tropical print on a cream background, green vines twining their way up curtains and across the bed as a background for brilliantly hued hibiscus blossoms.

Hibiscus, of course, didn't grow on a vine. The person who had designed the print should have been shot.

"God," she said again, trying to grasp the full extent of the chaos her life had become. Apparently it was possible for there to be something worse than divorce, worse than being cheated on. An invasion, that was what it was. An invasion by barbaric hordes off the steppes of Massachusetts.

The metaphor was ludicrous, of course, but somehow she couldn't manage to see the humor in it as she flopped into her bed and wondered how the hell to get all these recently divorced problems out of her life.

Closing her eyes, she forced herself to draw some calming breaths and let go of the irritation. What she had to do, all she had to do, was focus on the things she wanted to accomplish and let everything else— namely her erstwhile relatives—roll off her back like water off a duck. And the only thing she really had to worry about right now was getting her bookstore up and running. Everything else could wait.

Relaxed at last, she rose from her bed and grabbed a change of clothes. She felt sticky from perspiration and gritty from the sawdust from her shop, and all she wanted to do right now was climb into the shower.

The bathroom door was locked.

"Mother is in there," Fielding said from the living room. "She's getting ready to go out to dinner with me. Why don't you join us?"

Jillie's temper was further frayed when she heard Harriet turn on the water in the tub. "She's taking a bath?"

"Of course."

A series of unladylike expletives rose to her lips, but she bit them back one after another. There was absolutely no reason to explode, she told herself. It wouldn't get Harriet out of the bathtub any sooner. Turning sharply, she went back to her bedroom and threw her clean clothes on the hideous bedspread.

"Mother did a great job in here, didn't she?" Fielding said from behind her.

Jillie whirled and glared at him. "Get out of my room, Fielding."

"Oh, don't be such a priss, dear. We used to live together, remember?"

"You get out of here right now or I'm going to call the police and have you removed."

Fielding put his hand on his hip and looked disgusted. "Ooh, you're going to call the big, bad chief of police, I suppose. Well, he doesn't scare *me*, dearie. He may be panting after you, but he still has to obey the law."

"The *law* says I can throw you out, Fielding. This is *my* house."

"Actually, sweetie, it's *mine*. I bought it two days ago. Paid *cash*." He examined his fingernails, obviously enjoying himself.

Jillie was aghast. "You bought it? Why?"

He shrugged and smiled at her. "Mother hated feeling like a guest."

"Fielding, if you fell into the bay and a whole bunch of sharks decided to dine on you, I'd probably cheer them on!"

"Hey!" He straightened, looking hurt. And damn it, Jillie thought, he probably *was* hurt. In some ways, Fielding Wainwright was still a four-year-old. "You should be nice to me! You don't even have to pay rent anymore!"

Grabbing a pillow off the bed, she considered throwing it at him, but then checked herself. No matter how frustrated, she would not allow herself to get even mildly violent, and throwing anything at all was violence. Even a pillow. Instead she dug her fingers into it so hard she thought she felt the fabric rip. "But I *will* pay rent, you toad. You're not going to make me dependent on you. I'm not that stupid!"

."I wasn't..." But something in her expression made him back off. "Okay," he said. "Okay. You can keep paying rent. What the hell is that thing on your wrist, anyway?"

She looked down and saw the green doggie collar. "It's a dog collar. It's sort of like those yellow ribbons people wear to remember hostages and things."

"A green dog collar? What for?"

"Rover." She suddenly felt like smiling. "You know, the dog that bit you. He escaped, Fielding. And I'm wearing a green collar because I hope he stays escaped!"

Moments later she heard Fielding pounding on the door of the bathroom, calling in to his mother, "Mother! Mother, that dog has escaped ... and Jillian's glad he did! Mother ..."

Whine, whine, thought Jillian, heading for the

kitchen. If she couldn't take a shower she could at
least have an icy glass of lemonade.

Glancing down, she saw the nylon collar on her
wrist and laughed. "Go, Rover, go!" she said, and
heard Fielding howl in response.

The guy never could take a joke.

Living next door to Jillian McAllister had both advantages and disadvantages, Blaise thought that evening, as the sun set over the Gulf in a blaze of
vermilion glory. On the one hand he could watch her
gorgeous legs and sweet little bottom everytime she
pranced up and down her driveway—or, at this moment, watch her as she dug in the garden with that
cute little bottom way up in the air.

Unfortunately, he could also tell when she was ag-
itated about something . . . as she was right now.
There was no mistaking the way that trowel was digging into the dirt. Rage was powering that down-
stroke, and the weeds around the azaleas were paying
for it.

The other disadvantage of living so close was that
for now at least, Fielding Wainwright was only a hop-
skip away. It made Blaise hesitate as he considered
walking over to see what had Jillie in such a tear. Just
popping his head up over there would probably open
him to another discussion about how the dog control
laws in the state of Florida were totally inadequate.
He'd already gone that round once, just yesterday,
apparently right before Wainwright had decided to
try bribing the mayor.

Well, what the hell. The worse that could happen
was that maybe Wainwright would give him an excuse to arrest his Yankee ass. The possibility was
worth taking the rest of the flak. Besides, Jillie was
upset . . .

Not wanting to think too closely about why he cared that Jillie was so upset, he popped the top on a soft drink and wandered over into her yard.

She heard him coming and sat back on her heels. Reaching up to wipe the perspiration from her forehead she painted a dark streak of dirt across her face. He wondered if he should say anything, then decided against it. She'd probably snap his head off, judging by the look in her eye.

"Hi," he said.

She nodded, looking as if she were grinding her teeth.

"Umm . . ." He hesitated then decided to risk the consequences. "I get the feeling you're mad."

"Yep." She turned and jabbed the trowel into the dirt, abruptly ending the life of another weed.

"Uh . . . what happened?"

"Fielding." She punctuated the brief word with another stab of the trowel.

"Oh." He sucked on his teeth, reconsidering. Things between exes could get pretty damn bloody; he had the scars to prove it. Maybe he should just stay out of this, but he'd never been a coward. "What did he do?"

"He bought the house."

"What?"

"He bought the damn house I'm renting!" She pointed with the trowel at the little bungalow.

"Why the hell did he do that?" It sure didn't look like a rich man's investment. It looked more like something some elderly couple would buy, planning to live in it only a few years and not wanting to burden themselves with a lot of expensive upkeep.

"Oh, I don't know," she said angrily. "Maybe because he likes control. He told me I wouldn't have to pay rent and his mother didn't like feeling like a guest."

"He must have a lot of money to burn." It was lame, but he wasn't quite sure what else to say, because he wasn't quite sure how Jillian was interpreting her ex's behavior.

"Oh, he has *plenty* of money to burn," she agreed bitterly. "Entirely too much of it. A lot of people think that must be wonderful, but *I* can tell you that all it does is cause a serious character flaw. He honestly thinks he should have everything he wants the minute he wants it. The concept of delayed gratification isn't in his psychological makeup."

"I see."

"No, I'm sure you don't." She tossed another weed on the heap of mangled cullings. "Not only is delayed gratification utterly alien to his nature, so is the whole concept that there might be something in the world that he can't buy. As far as Fielding Wainwright is concerned, everything has a price tag."

"Ah." He could understand how that would annoy her.

"If he thinks he can buy *me* for seven hundred bucks a month—"

Blaise interrupted, appalled. "He offered you seven hundred dollars a month? For what? Remarrying him?" It sounded like prostitution to him. He was already mentally running through the penal code, trying to figure what he could nail the guy for.

"No!" She shook her head and sent another weed to Nirvana. "He bought this house and then told me I didn't need to pay rent anymore. How insulting can you get?"

He hesitated, thinking he'd better check out her reasoning before he made another mistake. "Insulting? Why is that insulting?"

"Because he thinks he can buy my affections in this underhanded fashion. Really, it isn't much different than if he'd offered to *buy* me. And *don't* tell me he only bought the house to make his mother feel more comfortable."

"I wouldn't dream of it."

"Fielding Wainwright has never in his entire life done anything altruistic. He used his mother as an excuse to buy that house so that he could put me in his debt. So that he could refuse to leave the premises because he owns it. So that he could—"

"Wait, wait, wait!" Blaise interrupted her. "Back up here, Jillie. What makes you think he can refuse to leave the premises?"

"Because he owns the house!"

"Don't you have a lease?"

"Of course I do! It's for nine months."

"Then for the next nine months you can throw both him and his mother out on their cans. If you want to."

She paused, trowel ready to assault another clump of weeds, and looked up at him. "I can?"

"You can. The lease transfers with the property."

"But he's the landlord."

"That doesn't give him the right to stay there all day every day. Check your lease. I think you'll find he's only allowed to be there with your permission unless there's some kind of emergency."

A slow smile began to spread across Jillie's face. "So when he comes back from dinner I can tell him to get lost?"

"And Harriet, too, if that's what you want."

Her smile faded and she sighed. "I'm beginning to feel as bad about her as I do about Fielding. She's completely redecorated the house since she arrived. She even bought new dishes." Shaking her head, she dug up another weed. "Today I came home to find my bedroom decorated in green vines and hibiscus blossoms. Tarzan ought to come swinging through at any moment."

"For somebody who usually has no trouble speaking her mind, you seem to be letting these two push you around quite a bit."

"You're right." Wincing, she pushed herself to her feet and tried to shake the stiffness out of her legs. "It's something about Fielding and his mother." She glanced at Blaise from the corner of her eye, looking almost embarrassed. "I don't know what it is, but . . . I even used to let Fielding tell me how to dress."

"You weren't intimidated by all that wealth, by any chance?"

She cocked her head and looked up at the remnants of the sunset. Blue was giving way to indigo, and vermilion had faded to a dull red. "You know, that might be it. I didn't exactly grow up poor, but the way Fielding and his family and friends were living . . . well, it was like another planet. And I . . ." She trailed off, hesitating. She hated to tell people that she had been orphaned, because it always sounded like she was trying to garner sympathy. "Anyway, I *did* feel out of place, and I guess I got into the habit of letting the two of them tell me what to do."

By a massive exercise of will, he kept himself from advising her to break the habit. He didn't want another lecture on how he was always telling people what to do. "I can see how that would happen."

Just then he happened to see Mrs. Herrera, Jillie's neighbor on the other side, peeking around the corner of her house, watching the two of them. "Don't look now," he said sotto voce to Jillie, "but Paradise Beach's biggest gossip is watching the two of us."

"Really."

He gave her high marks; she didn't even glance in Mrs. Herrera's direction.

"Maybe we ought to give her something to talk about," Jillie said, a mischievous sparkle coming into her eyes. "Wanna arrest me?"

"I'd rather do something much more exciting." Without another word, he swept her close, bent her back over his arm, and proceeded to kiss her with thorough wickedness.

Jillie was stunned. Not only had she not expected to be bent back this way, but she hadn't been in any way prepared for his kiss. Not that that would have made much difference. Something about being wrapped in Blaise Corrigan's arms with his hot mouth pressed to hers was enough to blow nearly every circuit in her brain.

Never had she imagined a kiss could be this dangerous. It was like taking an unexpected roller coaster ride in the dark, with no idea what curves and dips lay ahead.

Her heart slammed into high gear, and an exhilaration not far from fear gripped her. No! shouted some rational voice in her mind. No! She couldn't afford this. Not now. Not with her life overflowing with problems. There was Fielding and his mother and her business . . . no!

But the lure was irresistible, the ride too exciting to refuse. With nothing but the hot pressure of his mouth, he lifted her to a high pinnacle and filled her with yearnings she'd sworn never to feel again. God, she wanted this man!

"Hey! What are you doing?"

The voice dimly penetrated the fog of pleasure that swamped her, sounding as if it came from far away. But suddenly the lips that clung to hers were gone, and reality washed over her like a tide of cold water.

"Unhand my wife, you . . . you . . . *pervert!*"

Jillie was suddenly upright, standing on her own two feet, watching an angry Fielding stalk across the yard toward her. *Unhand my wife, you pervert*? She had to slap her hand across her mouth to stifle the laugh. A glance at Blaise showed he was feeling much the same way. The crinkling in the corners of his eyes was a dead giveaway.

When and how had she come to know him so well? she wondered with a sickening lurch of her stomach. She could read those minute little changes. Unnerved, she looked back at Fielding. Annoying as her ex was, she could deal with him a whole lot better.

"Damn it, Fielding, I'm not your wife!"

"And I'm not a pervert," Blaise added, although much more calmly.

"Get the hell off my property, Corrigan," Fielding ordered imperiously.

Blaise looked at Jillie, waiting. The decision had to be hers.

She thrust her chin forward. "He's here at my invitation, Fielding."

"It's *my* property."

Jillie shifted from one foot to the other and clenched her hands tightly. "No, Fielding. You know better. I have a lease that says it's *my* property. *I* decide who is welcome and who has to leave."

Fielding stared at her, his jaw working, then he suddenly rounded on Blaise. "What kind of crap have you been feeding her, Corrigan?"

Jillie took offense at that. "What makes you think anyone has to feed me anything, Fielding?"

"Because you didn't know about this earlier when I told you I'd bought the place!" He turned again to Blaise. "Keep your nose out of other people's business, Corrigan. Why aren't you out there doing your damn job, anyway? That beast that bit me is on the streets again!"

"I'm not the city dogcatcher, Mr. Wainwright," Blaise replied equably enough. "Nor do we know that the dog is on the street. As near as we can tell, Rover was stolen."

"Stolen? Stolen? Hah! His damn owner stole him, I'll bet. Have you bothered to look at him?"

"The dog is *not* with its owner." This time Blaise's tone was scathing. "Much as it may shock you, the Paradise Beach police department *does* know how to investigate these matters. In fact, you're one of our suspects."

Jillie sucked a sharp breath and looked at her ex. Fielding was puffing like an angry blowfish.

"Me?" He spluttered finally. "*Me?* Why, I . . . I wouldn't ever stoop—"

"Stooping has nothing to do with it," Blaise interrupted ruthlessly. "You've made it known far and wide that you want the dog dead. That makes you a likely suspect in dognapping."

Fielding spluttered again, finally jabbing his finger in Blaise's direction and roaring, "You'll be speaking to my lawyer!"

"Your lawyer can speak to me all he wants, but I'm not required to discuss an in-progress investigation with him." Then, pointedly, Blaise turned to Jillie. "Unless you want me to eject the jerk from the premises, I'll be on my way."

"You can't eject me!" Fielding roared. "I own the place!"

Blaise stepped toward him, and although he was dressed in white shorts and a blue-and-white striped shirt, there was no mistaking that he was a cop playing a cop's role. He didn't have to puff himself up any; he carried all the necessary authority in his posture. "Listen, Wainwright. The decision is Jillian's. If she says you're going, you're going. What's more, you're disturbing the neighborhood with this shouting, so hold your voice down or I'll take you in for disturbing the peace."

The last of the twilight was fading from the sky, but even so, Jillie could see how red Fielding's face was getting. She was also aware of Mrs. Herrera watching avidly from her yard, and Harriet looking positively aghast in the front seat of Fielding's car. She had to resolve this quickly, she decided, but she didn't know how. Fielding was determined to be confrontational, and she couldn't blame Blaise for responding the way he was.

But just then Harriet Wainwright climbed out of the car and raised her voice. "Fielding Wainwright, start behaving yourself right this minute."

"Mother—"

"Don't *mother* me, young man! You're making a scene!"

"*I* am? May I remind you who was involved in a disgusting clinch when we came out?"

"Now, you wait one minute!" Jillie flared. "That's nobody's business but my own! I'll kiss anyone I want, anywhere I want!" She saw Blaise suddenly avert his face and wondered if he was laughing. What the hell did he have to laugh about, anyway? Irritated, she wanted to bark at him, too, but couldn't think of a thing to say. He hadn't actually *done* anything.

"It damn well *is* my business," Fielding said hotly. "When I find my wife in the arms of another—"

"I am *not* your wife!"

"Fielding," snapped Harriet, "don't say another word! Have you completely forgotten what you came here to accomplish?"

Fielding seemed to have the sense to realize he was

heading into deep waters. He couldn't have back-stroked any faster if he'd been wearing swim fins. "Okay," he said, lowering his voice greatly. "Okay. I'll shut up but I don't have to like it!" He glared at Jillian who glared right back.

"Now, you two youngsters," Harriet said, looking at her son and Jillie, "just go inside and make up. I'm sure Chief Corrigan has better things to do with his time than listen to the two of you squabble."

That was just too much. Jillie erupted like Mount Saint Helens. "I will *not*! How dare you tell me what to do. I am going inside, alone, away from all you interfering busybodies. I want everyone out of here now! Everyone! And Fielding, I wouldn't have you back if you were the last man on earth, so you might as well go home tonight! And take your mother with you!"

Turning, she stormed into the house, catching a glimpse of Mrs. Herrera's gaping face as she slammed the door hard.

Only then did she realize that she had included Blaise in her indictment of busybodies.

Oh, hell.

Nine

"Hey, Chief?"

Blaise looked up to find Elaine Barbera, the desk sergeant, standing in his doorway. "Yeah?"

"I thought you might want to hear this. There's been some vandalism down on the boulevard. Looks like gang activity."

"We don't have any gangs."

"Yes, sir. That's why I thought you'd be interested. If some gang is after your lady friend—"

"My *what?*" Blaise interrupted sharply.

Elaine blinked and looked as if she were thinking about taking a step back. She was petite and dark-haired, but her appearance was deceptive: Elaine Barbera could hold her own against tough guys twice her size. "Lady friend," she said finally, holding her ground. "You know—your girlfriend."

"I don't have a girlfriend," Blaise said irritably, as

159

he wondered what the gossips of Paradise Beach had invented this time.

"Oh." Elaine shrugged. "Well, it wouldn't be the first time rumor's been wrong. So I guess you don't want to hear about this vandalism?"

"Well, of course I do! Especially if gangs are turning up out here."

Elaine nodded. "Well, it's nothing major, really. I just thought you'd be interested because of the involvement of—" She broke off sharply. "Never mind. It's just some graffiti on one of the businesses on the boulevard. Strange symbols. The guys who checked it out thought it looked like gang markings but they could be wrong."

"Which building?"

"Next to Belinda's Bathingsuits. The one that's being turned into a bookstore. At least, that's the rumor, but I guess that could be wrong, too, since you weren't really seen kissing the woman in her front yard the night before last . . ." Elaine was gone already.

Blaise stared after her, knowing she was laughing at him and that she hadn't believed his protestation at all. But why should she? Damn Mrs. Herrera and her big mouth.

But Jillie wasn't his girlfriend. In the first place, they'd had only one date. In the second, she was entirely too attached to her former in-laws for his taste. Just look what had happened last night. He'd gone over merely to find out what was bothering her and had nearly wound up in a fight with Fielding. Being around the woman was dangerous! And finally, he was never again going to make the mistake of developing any kind of attachment for a woman. They were attracted to the police uniform and the authority it represented, but when it came down to the nitty-gritty of putting up with the long hours, the occasional dangers and the lousy pay, they were all quick to take a hike. Like his ex-wife. Thank God they hadn't had any kids.

Jillian McAllister was merely . . . well . . . someone he'd like to have some fun with—if she ever got rid of her ex. And since that apparently was never going to happen, he was not going to elevate her to the status of girlfriend, however briefly. In fact, with Mrs. Herrera living right next door to her, it might be wise to quit talking to the woman entirely.

"Chief?"

Stifling a sigh, he looked up and saw Buck Kraft in the doorway. "What is it?"

"Some of the guys wanna wear green dog collars and we were wondering if that'd be okay."

"Green *dog* collars?"

Kraft grinned. "Yeah, you know. To support Rover. Most everybody in town is wearing them."

Ordinarily Blaise would have nixed the idea, because he didn't want his officers involved in politics while in uniform. On the other hand, when he thought of how it would affect Dan Burgess, he couldn't resist. He had to hide a grin of his own. "Sure, it's okay. Just don't wear them around the neck. It'd be too easy for somebody to grab one and hurt you."

Buck nodded. "I was just going to wear it around my wrist."

Well, Blaise thought, that shouldn't be much more dangerous than a wristwatch. "Okay, then." Why the hell not? Burgess was after his hide. It wouldn't hurt to get one back.

"Hey," he called after Buck, "can you get me one of those collars, too?"

Then he forced his attention back to the report he

was reviewing and tried not to think of Jillian Mc-
Allister, and how she must be feeling with her shop
having been vandalized.

"I really think you ought to come out and look at
this graffiti, Chief," Wes Tamlin told him on the
phone. "It's the second day in a row, and it's getting
vicious."

If the graffiti had been on any other business in
Paradise Beach, Blaise would have hotfooted it down
there for a personal look. Seeing as how it was Jillie's
business, he floundered around for an excuse. He
didn't want to see that woman again, ever. No way.
Christ, the whole damn world was giving him sly
looks and knowing winks, thanks to Mrs. Herrera's
big mouth. If anyone saw him within shouting distance of Jillian McAllister, the rumors would never
die.

Besides, it was Sunday morning and he was on the
way out the door. "I'm on my way to church, Wes."

"I'm telling you, Chief, you want to see this."

"Then I'll come by after service," Blaise said firmly.
"Take good pictures."

"I'll keep 'em from getting rid of it until you get
here. You gotta see this."

Wes's insistence both piqued Blaise's curiosity and
annoyed him. On the one hand, he didn't like being
pushed. On the other, Wes wouldn't be pushing if it
wasn't important. And whether he wanted to admit
it or not, he was getting concerned. One instance of
graffiti on her store could be taken as some kind of
prank by some kids with too much time on their
hands. A second outbreak indicated purpose and in-
tent. Jillie was being deliberately targeted, and he
couldn't ignore that.

But he also had to be in church. His failure to show

up in his accustomed pew at his accustomed time would start another rumor running around: that something was seriously wrong in Paradise Beach. It had happened once before, just last winter, when he'd caught some flu bug some damn tourist had brought in from up north and he'd missed church. It had taken *months* to stamp out all the rumors, tales ranging from his having been fired to there having a major drug bust to there having been a catastrophic accident.

Not this time. This time, everything short of massacre and riot was going to have to take a back seat to church service.

Because of Wes's phone call, he arrived a few minutes later than usual. The only parking space he could find was alongside the road, and a lot of people had already gone inside.

As he was striding up the sidewalk to the front doors, he was struck by the fact that nearly everyone was wearing a green dog collar. Most had them wrapped around their wrists, but a surprising number of youngsters were wearing them around their necks. Instinctively, Blaise looked around to see if Dan Burgess was anywhere in sight but failed to locate him.

He hadn't worn his own collar this morning, feeling it was inappropriate to wear at a church service, but it was tucked into the pocket of his khaki slacks. For a moment he toyed with the idea of putting it on, then decided not to. It was neither the place nor the time.

As always at this time of year, there were a lot of tourists in church. Among the regulars, his seat on the outside end of the fourth pew was considered sacrosanct, but today a woman in a pink cabbage-rose print and wide-brimmed straw hat occupied it. Blaise sat on the other side of the aisle and hoped his arrival had been noticed. He did *not* need another month of phone calls asking him if he'd caught the rumored drug dealer, and whether the family that had supposedly drowned had ever been located.

One of the subtle irritations of tourist season, one he had recognized years ago, was the way everything changed. Like not being able to get his regular pew in church unless he arrived extra early. Traffic became difficult to predict, other drivers became difficult to predict—well, hell, they'd learned their driving styles all over the world, and there was just no telling what they'd do in a given set of circumstances. Everything one had to do in the course of a day became more difficult because of crowds and crowding.

But most important of all was the loss of the comfort zone of habit. Everyone felt the irritation, and by the time the season was over, just after Easter, most locals were seriously on edge.

Blaise shook his head and refused to think about it. It was only January, and if he started letting the little stuff get to him, he'd be a ticking time bomb well before Easter.

Scanning the rapidly filling pews, he saw Stan and Cherry Potter, the tourists who had been involved in that collision on the boulevard. At this distance it looked like Cherry was still giving Stan a piece of her mind. Blaise was surprised they were still here. Most tourists would have packed up and flown, sure that any charges against them wouldn't follow.

This morning's hymns were all familiar selections, among them his perennial favorite, "Pass Me Not." Joining in, he tried to keep thoughts of Jillian McAllister at bay. Unfortunately, the Reverend Archer seemed determined to bring her to mind, through the indirect route of Rover.

"Today," said the minister, as he stood in the pulpit and frowned down at all of them, "we'll take our lesson from Psalm 36. 'Your steadfast love, O Lord, extends to the heavens, your faithfulness to the clouds. Your righteousness is like the mighty mountains, your judgments are like the great deep; you save humans and animals alike, O Lord.' "

Archer leaned forward, gripping the corners of the pulpit. The sleeves of his robe fell back a little and Blaise could see the green dog collar around the minister's arm. He almost laughed out loud but caught himself in the nick of time.

Archer repeated the last words of the verse in slow, measured tones. ' "You save humans and animals alike, O Lord.' " Straightening suddenly, he spread his arms wide. "Are we to do less than God for our fellow creatures? Are we to stand idly by while evil forces in this community wreak devastation on our little friends?"

Blaise all of a sudden had a clear idea of the direction this sermon was going to take. He glanced swiftly around, trying to gauge the mood of the congregation, and caught sight of Dan and Doris Burgess near the back. This was certainly going to be interesting.

Archer lifted his hand high. "A dog," he thundered. "A small furry little animal that wants nothing more than to adore its master. Not so very different from those of us in this church today who seek to adore our beloved and holy Master. A dog, a simple creature who loves us patiently throughout the days of our lives, seeking nothing more from us than a gentle hand and a meal."

Blaise settled back to watch Archer rev up, his hands waving, his voice thundering in righteous indignation as he talked about saintly dogs and the evil serpents who would have them untimely killed for the minor trespass of escaping their leashes.

"Those dogs need to be leashed *only* because we have left them no place to run free as they were intended to!" Archer's face was beginning to turn red, and voices from the congregation were beginning to reply with "Amen!" to his every statement.

From the corner of his eye, Blaise saw Dan Burgess trying to ease out of his pew only to be grabbed by his wife and forced to remain. Doris Burgess, Blaise noted, was wearing a green collar on her wrist, too. Oh, he could just imagine what life at home was like for the mayor right now. Doris was famous for ramming her opinions down people's throats, Dan's included. The mayor was probably sorry ever to have gotten involved in this.

"Rover!" shouted the minister, and the congregation responded with a hum of approval. "Rover! Nothing but a mutt, lineage unknown, color indiscriminate . . . Rover spends his days looking after Cal Lepkin, an elderly gentleman in our community, a man who has no family left on earth, who has only the companionship of one shaggy dog to keep loneliness away! Are we going to deprive Brother Lepkin of his only comfort? Are we going to tell him he can't have his dog only because Rover acts like a *dog*?"

"No!" said the congregation.

"Or are we going to save him as our Master would save him?"

"Yes!"

The place was beginning to sound like an old-time revival, Blaise thought, hiding a smile. He hadn't guessed Arthur Archer had it in him.

"Now," said Archer, raising his hands for silence, "there's another evil afoot in our community, one which we need to consider. Among us are people who would sell out their sacred public trust. People who come into our community from elsewhere and entice our public servants to commit acts of greed. We have among us in Paradise Beach a serpent, a slithering, crawling serpent with a forked tongue! A man who wants to see Rover dead and is willing to use all his personal influence and wealth to bring about the end of that poor dog. One terrible, terrible man against one little dog. One terrible man who would have *all* our dogs killed if they get off their leashes . . . and he doesn't even live here!"

At this point tourists began to look nervous. Blaise wondered what the hell he'd do if Archer stirred up the congregation into a free-for-all. This wasn't supposed to happen in church.

"Now, brothers and sisters," Archer said in a quieter voice, "I don't want you to go mistaking all our visitors as being serpents. Most of our visitors are wonderful people, and we're glad to see them year after year. But there is one—*one man*—who must be stopped before he exterminates all our furry friends! What will happen if we let him have his way with the city council about our dogs? Will he want to kill our kitty cats next? Our pet turtles? If he bends the council to his will on this issue, will he have his way with them on every issue in the future?" He paused, allowing the implied threats to fully sink in before he plunged ahead to his final exhortation.

"That is why, my dear neighbors and friends, you must make every effort to attend the city council meeting on Thursday evening. Save Rover! And save Paradise Beach from the predations of another carpetbagging snake!"

Mary Todd cornered Blaise outside the church. "Hah!" she cackled gleefully. "Now what did you think of *that* sermon?"

"I don't suppose you had anything to do with it?"

Mary put on her most innocent face. "Me? What could I possibly have to do with anything the Reverend Archer says in his sermon?"

"A whole lot, I imagine." Blaise couldn't quite smother his smile. "I guess this Thursday's city council meeting ought to be exciting."

"Hellzapoppin', as my daddy used to say. I don't know how it is, Blaise, but I get downright ornery when somebody tries to buy a politician. I get even ornerier when the politician is on the take."

"Just be sure you stay on the right side of the law."

"Gads!" Mary pursed her lips and frowned at him. "When did you become so straitlaced? This chiefing business hasn't done you a bit of good, Blaise. You're turning into some kind of . . . martinet."

"Martinet!"

"Oh . . . maybe that's not the right word," Mary said huffily. "My point is, you're always right and you're always telling everyone else what to do! That halo must be getting just a wee bit heavy!" Turning, she started to hobble away, leaning heavily on her ebony cane. After only three steps, she looked back at him.

"You really have to do something about the vandalism at Jillian's shop. The poor girl must be nearly out of her wits with worry! Two days running." She shook her head. "Damned if I know what this world is coming to."

Blaise, feeling stung, watched her hobble to her bright lavender golf cart and drive away. If Mary Todd could drive a car, he certainly didn't know. She'd been driving that golf cart forever, it seemed. Sometimes when she drove down the boulevard she caused traffic jams, but no one ever thought of telling her to stop. Mary Todd, her cane, and her golf cart were fixtures in the community.

Sort of like Rover.

And what the hell did she mean calling him a martinet and telling him his halo must be getting heavy?

Damn, Jillie had said practically the same thing—without the martinet accusation.

This unexpected view of himself made Blaise seriously uneasy. He had been able to dismiss it when it had been only one person, but now two people had seen him in almost the same light, and it was a light he didn't like.

Scowling, he made his way to his cruiser, barely nodding in response to the friendly greetings of other members of the congregation. Already there was a banner being strung between the two Washingtonia palms that fronted the church. In huge red letters on a brilliant yellow background, the banner begged Paradise Beach to *Save Rover!*

It was incredible, Blaise thought, as he climbed into the cruiser. This town didn't get exercised about anything except a threat to the free flow of tourist dollars. If someone had proposed closing the drawbridge, or putting an additional tax on hotel rooms, he would have expected this kind of response.

Yes, the people of this community loved their pets, though most of them kept their dogs within the boundaries of the leash law. Only Rover managed to rove on a regular basis, and most people were convinced that the dog was satanic. He seemed to have an absolute knack for doing the one thing that would get people angry—which made it all the more interesting that the town was so eager to come to his aid.

Posters supporting Rover were everywhere in evidence as he drove down the boulevard toward Jillie's store. He wasn't as indifferent as he wished he was. Having two incidents of vandalism directed at a single store was definitely cause for concern. He'd have felt a whole lot better if the graffiti had been sprayed the entire length of the boulevard. This, however, felt personal.

. When he pulled his cruiser up in front of the stucco building that housed the swimsuit shop and Jillie's budding business, he stared with dismay at the spray paint on Jillie's side of the building.

Wes Tamlin was still there, standing out in front of the building talking to Jillian. The street was Sunday-morning quiet; the only other people abroad were an elderly woman walking a Scottish terrier and a middle-aged man in swim trunks, T-shirt, and thongs. Blaise recognized the woman as a winter resident of the beachfront condos. The man had to be a tourist on his way back to his hotel.

Blaise climbed out of his cruiser and wished he was wearing his sunglasses. The look Jillie gave him wrenched his heart.

"Hi," he said, unable to think of anything else to say.

"Hi," she replied. Wes Tamlin nodded his greeting.

Compressing his lips, Blaise forced his gaze to follow the slashing red and black lines of the graffiti that ran across the storefront and around the side of the building. The miscreants hadn't been very tall, apparently, because all the damage was at or below eye level.

"Yankee go home!" was the most prominent phrase—and the least offensive—along with a few arcane symbols that he had to assume were some kind of gang signature.

"I don't recognize the markings," he said to Wes.

"Me neither." Wes hitched his gun belt a little higher and folded his arms. "Been tryin' to think, but they don't look like any I've seen before. Must be something new."

Blaise studied the black and red spirals and bursting suns and wondered about the minds behind them. Fascinated with science fiction, maybe?

"I don't even know anybody around here," Jillie said. "Why would they want to pick on me?"

The obvious link, but one Blaise kept to himself, was Fielding Wainwright. That man was one Yankee who'd managed to garner a lot of local attention in record time. In fact, he'd be willing to lay odds that before this day was out, everyone in Paradise Beach would have heard Fielding Wainwright's name in connection with the proposed dog ordinance.

"It does seem strange," he said finally.

"Strange?" Wes wasn't going to let it go that easy. "It's downright weird! I mean, I could see it if Miz McAllister here had been running her store awhile, and had maybe run off a bunch of punks who were disturbing her customers. But heck, she ain't been hereabouts long enough to run crosswise of anybody."

"That *will* make it difficult to run them to ground," Blaise agreed. Trying not to shake his head, he strode around to the side of the building. There, supremely visible against the white stucco, were more symbols and a telltale warning that this was the turf of the Thunderbolts. A crazy red zigzag apparently stood for lightning.

"Great."

Jillie, who had followed him around the building trying to think of some way to bridge the chasm her small temper tantrum had put between them, heard him. "What's great?"

He pointed to the turf claim. "They don't usually spell it out this way. It must be some new gang."

"And that's great? What would they want with my store, anyway? Why don't they just claim the city park, or something?"

"I was being sarcastic when I said it was great."

"Oh."

"As for your other questions, I'm afraid I don't have answers for them."

"Oh." Jillie looked at him, feeling as close to tears as she had in a long time. She had the worst urge to throw a temper tantrum at the injustice of all this. Fielding had messed up her life for five solid years, ever since she had first learned about his cheating. All she had wanted to do was start all over again in a new place where no one knew of her past and her humiliations. Instead, Fielding had followed her down here, bringing with him a miserable truckload of memories . . . and now this. Unshed tears burned her eyes.

She also had the worst urge to just throw herself into Blaise's arms. He looked awfully good in khaki slacks, dress shirt, and tie, but more than looking good, he looked *strong*. He looked like someone who'd be a bulwark against life's storms. In all her life she had never had anyone she could turn to for shelter.

"I'm sorry," he said finally, turning to face her.

"I'm not going to paint it over," she said, lifting her chin in unconscious defiance. "Not right away. They'll just come back tonight and do it again if I do."

"I don't know how long the city will let you leave it, though. There are codes covering the appearance of buildings . . ." He shook his head and gave her a mirthless smile. "The mayor is picky about these things."

Jillie thrust out her chin. "That man had just better stay clear of me. I'm picky about some things."

Just then, like a bat out of hell, Rover came tearing around the corner of the building, barking wildly. The dog pulled to a sharp halt as it saw them, but before any of them could react, it charged again, straight at Jillie. Instinctively she tried to twist away, but the dog leapt—and knocked her straight into Blaise's arms. No longer barking, the dog continued its wild dash with Wes Tamlin in hot pursuit.

Blaise and Jillie looked at one another, both acutely aware of their sudden proximity, neither quite knowing what to do about it after the way they had parted the other night.

Jillie wanted to apologize for the way she had lumped him in with Fielding and his mother, but she didn't know how to broach the subject. And what difference would it make, anyway, said that angry part of herself that just wouldn't shut up anymore. Fielding and his mother would queer any relationship she might develop with any man—and Blaise was just a man. Hadn't she had enough of men?

Blaise felt her starting to withdraw, but he couldn't let her go. The other night he had kissed her as much as a joke as anything, but in the process he'd discovered just how sexy and enticing Jillian McAllister really was. Now, with her pressed full-length to him, he could feel every succulent curve of her. That, combined with the kiss the other night, locked his arms around her as if she were a lifebuoy. He couldn't have let go of her to save his soul.

His whole body leapt in response to her closeness. His heart was hammering as hard as a drill press, and his every cell was reminding him of his most primitive instincts. Damn, he *wanted* this woman.

She tried to pull back, felt the resistance of his arms, and with a little sigh sagged against him once more. Her head came to rest in the hollow of his shoulder and he felt a wild triumph.

But then he remembered Fielding, and the dog, and the graffiti, and that this was a sunny street where anyone might see him holding Jillie like this.

"You know," he murmured roughly to her, "the

worst part about getting older is that you develop common sense."

"Common sense?" She looked up at him, blinking as if he'd roused her from some delicious dream.

"Yeah. Do you want the whole town talking about us hugging in an alleyway in broad daylight?"

She surprised him with a little laugh when he had half expected anger. "I guess not."

Slowly, reluctantly, they edged apart. They turned to look at the graffiti. Jillie finally broke a silence fraught with all the things neither would say.

"So, I should paint it soon?"

Blaise hesitated. "You might get away with leaving it for a few days, but sooner or later someone will complain and we'll have to cite you."

"I see." She sighed.

"On the other hand, if you paint it, you might entice the vandals to come back. Then we can stake the place out and maybe we'll catch the sorry s.o.b.'s."

She looked at him. "You'll watch the store all night?"

"You bet."

A wide smile spread across her face. "Okay, I'll paint it. I won't guarantee a great job, but I can probably get most of this covered up by tonight."

He felt himself nodding and smiling back at her. Only the other night she had lumped him in with her ex-husband and mother-in-law—company he certainly didn't like being placed in—and now he was forgiving her without receiving so much as an apology. Alarms were going off in every one of his besotted brain cells.

Instead of walking quickly away to safety, however, he heard himself saying, "I'll help you paint."

He figured he might as well have put his foot in quicksand.

*   *   *

"You really need a paint sprayer," Blaise told Jillie an hour later when they got together again, this time in old clothes. "You could cover this stuff up in no time at all, but you're going to go nuts painting this stucco with a brush or roller."

"Are they expensive?"

"I have a friend who owns a painting business. I bet he'd lend one to us. Can you wait while I run over and ask?"

Jillie looked at her shop. "Sure. I'll just work on scraping the windows."

And there was certainly enough of that to do, she thought unhappily as Blaise drove away. It was bad enough to have to do this at all, but to have to do it two days in a row seemed . . . unfair. But as one of her foster mothers had been fond of saying, where on one's birth certificate did it say life would be fair?

Smothering another sigh, she let herself into the building to get a scraper and a soft brush. Maybe she'd leave a note out for the vandals tonight: *Please just don't paint the windows!* As if they might listen.

Shaking her head over her own silliness, she dug the scraper and the brush out of a bucket where she'd stashed them along with other tools yesterday. Back on the sun-soaked street, she started scraping at the paint smeared across the windows.

"You poor dear!"

Jillie turned to say hello to Mary Todd. The woman was driving a lavender golf cart at curb's edge and pulled up in a parking place right in front.

"I saw this mess on my way to church. What in the world happened?"

"Vandals. The second night running."

"Oh, my." Mary climbed out of her cart, reached for her ebony cane, and hobbled up onto the sidewalk. Tipping her head back, she tried to read the words and symbols splashed everywhere. "You've called the police, of course."

"Of course." Jillie started scraping at "Yankee go home." Whoever had written it had surprisingly good penmanship. The words were legible, and they irritated her.

"What are they going to do about it?"

"Stake the place out tonight and see if the vandals come back." Glancing at Mary, she was surprised to see a smile twitch the older woman's lips. "You think this is funny?"

"Oh, my dear, no. Certainly not all the work you have to do to clean it up. But . . . the damage isn't permanent, is it? I mean . . . it could be worse."

Jillie stopped scraping and took a moment to wipe her brow with her sleeve. Damn, it was going to be hot today. Maybe in the upper eighties. And why was she getting the feeling that Mary Todd's sympathy wasn't quite genuine? "I suppose it could be worse. I could also go broke buying paint to cover this stuff up. You'd think they could at least avoid spray-painting the windows, wouldn't you?"

Mary frowned. "I agree with you about that. In fact, I really *can't* imagine why they painted the windows."

Jillie looked at her oddly. "Actually, I can't imagine why they painted any of this, to tell you the truth. What have I done to anyone?"

"I don't know. What have you done?"

Jillie swallowed a sudden burst of exasperation. "Nothing! I haven't been here long enough to have done anything to anyone."

"True." Mary nodded sagely. "Of course, some people might consider you associated with Fielding Wainwright."

"Fielding!" All of a sudden Jillie felt sick to her

stomach. That man had ruined more than five years of her life with his shenanigans, and now he was going to give her a bad name in a new town. Oh, she could just see it! Everyone in Paradise Beach probably thought she shared Fielding's opinion about Rover. Divorced or not, the man had been seen at her house, and his mother was living with her. Of course people would think she agreed with Fielding.

"Oh, my God," she said miserably, and sat with a thump on one of Belinda's cast-iron chairs. "I'm going to kill him."

"Well, I'm not sure that would help matters any," Mary said. "It might even get you sent to Raiford."

"Raiford?"

"That's the prison where they have Ol' Sparkey—the electric chair."

"I'll kill him anyway. There are always appeals."

"No, you don't want to do that. Just think, once he's dead, you can't make him miserable anymore. I'm sure you can come up with something much more diabolical if you give it a thought."

Jillie looked at Mary. "I can?"

"Of course you can. In fact, if you want, I'll be glad to help you."

The offer seemed surprising, but Jillie was in no mood to wonder about it. "Thanks," she said grimly. "It's about time somebody taught that man a lesson!"

Ten

When Blaise returned to Jillie's store, he was followed by a white van. On top of the van were aluminum ladders, and on the side was colorfully blazoned *Paradise Painting, Antonio Escobido, Owner* followed by a local telephone number.

"Tony wanted to help," Blaise explained to Jillie, as he and his friend started to unload the van. "That wall will be painted in no time."

"It's terrible," Tony said to her as he lugged his commercial paint sprayer into place. "It's an embarrassment to the community to have you treated this way, especially when you've so recently arrived. I felt it was the least I could do to come over here. Besides," he winked, "I don't want Blaise using my sprayer."

"Well . . . thank you," Jillie said, not quite sure how to respond. "Miss Todd thinks the vandalism has something to do with my ex-husband's campaign to rid Paradise Beach of Rover."

Tony cocked a dark eye her way. "Your husband is behind that?"

Here we go, thought Jillie. He'll probably pack up his paint sprayer and vanish. "*Ex*-husband," she said emphatically. "Rover bit him, and I guess he doesn't think quarantine is strong enough punishment."

"Well," Tony said as he clamped a hose to the sprayer, "I can understand how he might feel that way. Nobody likes being bitten. But I wouldn't blame this graffiti on pro-Rover forces in town."

"Why not?"

"Because all the support has been pretty good-natured and law abiding, hasn't it? I mean, posters and dog collars . . ."

Tony was wearing one, too, Jillie noticed. Around his neck. And Blaise had one on his wrist. "So far," she agreed.

Tony was a friendly, easy-to-be-with fellow who soon had the paint sprayer smoothly covering the offensive words and symbols. Blaise stood at the window beside hers and scraped industriously at the paint smears with a razor.

Wes Tamlin showed up twenty minutes later, sweat-soaked and weary. "I chased that ornery dog to hell and gone," he told Blaise, "but the dang animal ducked under O'Mallory's and a couple of the reg'lars got involved. The point bein' that the fool dog got away."

"How were the regulars helping?" Blaise wanted to know.

"I think they wanted the dog to get away, Chief." Wes grinned sheepishly. "I did my duty as a deputy, but I'm glad I didn't catch that mutt. You know, he's got a lot of spunk."

"Spunk?" Jillie asked, inescapably amused. "The dog has gone from being demon-infested to spunky?"

The three men laughed and Mary Todd's cackle joined them.

"Rover's turning into a folk hero," Mary said. "All he had to do was bite a tourist in the seat of the pants!"

"Robin Hood," Blaise suggested. "But where's his band of thieves?"

A while later, the owner of the cafe across the street came over with a glasses of ice-cold lemonade for everyone. He told Jillie how sorry he was that her store had been vandalized and offered to keep an eye on things for her.

By this time Mary Todd was holding court at Belinda's sidewalk tables. Locals passing by stopped to ask what was happening, and Mary made it very clear the Jillie had *divorced* the man who was behind the persecution of Rover, which caused a great deal of sympathy to come Jillie's way. Before long, it seemed they were holding an impromptu rally for Rover.

Jillie kept scraping, pausing only long enough to be introduced to another of her new neighbors. Blaise, too, kept working while he chatted over his shoulder. Tony finished painting the side of the building in no time, and after he put his equipment away, he joined the growing congregation at the tables.

The street was crowded now, with tourists exploring the shops, locals out for a stroll, people headed to the south beach. Someone set up a sign exhorting passersby to Free Rover.

And all of a sudden there was a TV truck at the curb.

"Look at it this way," Blaise told Jillie when she expressed dismay, "everyone in the entire Bay area is going to know about your bookstore by tonight."

"That might not be a good thing," Jillie said unhappily. "It'll depend on what they say."

"Nah. Any publicity is good publicity."

"How do you figure that?"

"Look at the politicians in Washington. Or better yet, Tallahassee." Tallahassee was the state capital.

Smothering a grin, Jillie turned her back to the TV people, hoping they wouldn't notice her. Maybe they'd be content to interview everyone else. Why should they want to talk to her, anyway? She wasn't even a ringleader in the Save Rover movement.

But only a few minutes later, much to her horror, a microphone was thrust into her face. "Ms. McAllister, is it true that you ex-husband, Fielding Wainwright, is behind the move to exterminate Rover?"

Jillie stared blankly into the camera lens.

"Is it true, Ms. McAllister?"

"I . . . don't know," she finally said, and tried to turn away.

"Are you protecting him?"

In an instant her mind became as clear as crystal. Protect that jerk? Not if her life depended on it. "No!" she said sharply, and tried again to turn away.

"How do *you* feel about Rover?" the reporter wanted to know.

"I've never met him personally, so I really can't say." She wanted to wince at the lameness of her answer but right now didn't feel it would be wise to tell the world that she held the dog responsible for causing her to have an accident and for thrusting her into Blaise's arms just a couple of hours ago.

"Do you think dogs should be executed for straying?"

"Of course not!" And then, savoring a sudden rush of power, she added, "I think anyone who could seriously suggest such a thing is an inhuman slug."

The reporter nodded as if he were taking everything she said seriously. "Someone mentioned that you bear a grudge against Mayor Burgess. That wouldn't have anything to do with your position on the ordinance?''

Jillie was beginning to feel a little like Alice in Wonderland. "Nobody cares what I think about the ordinance," she said. "I just moved here!"

"Then you're not denying that you have a grudge against Mayor Burgess?"

"I don't bear grudges," Jillie said sharply. "The fact that the man fired me because I wouldn't let a customer feel me up doesn't have any bearing on my opinion about the proposed dog law!"

It was only as the TV crew moved on to a new victim that Jillie realized she should just have kept her mouth shut. Here she was, new in town, opening a business and shooting off her mouth about a man who was presumably popular or he never would have been elected.

"Actually," Mary Todd said later, when Jillie shared her fear, "Dan got elected because no one else wanted the job."

Jillie almost laughed. "You're kidding!"

Mary shook her head. "It's not a great job, not in a community this size with so many residents who hail from all over the country. One of our past mayors likened it to being nibbled to death by ducks. Another said it was like being drawn and quartered in slow motion. Unfortunately, with the job comes some power—mainly the power to get a public podium the way he has over this issue of whether we should keep the city police." Mary smiled. "Don't worry, dear, he can't do anything to you that I can't undo."

Jillie didn't quite know how to take that. Her gaze wandered to Blaise, who was scraping the last of the paint off the front window, and she wondered why she had never before noticed just how good a man's legs could look in shorts. Of course, she hadn't seen many legs as good as Blaise Corrigan's. "Well," she said absently, "I'll bet that all my stupid comments wind up on the editing room floor. It's not as if I said anything really scintillating . . ."

At five that evening, she watched in horror as the local news butchered her. While the video showed her talking silently, the reporter's voice-over said, "We asked Jillian McAllister what she thinks of her husband's push for the execution of Rover . . ."

The volume came up then, allowing the audience to hear the tag end of her comment: "I think anyone who could seriously suggest such a thing is an inhuman slug."

"Paradise Beach mayor Dan Burgess doesn't agree," the reporter continued. "Mayor Burgess supports the passage of an ordinance that would order the execution of dogs that repeatedly stray. When asked if her opposition to the new ordinance was rooted in her feud with Mayor Burgess, Ms. McAllister said . . ."

"The fact that the man fired me because I wouldn't let a customer feel me up doesn't have any bearing on my opinion about the proposed dog law!"

"Lifelong Paradise Beach resident Mary Todd firmly offered her support to Ms. McAllister and her fellow Rover supporters . . ."

How, Jillie wondered as she switched off the TV, had she become the ringleader for the pro-Rover faction? She had hardly moved to this town and now here she was in the middle of an imbroglio!

"How could you say that about Fielding?" Harriet demanded. She hadn't taken Jillie's temper tantrum of the other night seriously and had moved back in

the following morning. After all, they were friends
and the house belonged to Fielding.

Jillie wondered if they were looking for volunteers
for the next moon mission. Or Mars. Maybe Mars was
far enough away for her to escape Fielding and Harriet.

"Really, Jillian," Harriet continued. "To say such
things about your husband on television—"

"My *ex*-husband," Jillie interrupted through
clenched teeth.

"Well, whatever! You simply shouldn't have said
such a thing about him."

"I didn't! They quoted only part of my statement,
and they did it out of context!"

"Oh, that's what everyone says when they don't
want to admit they've said something awful!"

"Are you accusing me of lying?"

Harriet abruptly fell silent, looking as if she was
astonished to find herself involved in this discussion.
"I beg your pardon," she said stiffly a few seconds
later. "I don't suppose my arguing with you is going
to make you feel any fonder toward Fielding."

"Hardly." Jillie's annoyance gave way to perplexity
as she studied Fielding's mother. "What's going on?"
she asked.

Harriet looked cautious. "Going on? Whatever do
you mean?"

"Neither you nor Fielding seemed particularly interested in keeping me around in the months preced-
ing the divorce, or even the months afterward, before
I moved down here. Why the sudden interest?"

"Oh, don't be absurd, child! Once you were gone
we discovered that we missed you. That's all."

But Jillie didn't believe her.

*   *   *

One of the worst parts of police work, as far as Blaise was concerned, was a stakeout. Since the department's budget didn't boast enough extra money to pay the overtime, he couldn't assign the task to any of his officers. Instead he had to designate himself as watchdog-in-chief for Jillie's business. Basically, he was going to sit out here all night until he caught the punks who were trying to make her life miserable.

He brought a couple of large insulated bottles full of coffee and some peanut butter sandwiches to keep his energy level up. Not that he expected to have much trouble keeping awake. The caffeine would have him wired.

The nights were cool at this time of year, at least to his Florida-acclimated blood, and Jillie's store wasn't heated yet, so he dressed warmly in a jacket and jeans. After nine, when all businesses were closed and the traffic was light, he let himself into Jillie's store with the key he'd gotten from Belinda earlier that day.

"Freeze."

He froze, uncomfortably aware that he was standing in front of the windows and was clearly silhouetted against the glow from the street lamps outside. "Who's there?" he asked.

"I'm asking the questions. Don't move, I've got a gun on you."

"Jillie?"

"Blaise?"

Something clattered as she moved, and then he could see her faintly in the little bit of light that came through the windows.

"What the hell are you doing here?" he asked her.

"Watching for the vandals."

"That's my job."

"It's my store. How did you get in here?"

"Belinda gave me the key. Damn it, I could have killed you."

"Actually," she said, her tone unmistakably dry, "I'm the one who had the gun on you."

"And what the hell are you doing with a gun? Don't you know how dangerous that is?"

"It's a squirt gun filled with vinegar," she admitted.

"A squirt gun?" He didn't know whether to laugh or to be furious with her. A squirt gun was absolutely no protection at all, but if it looked anything like a real gun, it could get her killed. "Just what the hell were you going to do with it? Make the vandals laugh themselves to death?"

Giving in to alternate waves of disgust and worry, he sat cross-legged on the floor beside her and put down his gear with a thud.

"You don't have to be so disparaging," she told him stiffly.

"Disparaging? I'm not being disparaging, I'm just . . . oh, damn it all to hell, anyway! Do you know what could have happened to you if you'd accosted these vandals with that squirt gun?"

"The vinegar was to sting their eyes without injuring them."

Blaise swallowed another oath. Turning to Jillie, he tried to read her face in the darkness. "Don't you see?" he asked her. "If they happened to be armed with real guns and they thought you were going to shoot them, don't you think they'd shoot first?"

She was silent for a long time. When she finally spoke, her voice was small. "I'm stupid. I should have thought of that."

"No, you're not stupid. Don't put yourself down. You just don't have a lot of experience thinking about these things." He sighed and looked out the window at the street. A group of young women walked by, laughing and talking, their voices muffled by the glass. "I'm sorry I got so angry with you. My adrenaline kicked into overdrive when you told me to freeze."

"Mine kicked in when you came through that door. It didn't look like you with all that stuff in your arms." She laughed self-deprecatingly. "I guess I ought to be glad you didn't come in here with your gun drawn."

He didn't want to think about that. A shudder started at the base of his skull as he pictured what might have happened, but he suppressed it and forced the image away. Best to change the subject.

"I saw you on TV tonight," he said.

"Oh, God, wasn't that terrible? They made me sound just awful!"

He chuckled quietly. "You didn't sound awful at all. Dan Burgess and your ex will probably have a problem with it, but I don't think anyone else will."

"And worse, they made me sound like the ringleader of the Save Rover movement."

"What's wrong with that? Don't you want to save the dog? I thought I saw you wearing a dog collar earlier."

"I was. It's just that someone else started all this stuff and did all the hard work, and it was embarrassing to have the story told as if I were claiming credit."

"Well, the real ringleaders can come forward anytime they want and claim all the credit. They don't seem in any hurry to, though." Scooting back, he leaned against the wall and stretched his legs out. "What I'd like to know is who let Rover out of quarantine."

"I thought you said he could escape any cage all by himself."

"Any cage Cal has ever put him into. Doc Kilkenny's cages are considerably more sophisticated. No, *somebody* let the dog out. They left a note, remember?"

"Wow." Jillie considered that and felt herself grinning. "There's a local Robin Hood."

A reluctant laugh escaped Blaise. "That's one way to look at it. Unfortunately, I get to be the Sheriff of Nottingham."

"Why?"

"Because the dog is supposed to be in quarantine for the public health and safety. That's not something I can sneer at. If I catch 'Robin Hood,' I'm going to have to arrest him."

"That ought to get you some wonderful publicity."

He shrugged, although in the dark she could barely see it. "I'm used to having people angry at me. It goes with the job."

"Doesn't it bother you?"

"It might if I brooded about it, but why bother? If I arrest the guy who freed Rover, all of Paradise Beach will probably be mad at me, but Dan Burgess will probably be thrilled."

"Meaning?"

"Meaning that people's anger with me flip-flops so fast there's no point in taking it seriously."

"I think I'm envious." In fact, she was. If she hadn't been so sensitive to people being upset with her, she wouldn't have put up with Fielding as long as she had, and she certainly wouldn't allow Harriet to be living with her now. "I need to learn to be that way."

"It's like any other callus. It grows thicker with constant irritation."

"Harriet's making a good start."

"Now, that woman's something else. She'd make an interesting acquaintance, but I sure as hell

wouldn't want her in the family. She's a born meddler."

Jillie felt instantly defensive. "She wasn't that bad
when Fielding and I were married."

He waved her to silence suddenly with a sharp
chop of his hand and a quiet "Shh."

In an instant all the adrenaline pumped into her
blood, causing her heart to stampede like a runaway
horse. She assumed he must have heard something
and she strained her ears trying to pick out the noise.
All she could hear, though, was the galloping of her
own heart.

Long minutes ticked by in nerve-stretching silence
before Blaise spoke.

"Sorry," he said, shifting to a more comfortable position. "I thought I heard something. I wouldn't expect them this early, though."

Outside there was a rumble as a car drove by. It
was still early, Jillie acknowledged. Not much past ten.
"It's a school night, though. Maybe they won't come
at all."

"You're making a couple of faulty assumptions
there. First, that they're school kids, and second, that
if they are, they have parents who give a damn. Too
many kids who pull stunts like this don't have parents who care."

He was right, of course, but Jillie was getting awfully tired of his being right. "There you go, being
perfect again." she said acidly.

"Shh," he said. "You don't want to make so much
noise you scare them away."

Fuming, she settled back with compressed lips and
folded arms. She most definitely did *not* think this guy
was attractive. No way. She *didn't* want to fall into his
arms and make wild love with him.

Which got her to thinking about why she had fallen

in love with Fielding in the first place. He certainly hadn't made her melt with a kiss the way Blaise had. She couldn't even claim that they'd had a meeting of minds. She and Fielding had rarely agreed on anything. So what had she seen in him other than that he was handsome and rich?

She squirmed a little, considering the possibility that her decision to marry him might have been utterly unfair to him. Had she really married him only because he offered the things her life had completely lacked, such as an established family and wealth? But maybe she wasn't being totally fair to herself. After all, even if she couldn't remember the feeling, she could remember that she had believed herself to be very much in love with Fielding. And incompatible or not, she would probably still love him if he hadn't betrayed her trust.

In fact, maybe she was rewriting history to salve her wounds. After all, he couldn't possibly have hurt her so deeply if all she had wanted out of him was his money and his family.

But that wasn't true. Even as she sat there trying to pick apart her feelings, wondering if she had been mercenary in her decision to marry Fielding, she found herself remembering just how very badly she had wanted someone, anyone, to love her. She'd probably have run off with a hobo if he'd professed to love her as Fielding had.

Aagh! The self-image she was painting was enough to make her throw up!

"You know," Blaise said, interrupting her miserable reflections, "I'm really not perfect."

"No?"

"No."

Jillie couldn't resist. "So what are your major flaws?"

"The biggest one, according to you, is that I have too many opinions and I'm always right."

Almost in spite of herself, Jillie laughed. "I *did* say that, didn't I?"

"That's all right. People are always telling me what's wrong with me. Let's see, I have a whole list somewhere . . . oh, yes, I'm intractable when it comes to the law. You'd be surprised how many people hate that, considering that everyone seems to be screaming for law and order these days."

"So it seems. So you've got this funny idea that you ought to uphold the law?"

"Yep. It's terrible, isn't it? Some folks call it an obsession. Others think I'm just too strict. Everything's open for interpretation after all."

"Sort of like five miles an hour above the speed limit isn't really speeding?"

"You got it. One of the most popular renditions of that song is that what's sauce for the goose is *not* sauce for the gander."

"I hear you. Fielding's a lot like that. He thinks he's a special case all the time."

"Are you going to get rid of him?"

For some reason she couldn't put her finger on, that question irritated Jillie. Maybe because that was exactly what she had been trying to do. Maybe because it wasn't any of his business. "I don't know," she said, being willfully perverse.

"You don't know? The guy cheated on you at least four times and you divorced him."

Jillie suddenly wished she had never told him about that. It was humiliating. Worse, because she had shared that with him, he felt free to comment. When was she ever going to learn discretion? "It's none of your business."

"You made it my business when you told me about

it. When you went out with me. When you moved to my damn town and drove over my mailbox!"

He wasn't being entirely rational, but she was past being rational herself. How they had come to this point was a mystery, but right now all she wanted was a screaming fight with someone. Anyone. Him.

"Look," she said tightly, "I am sick of your advice, and I don't want your opinion. I suppose everything looks all black and white to you, but you have the luxury of not being involved!"

"Do I?"

"What are you implying?"

"Not a damn thing."

They sat in silence for long moments but finally Jillie began to feel like an idiot. The feeling crept over her slowly and she wished she could drive it away, but it just kept getting stronger. She was trying to pick a fight with a man who, other than arresting her for drunk driving, had been nothing but friendly, kind, and helpful. A regular boy scout.

"Look," Blaise said, just as her humiliation was getting the better of her, "I know it's none of my business, but I think what you need more than anything else is to get a focus on what *you* want. Right now everyone is running over you, trying to get you to do what *they* want. Including me, I guess."

On the one hand, Jillie wanted to deny that he was trying to get her to do anything; so far he'd been nothing but helpful. On the other hand, what was he doing right now except trying to get her to do something? She seesawed, irritation warring with kinder feelings.

"I know," he said finally. "It's none of my business."

"I'm sorry," she said.

"So am I."

She didn't like the sound of that. It was so final, somehow, as if he were writing her off. And that really disturbed her because she didn't *want* Blaise Corrigan to walk out of her life. What she *wanted*, what she really, *really* wanted right now was for him to reach out, take her in his arms, and make her forget Fielding Wainwright had ever been born.

The coward's way out.

"Aw, hell," said Blaise, as he reached out. He was probably going to regret this later, but right now all he needed was to hug this little cactus of a woman and tell her it was okay to lean on him, to assure her she could trust him.

She came willingly, which surprised him, and settled comfortably against his side with her head on his shoulder. He'd half expected a fight.

"Don't you have any family you can turn to?" he asked her. "Somebody who could maybe come visit you and help you deal with the Wainwrights?"

She hated this question. It always made her feel as if there was something wrong with her. Stupid, of course, since she had done nothing to bring about her orphaned state, but there it was. She felt . . . flawed. "I'm an orphan."

"Really?" He turned his head, trying to see her expression in the pale yellow light that found its way from the streetlights through the windows. "You weren't adopted, either?"

"If I'd been adopted I would have a family."

"True." He wanted to kick himself for that stupid question. "How old were you when . . ." Christ, he didn't even know how to ask the question.

"I was six. They were killed in a car accident."

"And after that?"

"I was in a number of foster homes."

"But none of them gave you roots?"

Jillie was having trouble thinking, and foster homes were the last thing she wanted to think about right now. She wondered if Blaise had any idea just how good he smelled. And not until this very moment had she realized how much she had needed just to be held. It felt so good to have his arm around her!

"I don't think I am capable of putting down roots," she said finally. "The families I had were all good ones, but . . . as soon as I got out of high school I went as far away as I could. I suppose a psychologist would have a lot to say about that."

"What do you have to say about it?"

His hand was rubbing her arm gently, making it even harder to think. Unconsciously she snuggled closer. "I guess they might be right."

"But you managed to form a strong enough bond to get married."

She was touched that he was trying to tell her she was normal, but she was beginning to suspect otherwise. "When I think about the reasons I married Fielding, I'm not so sure I was attached at all."

And maybe, she thought, that was why she was keeping Fielding around now: so she wouldn't get attached to Blaise.

"You know, I wondered about the same thing myself. I mean—" He broke off, hesitating. "It's really not easy to talk about this," he told her on a self-deprecating chuckle. "I buried it so deep for so long."

"That's okay." She patted his thigh reassuringly and momentarily found herself almost breathless at the way muscle felt through denim. She snatched her hand back.

He rubbed his chin, then tried again. "After Millie left me, I had to do some soul-searching. It was kind of hard not to. I mean, sure, I was angry, and I felt betrayed, and it was easy at first to put all the blame on her. But when I calmed down, I realized she was justified in a way."

"You mean because you weren't there enough?"

"I mean because I don't think I really loved her. Oh, I thought I did. I wouldn't have married her otherwise. But in retrospect, I'm not sure I did. If I'd really loved her, would I have always put my career first? Would I have always taken all those evening and night shifts when other people wanted out of them? Would I have risked my neck quite so heedlessly? Would I have kept putting off the question of children year after year?"

He shook his head. "I was a selfish, self-absorbed son-of-a-bitch, and I got what I deserved. I won't ever do that again."

She wondered if he meant he would never treat a wife that way again, or if he meant he wouldn't marry again. She didn't know how to ask, because she was so afraid of the answer.

"Sometimes," he continued, "I've wondered if *I'm* incapable of forming a real attachment. It's been a long time since my divorce, but I've never even come close to falling in love again."

"Maybe you just haven't met the right person."

"Maybe. And maybe that's all that happened to you."

Before she could pursue that avenue of thought any further, she heard a tapping sound and felt Blaise stiffen beside her. Her heart slammed into high gear as she saw a dark figure on the street in front of the building.

The tapping came again.

"He's knocking on the door," Blaise whispered.

"Maybe to be sure no one's here?"

He shook his head. "I don't think so. Let me go answer it."

Jillie hated moving away from him. He had been so warm and so reassuring! Her gaze followed him as he stood and walked quietly to the door. If the person out there thought there was no one here, they were going to get a shock, she thought.

"For heaven's sake," Blaise said, as he neared the door. "It's Rainbow Moonglow. Do you know her?"

Jillie sat up straighter. "I . . . talked to her once."

Blaise opened the door and Rainbow, dressed in slacks and a sweater, walked in, her arms full of brown bags. "Hi! I figured you could use some hot food, since you're planning to be here all night. It's going to be chilly. I brought cocoa and coffee, and some cinnamon buns I baked. I hope they're still hot."

Apparently undisturbed by the poor lighting in the shop, Rainbow found some two-by-fours that had been laid over a couple of sawhorses and put her bags on them. Then she began to quickly set out cups and plates.

"Rainbow?" Blaise asked, after he closed the door. "Yes?"

"How did you know we were going to be here?"

"Oh, it just seemed logical. I mean, if a place has been vandalized two nights running, it would be intelligent to stake it out the third night."

Blaise looked at Jillie. In the poor light she couldn't make out his expression. "It's only logical. I hope the vandals aren't equally logical."

"Oh, they are," Rainbow said serenely. She lifted her hands a little and tilted her head back, growing still and silent. Finally she shook her head briskly and went back to emptying the bags. "No, they won't be coming tonight. Oh, good, the rolls are still warm," she added, as she pulled a large foil-wrapped package out. "See? You'd better eat them now while they're hot. That's when they taste best."

Quickly opening the foil, she pulled out a roll and passed it to Jillie.

"Uh, Rainbow?" Blaise asked, pausing as she handed him a bun.

"Mm?"

"How do you know they won't be here tonight?"

"Who?"

"The vandals."

"Oh. I just have a feeling."

"Oh."

The psychic wagged a finger at him, a ring on her finger catching enough of the streetlight from outside to twinkle in the dark. "I know you don't believe in it, Chief. But do you really want to spend all night here when they're not going to come?"

"I don't know that, Rainbow."

She laughed. "I just told you. Well, you'll see. The feeling is very strong this time. I'm sure I'm right. But there's really no point in Jillie sitting here getting cold and tired, too, is there?"

"Only that it's *my* business," Jillie said firmly. "I couldn't sleep for worrying, anyway."

"I guess I can understand that. Well, I'll just be on my way then. You really should reconsider, though. The vandals *won't* be back tonight. They know you're here." Waving, she walked back onto the street and disappeared.

Blaise spoke finally. "Well, if they didn't know we were here ten minutes ago, Rainbow took care of that."

Jillie bit into her cinnamon bun and savored the explosion of flavor. "She may be ditzy, but she makes one of the best cinnamon rolls I've ever eaten."

"She's an outstanding cook, and she's not at all ditzy."

Jillie felt a sudden stab of jealousy. Rainbow Moonglow was a lovely woman in her late thirties, and she didn't have the added disadvantage of a bunch of Wainwrights clinging to her apron strings. And how would Blaise know that Rainbow was a good cook if he hadn't eaten her cooking on several occasions?

Jillie all of a sudden wanted to strangle the woman.

"She only seems ditzy because she believes in stuff most of us dismiss," Blaise said. He found a perch on a sawhorse and sat swinging one leg while he munched on his roll. "Take her insistence that the vandals won't show tonight. If she'd called it a hunch or intuition, she wouldn't have sounded ditzy. Fact is, no matter what you call it, it's probably based on the same thing: unconsciously she reasoned that our presence would prevent the vandals from showing up."

"Makes sense," Jillie agreed through a mouthful of bun.

"If nothing else, having her show up like that will warn anyone off."

"If they saw her."

"Yeah." He chewed another bite of roll.

Jillie's curiosity got the better of her. "Did you date her?"

"Rainbow?" He smiled. Even in the shadows she could see the gleam of his teeth. "Yeah."

"Oh." She bit her lip, not wanting to ask more for fear he would guess how jealous she was feeling. The silence stretched for several endless seconds.

"A long time ago," he said finally. "I dated her maybe three times. She's a sweet lady, and I like her loads, but the sparks just weren't there."

"Sparks?" She suddenly found it difficult to breathe. Around Blaise, she felt very little but sparks of one kind or another.

"Yeah, you know. Sparks. I realize you'll probably

say it's a typical, disgusting male attitude, but you may as well know. I want to want my woman the way I want a tall glass of water on a hot, dusty day. I want to crave her. If I don't, then the relationship is going nowhere. I'm still looking."

Jillie found herself wanting to be craved just the way he described. Fielding had never craved her that way, at least, not after the first couple of times they'd made love. Then he'd started craving everyone else. But Blaise—oh, how much she would like it if he felt that way about her!

As soon as she admitted the yearning, she felt a wild rush of panic. No! She wasn't going to get tangled up with a man again. It was too messy and painful. Didn't she have the scars to prove it? It was definitely time to change the subject.

"It's still too early for anyone to come spray paint this place isn't it? I mean, people are still on the streets."

"Maybe. It's hard to say."

An unsatisfactory answer at best. Popping the last bit of roll into her mouth, she licked her fingers clean. "Maybe they'll show up later."

"We can hope. This kind of police work tends to be rather time-consuming and boring. Chances are I'll have to sit out here a lot of nights to catch the culprits. Why don't you just go home to bed and leave all this to me?"

"I can't. As I told Rainbow, I couldn't possibly sleep for worrying about it."

He passed her a foam cup full of cocoa. "Careful. It's hot. What's to worry about? It's just a little spray paint, and if they keep coming back we're bound to catch them sooner or later."

"I'm worried they might do something more than paint. With each passing day, Belinda has more money invested in this place. And next week I'm going to start receiving shipments of books and other supplies. What if they decide to break in and tear things up? Or steal things?"

"There's no way to guarantee that won't happen."

"I know that, but . . ."

Blaise slipped off the sawhorse and came to sit beside her again. "What are you going to do? Sleep here every night?"

"Only until these people are caught."

"We may never catch them. They may never come back."

"I'll just have to wait and see."

He turned a little, watching her as she sipped her cocoa. "You're really worried about this."

"I've never had anything before that was really mine." She put her cup down and wiggled around so she could look straight at him. "I was always given things that were taken away when I left. Even Fielding did that to me. It was just like leaving a foster home. I walked away from our marriage with almost nothing of what we had put into our life together. This time it's mine. I'm building it and it'll belong to me, and nobody can take it away." She shrugged a shoulder, feeling embarrassed at having told him so much. "No big deal, really, but it . . . means a lot to me."

"Then it's a big deal. A very big deal." He wanted to reach out and gather her close, but he held back. Everything was out of whack somehow, and he was uneasy about his own emotional responses to her. He must just be feeling sympathy, he told himself. Anyone would.

He also understood that she wanted to protect her business so he didn't suggest again that she go home and let him do it. This was something she needed to do herself.

"It's going to be a long, cold night," he said finally, not knowing what else to say.

"That's okay. I've had long, cold nights before."

That simple statement—profoundly brave, yet speaking of many years of loneliness—overruled Blaise's common sense and made him ache for her. He went to sit beside her and drew her snugly into his arms.

"I'll keep you warm," he said huskily. "At least for tonight."

He felt her look up at him in the dark, trying to read his face, then she sighed and snuggled even closer. Her breasts were pressed to his side and her leg came to rest trustingly over his. He felt as if he'd just been granted a major victory.

He waited a little while, enjoying her closeness, and felt her gradually soften even more as sleep began to creep up on her.

"Jill?" He whispered it.

"Mm?"

"Can I kiss you?"

He felt her face turn slowly upward. "Just a kiss?" she asked, whispering too. He couldn't tell if she wanted more or was afraid of more.

"Just a kiss," he promised. "Just a kiss . . ."

But with Jillie, there was no such thing as just a kiss, he discovered, as he kissed her for only the second time. With Jillie there were sparks, explosions, and a soul-deep yearning. Christ, it terrified him!

With his loins throbbing and his heart aching, he gently broke away and tucked her head against his shoulder. "Doze if you need to," he told her. "I won't have any trouble staying awake."

No trouble at all. She'd rocked his entire world.

"Blaise?" she said sleepily, a long time later.

"Mm?"

"Fielding and Harriet are up to something. I just wish I could figure out what it is. They never wanted me back before . . ." Her voice trailed away as sleep won the battle.

Blaise thought about her comment for a while. The Wainwright clan was Jillie's biggest flaw, the one that made him keep checking himself when he would otherwise have just reached for what he wanted. He didn't want to be involved with them. They were trouble.

But he didn't want Jillie to be involved with them either. Thinking about it, he was inclined to agree with her. Why did they suddenly want her back?

Sitting there in the dark, aching so badly for her that it was all he could do not to wake her up and make love to her, he decided he was going to hire somebody to look into it. Or maybe he'd look into it himself. One way or another, he was going to find out what Fielding Wainwright really wanted.

Eleven

The morning sunlight was so strong it seemed to hurt Blaise's eyes as he stepped out the front door of his house. Of course, he realized, his eyes were probably extra sensitive after he'd sat up all night waiting for vandals who had never appeared. He'd learned a lot about Jillie, though, and still felt like chuckling at the way she'd finally fallen asleep, succumbing reluctantly to the demands of nature.

He'd showered, shaved, and changed and was now headed down to the station to put in a couple of hours of necessary work before he came home and crashed. Every bit of sleep he could get was going to be necessary if he intended to stake out Jillie's place another night. And he fully intended to.

As he was walking from his door to his driveway, Fielding Wainwright pulled his car in behind Jillie's and got out, stalking toward the door of her house. Some instinct made Blaise pause. He leaned back against the fender of his car, folded his arms, and waited.

Clearly Wainwright was angry. Blaise's only question was how much, and what the man was going to do about it. This little visit of Wainwright and his mother to Florida to try to persuade Jillie to return smacked of stalking, and stalking could turn ugly.

Of course, it wasn't yet stalking. Nothing Wainwright or his mother had done qualified as that, but their refusal to get out of her life might be just the first symptom.

He'd wait awhile to make sure everything was okay, he decided, tipping his head back so he could look up at the cloudless blue sky. A huge white egret flew lazily in for a landing on Jillie's lawn and stood as motionless as a statue while it assessed its surroundings. Evidently deciding Blaise posed no threat, it began to search the ground for insects, moving at a slow, stately pace. Watching the bird now, no one would ever guess how fast that bill could strike.

A breeze caused palm fronds to clatter, and the distant sound of a cigarette boat on the waterway gave a lazy feeling to the morning. It was the kind of morning when a man could settle into a hammock and doze. Unfortunately, he didn't have the time right now.

Just as he had concluded that everything was okay at Jillie's, he heard Fielding's voice raised angrily.

"Dammit, Jillie, how could you say that about me?"

Jillie's response was restrained; from where he stood, Blaise could hear only the soft murmur of her voice. He could hear Fielding's reply, though, and fill in the blanks.

"You can't possibly expect me to believe you weren't talking about me! I heard the question, and I heard what you said!"

Christ, thought Blaise, the man couldn't be serious. Hadn't he ever heard of editing? He couldn't hear the next couple of exchanges, but then: "You've been avoiding me since I got to town," Fielding went on, his tone altered somewhat. "I'm not going to go anywhere until you at least give me a chance . . ."

The rest faded away, leaving Blaise uneasy and impatient. What were they talking about? Surely Jillie couldn't seriously consider giving the jerk another chance! But what if she did?

Damn it, he had to stop thinking with his hormones, but every cell in his body rebelled at the idea of Jillie giving that man so much as the time of day. She had loved him before, or she'd never have married him. She might actually be harboring some feelings for him still . . .

It didn't matter, he told himself—absolutely, positively did not matter. He wouldn't let it matter. He absolutely, positively was not going to let himself get drawn in any deeper with these Wainwrights. Get someone to look into the reasons behind their visit, yes. But get involved in another test of wills with a wacky Wainwright? No way.

None of which explained why he was suddenly halfway across Jillie's lawn, hell-bent on making sure she didn't give that jerk another chance.

As he rounded the huge azalea, he spied Jillie standing in the doorway of her bungalow, looking for all the world like a woman who was barring the entrance of her home with her body. Her hands were firmly planted on the door frame to either side of her head, as if she were braced for an invasion. Behind her he could see Fielding's mother, who was apparently talking as furiously to Jillie's back as Fielding was talking to her face.

Over Fielding's shoulder Jillie threw Blaise an almost despairing look.

That look froze him. It suddenly occurred to him that he had no right to intervene, nor any excuse he could give for doing so. The look he shot Jillie was probably identical to hers.

Then he decided it couldn't hurt to be a nuisance. After all, he was the chief of police; he was entitled. Settling his hands on his hips, he cleared his throat noisily.

"Are you having a problem here, ma'am?" Damn, he hadn't said since his patrol days. "I heard angry voices."

Fielding whirled around and shot him a glare that would probably have withered most folks. Blaise had experienced such looks from people who could actually do something about it—most of them armed felons—so he wasn't fazed.

"Who asked you to butt in?" Wainwright demanded.

"I don't need an invitation," Blaise replied mildly enough. "I'm a cop. I heard shouting."

"There's no law against shouting," Fielding retorted. "What there is is a law against cops trespassing anytime they get the urge."

"You're out in plain sight, Mr. Wainwright, and I'm not trespassing until Jillian tells me to get out of here. Even so, I could remain if I suspect there's danger of a law being broken."

"I don't break laws. Now get out of here. Jillian, tell the man to go."

"I don't think so, Fielding," Jillie said firmly. "You were shouting at me and I don't like it."

"Why wouldn't I be shouting? You humiliated me in front of the entire state of Florida!"

"I told you I wasn't talking about you!"

"And I'm supposed to believe that just because you say so? Like I didn't hear you with my own ears."

He turned again to glare at Blaise. "As for you, you crummy cop, I know what you're up to! You're trying to steal my wife!"

"I'm not your wife, damn it!"

"That could change," Harriet said from behind her. "So you should be very careful what you say about Fielding. It could affect your entire future."

Jillie looked at Blaise. "I'm losing my mind, right? I only *think* I'm talking."

"You're talking. They're deaf."

Before the situation could get any more interesting or explosive, a car pulled up and began disgorging its occupants. Moments later a second car pulled up, and out climbed Mary Todd and the Reverend Archer.

"What's going on?" Fielding demanded. "I don't know these people!"

The Hole-in-the-Seawall Gang—minus city attorney Felix Crumley who was wisely lying low—bore down on him with utter unconcern.

"You don't need to know us," Mary Todd said sharply. "We've come to see Jillian."

Jillie looked at Mary and the four men who followed and wondered what she'd done now. Something she had said must have upset this band of upstanding citizens to bring them to her door. What if that damn TV station had taken something else she'd said out of context and put it on the morning news? But what else *had* she said? She racked her brains trying to remember and discovered only that she was so tired, remembering anything was impossible. Yesterday had become a big blur followed by the even bigger blur of last night. About all she could remember about the vigil she had shared with Blaise was that Rainbow Moonglow had shown up—and that Blaise had kissed her. The thought warmed her even now.

Rainbow knew Blaise fairly well. Once again a snake of jealousy tried to worm into Jillie's brain, but she shut it out. Nothing, absolutely nothing, was ever again going to make her jealous over anything as insignificant as a man.

Fielding was saying something unpleasant to Mary, telling her to remove herself from his property. Jillie had had enough.

"Shut up, Fielding."

"What?" He looked at her, annoyed.

"I said shut up. Leave my friends alone!"

"You haven't been here long enough to make friends."

"You wanna bet?"

The childish response seemed to leave him with nothing to say. Satisfied, Jillie turned to Mary. "How are you today, Miss Todd?"

"Fair to middling," was the response, but Jillie caught the twinkle in the older woman's dark eyes. "It appears you're not doing so well yourself."

"I'm all right, really." She managed a wan smile. "I just didn't get enough sleep last night."

"You and Blaise were up all night, eh?"

Miss Todd might as well have set a match to dry pine needles, Jillie thought, as she watched Fielding's face pass through a range of colors from magenta to fuschia. He stared at Jillie as if he could scarcely believe his senses.

"You were up all night with *him*?"

Jillie's instinct was to explain that she had been staking out her store to prevent further vandalism. She didn't want to support the start of a rumor and she was absolutely sure that Fielding's notion of what it meant to be up all night with someone was a far cry from what had happened last night.

But it was that very thought that stiffened her backbone. Fielding had often been "up all night" with women. Why should she explain anything to *him*? "It's none of your business what I was doing, Fielding."

Mary Todd laughed outright, and her companions all smiled. But Harriet's reaction was entirely different.

"Jillian, no! You didn't!"

Jillie turned to her former mother-in-law. "What's sauce for the goose is also sauce for the gander, Harriet. It doesn't matter anyway. Fielding's goose was cooked long ago." Then she smiled, feeling good about telling the woman off—albeit fairly mildly.

"Mother, just stay out of this! Jillian, you're coming with me."

"I'm not going anywhere with you, Fielding. Not now, not ever."

"For God's sake, woman, I just want to take you to breakfast!"

She thrust out her chin. "Don't you glare and thunder at me, Fielding Wainwright. I've taken all the male macho meathead garbage from you that I'm going to take!"

"Male macho meathead?" He roared the words. "You and your liberated crap—"

"Hold it down," Blaise interrupted. "We have noise ordinances, and you're exceeding them. I'll have to arrest you for—"

"Arrest me?" bellowed Fielding. Evidently it was a very bad day for him. He didn't seem able to believe anything anyone was saying to him. "Just you try it, you stupid jerk. My lawyers will tear you a new—"

"Fielding!" snapped Harriet. "You're in the presence of ladies!"

"A lady who just called me a macho meathead!"

"And two other ladies who haven't called you anything at all. Behave yourself."

"I'll behave myself when I'm damn good and ready. Jillian! Are you coming with me or not?"

"No."

"The loss is yours." Fielding turned to stalk away, but came face to face with Mary Todd and her friends. "What the hell do you want?"

Blaise took a menacing step forward. "Watch how you speak to her, Wainwright."

"What we want," Mary said, lifting her ebony cane and wagging it at Fielding, "is for Jillie to chair our organization."

"What organization?" asked Jillie and Fielding at the same time.

Mary looked at Jill. "Our ad hoc group to save the dogs of Paradise Beach."

Fielding rounded on Jillie. "You wouldn't!"

Her chin lifted. "I might. I need to know more about it." She smiled at Mary and her friends. "Would you like to come in?"

"No!" shouted Fielding. "That's *my* house and I'm not going to let you use it to make a laughingstock of me!"

"It's *my* house and nobody can make a laughingstock of you except yourself, Fielding!"

"Hear, hear," said Mary Todd, thumping her cane.

But Fielding was in no mood to listen to anyone else. "You can't treat me this way, Jillian! I won't have it." He loomed over her, glaring and poking at her with his index finger in a way that she had always loathed. "You want to know why I had girlfriends while we were married?"

Jillian felt a roaring begin in her ears, though she didn't know whether it was anger or humiliation that was making her blood pound and her field of vision narrow. Dimly she was aware that Blaise was saying something sharp and that Harriet was imploring Fielding to shut his mouth. Mary Todd and her friends seemed to be shouting something at Fielding, and surely all those voices would drown him out as he said out loud what she had always feared.

But a quick movement caught her eye, tearing her attention from Fielding's ugly, open mouth. Turning her head a hair, she saw Rover.

As if in slow motion, she saw him bound forward out of the shrubbery between her house and Mrs. Herrera's. She saw Mrs. Herrera standing over there with huge eyes taking in the entire scene as Rover charged straight at Fielding and then, as if he had taken wing, leapt into the air. In amazement she watched the dog sail toward Fielding, butt his head against Fielding's arm and shoulder, and continue his arc to the ground.

Everything suddenly sped up as Fielding fell back and landed on his rear. Rover hit the ground at a dead run, evaded Blaise's reaching hands, and disappeared down the road just as Jim Knapp pulled his postal truck up to the driveway.

"Get that dog!" bellowed Fielding. "That animal has attacked me twice now! He's a menace to society."

Something inside Jillie snapped. She pointed her finger straight at Fielding. "He's only a menace to *you*, you jerk!"

Mary Todd spoke. "Looks to me as if he was protecting Jillie from *you*, Mr. Wainwright."

"That's how it looked to me," Jim Knapp said, as he came up the drive with a handful of mail. "Ms.

McAllister, you didn't move that bird's nest out of the box like I asked."

It took Jillie a moment to reorganize her thoughts. "I'm sorry, Mr. Knapp. I couldn't bring myself to do it. The birds have laid eggs in there and I don't want to disturb them."

Knapp handed her her mail. "Well, seeing as how there are eggs in there, I can just bring the mail to your door."

"Thank you. Tell you what. I was thinking about getting another mailbox and just putting it up beside that one."

Knapp waved his hand dismissively. "There are times when rules are meant to be bent, and I guess this is one of them. It's not that far a walk that I can't carry your mail to the door. Of course, if you're not here . . ."

"I'll get the mailbox, but thank you for being so understanding."

Knapp astonished her with a wide, toothy smile. "My pleasure. And wasn't that Rover something?"

Jillie watched him walk back to his truck and felt a wide smile dawning on her own face. "Yeah," she said, "he was something."

Fielding moaned. "Jillian, how can you! That dog attacked me! He's dangerous! I'm going to sue the damn police department for failing to catch him. Hell, I'm going to sue that whole damn town!"

Jillie didn't spare him a glance. Instead, she turned to Mary Todd. "Miss Todd, I'd be honored to join your ad hoc committee to save the dogs of Paradise Beach."

She never heard the rest of Fielding's diatribe because she turned and walked into the house, forcing Harriet to stand aside. Mary Todd and her friends followed her and gathered in the living room.

The room, which had once been simply decorated in white and green, had turned into a tropical paradise overrun by huge plants. Harriet had evidently bought out the better part of an entire nursery to "bring the outdoors inside," as she had told Jillian. Jillie figured there was enough of Florida right outside her door that she didn't need to turn her living room into a jungle. The small room didn't have a square inch of space left.

"Can you breathe in here?" Mary Todd asked, looking around with an arched brow.

"It's difficult," Jillie replied, not caring if Harriet overheard. "If I didn't have a lease, I'd move out."

"Just move some of the plants out, my dear. If you need help, ask Chief Corrigan. He's a strong young man. Now, let me introduce you to my friends."

Jillie shook hands with Hadley Philpott, Arthur Archer, David Dyer, and Luis Gallegos.

"We, my dear," Mary said proudly, "are the Ad Hoc Committee to Save the Dogs of Paradise Beach— AHCSDPB, for short."

"We couldn't come up with an acronym that was pronounceable," Arthur Archer said. "Heaven knows we tried."

"And had a great deal of fun at it," Mary said, tapping her cane impatiently. "What does it matter what we're called? We'll only be in existence until after we stomp out this ridiculous ordinance. We could just as easily have called ourselves the Committee to End Political Corruption, but dogs garner so much more sympathy and interest."

Jillie wasn't sure how to react to that. "So you're not really interested in Rover?"

"Of course we are," Philpott said emphatically. "But we're also dead set against some outsider coming into this town and buying laws to suit his own self-interest. It just happens that two of our concerns come together in this single cause."

"Oh. Well, it's not that I'm not against political corruption, because I am, but I feel a much stronger desire to protect the dogs."

"So do we, dear," Mary Todd said warmly. "But we're not averse to getting two birds with one stone."

"Well, of course not. Would anyone like anything to drink? I have tea, coffee, water . . . and I think some orange juice."

At the kitchen sink, she could see Fielding was still in the front yard, toe-to-toe with Blaise. Harriet was standing there watching the two of them, looking as if she couldn't quite believe what was happening. Jillie wondered if Fielding was going to wind up spending the night in jail.

Not that he didn't deserve to, she thought, as she filled a tray with beverages. Had he always been this obnoxious?

Probably. She didn't have a whole lot of difficulty recalling other times when he'd behaved this unreasonably. The difference now was that she didn't feel a wife's duty to believe the best of him. Fielding Wainwright was a horse's ass!

Despite the crowding of the living room, everyone was seated comfortably on Jillie's couch and the two chairs Harriet had bought. Jillie pulled a kitchen chair in for herself.

"What are we going to do about this ordinance?" she asked everyone. "Were you responsible for all the posters and the collars that were passed out around town?"

Hadley Philpott smiled modestly. "We had a little something to do with that."

"I wondered who had gone to the trouble. What's next, and what do you need me for?"

"Well, my dear," Mary said, "you've been seen on TV speaking out against the ordinance, so you're already highly recognizable. We thought if you joined the picketing in front of City Hall, the TV people would be sure to interview you. So now you can tell them you're our president and you can speak for us."

"But any one of you could speak for the group."

Mary shook her head. "We're all elderly. Trust me, in Florida nobody has respect for the elderly. We move too slowly and we don't understand what's important."

"To be fair, Mary," Philpott said, "too many elderly people in this state have been far too selfish about things like money for schools. Young people naturally doubt our wisdom when so many of us appear to be concerned with nothing but having our way. I think if I hear one more well-heeled person argue about the proper size of a senior citizen's free cup of coffee, or insist that they shouldn't have to wait in line like everyone else, I'm going to die of mortification."

"There is entirely too much of that attitude," the Reverend Archer agreed.

"But not everyone's like that," Jillie protested. "Like anything else, it's a few bad apples in the barrel. Look at all of *you*."

They all smiled fondly at her, making her feel she'd just been adopted by a whole band of doting parents.

Mary Todd rapped her cane for attention. "Bad attitudes among the elderly are mirrored in bad attitudes among the young. And those attitudes have nothing to do with our current purpose. The question is: what additional things can we do to prevent the passage of the dog ordinance on Thursday? We need to get everyone involved."

"Well," said Luis Gallegos, "we *could* let a lot of dogs loose at the same time."

Jillie got the distinct impression that this was a new idea, something that hadn't occurred to any of them until this very moment. "What good would that do?"

"If your dog had recently strayed, it might make you a little more sensitive to the issue of whether stray dogs ought to be killed."

"I don't know about that," the Reverend Archer said. "Letting all those dogs go—well, it doesn't sound quite legal. And what if some of them were to get hurt—run over by a car, for example. No, I don't think this is a good idea."

Harriet came through the front door and regarded Jillie with an expression rife with disappointment and anger. "I can't believe you, Jillian. I can't believe you would hurt Fielding this way."

Jillie lifted her chin. "I'm not hurting him, Harriet. I'm opposing his political position. If *that's* tantamount to hurting him, then he ought to stay out of politics."

"Hear, hear," said Mary.

Harriet glared at Miss Todd and shook her head at Jillie. "You really haven't considered what you're doing here, young lady. You ought to think about what you're tossing away with your foolishness. Fielding Wainwright is a very wealthy man with a great deal of influence and prestige! You could share that with him."

"Prestige didn't keep me company in the middle of the night, Harriet, nor did money. Believe me, *nothing* could induce me to take that man back."

Harriet drew herself up, frowning deeply. "Then I'm going to leave. We have nothing more to say to one another. Ever."

Jillie felt a pang at that. She was startled to feel a

hand pat hers and turned to find Mary Todd leaning toward her.

"It's all right, my dear. She'll calm down. For the moment it's best just to let her go."

Jillie nodded and forced herself to smile brightly. "I don't understand it. Neither of them has wanted to speak to me since the divorce six months ago. Back home in Massachusetts, Fielding even got a restraining order against me, claiming I was stalking him because we used the same auto mechanic. I can't imagine why all of a sudden they both want to see me reconcile with him."

Mary Todd's eyes narrowed. "That does seem awfully strange."

The others nodded their agreement.

"I'll tell you what, Jillian," Mary continued. "I happen to have one of the world's best attorneys—hell, he kept me from being declared incompetent a couple of years ago when my nephews ganged up on me. They wanted my property, you see, because developers are willing to pay millions for it. They said I was crazy because I preferred to keep it just as it is and pass up all the money. Anyway, they did some really dastardly things, but Cleveland kept them from getting away with it. I'm going to ask him to look into some things to see if we can't discover what these two are up to, hmm?"

Jillie nodded, already feeling better simply because she had an ally. "It would be nice to know."

"I somehow doubt it's going to be nice at all."

Blaise woke in the early evening with the feeling that someone had driven an ax into his skull. That was what came of staying up all night when he wasn't used to it anymore.

Damn. His eyes burned and felt too big for their

sockets. Every old injury he'd ever had, from the knee he had twisted playing high school football to the wrist he'd broken wrestling with a murder suspect years ago on the beat in Jacksonville, shrieked an aching protest when he moved. He was getting too old to spend all night on a hard floor with his back propped against an equally hard wall. Maybe he ought to bring a lawn chair along tonight.

A hot shower went a long way to easing all the aches and once again making him feel a young thirty-eight. A meal of eggs and bacon also helped. With a second mug of hot coffee, he stepped outside into the warm twilight and trekked next door to find out if Jillie was planning to join him on the stakeout tonight or if he was on his own. No point in taking two cars when they could get by with one.

Besides, he really wanted to know if Jillie was all right after the confrontation in her yard. Fielding was an abusive son-of-a-gun, and he had a feeling Jillie had put up with more in her marriage than she'd realized.

Chances were she had been emotionally and psychologically abused by a man who felt himself better than her in every way. In fact, Fielding had probably married her because he had so much to lord over her, from his wealth to his long-established roots. Fielding Wainwright struck him as that kind of guy, a man who needed to bolster his own importance and manliness by surrounding himself with people he could bully and put down.

And Jillie, coming from the background she had, had probably been impressed enough to believe that Fielding had every right to act as if he were God's gift to the rest of the world. Hell, she had probably even believed he was—for a while.

But this was all only a lot of amateur psychology.

It was just that he'd seen plenty of men like Fielding, men who didn't have as many advantages or as much clout. Men such as pimps and petty crooks who used women to make themselves feel important and strong. He recognized the type.

Well, thinking about it wasn't fixing anything, and he was a man who preferred to fix things. He knocked on Jillie's door and waited.

A couple of minutes later, she opened the door a crack and peeped out. "Oh!" she said, and opened the door wider. "I was afraid it was Fielding or Harriet."

"Just me," he said with a smile. "I came over to see if you were planning to stake out the store tonight. If so, we might as well go together."

"Harriet spent a lot of time moving out this afternoon and I didn't get much of a nap. I'd probably just fall asleep on you."

"That's okay." He didn't elaborate on whether it was okay that she would fall asleep, or okay if she didn't want to come, simply because he didn't trust himself to say anything one way or the other. Either way he'd probably reveal just how disappointed he was. "I'll see you tomorrow, then. Good night." He turned and walked resolutely away, telling himself that he'd just had a lucky escape. He was getting entirely too involved.

"Wait!" Jillie called after him. "I'll come along. Just let me get a sweater and something to sit on."

He smiled, realizing she didn't want to sit on the damn floor again, either. "I'll wait."

"It's not working," Mary Todd told the rest of the gang, as they sipped decaffeinated tea and nibbled sugar-free cookies in her living room. "Did you see how restrained Chief Corrigan was? He should have popped that despicable Wainwright man in the jaw for the way he talked to Jillian!"

"He could hardly do that," Hadley Philpott said. "He's the Chief of Police. He just can't go around acting like an ordinary man."

"Nobody should be popping anyone else in the jaw anyway," Arthur Archer said sternly. "What an un-Christian attitude, Mary!"

"We're not talking about religion here, Arthur. We're talking about *romance*. It has an entirely different code of conduct!"

The reverend rolled his eyes. "God help us if that's true!"

"Don't be such a prude, Arthur. Jillian needs to know that Blaise wants her enough to fight for her."

"Ridiculous," said Hadley. "For all you know, if Chief Corrigan socked Fielding Wainwright in the jaw, Jillian might well find her sympathies falling with Wainwright. Women, after all, have a strong desire to nurture and protect. She might very well turn on Corrigan."

Mary scowled at him. "What would you know about women's sympathies, Hadley?"

"Something, I should think. After all, I've been married to one for forty-six years, I've got three daughters and seven granddaughters, and I've taught scores of women at the university. Sorry, old girl, but I don't think women are mysterious beyond the comprehension of a mere male—at least, not if he's willing to pay attention and give the matter some thought."

Luis Gallegos chuckled, and David Dyer grinned.

Mary sniffed. "It's been my experience that men prefer not to devote the effort."

"That may be true," Hadley agreed, tapping his pipe gently against the side of an ashtray. "I'm willing to concede that most men believe women to be mysterious simply as an excuse not to expend any effort in understanding them."

"Oh, please," said Luis, "don't do this. The mystery is so much more enticing! If there's one thing wrong with the world today, it's that there isn't enough mystery. A human being needs the miraculous to give him a sense of awe and wonder. Explain all the miracles and what do we have left?" He waved a hand. "Me, I prefer to think women are mysterious and miraculous, *including* our lovely Mary."

Arthur interrupted. "None of this has anything to do with whether Chief Corrigan should be expected to pop Fielding Wainwright in the jaw in order to win Jillian's affections."

"True," David agreed. "But socking a rival in the jaw is so *satisfying*."

They all looked at him, the question plainly written on their faces, but he didn't answer. David rarely said much, even when prodded.

"Well," said Arthur finally, "I guess that will remain a mystery until the end of time."

Hadley and Luis both laughed.

"We're not coming to the point," Mary said, mildly irritated by the way the agenda seemed to keep slipping from her grasp. "We're here to discuss what we can do to bring Jillian and Blaise together."

"Maybe we shouldn't push, Mary," Luis argued gently. "If it's meant to be, the two of them ought to be able to figure it out themselves."

Mary snorted. "You agreed to help me."

"And we did. We created the Ad Hoc Committee to Protect the Dogs of Paradise Beach—or whatever nonsense it was that we created. Jillian and Wainwright are now on opposite sides of an issue, and Wainwright definitely doesn't strike me as a man who likes to lose. If he doesn't win this—and I don't think he will—he'll never forgive Jillie for opposing him."

"We also vandalized Jillian's store," Hadley reminded her. "And if I didn't feel like an absolute cad doing that! But we succeeded in giving her and Blaise an opportunity to be together, and it exceeded our wildest expectations. After all, they spent all night sitting together in that store waiting for us to show up. And they'll very likely spend tonight doing the same thing. How much more can we expect?"

"A great deal," said Mary. "I've never seen two people so afraid of getting closer! They need help."

"Actually," said Arthur, "considering that they've only known one another for a brief time and that they're both divorced, they're doing just fine. Jillie in particular is apt to be reluctant to get involved right now."

"Which is exactly the attitude we need to help them overcome."

"So now we're supposed to get Chief Corrigan to fight with Wainwright."

"It would help," Mary said firmly.

Luis sat back. "Are women really this bloodthirsty?"

"Bloodthirstiness has nothing to do with it!"

Arthur intervened before the discussion could escalate into anger. It wouldn't be the first time the Hole in the Seawall Gang had come to voluble disagreement, but none of them particularly enjoyed it when it happened. "I think we're getting away from the real point here. Mary is fixating on a specific act—namely, that of Blaise fighting Jillie's ex—but I think she's really after something much broader."

Mary looked doubtfully at him. "I am?"

"Of course you are. What you really want is for Blaise to make some gallant gesture that will make Jillie aware of him as a romantic possibility."

"I guess you could put it that way. I want the man to get off his duff."

"He's not ready to," Luis said. "Give him time to get to know the woman."

Mary waved an impatient hand. "It doesn't take time to know you're in love."

"Perhaps it does when you've been burned before," David said. The group fell silent, once again wondering about David's romantic past.

"All right," said Mary finally. "We can sit back and see what happens. But only for a while. I'm petrified that girl might go back to Wainwright if she thinks he's the only one who wants her."

"I think she has more intelligence than that," Hadley remarked. "At least from what little I've seen."

Before Mary could answer, someone knocked on her front door. Rising from her chair, she leaned heavily on her cane and went to answer it. Her beau, Ted Wannamaker, stood there looking as dapper and elegant as he always did.

"Well," he said, smiling, "what are the lot of you up to now? And have you disposed of the body yet?"

Mary gave him an annoyed look. "We're merely discussing methods of bringing Blaise and Jillian together." She stepped back to let him in.

"The young woman we met with the chief out on the beach that night?" He removed his hat and nodded to the other men. Ted wasn't a member of the group—he was far too conservative to indulge in some of the hijinks the gang sometimes took pleasure in—but he was the only one outside the group who knew of its existence. "I thought they looked as if they were doing just fine on their own."

"That's what we're trying to tell her," Hadley said. "But Mary thinks Blaise should punch Jillie's ex-husband in the jaw to let her know he's interested."

Ted looked down at Mary with an arched brow. "A punch to the jaw? Is that all I've needed to do these many years?"

And to the amazement of the entire gang, Mary Todd blushed bright red to the roots of her hair.

Twelve

For the second morning in a row, Blaise and Jillie faced the dawn with burning eyes and aching, exhausted bodies.

"This isn't working," Jillie said, as they stepped out onto the street and looked east into the pink and tangerine glow of dawn.

"It sure isn't," he agreed. The cool morning breeze stirred the fronds of the palms decorating the boulevard and made them clatter softly. The dawn's light turned Jillie's hair even redder than usual and cast a soft glow over her face. Never, Blaise thought, had he seen a woman more beautiful.

"Listen," he said, "why don't I run across the street to the bakery and pick up some bagels and coffee? We can take them down to the beach and enjoy the morning before the world gets up."

The world was already getting up, but Jillie didn't point that out. It was a beautiful if cool morning, and having breakfast on the beach appealed to her. "Sounds wonderful. Just don't get us arrested."

He laughed, then trotted across the street.

Jillie had slept quite a bit during the night, so she didn't feel as bad as she might have. The morning still had a dreamlike quality to it, though, and that gave her a soft, silly smile. Sometimes, she thought, it was good just to be alive—something she seemed to have forgotten of late.

She had her head tilted up to the sky and was watching the sunrise spread, so until the car stopped right in front of her, she didn't pay any attention to its approach. When she looked down and saw Fielding, she wanted to throw a temper tantrum.

He climbed out and faced her over the hood. "I know," he said. "I'm the last person on earth you want to see. But . . . I had to tell you I'm sorry for the way I've been acting."

A bolt of lightning out of a clear blue sky couldn't have shocked her more. She gaped at him.

He colored faintly, as if he had correctly interpreted her reaction. "Look, can I buy you breakfast?"

"Sorry, I'm having breakfast with Blaise." She said it defiantly, determined to let him know she didn't feel in the least apologetic.

"Oh."

She half expected him to begin arguing with her, but he didn't. Instead he stood there, glancing away, then looking at her as if he didn't quite know what to say.

"Well," he said finally, and cleared his throat. "You're really going to fight this dog ordinance?"

"Yes."

"Because of me?"

She could hardly believe his egotism, even though she had lived with it for five years. "It has nothing to do with you, Fielding. It has everything to do with the fact that I don't think dogs should be killed merely because they slip a leash or burrow under a fence. That's like ordering the execution of all children who spill a glass of milk."

"That's an analogy by false extremes," he said. "Not a good comparison at all."

"Isn't it?"

Again he didn't answer. He gnawed his lower lip for a minute or so, then said, "How about we discuss it over dinner?"

"Discuss what?"

"The dog law. I'll buy dinner and you can try to talk me into dropping my support of it. I'll try to talk you into reconsidering your position."

"Which position?"

He shook his head and smiled almost mischievously. "Any position. Hey, Jillian, I'm serious here. I'm going to give you a chance to lobby me. In exchange, all I want is a chance to convince you that I'm not the devil incarnate. Fair enough?"

"Just dinner?" she asked him.

"Just dinner, I swear."

"And if I hear you out and still don't want to get back together, will you go away?"

He hesitated, then nodded.

"Okay."

He flashed her a huge smile. "All right! Tonight. I'll pick you up at seven. Wear something nice."

Then he climbed back into his car, made a quick U-turn, and roared away up the street.

Only then did Jillie realize that Blaise was standing across the street holding a bakery bag and two cups of coffee. When Fielding drove away, he crossed the street to her.

"Everything okay?" he asked.

"Just fine." Reaching out, she took the coffee cups from him. "He wants me to go out to dinner with him tonight and I agreed."

"Oh."

Something about the way he said that made her look closely at him, but his face was as blank as a stone wall. "He offered to give me a chance to talk him out of supporting the dog ordinance, so I agreed. It's worth a shot."

"What does he get out of it?"

Jillie felt the sting of color rising to her cheeks. "The opportunity to convince me he's not such a bad guy after all." Something compelled her to add, "He won't succeed. I've had too much experience with him."

"Right." He gave her an enigmatic smile. "Well, let's head down to the beach before we miss the sunrise and the place fills up with tourists."

He took her to one of the prettier spots midway up the island, where the public access area, sandwiched between high-rises, was beautifully landscaped. They mounted the dunes on the boardwalk and crested them to discover that the beach grooming crew was out. Instead of going down onto the sand, they decided to balance their cups on the railing and watch.

Before she had come to this place, Jillie had never imagined that beaches were groomed on such a scale. In fact, she'd never thought they were groomed. Out there on the sand right now, however, was a parade of heavy equipment that moved in tight formation and with astonishing precision as they graded and raked the sand into a smooth, even surface.

The waves were high this morning, and clouds on the southwestern horizon hinted at a storm out over the Gulf. The pounding of the surf blended with the roar of machinery to preclude conversation as they sipped coffee and munched on fresh bagels.

Having finished one segment of beach, the heavy equipment formed an evenly spaced single-file caravan and moved to the next section. Beside them trotted men with rakes and shovels.

Jillie leaned toward Blaise, shouting, "It looks like a military drill."

He nodded and flashed a grin, giving her a thumbs-up. When the beach in front of them was clear of equipment, he suggested they go down to the water. They tossed their empty coffee cups into a trash bin along with the empty bagel bag and set out. Two steps later Jillie decided to take her sneakers off.

The sand was cold and damp beneath her bare feet, and the sensation invigorated her. Laughing suddenly, she ran down to the water's edge and let the surprisingly warm foam lap at her toes. The next wave was a little higher, though, and it soaked her jeans above her ankles. She didn't care.

It was as if she had shed all her worries and concerns, though she didn't know why she suddenly felt as light and free as a balloon. All she knew was that it had been a very long time since she had last felt young and free, and right now she was feeling as young and free as she ever had.

She stepped further out into the water and laughed again when a wave hit her above her knees. The sand beneath her feet washed away, and she felt herself sinking and sliding deeper into the water.

Suddenly a hand gripped hers and she looked around. Blaise had come into the water beside her and was smiling as broadly as she as the waves soaked his jeans.

Another wave swept forward, and this time it caught her sneakers, filling them with salty water. Jillie laughed again and turned them upside down to drain them. "So much for staying dry," she said to Blaise. He was laughing, too.

Then their eyes met and their laughter died. Jillie felt her breath lock in her throat, and her heart began to hammer wildly. Blaise's gaze held hers, growing intense and as hot as blue fire. He wanted her; she knew it with every fiber of her being. He wanted to throw her down on the damp sand and make love to her.

The impulse was primitive, and she responded to it in a primitive fashion. The blood in her veins seemed to grow heavy even as it pulsed with a pagan rhythm. Her mouth opened, dragging in a soft gasp of air, and her awareness seemed to spiral downward to her womb until she felt she was nothing but a living hunger.

The beach crews had moved way up the beach, so far away now that the roar of the engines was drowned by the surf. The windows on the houses lining the beach were dark, and probably concealed nothing but people still soundly asleep. One by one the dregs of her mind cast away objections.

His gaze, hot and hungry, moved over her, tracing her damp contours, telling her how his hands wanted to do the same. She felt his eyes touch her breasts as surely as if his hands did it. She felt his gaze trail lower to the cleft at the juncture of her thighs, and she drew a sharp breath, just as she would have if he had reached out and touched her there.

She wanted him, and it suddenly didn't matter at all that people might be watching, that she didn't want to get involved with a man, that . . . that what? All her objections drifted away like flotsam on the tide.

She saw him swallow, saw him look away. The spell snapped like a thread drawn too tight. Then he looked at her again and smiled, a smile full of regret and determination.

"Come on," he said. "Let's take a walk and warm up." He touched her hand.

Warm up? His touch felt like fire to her, his palm branded hers. Warm up? What she needed to do was cool down. She only wished she didn't have to.

Neither of them moved.

"I want you, Jillie."

She couldn't answer, couldn't move. Her mouth was dry and her brain was as silent as the depths of the ocean. She felt open, more open than she had ever felt, a ready receptacle for whatever life handed her.

Blaise gave a gentle tug on her hand. "We can't," he said. "Wanting isn't enough for either of us. I know I need more. A lot more. And you're not ready to give it. So let's get moving before we do something we might regret."

He was right. Reality washed over her, jarring and cruel. She closed her eyes a moment and felt herself slip back into gear. The moments past were best forgotten.

Still holding hands, they started walking down the beach toward some of the older, wealthier homes on the island. The sun had risen above the rooftops and bathed them both in warmth, welcome now that they were half soaked.

"I guess there's no point in staking the place out again tonight," Jillie told Blaise. "Apparently the vandalism has stopped."

"Maybe." He kicked up some sand and spied a perfect seashell, a rarity on the picked-over shores. He scooped it up and handed it to Jillie.

She smiled with delight. "I'd given up hope of ever finding one that wasn't broken!"

"This place is combed pretty thoroughly every morning by shell hunters."

"I've seen a lot of metal detectors out here, too. Do they ever find anything?"

"Plenty of coins, sometimes some lost jewelry or watches. I've often wondered if they make enough to pay for the equipment."

The clouds on the horizon seemed to be growing thicker and heavier, and Jillie wondered if they'd get some rain today. She didn't think it had rained twice in the all the time since she had moved here, a marked change from the climate she had recently left behind. Of course, back home in Massachusetts, everything was under snow now.

"One of my foster fathers was a cop," she heard herself telling Blaise.

He looked down at her. "There's a reason you're telling me this. Should I duck?"

She laughed. "No . . . no. It's just that he was . . . well, he was a really nice guy, you know. But authoritarian. He was always telling everybody what to do, and we were all expected to do it unquestioningly. I think that's why I react so poorly when you give me advice."

"Well, I give too much advice too freely, I guess. I'm working on it, though." He turned to face her, capturing her other hand and drawing her closer. "What I really can't understand is why you weren't adopted."

His face was swimming closer and Jillie felt weakness steal through her. He was going to kiss her, and she was going to find out if she had just imagined the effect of his last kiss, or if he could do that to her again. Everything inside her hushed with anticipation.

"Oh, hell," he said, giving up the battle.

His mouth was warm, gentle, and persuasive, instantly making her want to melt into a puddle on the sand. Never had she imagined that the touch of a pair of lips could make her feel so soft inside, so eager to yield.

She tipped her head back even further, silently asking for more. When his arms wrapped around her, they felt so good that a sigh seemed to rise from the tips of her toes. Never had she felt so welcome and safe.

Hard on the heels of the feeling of safety came a rush of sexual desire that left her feeling warm, weak, and heavy. All she wanted to do was sink to the sand and let this man take her on a journey of the senses.

He drew her more snugly to him, letting her feel every contour of him, from his hard chest to the thrust of his pelvis. The sensation of his hardness against her was even more arousing, and she began to have dizzying mental images of him touching her breasts, cupping her bottom, removing her clothes. Just please don't let it end . . . ever . . .

But a seagull apparently had a very different idea. It came so close so suddenly that Jillie was startled out of the growing haze of desire by a shriek and a loud flap of wings that felt as if it had barely missed her ear. She jerked her head back and stared up into Blaise's face. His eyes were heavy-lidded and looked at her with sultry passion. Her heart skipped a beat.

The seagull attacked again, squawking loudly and flapping its wings.

"I guess," Blaise said, "we must be too near something important."

"Eggs?"

"I don't know. I haven't the foggiest idea where a seagull lays her eggs. Nor does it matter. I suggest we move."

The gull swooped down on them again and they separated, breaking into laughter as they stumbled and fell in the sand. All at once Jillie was aware of how cold and wet her jeans were. And her shoes . . . where had she left her shoes?

The seagull squawked again and landed right where they had been standing. It made threatening moves in their direction, flapping its wings and puffing its feathers.

"That's definitely mama bird behavior," Jillie said. "I've seen it before. I don't know where the babies are, but we'd better be on our way before the poor thing wears herself out."

Her shoes had fallen in the sand next to Blaise's. She scooped them up and together he and she began to walk back. Her heart squeezed a little with happiness when he reached out and took her hand. His touch made her forget just how cold and wet her jeans were, and just how tired she was.

In fact, she felt as if she were walking on air. It was a beautiful morning in Paradise Beach.

Clothing was a little bit like armor. When Jillie put on a black silk slacks suit that evening, she honestly felt she was girding for battle. Primarily she wanted to make Fielding feel regretful over what he had flung away—if it was possible to make Fielding regret anything—and she wanted to look her best so that she wouldn't be easily intimidated if he tried to put her down.

The only jewelry she had taken from her marriage was a pair of gold earrings that she had bought for herself with her own earnings. She put them on now knowing full well that Fielding had never liked them—primarily, she suspected, because he hadn't bought them.

In fact, with twenty-twenty hindsight she could see just how controlling Fielding had been throughout their entire relationship—and how she had retaliated by becoming more and more mouthy. A sigh escaped her as she acknowledged that she had probably given Fielding plenty of reason to want to hit her over the head with a shovel and bury her remains in the root cellar.

Not that he would ever do such a thing. Fielding was not at all violent; he simply bought what he wanted.

Oh, well. A knock sounded on the door and she turned from the mirror. Snatching her bag from the bed, she went to answer the door. As she expected, it was Fielding. Before he could attempt to step inside, she stepped out and locked the door behind her.

"In a hurry?" he asked.

Actually, she didn't want him inside her little bungalow, not even for a minute. Truth be told, she didn't want to spend this evening with him. He made her skin crawl, which in turn made her wonder what she had ever seen in him. She gave him a wide smile. "No, I'm not in a hurry. Would you like to sit on the patio out back?" The patio that consisted of a six-by-six slab of concrete. "Or take a walk up the block?"

"No, thanks." The promised rain had never developed, but the air was thick with unshed moisture, making the evening uncomfortable. "Let's just go."

He had selected a restaurant on the next island in a town Jillian didn't like nearly as much as Paradise Beach. Here the buildings were crowded together, old motels and shops abutting newer, glitzier high-rise constructions. If there had ever been any zoning laws, they had been utterly ignored.

There was, however, a really nice restaurant in one of the big hotels, and it was there that Fielding took her. To Jillie's way of thinking it couldn't begin to compare with the dinner she and Blaise had enjoyed at the beach bar that night, watching the sunset.

Fielding did get them a table overlooking the beach and the sunset, though, and Jillie made up her mind to take what pleasure she could out of the evening. She began by ordering the surf and turf.

Fielding raised a brow. "Still in love with lobster, I see."

"It's only been a year and a half since we last dined out together, Fielding—not a lifetime."

Whatever annoyance he felt was masked swiftly. "The last time we dined out together, you said you wanted a divorce."

"I remember." Indeed she did. It had been a waste of an excellent lobster tail. "And as I recall, you agreed."

"The point being?"

"The point being that I can't imagine what we're doing eighteen months later dining out together. We divorced. You didn't oppose it."

"Not then."

"What has happened?"

He looked down at his napkin and began to crease it into accordion folds. Since the napkin was thick cloth, it kept springing open on him. "I've had time to reconsider."

And pigs fly, she thought. "You know, once the first flush wore off, I got the distinct impression that you really didn't like me all that much."

Fielding looked pained. "People change. I've changed. Listen, I agreed to give you time to talk me out of supporting the dog ordinance."

He was avoiding the subject. Jillie had had enough experience with Fielding to know that he was trying to avoid lying. Not that he was always truthful, but he was inclined to avoid direct lies if he could. Oddly, she felt disappointed. Silly as it was, some part of her had been hoping that this man might regret, just a little, the way he had treated her.

Not that she wanted him back. Not even under threat of having her toenails ripped off would she take Fielding back. But she wondered what had made him come after her when he obviously didn't really want her back, either. Her curiosity was aroused, making it difficult for her to concentrate on the dog issue.

Fielding's thoughts had taken a different turn. "Did you accept the leadership position with that ad hoc committee just to spite me?"

She'd go cheerfully to the gallows before she'd admit that. "No. I honestly believe the proposed ordinance is wrong. Come on, Fielding. One dog nipped you. And that's all it was—a nip. Can you really be so cold-hearted as to want dogs killed simply for straying just because one dog happened to nip you? Especially when you're going to leave in a few days and never come back?"

He shifted uneasily. He was never comfortable with appeals to his better nature. "That dog is a menace! Look how it jumped me yesterday."

"That dog is *one dog.* You can't blame all the dogs in the world for Rover's behavior."

"And I'm really angry at the police in that pissant town. You'd think they could catch one lousy dog!"

"The dog keeps running away, Fielding."

"I forgot . . . you're sweet on the police chief."

Jillie didn't bother trying to deny it. What was the point? "Aside from trying to kill all these poor little doggies—" she watched Fielding wince, as if she'd accused him of stealing some baby's teddy bear, "—you've got no business bribing the mayor."

"Now, who said that!" he demanded disgustedly.
"I did no such thing."

"Promising him a campaign contribution—"

"Is *not* a bribe," he interrupted hotly. "Jeez, Jillian,
there's no comparison between the two. A bribe
would go into the man's own pocket. A bribe would
be offering him a vacation in Waikiki or a fancy new
car. Promising a politician a campaign contribution if
you're pleased with what he does is the way politics
is run *everywhere!* I didn't do anything illegal, and neither did that stupid mayor whatsisname."

Jillie felt the ground slipping from beneath her, and
her indignation turned up a couple of notches. "People in Paradise Beach are very upset about it."

"Let 'em be. They're upset because I'm not a local.
But trust me, babe, this is how it's done. Legally."

She hated it when he called her babe. She chalked
it up as another reason he made her skin crawl. "Legal or not, what you're trying to do is wrong. It's my
understanding that the mayor agreed to push this ordinance through without public discussion. Now,
that's an attempt to circumvent the process."

"Yeah, sure." He shrugged. "So? Legally, the guy
can propose an ordinance, and legally the city council
can vote for it, all without any person from the public
offering so much as a peep. In my experience, city
council members get together in the presence of one
bored reporter and two or three flakes who come to
kibitz every meeting and then conduct their business.
It's not as if I was asking the mayor to have a meeting
behind closed doors with everyone else in the world
locked out. I just didn't want him to publicize it." He
shrugged. His eyes flicked to the green dog collar
around Jillie's wrist. "Too damn late for that now."

The waiter brought their dinners just then, and Jillie
was glad to have an excuse to pause in the discussion.

Okay, so maybe offering a contribution wasn't illegal. All that meant was that she had to try a different tack to get his cooperation.

The sixty-four-thousand-dollar question, though, was why Fielding was seeking a reconciliation, and could she use that to save the dogs of Paradise Beach. But that seemed so . . . so calculating. Not like her at all. Not like the person she wanted to be.

But what about the dogs?

The lobster was exquisite, satisfying a craving she hadn't realized she'd had. The filet mignon was equally good and gave her cause to reflect that you couldn't get a meal like this from a supermarket.

"Well, then," Fielding finally asked, "is the dog subject closed?"

She shook her head. "What is it you really want from this, Fielding? Revenge? Because killing all the dogs that stray in Paradise Beach isn't necessarily going to kill the one you're mad at. Worse, it'll kill a lot of dogs that never hurt you. What's the point?"

"It's the only way I can get at Rover."

But he was a little uneasy with the idea; she could see that. Fielding wasn't mean or cruel; he rarely set out to do harm to anyone. But he *was* like a child, taking what he wanted without any thought of consequences. To his way of thinking, Rover deserved to be punished, and if that meant punishing all the dogs, fine. But childish or not, it was possible to reason with Fielding. All she had to do was find the right argument. She was sure that in his heart of hearts, Fielding didn't want to hurt a lot of innocent dogs. At this late stage, his desire to punish Rover had probably waned a little, too.

"Look," she said, "you need to be reasonable about this, Fielding. The primary thing you should want to accomplish here is to avoid having to get rabies shots."

"Do you know anything about rabies?" he asked her, and shuddered. "I read up on it. It's a terrible way to go. And that damn dog could have given it to me. He shouldn't have been running around free!"

"Granted."

"And now he's running around free again because somebody let him out of the kennel. And I'm going to have to have rabies shots."

"Rover doesn't have rabies."

Fielding colored faintly. "That's what the vet says. So my doctor doesn't think I really need the shots. But I might have had to have them if you hadn't known which dog bit me! And that's my point. Nobody's dog ought to be running around without a leash. It's a menace to public health!"

Jillie also thought it was a menace to the dog, which might well get hit by a car, but she didn't figure Fielding felt much sympathy for dogs right now. "I agree. But dogs will get loose. There's already a leash law, and the owners get fined. What's the point of killing the dog for the crime of being a dog?"

Fielding harumphed and poked at the remains of his prime rib. "The law would specifically deal with animals that are found unleashed more than once. No one seriously proposes exterminating an animal for getting away once. But twice or more shows a pattern of conduct—namely, that his owner isn't taking proper care."

"So kill the owners," Jillie suggested. She didn't mean it seriously, but a little shock to his worldview might help him see the light.

"Don't be absurd, Jillian! The liberals would never allow it!"

Jillie found herself rendered absolutely speechless.

Apparently it would never occur to Fielding that conservatives might also object. She found herself wondering if that was a measure of Fielding's view of politics, or a measure of his view of the value of human life.

She also found herself wondering why she was wasting any time wondering. Fielding was in a class by himself and always had been. She turned to look out at the beach, seeking the soothing effect of sea and sky, but instead found that the night had turned dark and all she could see in the window was her own reflection.

It was not a happy sight.

"I can't do this, Mary!"

"Of course you can," Mary Todd said bracingly to Ted Wannamaker. She had exacted a promise from Ted to bring her here for dinner, and then she had invited her Hole in the Seawall Gang to join them. Only Hadley and Luis had taken her up on it, but that was sufficient. The instant Felix had told her the mayor was bragging that Wainwright was taking his ex out to dinner to settle her dog opposition, Mary had known that action had to be taken.

"No, Mary, it would be inutterably rude to barge in on that young couple that way."

"We're not barging in, Ted. When you see an acquaintance in a restaurant, you naturally stop to say hello."

Ted looked pleadingly at her. "Stopping to say hello is one thing. Actually forcing ourselves on them is another!"

"Trust me, Jillian will be grateful."

"But what about the young man?"

"He's the one who's bribing the mayor to pass the dog ordinance without public discussion."

Ted frowned. "The promise of a campaign contribution is *not* a bribe."

"In *your* worldview, perhaps." Mary shook her head and looked at her friend of sixty years with sad disappointment. "Dear Teddy, you're reminding me of why I would never marry you."

Now it was Ted's turn to look dismayed. He appealed to Hadley and Luis. "Are you comfortable with this?"

"Certainly," said Hadley. "The man's a fool and the woman's heading up our ad hoc committee. Of course we ought to join them."

Luis merely smiled, amused by the entire thing.

Ted looked back into the dining room and squared his shoulders. "I suppose," he said.

Mary tucked her arm through his and smiled approvingly. "There," she said. "I knew you were made of sterner stuff."

"Sterner stuff has nothing to do with it," he answered. "I'm a pushover!" But he marched forward with Mary on his arm straight toward the table where Jillian and Fielding sat. Once committed, Ted Wannamaker followed through.

Fielding saw them coming and frowned. His expression made Jillie turn around to look, and when she saw Mary Todd and her flotilla of friends, she smiled.

"See?" Mary said to Ted. "We're welcome."

Ted, measuring Fielding's expression, wasn't quite so sure.

"Jillie," Mary said warmly as they reached the table. She bent and kissed Jillie's cheek. "You remember Ted, don't you?"

"Yes, we met at the beach bar." Jillie shook his hand.

Mary turned her gaze on Fielding. "Mr. Wainwright, I believe you've met Hadley and Luis, and this is Ted Wannamaker. Of the West Palm Wannamakers."

Jillie seriously doubted that Fielding had ever heard of anyone named Wannamaker, let alone the West Palm Wannamakers, but the form of the introduction was a code that Fielding instantly recognized. His greeting to Ted was friendly, even as Jillie noted that Ted looked distinctly uncomfortable.

Mary looked triumphant. "Look, wouldn't it be silly for us to sit at separate tables?" Before anyone could say anything one way or another, she'd told the waiter to bring some more tables over so they could all sit together.

Fielding looked poleaxed; his plans for this evening hadn't included an invasion by the Ad Hoc Committee to Save the Dogs of Paradise Beach. Some of his annoyance waned, however, when he found himself seated next to Ted.

"The West Palm Wannamakers, eh?" Fielding asked him jovially. "What are you in?"

"I'm in retirement," Ted said acidly, glaring at Mary.

Fielding laughed. "Right. Right! Good line. I'll have to remember it."

Mary, seated next to Jillian, leaned over to murmur, "I thought you might need rescuing. Was I wrong?"

"You couldn't have been more right."

"Right about what?" Fielding asked testily. He had never liked being excluded from conversations.

"Right that it's so tacky to discuss business at dinner," Jillie said sweetly.

Fielding huffed. "I wasn't trying to discuss business. I was merely trying to find a common ground for conversation."

"No one accused you of anything, Fielding."

"Certainly not!" Mary said firmly. "Luis is in the restaurant business, Mr. Wainwright. And Hadley, dear Hadley, is still occasionally responsible for warping young, impressionable minds."

Fielding looked startled. "What?"

"He teaches philosophy at the university," Mary elaborated.

"Oh." Fielding didn't get the humor. Fielding rarely did.

Mary signaled the waiter again and asked him to bring wine to the table for everyone. Fielding, who had been drinking Manhattans and hated wine, didn't say anything when a glass of sparkling white was placed before him, but he stared at it as if it had come from another planet.

"It's a Portuguese vintage," Mary told them. "Absolutely one of my favorites."

Fielding obediently raised his glass and sipped. "Excellent. Thank you." His lack of enthusiasm couldn't have been more apparent.

"Oh!" Mary said suddenly, "I wanted to tell you, Jillie. There's a wonderful protest planned for tomorrow on the dog ordinance—"

Fielding interrupted, wagging his finger and tsking. "It's tacky to talk business at dinner, remember?"

Mary smiled brittlely at him. "Of course." She turned back to Jillian. "Remind me to tell you later, then."

Conversation became general, bouncing around the table as dinners were ordered for the new arrivals. Fielding was conspicuously quiet, although no one seemed to notice, and he barely touched his wine. Instead, he pouted.

Just as dinners were being served and Fielding was making the kind of movements that seemed to indicate he was going to leave, Blaise Corrigan walked in.

Mary waved at Blaise to come over. Fielding looked as if he had just swallowed something very bitter.

"Oh, hell," Fielding said to Jillian, not caring who might hear, "not him, too!"

Blaise looked scrumptious in a dark blue suit, white shirt, and tie. Jillie could hardly tear her eyes from him and wondered rather unhappily how it was that she was out for dinner with Fielding instead of him.

"Now, wouldn't he make a wonderful model for the cover of a romance novel?" Mary asked Jillie.

"I'd rather see him on blue satin sheets." The words slipped out of Jillie's mouth almost before she was aware of thinking them, and she blushed furiously. Fielding glared at her, and Mary cackled delightedly.

Blaise reached the table and greeted everyone pleasantly as a chair was brought for him. The look he gave Jillie was enigmatic.

"I asked Blaise to join us," Mary announced. "I figured he might as well be in on the Ad Hoc Committee's discussions, since we don't want to do anything that might cause trouble. However, since we can't discuss business now that the archenemy is here—"

"Archenemy?" Fielding repeated.

"Well, I don't know how else to refer to you," Mary said. "You're bribing the mayor to pass a despicable ordinance."

"I'm not bribing anyone! Furthermore, you interrupted my dinner with Jillian, not the other way around. If you want to have your meeting, go elsewhere."

"We can't." Mary smiled sweetly. "Our dinners, you see. But *you* can leave."

"Fine!" Fielding rose. "Jillian?"

Jillie hesitated, particularly since Mary had gripped her forearm.

"Stay," Mary said. "You're our president, after all. We need you for this meeting."

Jillie hesitated. On the one hand, she felt that manners required her to leave with Fielding; he was her date, after all. On the other, she would rather do almost anything than go with Fielding. And if she refused, maybe he'd get out of her life.

Etiquette lost. "I don't want to leave yet, Fielding. Stay and have dessert."

"I will not stay and allow myself to be insulted."

"No one's insulting you," Mary told him. "I simply stated the facts as they stand. If you find them insulting, perhaps you should change your conduct."

Fielding turned dangerously red. In the past Jillie would have tried to smooth things over and get him out of there quickly, not because she was worried about him, but because his temper tantrums were so ugly. This time she didn't do a damn thing. Fielding, she told herself, was no longer her problem.

But then, much to her amazement, he sat back down. He reached for his wine, gulped it down, and manufactured a smile of sorts. "You're right," he said to Mary Todd. "Perhaps I should reconsider my conduct. Perhaps dogs have an inalienable right to roam wherever they wish and bite whomever they wish. Hm?"

"I don't believe any of us is saying that," Mary answered.

"Then just what *are* you saying? I have twice been attacked by that mutt that everyone's so eager to protect, and once I was actually bitten. I have had to endure painful medical care and the threat of rabies shots. I naturally want to ensure that this won't happen to anyone else."

"No," Jillie said. "You're not worried about anyone else. You just want to get even with the dog."

Blaise quickly covered his mouth with his hand, and Jillie wondered when she was going to learn to shut her own mouth. It wasn't that she was worried about Fielding's response to her accusation, but she figured by now Blaise must have decided she was an utter shrew.

"That's not fair, Jillian," Fielding said petulantly.

"But it's perfectly accurate," Jillian said, deciding it was already too late to fool Blaise. He certainly knew by now that she was a shrew. "The equation is simple, Fielding. Owners are fined for loose dogs. I can't imagine why you think the threat of death to the dogs will be a greater deterrent. Heck, the death penalty hasn't prevented a single murder yet that I can tell!"

"It's true," Blaise said from his end of the table. "We have more murders than ever."

"We're a violent society," Hadley observed. "Only look at Mr. Wainwright's bloodthirsty approach to the problem of dogs!"

"Please, Hadley," Mary said, "let's not get philosophical. This isn't the right time to debate weighty matters. The issue at hand is whether Mr. Wainwright is seeking social justice or revenge. My vote is with revenge."

Everyone except Fielding nodded.

"That does it," he said, rising and throwing his napkin on his plate. "I will not sit here and listen to you question my motives. Jillian?"

The last thing Jillie wanted to do was give the appearance of supporting Fielding's behavior, but she *had* come with him and the rudeness of not leaving with him . . .

But apparently she hesitated just a moment too long. Fielding tipped his head backward a little, registering disapproval. "Very well, then," he said sharply, and stalked away.

Jillie, who had just started to rise, sank back into her chair. It was ridiculous, but she felt enormously relieved.

"For a man who's trying to win you back," Mary remarked, "he's doing an abysmal job of it."

"He doesn't really want me back," Jillie said. "I don't know why he's even trying. It wasn't so long ago that he was thrilled to see the last of me."

"Regrets?"

"Fielding doesn't know the meaning of the word."

Just then a waiter approached and placed a leather folder in front of Jillian. She opened it and started to laugh. "And I get stuck with the bill," she said.

"Absolutely not!" Mary snatched it right out of her hands. "We're the ones who drove him away, and I absolutely will not let you bear the cost of it."

"Really, Mary, I don't mind." Jillie reached for the bill, but Mary held it out of reach.

"You *should* mind," Mary told her sternly. "That impossible young man asked you out to dinner and he shouldn't have stiffed you this way! Given that he did, it's my responsibility, because he certainly wouldn't have abandoned ship if we hadn't barged in on you."

"Believe me, this isn't the first time."

Mary arched a brow. "What a boor! But that's neither here nor there, gal. I'll pay the bill. I have more money than I'll ever know what to do with and I can certainly afford a couple of dinners."

"And I'll drive you home," Blaise said from his end of the table.

Jillie looked ruefully at him. "I seem to need a lot of rescuing."

"Only since the Wainwrights arrived in town."

Thirteen

"What I'm going to do," Blaise told her, "is drive by your shop every couple of hours through the night. I think we've seen the last of the vandalism, though."

"So do I."

The night breeze was soft, just a touch cool, and it felt good to lie back in the chaise on Blaise's deck and let it whisper over her. She guessed at some level she was a dyed-in-the-wool Yankee, because she was having the most ridiculous craving for cold weather and a roaring blaze in a fireplace.

Blaise had changed into casual clothes and sat nearby.

"This deck of yours is wonderful," Jillie said. "I feel as if I'm way above it all, right up in the tops of the trees."

"Feel free to use it anytime." It *was* above it all. The surrounding homes were mostly one-story concrete structures built before federal flood management had decreed that no one in a flood zone ought to be living on the first floor. Consequently his deck had a unique bird's-eye view over the surrounding rooftops and he found a great deal of serenity here at the end of a long day.

"You know," Jillie said presently, "I think Mary Todd planned it."

"Planned what?"

"That scene at the restaurant. I know it sounds paranoid, but it seemed kind of strange the way they all showed up and then insisted on joining Fielding and me."

Blaise tensed a little, wondering if that bothered her. Maybe she had actually been enjoying her time with her ex. "I don't know" was all he said.

"It *does* sound paranoid," she repeated. "Or megalomaniacal. There's no reason to think Mary would do anything at all because of me. No reason she should. It just felt weird, is all."

"Mary does meddle from time to time."

"She does, huh? Well, she certainly doesn't like Fielding—not that I can blame her—so maybe she's having some fun making his life miserable."

"That might be."

Jillie chuckled quietly. "She sure doesn't fit the stereotype of the typical elderly lady."

"I don't think Mary has ever fit any stereotype— except when it suited her to be underestimated."

"You really like her, don't you?"

"I sure do. She can be absolutely maddening at times, but I've never known her to act out of malice."

"Unlike a great many people." She stretched her legs, pointing and flexing her feet. "I wonder what's happening with Rover. I gather he hasn't gone home yet."

"Apparently not. And that really bothers me. Cal's

whole life is wrapped around that dog." Rover's the only living being that loves Cal Lepkin. He sits for hours on the porch with that man, plays fetch with him—you know, without the dog, Cal wouldn't have any reason to get up in the morning.

"Well, nobody made Rover bite Fielding," Jillie pointed out. "All of Fielding's dastardly plans aside, the only reason Rover was in quarantine was because he bit someone."

"Personally, I think the dog is sweet on you."

"Sweet on *me?*" Jillie laughed at the very idea. "That's the same dog that caused me to run over your mailbox! If he's sweet on me, he sure has a strange way of showing it."

It was his turn to laugh. "Well, he sure seems hell-bent on protecting you from Fielding."

"After tonight, I think a lot of people may be trying to protect me."

"Do you need protection?"

She shook her head. "I've been spending most of the last couple of days trying to figure out how I fell in love with the guy in the first place. Or if I ever was really in love with him."

"That kind of question won't get you anywhere. There's really no point in second-guessing yourself, Jill." Suddenly he chuckled, his laugh warm in the darkness. "Oops. There I go again, giving unwanted advice."

"That's okay. I know you're right."

"So giving advice is okay when you already know it?"

Jill shot him a glare, which he didn't see, but that was okay because it wasn't a serious glare. "That isn't at all what I meant. I just meant that it's okay that you gave me advice and that I agree with you."

"Oh."

"Didn't you ever wonder why you married your wife?"

"Sometimes." He hesitated and then decided just to lay it out. "And in most of my relationships since, I've had a reason to wonder. You have to wonder when you walk away—from someone and nothing hurts. In fact, it feels like a relief."

Jillie nodded. "By the time I finally left Fielding, that's how I felt. Relieved. As if I had shed a really big burden."

"From the looks of it, you had."

She laughed again, realizing how much she really enjoyed Blaise's company—and how much more relaxed she felt sitting here and talking with him than she had felt with Fielding at dinner.

Had she ever really felt relaxed with Fielding? No, she seemed to recall that she had spent much of her early time with him on tenterhooks for fear he would find something wrong with her. And then, when she'd learned of his affairs, she had been forever on the edge of her seat wondering how she measured up, if he was going to leave her, why he had found her wanting, and whether she was going to discover some other unsavory bit of information.

All in all, she thought now, life with Fielding had been hell. Why had she put up with it for so long?

And why was she ruining a perfectly good evening worrying about it?

"Can I get you something to drink?" Blaise asked. "Coffee, tea, milk, soft drink?"

"Tea sounds really good."

She followed him into the kitchen and leaned back against the counter while he boiled some water and dug out some tea bags. "You have a wonderful kitchen," she told him. "Most newer homes have these tiny little galleys."

"I'm too big for something like that. I prize room. Lots of it. I want to be able to move around without bumping into something at every turn. Besides, I hate clutter."

"Hey, clutter is a wonderful thing! That's what flat surfaces were designed for."

He smiled over his shoulder at her. "Let me guess . . ."

"You'd be absolutely right. I believe table tops were meant to hold things, as were counters, dressers, mantels . . ."

"Hey, so do I," he protested with a hand over his heart. "But I don't want a place to feel cluttered because there isn't enough room for the necessary furniture."

"Well, I can agree with that. But I've never before had a kitchen big enough to hold a center island."

"Nice, isn't it?" He set their cups of tea on the island and pulled out a stool for her to sit on. "It also makes a great table for a bachelor who doesn't want to be bothered carrying all that stuff into the dining room."

"That's a definite plus." She dipped her tea bag a few more times, then set it on the saucer and drank. The warmth was surprisingly welcome, and she cradled the cup in her cold hands. "Do you do a lot of entertaining?"

"Fancy stuff, you mean? Some. Chief of police is a political position to the extent that I'm answerable for my policies, so I throw a couple bashes a year and invite all the people who might get me fired."

He said it humorously, and she laughed. "Well, if there's anything I can ever do to help, don't hesitate to ask. Fielding used to do a lot of formal entertaining. I can even make palm trees out of carrots and green peppers."

"Now, that's a talent beyond compare."

"I think so." She buffed her nails ostentatiously. "I'm afraid I didn't graduate to ice sculptures, though. But hey, you can't have everything."

The look he gave her right then caused her breath to lock in her throat.

The windows were open, letting the night breeze blow through the room. As if her nerve endings had suddenly wakened from a long sleep, Jillie felt the whisper of the air across her skin as a sensuous caress. Her heart began to thud heavily in anticipation.

"Can't I?" he asked. His voice had gone husky, and the sound sent a shiver of pleasure dancing along her nerves.

Some little warning bell went off in her mind, reminding her that she was dangerously susceptible right now. It had been a long time since a man had looked at her with desire and a long time since she had last had sex. Her hormones and her bruised ego were both crying out for first aid. She'd be a fool to forget her common sense simply because of Blaise's hungry look.

And it was a hungry look. As if he sensed her susceptibility and interest, he let his eyes wander from her face down to her chest. Jillie was suddenly achingly conscious of the weight of her own breasts, of the way they moved with each quick breath she took. Her nipples were swelling, nearly causing her to cry out her need to be touched.

The warning gong in her head became nearly deafening. No. No, she couldn't let another man do to her what Fielding had done. No way was she going to allow another man to hurt her, to leave her feeling as if she were a poor second-best.

But his gaze held her, locked her in place. The warnings quieted to mere whimpers, then faded away. When he came around the island to her, her only thought was that he wasn't moving fast enough.

When he reached her, he turned her gently on the stool, then bent to kiss her. The first brush of his lips caused her heart to slam into overdrive. With gentle hands, he guided her arms up around his neck. The pressure of his mouth deepened and she responded by opening her lips to welcome him. The first thrust of his tongue caused rippling thrills to run through her, softening her, filling her with an anticipation that was almost painful.

Oh, how she wanted him! One night. Just one night. That wasn't too much to ask, was it? One night to forget all her hurts and doubts, one night in which she could believe herself to be adequate. One night of balm for her soul and her heart . . .

His hands closed on her breasts, cupping them gently through the layers of her dress and bra. The effect was electric. Her entire body grew heavy, filling her with delicious languor, and her center began to throb gently with longing.

One night. Just one night. One night to feel like a woman again, like a desirable woman. Fielding had stolen that from her, and Blaise was offering to give it back. Just one night . . .

She gasped as she felt her dress fall open and slip off her shoulders. When had he unfastened the zipper? And then her black bra, a simple front clasp that he opened with a single flick of his wrist.

Open. She was so open, so exposed, so helpless in thrall to the feelings that filled her like a mighty tide, growing, growing . . .

Ah! Another gasp escaped her as his round, rough palms covered her naked breasts with their heat. Fielding's touch had never felt so good . . . and then she stopped making comparisons. When his thumbs brushed over her aching nipples, there was no longer anyone left in the world but Blaise Corrigan.

She arched, trying to press herself closer. He took it as an invitation and lifted her onto the island so that he stood between her legs. Jillie leaned back on her arms, silently begging him for more, and he obliged, bending to take one of her nipples into his hot mouth.

"Jillian!"

The voice was far enough away that it seemed like a mere nuisance, no more troublesome than the buzzing of an insect. The only thing that mattered was Blaise's hot mouth sucking on her breast as if she tasted of ambrosia.

"Jillian!" There was a distant pounding now, and it vaguely registered that Harriet must be at her door, knocking and calling for her. She'd go away . . .

Blaise's mouth moved to her other nipple and she gasped as fresh spears of sensation shot through her. Nothing, nothing had ever felt this good, this wonderful, this—

"Jillian! Jillian, answer this door or I'm going to call the police!"

Blaise lifted his head sharply and Jillie jerked with horror as she heard Harriet's threat. She spilled one of the cups of tea, and she felt the tepid liquid soak into the seat of her dress. Great!

"Oh, my God," she said, as she realized what she had been doing . . . and worse, what she had been about to do.

"I'll go calm her down," Blaise said reassuringly. He made an ineffectual effort to fasten her bra, but her breasts persisted in tumbling back out.

"Let me," she said, sliding from the island to stand. Standing made her feel better, as if she had some control. Control? Her hands were trembling so hard she couldn't fasten her own bra.

"I'll go talk to her."

"No! No." Fumbling she managed to fasten the clasp. Without thinking she started to arrange herself inside the cups and caught Blaise watching with approval. A flush stained her cheeks.

"Sex," he said, "is really funny if you let yourself think about it."

She didn't appreciate the comment as she tried to button her shirt and kept getting the buttons all mixed up.

"Jill, just let me go talk to her. I'll tell her you're here having a cup of tea."

She shook her head emphatically and groaned when she realized she had done the buttons all wrong again. "No, please. She'll tell Fielding some wild story and he'll be all over me . . . dammit! Why doesn't he just go back home? Why is he hanging around like this?"

"Why don't you ask him?"

"I did! All he'll say is that he's discovered he misses me."

Something in Blaise's expression softened, nearly depriving her of breath all over again. "Is that so hard to believe?" He brushed her hands aside and zipped her dress with swift efficiency.

The question, and the gentle way he'd asked it, unlocked walls of reserve that she had erected with painful determination in the years since her parents had died. "Yes," she said, admitting her weakness. "It's impossible to believe."

"Stay here." Leaning toward her, he brushed a soft kiss on her lips.

"No, I can't." She headed for his front door, but before she could begin descending the steps, she heard Fielding's voice and she froze, listening. Blaise, too, stood still.

"She's probably with that cop, Mother," Fielding said.

"And you're not going to do anything about it?" Harriet demanded.

"Why should I? We're divorced. She can do anything she wants now."

"You stupid twit! Have you forgotten what we came here for?"

"I haven't forgotten anything, including the fact that you didn't want me to marry her in the first place. She wasn't good enough to be a Wainwright, you said. My, how your tune has changed!"

"How dare you!"

"Oh, shut up!"

Their voices faded away and Jill turned to look at Blaise.

"The plot thickens," he said.

She nodded, then hurried down the stairs and out into the front yard, where she caught Fielding and his mother just as they were about to get into his car.

"So!" Harriet said. "I was right! What are you doing with that man, Jillian?"

"It's none of your business, Harriet."

"You were married to my son! Everything you do is my business."

"Not anymore. I only came out here to tell you not to call the police. I'm not missing." Turning, Jillian prepared to walk away before her temper got the better of her. How could Harriet possibly believe she had anything at all to say about what Jillian did?

"You wait one minute, miss," Harriet said sternly. "I'm not done with you."

"But I'm done with you!"

Porch lights were beginning to come on at nearby

houses as people leaned out their doors to see what was wrong. Mrs. Herrera did more than lean out. She came out to where she had a better view.

"How can you do this, Jillian?" Harriet demanded. "We took you in and made you one of us, and this is how you repay us? By dating a . . . a cop? It's so . . . blue collar!"

"God, Harriet! That's so snobbish!"

"It's not snobbish, it's merely discriminating! You had *everything* when you were married to Fielding! How can you consider allying yourself with a . . . with a mere police officer? What can he give you?"

Jillie felt herself shaking with rage and half doubted she would find voice to speak. "When I was married to Fielding, Harriet, I didn't have a *husband*. As for Chief Corrigan, the only thing I want from him is friendship, something Fielding was never capable of providing!"

Fielding looked as if she had struck him. "Now, wait one minute, Jillian. I have a lot of friends, good friends. I know how to provide friendship!"

"Actually, Fielding," Jillie told him frankly, "you have a lot of sycophants who would be gone the instant you lost your money. But I'm not one of them. And I'm not going to *be* one of them. You'll just have to learn to live without me."

"I have! I mean. . . ." He trailed off, looking uneasy. "I meant to say, I can't. Come home, Jillian. We can work it all out. Really."

"*This* is my home now. I'm not going anywhere."

"It's the bookstore, isn't it? You can have a bookstore in Worcester, I promise. A bigger and better one."

"I don't want a bookstore anywhere else. I don't want a bigger and better one. I want exactly what I have here, and I want to do it myself."

Fielding stepped toward her, reaching out a hand, but froze instantly as a low growling issued from the azaleas. "What's that?" he asked in a horrified whisper.

The growl, long and low, stopped.

"Oh, God!" Fielding said, covering his butt with his hands. "It's that dog! I know it's that dog!" Looking around wildly, he began to back toward the car.

"Fielding!" Harriet looked appalled at her son's behavior. "Where's your backbone? All the dog did was growl."

"Every time I come anywhere near Jillian that dog turns up," Fielding wailed. "It's trying to kill me, I know it." He pointed at Blaise. "Why doesn't he do anything about it? He's a cop! He ought to be protecting me!"

"You're absolutely right, Mr. Wainwright," Blaise said briskly. Stepping forward, he took Fielding by the arm. "Let me escort you safely to your car, sir. Once you're inside and driving away, stray dogs can't possibly be any threat."

Fielding tried to yank his arm out of Blaise's grip, but failed. "Let go of me, damn it!"

"Sorry, sir, that would be unwise while the dog remains in the vicinity."

"I can walk by myself, thank you!"

Blaise let go quite suddenly, so suddenly that Fielding was thrown off balance and stumbled. "Very well, sir. Just keep walking steadily toward your vehicle. You, too, ma'am," he added to Harriet.

Harriet was aghast. "You have no right to tell me to leave."

"Ma'am, I'm suggesting you go home before I have to arrest you and your son for disturbing the peace. This is a quiet neighborhood, it's after ten o'clock, and there's no question that you've been exceeding local noise ordinances."

"You wouldn't dare!"

Fielding took one look at Blaise's face then grabbed his mother's arm. "Come on, Mother. It's time to go."

"I will *not* be thrown off property you own."

"We're not being thrown off it, Mother. And really, we can continue this discussion with Jillian tomorrow." Alternately swearing and cajoling, he bundled his mother into the car and drove off with her.

Blaise looked at Jillie.

"My hero," she sighed, and batted her eyelashes.

He grinned. "Where did those two get the idea they're better than everyone else?"

"I think it was fed to them with their Pablum. I've certainly never seen any sign that either of them has ever doubted it."

When the taillights of Fielding's car vanished around a corner, Blaise slipped his arm around Jillian. He didn't care who saw, although it appeared that everyone had gone back inside their homes . . . with the possible exception of Mrs. Herrera.

A chuffing sound came from the azalea, then Rover trotted out, looking dark and mysterious in the light from the street lamps.

Blaise immediately squatted and held out his hand. "Hey, guy," he said quietly. "Where have you been and what have you been up to?"

Rover chuffed again and wagged his tail. The dog came closer, but not close enough to touch.

"You should have stayed in the kennel," Blaise told the dog. "It's only for ten days, and I told you I'd bring doughnuts every day. Think what you're missing."

Rover yawned and sat on his haunches. He

watched Blaise attentively, and his stubby tail never stopped wagging.

Jillie squatted, too, hoping that by doing so she would diminish any threat the dog perceived. Rover thumped his tail harder.

"Cal misses you, guy," Blaise said quietly.

Jillie could have sworn the dog recognized his owner's name. He cocked his head inquisitively and wiggled closer to Blaise, never quite lifting his butt from the ground.

"Life on the lam can't be a whole lot of fun," Blaise continued, his voice pitched soothingly. "Maybe the food at Doc's joint wasn't as good as what you get at home, but at least it was regular. Aren't you getting hungry?"

The dog wormed closer and Blaise's hand shot out with lightning speed, seizing the animal's collar. Rover tugged a little, making a token attempt to escape, then gave up and settled down, resting his head on his forepaws.

"Good dog," Blaise said. He then scooped Rover up in his arms and carried him to the police cruiser, putting the dog in the backseat, behind the protective grille.

"What are you going to do with him?" Jillie asked.

"Take him back to Doc's to finish out his quarantine. Then I'm going by Cal's place to tell him his dog is okay. And I'll drive by your store to check it out. Want to ride along?"

Blaise radioed Sean Kilkenny before he pulled out of the driveway. By the time they arrived at the veterinary clinic, Doc was there to meet them.

"Ah, the prodigal returns," Kilkenny said, as he leaned down to peer into the backseat of the patrol car. Rover was lying stretched out on the seat in apparent indifference. "Dog, I am sorely embarrassed at your escape."

"Somebody had to have let him out," Blaise said.

"That goes without saying. However, it leaves me in the awkward position of having to explain to all my other patients' humans that this isn't something they need to worry about. I've never had another dog escape or get stolen."

"Rover is a unique animal in a lot of ways," Blaise said humorously. "I'd dearly love to know who staged the escape."

"Well, it wasn't Cal. He's no cat burglar, not at his age." Kilkenny spied Jillie. "Miss McAllister! Have you considered adopting a pet?"

"Well . . . not really . . ."

"You should think about it. Think of the comfort and the security of owning a dog. It's a live-in burglar alarm with a personality. It can drive away loneliness, occupy your bored hours, provide companionship on long walks, and bring your blood pressure down."

Jillie felt a huge grin starting to spread across her face. "Sounds like snake oil to me."

Kilkenny adopted a serious expression. "No, it's just a dog. Mongrels are the best, you know. They tend to be more intelligent and less likely to develop serious abnormalities, such as hip dysplasia. That having been said, let me assure you that it's not every day I can offer you your choice of mongrel pups, absolutely free. And these are especially cute, half Husky and half Lab. One in particular has blue eyes and a coal-black coat . . ." He tilted his head to one side. "I'll even throw in shots and neutering for free."

Blaise smiled at Jillian. "You can't beat that deal."

But life had taught her to be more suspicious. "What's wrong with these pups?"

"Not a thing," Sean said. "They were abandoned

and a friend found them and brought them to me. I've checked them out and they're perfectly healthy. All I want to do is find good homes for them."

"I don't know. I really haven't thought about having a pet just yet. I'm so busy . . ." But she was wavering. She could feel it. It *would* be nice to have a dog.

"Well, come on in and see them," he suggested. He got Rover out of the backseat of the car with a minimum of fuss and led him inside on a nylon lead. Rover appeared resigned and entered the cage with nothing but a heavy sigh.

"Tomorrow," Blaise promised the dog. "Tomorrow morning I'll bring you a jelly doughnut."

"I'm telling you, Blaise," Sean said sternly, "that's not good for the dog."

"Neither is being quarantined like this."

Sean sighed but didn't argue.

There were five pups, all about six or seven weeks old, Sean thought. The cutest, though, to Jillie's way of thinking, was the coal-black one with the bright blue eyes. Blaise was drawn to one that was black and white and showing signs of developing a huskie's mask.

"Go ahead and pick them up," Sean said. "It's good for them to socialize with a lot of different humans while they're young. They're less apt to become a problem later."

Jillie knew she shouldn't handle the pup, but she did anyway. Its coat was as soft as silk, and it nuzzled close to her right away, trying to burrow into the warmth between her neck and chin. She knew she was lost when she felt the little pink tongue licking her and felt the tail wagging wildly.

"I don't know anything about housebreaking," she said desperately.

"Basically, it's easy," Sean said. "Get a pet carrier and keep her in it whenever you're not at home. She'll sleep and she probably won't mess much because she doesn't want to sleep with it. Dogs don't soil their dens. When you're home, walk her frequently and praise her extravagantly when she does her business outside. It won't take long. Trust me."

Somehow Jillie felt it couldn't possibly be that easy. Nothing ever was. But she wanted to *believe* it would be that easy because she couldn't imagine going home without this adorable little puppy that seemed to be perfectly content to curl up on her shoulder and lick her ear.

She looked at Blaise and saw that he was getting attached, too.

"I can help you with housebreaking," he told Jillie. "I've had pups before."

"I never have," she admitted. In only one home where she had lived had the family had a pet, and it had been a guinea pig.

"I'll be glad to help," Blaise said again.

"Look," Sean said, "if it doesn't work, you can bring her back to me. Consider it a warranty."

Blue eyes looked up at her and a pink tongue stretched out to lick her face. Jillie sighed and gave up the battle. "Okay. Okay." Then a bubble of laughter rose in her. "I'm such a pushover!"

"Everybody needs a pet," Sean said soberly, but then he laughed along with her. "Make her a bed with a cardboard box and a towel for tonight, but get her a pet carrier as soon as you can."

When she left, she was carrying the puppy and a nylon leash. Blaise carried a bag of puppy chow the vet had given her.

"How come you didn't succumb?" she asked Blaise, as he opened the car door for her. She slid in and cradled the dog on her lap, where it seemed perfectly happy to curl up and go to sleep.

"I probably will," he admitted. "But not tonight. Tonight my mind is on other things."

A pleasant shiver ran through Jillie at the way he was looking at her, reminding her that they had come very close to sharing the most intense experience a man and woman could have together.

Blaise slammed the door and came around to climb in behind the wheel. "Next stop," he said. "Cal Lepkin's house."

Blaise was in trouble and he knew it. Despite all his resolutions not to get involved with Jillian, his willpower was waning. He wanted her . . . no question of that. But he also felt she wasn't built for a casual affair. Come to that, neither was he. Every time he tried to have one, he wound up walking away full of self-disgust. Relationships shouldn't be that empty.

And that was why he knew he was in trouble. As long as his need for Jillian was purely sexual, he could control it. But lately he'd begun to feel very protective of her, and very concerned about her emotional state. He had begun to spend an inordinate amount of time worrying about her problems, and then he'd even gone so far as to hire a friend who, conveniently, was a private detective, to see if he could find out why the Wainwrights were suddenly so interested in Jillie.

That was another cause for alarm. It wasn't that his need to protect her was causing him to spend large sums of money—that was nothing—but he didn't have the foggiest idea how to tell her that he'd involved himself in her life this way. She'd probably kill him if she knew.

Which wouldn't have mattered if he didn't give a damn about her.

Christ!

Tonight's scene with the Wainwrights should have reinforced all his reasons for keeping clear of her. Instead, all he had wanted to do was step between her and those idiots . . . to make rash promises that he'd keep them out of her life forever if she'd just let him.

He was losing his marbles. Here he was, riding around on official business and dragging her along with him because he couldn't stand to let her out of his sight. He really, really needed to get his head screwed on straight—one way or the other. Commit or stay away. Was it really such an impossible choice?

Well, yeah, considering that Jillie herself didn't seem particularly eager to get involved.

Stifling a curse, he jammed the key into the ignition and started the car. Focus on Cal Lepkin. Focus on the job. It was the only way he could stay sane.

He took Jillie down one of the few streets she had never been on. Here the houses became poorer and more ramshackle, a far cry from the touristy glitz only a few hundred feet away.

"This part of town was settled a long time ago," Blaise told her. "Back when most of the folks living out here were fishermen, before tourism became such a big thing and just about ran everything else out of town."

"It's hard to imagine."

"It is, isn't it? Anyway, these houses haven't changed much, and for the most part the people living in them have been living here since birth. The neighborhood's steadily shrinking, though."

They pulled up in front of Cal Lepkin's house, and Jillie was appalled. The place was little more than a tarpaper shack with a dirt yard. Out on the front porch, in a battered old rocker, sat a man who looked nearly as old as Methuselah. He rocked steadily back and forth, not even pausing when Blaise got out of the car and walked up to him.

The window was open a crack, so Jillie was able to hear the conversation.

"I found Rover, Cal. He's okay. I put him back with Doc Kilkenny to finish out the quarantine."

"That's good." Cal kept right on rocking. "That dog ain't sick."

"I know it, but we gotta follow the law."

"I s'pose."

"Doc's giving away some pups, Cal. You might want to take a look at them tomorrow. They're cute little things."

"Only got room for one Rover at a time," Cal said.

"But Rover is always wandering. If you get a new pup, maybe you'll have one dog around to keep you company most of the time."

At that, Cal cracked a laugh. "One's enough to chase these days. I don't get around the way I use ta. Naw, jes' get me my dog back."

"Just a couple more days now, Cal."

"I know. I know. I'm a-countin' 'em on my calendar."

Blaise climbed back into the car and headed them toward Jillie's store.

"That's sad," Jillie said.

"What? Cal? Believe me, he doesn't see himself that way."

"I'm sure he doesn't, but it's sad anyway. What's he got besides a dog? And Fielding is trying to take even that away."

"He won't succeed. That law is going to go down in flames tomorrow night."

"You're sure?"

"I'm sure. Now, what are you going to name your puppy?"

"I haven't the foggiest idea. This calls for some thought."

The bookstore appeared to be untouched. No sign of graffiti could be detected, even when they pulled into the alley.

"Safe and sound," Blaise said, and began to back out onto the street. "I'll come back again in a couple of hours, but I think we've seen the last of the vandalism."

"I wonder who was behind it. I mean, it seemed to be directed at me personally. I'd kind of like to know who hates me."

Blaise shook his head. "I don't think anyone hates you, but we've never had anything like this happen here before—at least, not that I know of. It's strange all around."

"You'd think that if it had been random gang activity some of the other places would have been spray-painted."

"You would, wouldn't you?" He drummed his fingers thoughtfully on the steering wheel as they drove slowly down the now quiet boulevard. "Whoever it was didn't leave a clue," he finally said. "The truth is, I don't know where to look next. We checked area stores that sell spray paint, and nobody remembered any kids buying the stuff. We questioned employees at surrounding businesses, we asked in the newspaper for anyone with information to come forward, we even checked into Belinda's friends to see if someone was mad at her. Nothing."

Jillie nodded. The puppy on her lap stirred and she petted it gently, soothing it back to sleep. "Have you ever thought how awful it must be to be a puppy? Taken from your mother and put in a strange place where you don't know anyone or anything?''

"Kind of like you moving to Paradise Beach."

She looked at him, surprised. "It's not the same."

"No?"

"No. I'm older. I understand things. It was my choice."

"I'll agree with the choice part, but age doesn't make it any easier to leave everything you know behind and come all this distance to build a new life among strangers. That takes a lot of guts."

"Or a lot of desperation."

"Don't put yourself down. Don't minimize what you did. Very few people would have done that."

"Well, I thought there would be some advantages to it. A fresh start where no one knew my sordid history, where there were no reminders of things that hurt." She gave a mirthless little laugh. "I never guessed the past would follow me."

"Which brings up another point. Those two are up to something."

"I'm convinced of it. I asked point-blank why Fielding got this sudden urge to reconcile, and he swore it was only because he missed me when I left. I'm not buying it."

"I wouldn't buy it, either. Not that I can't see someone missing you when you're gone, but . . . I don't know. It doesn't fit with what you told me about the divorce and the restraining order. And his mother showing up as well—that fits even less."

"I keep thinking about that," Jillie agreed. "Especially about Harriet. I can't imagine why it would be important to her for us to reconcile. She swears she loves me and wants me back in the family, but it still doesn't fit. I mean . . . oh, I don't know what I mean. I'm fond of her, but I'm not at all sure she's that fond of me. She's said some things that have really hurt."

"People *do* hurt people they care about."

"But she was blaming me for the divorce. If she really thinks I drove Fielding to have affairs—"

"She *said* that?" Blaise interrupted, his voice loud with indignation. The puppy whimpered and stirred.

"Basically." She was trying to pretend she didn't believe it, but the simple truth was, Fielding's infidelities had gutted her self-confidence as a woman. And come to think of it, she was getting awfully tired of strumming that particular chord. So what? Plenty of women had been cheated on and they didn't let it drive them into a deep, dark hole of self-pity.

"Well, you may not have been to Fielding's taste," Blaise said, "but you're certainly to mine!"

"Oh, how would you know?" Jillie said without thinking. "We haven't even—" She broke off sharply. Oh, heavens, what was she saying? How could she even refer to . . . *that*? He would misunderstand!

Which was precisely what he did. "We can remedy that," he said, and glanced at her with a faint smile. "I fully intend to, you know. If not tonight, some other time. That's a promise."

Her heart started hammering frantically and she began to gulp air. "I . . . ah . . . um . . ." She gave up. Speech had deserted her. Half of her wanted to run and half of her wanted to fling herself into his arms— as soon as they were safely parked, of course.

She didn't know what she was more scared of: the possibility she might disappoint him, or the possibility she might become involved with him and get hurt the way Fielding had hurt her. Nor did it matter. The only thing that mattered was that she was suddenly scared to death.

He wheeled the car into the driveway and turned off the ignition. The night was dark and wind-tossed. Moonless. Beckoning and frightening all at once. Like

Blaise. Blaise made her feel the same way.

He climbed out of the car and came around to open her door. "Here, let me help you," he said, and reached in for the puppy.

She missed the warm weight of the dog on her lap and felt suddenly defenseless, as if he had just removed a shield.

"Let's go in and make her a bed," he said. "Do you have a box, or do I need to get one?"

"I have one." She was amazed that she could speak. She was even more amazed that he didn't seem the least bit rattled or awkward after what he had just said. Didn't he feel embarrassed?

They walked together to her front door. From ten feet away, despite the darkness, she could see that something was wrong. "I've been vandalized!"

Fourteen

In the darkness under the eaves, she couldn't make out the words, but she could see that paint had been sprayed all across the front of her house.

"Here." Blaise turned and handed her the puppy. "Go get in the patrol car while I check this out. They could still be here."

She stood frozen for a minute, unable to believe this was happening to her, then did as she was told because there was nothing else she could do. With her hands full of puppy, she wouldn't even be able to defend herself if she ran into the vandals.

The inside of the patrol car was warmer than the night air but still chilly. Blaise had taken the keys so she couldn't turn on the heater, but that was okay. She shivered, but she suspected that had more to do with events than with any chill.

The puppy squirmed on her lap, seeking warmth, and found her finger. It began to suck eagerly, its little teeth sharp. Jillie ran her hand over the tiny dog and murmured something comforting.

Blaise was back in under five minutes. "They're gone," he told her.

"Who's doing this?"

He didn't have an answer for her, and she knew it, but the question expressed her frustration and worry. "Actually," he said, "I'm beginning to wonder if your ex isn't behind this."

"Fielding?"

"Do you have another ex I don't know about?"

"No, I do not!" Men! Good heavens, why was she allowing one of them to get this close to her? They were all— She cut off that mental diatribe abruptly because it wasn't true. It would be wrong to tar all the men of the world with Fielding's brush. Especially Blaise, who had been nice to her from the outset— except for that little arrest, but then, nobody was perfect.

"Well, who else would want to drive you out of Paradise Beach? It's stretching credulity now to think this is the random work of some misguided kids."

"I know. But . . . Fielding?" She couldn't imagine him doing anything of the sort. He wasn't the kind of person to get his hands dirty.

"Maybe he's paying someone to do it."

Now that brought it within the realm of possibility. She could easily see Fielding paying someone to spray-paint her store and house.

"At the very least, I'm going to question him about it in the morning," Blaise continued. "But as for tonight . . . would you feel safer staying with me?"

The offer was tempting on so many levels, all of them purely selfish. It was also terrifying. "I'm not scared, Blaise. Whoever's committing this vandalism doesn't want to hurt me physically. They're just trying to scare me."

"Probably. But to tell you the truth, if you spend the night in your own bed I'm not going to sleep because I'm going to be up keeping an eye on you. I'd sleep a whole lot better if you were under *my* roof. I'll even give you the guest room. No strings."

It was an offer she'd have felt churlish refusing. "Thanks."

They cut down the sides on one of her empty moving boxes and lined it with a towel for the puppy.

"I've got dishes you can use for water and food tonight," Blaise told her. "We'll put her in the utility room where she won't be able to mess anything up."

Jillie grabbed a nightgown and some necessaries, like her toothbrush, and followed Blaise back over to his place. The dog settled happily into its little box after lapping some water and went instantly to sleep.

"The little tyke is exhausted," she said softly, feeling a warm maternal rush.

"Seems to be." Blaise led her to the guest room on the third floor, a pretty one with soft, feminine appointments.

Jillie looked around, at once admiring it and wondering at a bachelor who would have such a room.

"My mom stays here when she visits," he said. "You'll probably run across some of her things, but don't worry about it. Make yourself at home. Good night."

She had to bite her tongue to keep herself from calling him back. He disappeared down the hallway into a room on the far end, and the door closed with finality.

Jillie closed her own door and sat on the double bed, wondering if she was being wise or foolish. Hell, she finally decided wearily, there was no answer to that question. She'd been acting on instinct since the moment she'd realized she had to either divorce Fielding or die.

Because he *had* been killing her, emotionally. Living with the constant pain of knowing her husband was cheating was not something she was equipped to do. Some women managed it. Heck, look at most of the Wainwright women. They claimed it was a natural part of being a woman. But not Jillie. Never.

So here she was, half a continent away and getting in over her head with another man. Maybe what she really needed was a psychiatrist.

Sighing in exasperation, she fell back on the bed and stared up at the ceiling.

And Fielding . . . what could that man be up to? If it *was* Fielding. She didn't know which possibility disturbed her more: that Fielding might actually be willing to go to these lengths to drive her out of this town in hopes she'd come back to him, or that some stranger might be doing it.

Fielding? Fielding. The more she thought about it, the more likely it seemed. Her ex-husband didn't like being thwarted, and from experience she knew he was willing to cross ordinary boundaries to get his way. But to break the law?

There were no answers. Finally, giving up, she went to bed.

Dawn came creeping through the window above the bed, a soft peach glow that filled the room with warmth. Jillie opened her eyes slowly, feeling as if she were drifting in a warm cocoon on a river of light. It would be so nice, she found herself thinking, if Blaise were with her now.

Almost as if in answer to her thoughts, there was a quiet knock at the door. In an instant her mind filled with a vision of him walking through it and seeing her in her comforter cocoon. He would approach slowly, uncertain whether she was asleep. When he saw that her eyes were sleepily open, he would bend over her and . . .

Her breath caught in her throat and her limbs suddenly felt as heavy as lead. A wave of desire flooded through her. Had she ever wanted anything so much?

The knock came again. With effort she managed to croak, "Yes?"

The door opened just as she'd imagined and she found herself perched on the knife-edge between hope and fear. Yes. No. Oh, please . . .

"Jill?" The door opened wider and Blaise peered around it. "I'm sorry to wake you, but most of the neighborhood is in your front yard looking for you."

He might as well have doused her with cold water. The languor of desire instantly turned into anxiety. She sat up, shoving her hair back from her face. "Looking for me? At dawn?" She hadn't spoken more than a few words to any of her neighbors in the brief time she'd been here, and visions of a lynch mob immediately sprang to her mind.

"It's not really that early," Blaise reminded her. "Most of us are getting ready to go to work."

She blushed, feeling like a slug-a-bed.

"I think you'll want to get dressed and come out," he continued. "I'll see you out front." He started to close the door, then paused. "By the way, I took care of your puppy. She's been cleaned up, fed, watered, and walked."

"Thank you."

"No problem." The door closed.

Jillie sat for a few seconds, trying to shake off the muzziness of sleep, the lingering twinges of denied arousal, and the anxiety about why her neighbors

were looking for her. After all, she hadn't done anything to them. They couldn't possibly be looking to
ride her out of town on a rail . . . could they?

Unfortunately, there was only one way to find out.
Shaking off the last of sleep, she quickly dressed and
brushed her teeth, wishing she'd thought to bring a
change of clothes over last night. A black silk dress at
this hour of the morning was going to be a dead giveaway.

Which was a thought that gave her pause before
she stepped out Blaise's front door. Did she want to
be seen emerging from the chief of police's house at
this hour wearing black silk? Did the chief want her
to emerge from his house looking as if she'd spent the
night in his bed?

Gloomily she contemplated the problem, wondering how she could get out of this fix. Maybe she could
sneak around back.

The house was on stilts, but part of the ground area
had been turned into a finished storage room or office
and enclosed stairway, so that one didn't have to de-
scend the outside stairs. She took the inside stairs
now, hoping there was a door at the back.

There was. Stepping through it, she found herself
in Blaise's backyard. Apparently he wasn't much of a
devoted gardener. At some time or other, someone
had planted bougainvilleas, hibiscus, azaleas, and
other, unidentifiable shrubs, but a lack of care had let
them run wild. The remains of a path could barely be
seen.

She darted down it, keeping low so the shrubbery
would conceal her. She didn't let herself think about
what she was going to do when she reached her own
yard, which was largely packed dirt and sand.

The path curved sharply and she turned, practically
duck-walking with her head down almost to her

knees. She barely had time to register a pair of jogging shoes in front of her before she bumped into one of the neighbors she was trying to avoid.

"It's all right," Mrs. Herrera said. "You don't have to hide. We know all about it."

Still crouched, her stomach sinking to her ankles, Jillie looked up at her. "You do?"

"Chief Corrigan told us everything. We understand. Come out front."

He'd told them everything? Panic clutched her. *What* had he told them? "I can explain."

"It's really none of our business, you know." Mrs. Herrera bent and tugged her to her feet. Her leg muscles cramped immediately and didn't want to straighten all the way. It had been a long time since she had duck-walked.

"Everyone's been looking for you," Mrs. Herrera continued. "You can call me Connie, by the way. It's short for Consuelo. I came here from Cuba in 1958, when I was just a little girl, you know."

"Really?" Her legs were doing the pins-and-needles thing as she stood there wondering wildly just what Blaise had told everyone. She knew men; they rarely said as much as needed saying. For example, he'd probably consider it quite adequate to simply say, "Jillie was afraid, so she spent the night with me." Aagh!

Connie Herrera gave her a smile. "Yes, really. My parents are still hoping to go home, but I've decided *this* is my home. I have only a faint memory of Cuba anymore, and I don't think we're going to get it back when El Barbo dies."

"El Barbo?"

"The bearded one. Castro."

"Oh." It suddenly struck her that she was standing in bare feet in the backyard of someone else's home wearing an evening dress in the bright morning light while someone she didn't know explained Cuban politics to her. All that was missing was the Mad Hatter.

"Come on," said Connie. "I'll take you to the back door and you can change out of that dress. Some people might find it difficult to believe the chief's story if you go out there wearing this."

"Which was precisely why I was creeping through the shrubbery." And what had Corrigan told them?

Connie laughed. "But creeping *looks* guilty, you know?"

Jillie managed a weak smile and followed the town's biggest gossip across the backyard. Connie scouted for her, telling her when the coast was clear and no one in the front yard could see her. Connie also followed her inside.

"I saw all that stuff your mother-in-law ordered for you," Connie said. "When they were unloading it from the truck. She made some changes."

"No kidding." Jill walked through the house and disappeared into her bedroom, closing the door firmly. Some nosiness she wouldn't tolerate.

"Do you like it?" Connie called through the door.

"Actually, no. It looks like a decorator's idea of a tropical paradise. It's not mine."

"I'm glad to hear it. I think it's awful, myself. It's too bad you're stuck with it."

Jillie yanked on her jeans and a sweater. "I'm going to make Harriet load it on a truck and take it back to Massachusetts with her."

"What if she says no?"

"Then I'll have a yard sale and get rid of it."

Connie's laugh floated through the door. "Are you always so outspoken?"

"Unfortunately, yes." She opened the door and

stepped into the hallway, feeling better about facing the mob out front.

"Come on," Connie said. "Everyone's getting impatient."

"What do they want?"

"You'll see."

At least now, she thought glumly, she wasn't wearing a skirt that would ride up indecently if they tied her to a rail.

The mob out front wasn't much of a mob, maybe fifteen souls strong. Nor did they look like they wanted to string her up. In fact, most of them were standing there holding paint brushes. Jillie looked at the brushes and wondered if this was some strange Paradise Beach custom. Or perhaps they were planning to use the brushes when they tarred and feathered her?

They looked at her and she looked at them, and for several seconds it seemed no one knew quite what to say. Finally one of them stepped forward, an elderly man she had given a ride to one day when his car wouldn't start. What was his name? Moranti. Mr. Moranti.

"Ms. McAllister," he said, then paused to clear his throat. "When we woke up this morning and saw the spray paint all over your house, we were appalled. Things like this don't happen in Paradise Beach."

Jillie nodded. "At least, not until I arrived."

"That makes it even more appalling. Blaise told us about the trouble you had at your new business, and then this." He waved his hand at the graffiti on her house, which in the clear morning light looked even more shocking than it had last night. "We can't apologize for actions over which we have no control, but I do assure you, we are ashamed that you've had this kind of welcome to our community. We're really very nice people, Ms. McAllister."

"I'm sure you are." And she was touched that they had cared enough to come tell her this.

"We thought that if we all pitched in it wouldn't take but a few minutes to get the front of your house all painted over. So if you don't object, just as soon as the police are through taking pictures of the damage, we'll get to work. We've got plenty of white paint, and everyone has a brush."

Jillie was speechless as she looked at her neighbors and saw them all smile and hold up their brushes.

"Fifteen, twenty minutes," said a man near the back of the group, "and it'll be like new."

"I . . . I don't know what to say!"

"You don't have to say anything at all," said a blue-haired woman in a shocking pink pantsuit. "You hear bad things about New York all the time, but I'll tell you, even in Brooklyn we helped when a neighbor had troubles."

There were nods and murmurs of agreement all around.

"And listen," said another woman. "You don't have to stay with a bachelor again if you get scared. You come stay with me. You're not alone anymore."

Jillie felt color stain her cheeks, and she couldn't think of a single thing to say. Finally she blurted out, "Thank you."

Mr. Moranti spoke again. "Now, go inside and have breakfast, or something. Take a nap. Blaise said you didn't get much sleep because of last night. In no time at all, you'll never know anything happened."

Jillie glanced at Blaise, who was dressed in uniform this morning. He stood to one side, his arms folded, smiling with obvious approval. "Paradise Beach is a great place," he said.

"Yeah," agreed one of the men. "Now all we have to do is stop the mayor from shoving that damn dog ordinance through tonight. Hey, Ms. McAllister—"

"Jillie. Please call me Jillie."

"Okay, Jillie. Is it true the man who's pushing that is your husband?"

"My *ex*-husband."

"Jillie," Blaise added, "is president of the Ad Hoc Committee to Save the Dogs of Paradise Beach."

A smattering of quiet applause passed through the group.

"I guess," said one of the women with a humorous smile, "that you're *not* planning to get back with him?"

Everyone laughed. Mr. Moranti and Connie Herrera urged her back into the house, and almost before she knew it, Jillie found herself sitting in her own kitchen, sipping a cup of tea out of one of the vine-covered china cups Harriet had bought to replace the melamine.

Vines everywhere, she thought, and suddenly burst into tears.

Blaise found her there a couple of minutes later. Without a word he drew her out of her chair and into his arms, cradling her close. "It gets to be too much, doesn't it?"

She had been trying to hold back her tears, but at the quiet understanding in his voice, her last reserve broke and she sobbed into his shoulder until his uniform shirt was damp. When her tears finally stopped, she felt headachy and exhausted. She didn't want to look at him.

"It's okay," he said, when she tried to pull away. "Really. Sometimes life just shovels too much shit."

She nodded but still felt foolish. "It's stupid. I mean, what has really happened?"

"Oh, I don't know. You've been hassled for well over a week by an ex-husband and a former mother-in-law who really aren't all that fond of you, from what I've seen. You've had your business vandalized twice, and now your home, and to top it all off, you haven't had enough sleep."

"Don't forget my arrest for DUI."

He pulled back his head and looked ruefully down at her. "You smelled like beer, you know."

"I know." She let her head fall against his shoulder again. "I need to wash my face and then get out there and help all those nice people paint this house."

"I don't think there's room enough for you. Besides, didn't they tell you to go have breakfast while they took care of it?"

"But I wouldn't feel right letting them do all the work."

"Okay, then." He gave her another squeeze and let go of her. "I have a couple of paintbrushes at my place."

Apparently, at some point, without even being conscious of it, she had named her puppy Corky. When she and Blaise got the paintbrushes, she used the nylon leash the vet had given her to tie the pup to a tree in the front yard where it could roll in the grass and chase bugs.

By this time a couple of cops had arrived to take pictures and statements. Jillie remembered Gary Melrose and Andy Clair from the day the tourist had blocked the intersection and argued about moving his car. Just as they were wrapping up their questions, Mary Todd pulled up in her lavender golf cart, Hadley Philpott beside her on the seat.

"This is outrageous," Mary declared, pointing at the graffiti with her cane.

"Have you no shame?" Hadley asked her softly.

She ignored him, turning her attention to Jillian. "You poor dear! You must be at wit's end!"

Before Jillie could respond, a black sports car pulled up and Dan Burgess climbed out. Behind him came another car, this one bearing a photographer who immediately started snapping pictures of the mayor as he surveyed the damage to Jillie's house. The neighbors, who were patiently awaiting police permission to start painting, stood back and watched with a variety of reactions.

Jillie simply shook her head. "I don't believe this."

Mary patted her arm. "He's never been one to miss an opportunity for publicity."

"But that man fired me!"

Once he had been photographed in front of the graffiti looking suitably appalled, Burgess immediately turned to the gathered neighbors and began shaking their hands, assuring them the city would do everything possible to catch the culprit or culprits who were defacing the fair city of Paradise Beach. None of the people to whom he spoke looked particularly impressed. In fact, a woman in purple leggings, gold lamé blouse, and huge glasses turned her back on him when he sought to shake her hand.

But then the mayor saw Blaise and his two officers. "Aha!" he said. "So the police finally arrive!"

Blaise folded his arms and smiled faintly. "Sorry to disappoint you, Mr. Mayor. I've been here for hours."

Dan's smile congealed. "So you've caught the vandals."

"Not yet."

"Why not? This is the third case of vandalism in Paradise Beach in less than a week! Are we to have our entire town painted by these hooligans before you and your officers do something about it?"

Blaise's expression never wavered. "We're working on it."

"Working on it?" The mayor flung his arms wide as if appealing to the bystanders to join him in his disbelief. "How hard can you be working? You should have found them by now!"

Still Blaise said nothing. Jillie opened her mouth to tell Dan that he was being a jerk, that Blaise had been working very hard indeed on this case, including staying up all night to protect her store from further vandalism. Before she could finish drawing breath, Mary Todd beat her to the punch.

"Really, Daniel," the woman said sternly, "you're making an ass of yourself."

Dan glared at her. "Stay out of this, Miss Todd. You have no idea what you're talking about."

"Don't I?" She waved her ebony cane at him. "You're the mayor of this town—although God only knows why so many people were fool enough to vote for you—and the last time I checked, I'm a registered voter and taxpayer in this town. That gives me a right to express my opinion, and I'm expressing it. You're being an ass!"

"I am not! I'm merely doing my job as mayor in demanding to know what the police are doing about this crime!"

"They're investigating! That was obvious to everyone here before you arrived. Right?" She looked around at the bystanders, a crowd which seemed to Jillie to be steadily growing.

Nods and murmurs of "Right" answered her. Mary turned to look at Dan. "So tell us, Mr. Mayor, just what do you know about this vandalism?"

He was taken aback. "What do *I* know?"

"Yes, what do you know?"

"Nothing! How would I know anything?"

Mary shook her head. "I thought since you were so sure that the police must have figured it all out by now that you must have figured it out yourself."

Jillie clapped a hand to her mouth to stifle a laugh while Dan spluttered.

"I don't know anything about it," he said finally. "It's not my job! It's *their* job."

"Then let them do it," Mary said dismissively. "Quit trying to turn it into a political circus for your own benefit.

"I'm concerned about this young woman whose home has been vandalized."

"Bull puckie," Mary said sharply. "If you were concerned about this young woman, you wouldn't have fired her for refusing to let one of your customers paw her all over."

"That's right," said one of the women in the crowd. "I heard about that, Dan. Just what kind of place are you running over there?"

"Just a minute!" Dan turned on the woman. "*She*," he said, jerking a thumb at Jillie, "dumped a beer on one of my customers!"

"It was an accident," Jillie said quickly. "He pinched me and I jumped!"

"Then you shouldn't have fired her," said one of the men in the crowd. "People shouldn't be pinching young ladies that way."

"Well . . ." Dan appeared to be backing up, unaware the photographer was still busy snapping photos. "Well, now that I know what really happened," he forced a smile to his lips, "of course Ms. McAllister can have her job back."

Ms. McAllister placed her hands on her hips and scowled at him. "You can take your job and shove it."

A cheer went up from the onlookers.

Just then Dan caught sight of the photographer still

taking pictures. "Stop," he said, and reached out to cover the lens with his hand.

"But, boss, you said to snap everything so we can get it to the newspapers."

"Just stop it! Now!"

The photographer shrugged and let his camera dangle by the neck strap. Dan turned to face the gathered crowd and tried to regroup. Jillie gave him credit for not just turning tail and getting out of there.

"Look," he said to her neighbors, "all I'm trying to do is let you know that I'm as deeply concerned as you are about this vandalism. And I'm just trying to make sure the police are doing their jobs! But as it stands now, they apparently haven't even got a suspect."

Heads all swiveled to look at Blaise. He hesitated a moment, then finally said, "We have a suspect. I'm going to question him later today."

Hadley and Mary exchanged glances. Hadley said quietly, "Now, this could get very difficult."

"There's no way he could know you're involved."

Hadley arched a brow. "Really? Are we going to let an innocent person hang for our misdeeds? An interesting moral dilemma."

"Quit talking like a professor!"

"I *am* a professor."

"And nobody's going to hang, not for this."

"I was speaking metaphorically."

Mary rolled her eyes.

It was at that moment that Fielding, with his usual impeccable timing, pulled into Jillie's driveway. He climbed out of his car and looked at the crowd with a mixture of curiosity and distaste. "What is going on?"

Jillie pointed in the direction of the house. Fielding studied the graffiti. "I see," he said.

Blaise looked him over. "You wouldn't happen to know anything about it, would you?"

"Of course," Fielding said acidly. "I routinely spray graffiti all over my property. It was just so beautiful last night that I couldn't resist."

"Mr. Wainwright," Blaise said, "you're under arrest. You have the right to remain silent. Anything you say can and will be used against you in a court of law. You have the right to an attorney . . ."

Fielding listened to his rights with an impatient expression, as if the entire thing was beneath him. Some of that faded when one of the other officers handcuffed him. "You can't arrest me," he told Blaise. "I haven't done anything."

Blaise paused. "Are you saying you didn't spray that paint on the house?"

"I'm saying that I can spray any kind of paint on it I want and you can't arrest me. It's *my house!*" He looked triumphant.

"Mr. Wainwright," Blaise said very patiently, "did you understand the rights I just read to you?"

"Yes, of course. It doesn't take an Einstein!"

"Then I suggest you be very careful what you admit."

"I'm not admitting anything! I'm saying you can't arrest me for vandalizing my own house."

"I'm not arresting you for vandalism. Under the laws of the State of Florida, I'm arresting you for stalking."

"Stalking!" Fielding squawked the word. *"Stalking?* I'm not stalking anybody."

"You, sir, are stalking your ex-wife and attempting to terrorize her into going back to Massachusetts with you. Put him in the cruiser, Gary."

The officer urged Fielding toward the patrol car, but Fielding didn't go quietly. Fielding never went quietly. "You can't do this! I'll sue you for false arrest! I'll own this town by the time I get done!"

"Oh, dear," said Hadley.

"Hush," said Mary.

"We've got to do something!"

"Obviously." Mary pressed the accelerator and drove her golf cart down the street at a quick clip. "But not too swiftly, Hadley. Not too swiftly. Mr. Wainwright is about to learn a long overdue lesson."

Jillie helped her neighbors paint over the graffiti. They were finished in short order, but the painting party quickly turned into a yard party, with everyone running home to throw together something for a pot-luck picnic lunch. By noon Jillie's front yard was full of lawn chairs and folding tables of every description and around two dozen neighbors.

Jillie sat in their midst, enjoying the company and the gorgeous day, getting to know the people who lived in a two block radius around her—and trying not to think of all the things she should be doing at her store today. That could wait until later.

Some of her neighbors were snowbirds who would be here only for the six-month winter season; some were younger couples who wanted to live in the more relaxed beach atmosphere; and two were business owners who offered her all kinds of help.

She didn't see Blaise again until late afternoon, when he pulled up in his cruiser and climbed out, looking at her across the expanse of yard.

He didn't look like Blaise, she thought. He looked like the cop who had arrested her for DUI. He stood stiffly, and something about the way the uniform fit him made her freshly aware of the breadth of his shoulders, the narrowness of his hips, and the strength of his arms and legs. Mirrored sunglasses did nothing to make him look any more approachable. And there was the gun. She looked at it nervously; she liked him much better without it.

"Jillie? Can I have a word with you?"

The few remaining neighbors fell silent and watched as Jillie walked over to Blaise. When she reached him, he turned his back on the gawkers and spoke quietly.

"Your ex is going to be released on bail. I thought you should know, since this is the first place he's apt to come."

She regarded the prospect gloomily. "I have to tell you, though, I'm not at all sure Fielding did it."

"He said he did."

"Not exactly. He didn't *deny* it. I thought he sounded sarcastic."

"He always sounds sarcastic, and if he didn't do it, he should have denied it. I asked him to deny it and he didn't. It's his own fault he got arrested."

Jillie couldn't argue with that, nor did she want to. "I know. I'm not criticizing you."

He looked down at her, his gaze hidden behind his sunglasses. "It's okay even if you do."

"Well, I'm not."

"Did Dan give you any more trouble?"

Jillie had to laugh at that. "Once you arrested Fielding, he could hardly stand around here claiming you weren't doing anything. I also got the feeling that it occurred to him it might not look too good if he was discovered to be accepting contributions from a man accused of stalking."

Blaise grinned at that. "A man accused of stalking a woman Dan had recently fired. Think what the press could do with that."

"As if the big papers really care what's happening in Paradise Beach."

"Oh, believe me, they do. Didn't you see the story about the two women I had to ticket for drinking coffee on the beach?"

"How'd they hear about that?"

Blaise snorted. "Our illustrious mayor shot off his big mouth about how tough he is on enforcing the ordinance. I guess he thought it'd make him look tough on law and order, or some such thing."

"But it didn't?"

"I thought it made him look like a persnickety, self-serving jerk, particularly when the article mentioned he owns one of the condos on that stretch of beach. But that's just my opinion . . . considering I don't object to the ordinance in principle."

"How can you? Considering the numbers of people who come to these beaches, I imagine cleaning up after them must be a nightmare."

"It's also a nightmare for the wildlife. Anyway, I don't really object to telling people they can't bring food or beverages onto the beach. But the enforcement of it can be so petty."

Jillie nodded, thinking he looked awfully tired. "You've been working too hard," she said impulsively.

He shook his head. "Not hard enough, actually. If you're right about Fielding, I need to get on the stick and find out who's terrorizing you."

"I don't exactly feel terrorized."

"But you don't exactly feel as comfortable as you used to, do you?"

She shook her head.

"Anyway, it's a crime no matter how you feel. My money's still on Fielding, but it would be stupid to stop investigating before we're a hundred percent certain."

Jillie bit her lip. "Do you really think he's stalking me?"

"That's how it fits together."

She leaned back against the patrol car beside him and stared off into the blue sky as she thought about it. The afternoon breeze was warm, tossing her hair gently and trying to coax the tension out of her. "It would fit together a whole lot better if I could just figure out one reason why he wants me back. He didn't want me this much even when we were married."

Blaise shrugged a shoulder. "Some men are just possessive. They hate it when a possession gets away."

"That should have struck him a while ago, though, shouldn't it? I mean, to me it looked like he couldn't wait to get rid of me once I told him I wanted a divorce. And he did his damnedest to make sure he never set eyes on me even by accident."

"Well, maybe it took a little time for reality to penetrate. I don't know, Jill. I'm not a psychologist."

She liked the way he called her Jill. It made her sound grownup and independent. Which she was, now that she came to think of it. But it was nice to feel that Blaise saw her that way. Neither Fielding nor his mother ever had.

"Listen," Blaise said abruptly, drawing her even further from the congregation on her lawn. "There's something I need to tell you."

Jillie looked up at him expectantly. "Yes?"

He hesitated, and she wished she could read his eyes through his sunglasses. Finally he spoke.

"I may not be much of a psychologist, but this thing with Fielding and his mother has got me really concerned."

"Me, too." Jillie shook her head. "All the excuses I can think up don't fit the bill."

"Me either." He sighed. "Look, don't get mad, but I . . . um . . . I hired a private detective."

"You did *what*?" She could hardly believe her ears.

"I hired a private detective. I told him what was going on, and asked him to see if he could find any reason for those two to want you back so desperately."

Jillie looked at him, feeling hurt but feeling stupid for it. "So you don't think my sterling charms and wonderful personality are enough?"

He almost cracked a smile; she saw it in the way the corners of his mouth twitched. "Your charms and your personality are wonderful, Jill. Why do you think I keep hanging around? But for those two . . ." He shook his head. "Something is fishy. You know it as well as I do. Don't be mad at me."

She ought to be, she supposed. She ought to be furious that he was sticking his nose into her life without so much as a by-your-leave. But even as she tried to whip up some minor indignation, she couldn't. All she could feel was cherished and cared for. It touched her that he had gone to so much trouble and expense.

"I'm not mad," she said, feeling all soft inside. "I'm not mad at all. Thank you."

"Thank me when he finds out something."

"I will." She smiled up at him. "I promise."

"Yoo-hoo!" Maggie Dewitt, the woman of the purple stretch pants and gold blouse, called to them. "Aren't you two going to join us?"

"That's my cue," Blaise said. "I've got to get back to work."

Jillie didn't want him to leave, but she certainly didn't want him to go without making plans for the two of them to get together again. "Can I make you dinner tonight?"

He looked surprised, then smiled. "Sure. I'd really like that. I get off at five."

"So I'll plan dinner for six?"

"Make it six-thirty. Then we can go directly to the city council meeting." Then, in front of all the watching people, he bent and pressed a quick kiss to her lips. After tossing a wave to the assembled people, he climbed into his car and drove away, leaving Jillie to face all the knowing smiles.

That was okay, since she was grinning like an idiot herself.

Fifteen

"This looks really great," Blaise said, as he sat at the table in her kitchen.

"Thanks." It wasn't much, to her way of thinking, but she didn't really know Blaise's taste in food, so she'd made a shrimp salad and served it with rolls from the bakery. He seemed to enjoy it, though, eating heartily.

"Where's the pup?" he asked.

"She's sleeping in the carrier I bought for her this afternoon. She seems to like it in there."

"Maybe the small space feels safe."

"Maybe."

He speared another shrimp. "Have you decided what you're going to say at the city council meeting tonight?"

"Me? Why should I say anything?"

"Because you're the president of the Ad Hoc Committee to Save the Dogs of Paradise Beach."

"That doesn't mean I have to speak!"

A smile crinkled the corners of his blue eyes. "Think about all the great publicity you'll get."

"Oh, yeah, right. Like the publicity I got on TV news on Sunday. No thank you. I've got enough problems without everyone in Paradise Beach thinking I'm a total idiot."

"Now why would they think that? Most of 'em are going to be on your side with regard to this dog ordinance."

"I'm not a public speaker."

"You do just fine when you're riled."

"Quit pushing, Corrigan, or I'll stay home."

He laughed. "You're a regular handful, aren't you? Okay, not another word. Just be sure to bring your dog."

"Corky? Why?"

"You'll see when we get there."

She certainly did. Five or six hundred people had shown up for the council meeting, and most of them were wearing green dog collars and leading or carrying dogs. She and Blaise managed to find seats only because Mary Todd and her friends had saved them—in the front row.

"I figured you'd want to be able to hear everything, my dear," Mary said with a smile. "Since you're our spokesperson."

"What?"

Blaise stifled a laugh. "Skewered," he said to Jillie, then laughed even harder when she glared at him.

"Really, Mary," Jillie said, "I can't speak for the group. I'm new in town and I really don't know anything about how people feel about this."

"You know how *you* feel, don't you?"

"Well, yes . . ."

"Then that's all you need to know." Mary patted

her arm reassuringly. "You'll do just fine, Jillie. You'll see."

Jillie gave serious thought to walking out right then and there, but when she glanced down at the puppy sleeping so contentedly on her lap, her resolve took over. This whole idea of Fielding's was unconscionable. She couldn't just walk away and leave the outcome to fate.

Blaise reached over and captured her hand, squeezing gently. "You'll be fine."

"When did you get that dog?"

Startled, Jillie looked up to see Fielding towering over her.

"When did you get that dog?" he asked again. "Good God, it's a mongrel."

Harriet was right beside him. She reached out to grab his arm, saying, "Fielding. . . ."

"No, Mother, I will not be silent. You know perfectly well how ferociously allergic to dogs I am, and so does Jillian. There is no way on earth I'm going to let her bring that mutt home to Worcester."

Jillie answered hotly. "There's no way on earth I'd go back to Worcester with you."

"Now, Fielding," Harriet said. "Jillian. Don't the two of you say things you'll regret later."

"I'm not going to regret one word of this later," Jillie said.

Surprisingly, Fielding said nothing to her. Instead, he looked uncomfortably at his mother, then said, "You're right of course, Mother. If Jillian wants a dog, she can have a dog."

"You don't have one thing to say about it anymore," Jillie told him angrily. "Will you just go away?"

Blaise cleared his throat. "You heard the lady."

Fielding's face reddened. "You stay out of this, Corrigan. I'm going to have your ass served to me on a platter before this is over!''

"The lady asked you to leave. You've already been arrested once for stalking. Do you want to try for twice?''

Fielding turned his glare on Jillie. "So now you can hide behind a cop. How cute.''

"Fielding!" Harriet snapped. "Just go sit down, before you make things worse.''

For a minute it looked as if Fielding was going to act like a temperamental two-year-old and refuse to obey. But then, thrusting out his lower lip, he walked away.

Harriet looked straight at Jillie. "Fielding didn't spray-paint the house or your store.''

Jillie just nodded.

"I can't believe you said he did.''

Blaise intervened. "Mr. Wainwright said he did it, not Jill.''

"Well!" Harriet lifted her chin sharply and compressed her lips. "Very well, then. But Jillian, I expect you to make some time to talk to me before I go home.''

"When are you leaving?''

"Monday.''

Jillie nodded. "We'll talk before then. Definitely.''

"Thank you." With great dignity, Harriet moved away.

"Gee," Jillie said under her breath, "dare we hope that Fielding's going home on Monday, too?''

"He can't," Blaise said.

"Why not?''

"Because he's been charged with stalking. He'll have to get a judge's permission to leave the area.''

"Oh, my God." Her heart sank to her toes. "You mean I'm stuck with him for months?''

"Uh . . . yeah." He looked as if he hadn't considered that before, either.

"Is there some way you can *un*charge him?"

Blaise shook his head. "We can approach the prosecutor and ask him to dismiss the charges."

"Let's do it. I can't have that man hanging around for months driving me crazy."

"There's no guarantee the state attorney will drop the charge, though, Jill. As for Fielding driving you crazy for months . . . he'd better not. He could be charged again for stalking."

"And then he'll be around forever! I just want him to go home." She shook her head. "Besides, Blaise, he hasn't really been stalking me. Driving me nuts, yes— but he never made me afraid."

"Unless he's been the one painting all the graffiti. Or paying someone to. That goes beyond driving you nuts, Jill."

She nodded reluctantly. "I guess my problem here is that I really can't imagine Fielding having anything to do with the graffiti. It's just not his . . . style, for lack of a better word."

"But who else around here could possibly want to target you like this?"

"I don't know. Dan Burgess?"

Blaise suddenly grinned. "Don't tempt me. Damn, that's almost too much to resist."

She had to laugh at that, mainly because she felt the same way. "But there's nothing to tie him to the crime. We're stuck."

Considering the room was full of dogs, it was remarkably quiet. Occasionally some of the dogs would start barking or growling, but Jillie guessed most of the animals were intimidated by the strange surroundings and the large number of strange dogs, and they sat quietly, albeit alertly, beside their masters' chairs.

But Dan Burgess wasn't about to settle for that. The city council members were all seated in deep leather chairs at a half-moon table. In front of each of them was a microphone. The mayor, seated in the middle, leaned forward and tapped his microphone as if to test it. He received the instant attention of everyone in the room.

Dan cleared his throat. "Before we begin the meeting tonight, we need to clear the room of all the dogs. Come on, folks, you know they're not allowed in here."

A disapproving murmur filled the room. A man a couple of rows back stood up.

"Forget it, Burgess," he said. "If you're going to sit here and decide the fate of these animals tonight, you can damn well look at 'em while you do it."

Applause rose loudly from the floor, and a few dogs started barking.

Dan tapped on the microphone again, signaling for quiet. Eventually he got it. "The dogs make too much noise. They'll interfere with discussion."

Jillie lifted Corky into her arms and leapt to her feet, incensed. "Now wait one minute, Mr. Mayor. It's my understanding that you planned to push this ordinance through without any discussion at all. Is that what you're trying to do by making us all take our dogs out of here?"

She was answered by a resounding chorus of *yeah*s from the audience.

Dan held up his hand, gesturing denial. Gradually the room quieted again, except for a string of yips from a Chihuahua near the back.

"I'm not trying to avoid public discussion of the measure," he lied manfully. "Not at all. But we have rules, and one of the rules is that no dogs are allowed in City Hall."

Mary Todd stood up. "We have other rules, too, Daniel. One of them is that proposed ordinances should be open to public discussion. We're the public and we're here to discuss it."

"But the dogs—"

"Will stay," Mary said. "There are only fifty or sixty of us here in this room, but have you looked outside?"

Dan suddenly looked nervous. "What do you mean? What's going on outside? Corrigan?"

Blaise rose. "Well, I'd estimate there are another four or five hundred dog owners with their dogs outside, Mr. Mayor. I've radioed for crowd control."

"And there are more of them coming, Daniel," Mary continued, rapping her cane for emphasis. "This time you've tried to gore *everybody's* ox." She looked over at Jillie. "Or is it *oxen*?"

Jillie shrugged. "I have no idea."

"Whatever." Mary turned her attention back to the mayor. "Did you even bother to count up the number of dog owners there are in Paradise Beach? It'll cost you a lot more than any campaign contribution can make up for if you offend all these people."

Dan's complexion turned even pastier. "Look," he said, "we have to follow the rules. I'll let everybody and their dogs stay, but we have to run this meeting decorously and according to the agenda. That's the way it's done. Now everybody sit down and be quiet."

Having gotten what they wanted, at least initially, everyone sat down. Except for the inevitable rustling of a roomful of people, and occasional whines or growls from the canine attendees, the room became quiet.

The meeting was called to order and the minutes of the last meeting were read. Jillie nearly fell asleep listening to the litany of boring issues: rezoning a lot, parking difficulties at a condominium, advertising Paradise Beach in additional travel magazines, installing another traffic light on the boulevard.

But then came the next item on the agenda. "New Christmas ornaments for the boulevard," announced one of the council member, Andrew Barkdale. "At the last meeting we had substantial discussion on the issue and concluded that the city needs new ornaments along the boulevard. The old ones are beginning to look frayed and dirty—"

"Beginning to?" interrupted Verna Curtis, another council member. "They look as if they were purchased fifth or sixth hand at a junk store. Now, admittedly they look fine at night when they're lit up, but in the daylight, when most people see them, they're pathetic."

"We already agreed on that at the last meeting," Barkdale reminded her rather impatiently. "We agreed they need replacing. We assigned Tess Lauder, of the public works department, to research the issue and come up with some suggestions for us that fit within the budget and will serve the purpose. Ms. Lauder?"

A severe-looking woman of about fifty-five stood up. "Considering the budget you gave me, gentleman, I was lucky to find anything at all that might work."

The council members and the mayor exchanged looks. Barkdale leaned forward. "Are you saying you need more money?"

"I'm saying that it's been so damn long since this city bought any Christmas decorations that you're pathetically out of touch with the cost of things. Then you gave me a whole list of your wants, which elevated the cost considerably. Let me see here . . ." She flipped through several pages of her yellow pad. "Yes, here we are. You wanted glittery tinsel, tiny lights, big bows. Everything shiny had to be tarnish proof because of the salt air."

She closed her pad and looked up at the commissioners. "It was a difficult task, to say the least. And no one, by the way, is prepared to guarantee anything against corrosion by salt air. Moreover, at the price the city is willing to pay for some one hundred decorations, nobody's willing to guarantee anything will last through a single season."

"Oh," said Barkdale.

Ms. Lauder pushed her glasses higher on her nose and continued, this time with slides projected on a screen to the right of the commissioner's dais. "Here we have them, gentlemen: Christmas stockings, candy canes, and wreaths. All the decorations are no more than a foot in height, which will look ridiculously small from the light posts, but we can't afford anything bigger unless you give me more money."

"Oh." The commissioners exchanged looks. Barkdale leaned forward, looking at Ms. Lauder. "Is that an ultimatum?"

She never blinked. "You get what you pay for. This is it."

"Then maybe we need to consider a bigger budget."

"Then maybe you need to consider getting someone else to do this thankless job," Ms. Lauder said, snapping her notebook closed. "You gave me a ridiculous set of parameters, a ridiculously small allotment of money, and a ridiculously short period of time. I managed to stay within all these ridiculous guidelines and present you with several options, and all you can say is that maybe you need to give me a bigger budget?

Maybe you need to make me do this all over again?"

The commissioners squirmed uncomfortably. "Now, Ms. Lauder," said Barkdale, "you've done all this work, and a small upgrade ought to be relatively easy—"

"What do you know about it?" Tess Lauder demanded. "You sit up there at your fancy desk and delegate people to do things and you never consider what you're asking of us. You never consider how much time and effort we put into these things, or how hard it is to meet your stupid requirements!"

"Now, Ms. Lauder—"

"Oh, shut up! All of us are getting sick to death of doing things according to your almighty specifications only to have you tell us to do it all over again when you don't like the results! Wake up. Think about these things before you assign the damn task!" She threw down her notebook with a bang and folded her arms across her breasts. "We're not slaves, you know. We're people. We have feelings. Needs. Hopes. Dreams!"

Utter silence greeted this outburst. A full minute ticked by before Verna Curtis finally cleared her throat. "Maybe we shouldn't buy decorations at all. Perhaps there's a First Amendment issue here, and we shouldn't use city funds to buy these things."

Felix Crumley started to speak, but was cut off by Tess Lauder.

"That's right," the woman said. "Weasel out of it now, after all the work is done! Don't put any decorations up at all! Who cares? Would *I* care?"

"Ms. Lauder . . . Tess . . ." Barkdale and the mayor spoke at the same time. They looked at each other and Barkdale, with a wave of his hand, deferred to the mayor.

Dan turned his attention to Tess. "I'm going to

move that the commission table the further discussion of Christmas decorations until the next meeting pending a study as to whether we can increase the decoration budget."

"I second," said Verna Curtis.

All hands were raised in support, leaving Tess Lauder nothing more to do or say. She bent and picked up her pad, resuming her seat as if she hadn't just thrown a fit.

"The next item on the agenda," Barkdale said, "is dogs. Somehow we have the draft of a proposed ordinance to consider." He looked over the top of his glasses at Burgess. "I don't recall the dog issue having been discussed before, Mr. Mayor. Did I miss something?"

Dan Burgess shifted in his seat. "No, Mr. Barkdale. I undertook the drafting of the ordinance on my own initiative to save time. Little more than a week ago there was an incident that made it apparent our current leash law may be inadequate."

Verna Curtis spoke impatiently. "I don't know how much more adequate you can get than a law that says all dogs must be kept leashed at all times."

"Well, *apparently*," Dan said, with a sharp edge of sarcasm, "the penalties aren't strong enough. Rover, a dog well known to the majority of us, strays all the time. Most of us have sworn at one time or another that we were going to kill that animal. This time, however, he did more than leave a pile in your yard or drag Andrew's garbage all over the street. He bit a *tourist*."

"Oh, for God's sake," said one man. "What if he'd bitten a local? Would we even be discussing this? I'm getting so damn sick and tired of the way you all pander to tourists!"

A murmur of agreement rose, but Dan was busy

banging a gavel and calling for quiet. "Sir, the chair hasn't recognized you."

"To hell with the chair," called someone else. "We don't need a law like this for every dog when only *one* dog is the problem!"

"Uh-oh," Mary said to Jillie. "I don't like the turn this is taking."

"Me either," said Blaise from her other side. "I don't want this to turn into a move to lynch Rover."

Jillian looked down at the dog on her lap and thought about how much the little puppy had already come to mean to her. In such a short time she had become emotionally attached. What about Cal Lepkin? He must be terribly attached to Rover.

She found herself on her feet, facing the crowd, Corky in her arms. "We don't need to turn on Rover, either. He has only bitten once. The injury wasn't even serious."

Fielding leapt to his feet. "You wanna bet? He gored my . . . uh . . . posterior."

"He *scraped* your fanny," Jillie corrected him. "Jeez, Fielding, you could hardly raise more than a couple of blood drops."

One of the standing men looked at Fielding. "*That* was the cause of all *this*? Cripes, man, my dog does that much to me when we're playing! If it didn't take stitches, you didn't get bitten! Do you know what a dog's jaws can *do*?"

"He bit me, I tell you!" Fielding was indignant that anyone would doubt his word.

"And he's in quarantine," Blaise added, rising also. "But he had all his shots, so you really don't have to worry about it."

"It doesn't matter whether he's in quarantine or had all his shots," Fielding insisted. "If he'd been on a leash, he wouldn't have bitten me to begin with!"

"So?" asked Barkdale. "So? Dogs get off the leash and out of their cages sometimes. It happens. That's why we have fines. And you didn't even get seriously hurt!"

"I *was* hurt."

Jillian shook her head. "Your *pride* was hurt, Fielding."

"What would *you* know about it?" her ex-husband argued. "You weren't bitten!"

"No, but I treated the bite, remember? It was nothing but a little scrape."

"It was still a bite!"

Blaise spoke. "Maybe you ought to tell all these people why the dog bit you."

"Why?" Fielding looked at him like he was out of his mind. "How the hell should I know why the damn mutt bit me?"

"It was obvious to me," Blaise said. "I guess you just don't know how to put two and two together."

"Huh?"

"Jillian was throwing you out of her house, remember? And you were yelling and waving your hands at her. I saw the whole thing from my driveway. That was the reason I came over when I saw her let you back in the house. I was afraid you'd threatened her."

"Threatened her!" Fielding looked thunderstruck.

"That's what the dog thought, too."

"How the hell can you know what a dumb dog was thinking?" Fielding demanded. "Did the two of you hold a conference to discuss it? Or maybe you exchanged faxes afterward?"

"Actually," Blaise said drily, "he radioed me on the police frequency, asking for reinforcements."

A laugh rolled through the crowd, but it only served to make Fielding angrier.

"That dog is a menace," Fielding said. "He came

after me again when he escaped from quarantine. How the hell did he get out of quarantine, anyway? Is there some kind of conspiracy in this town?"

"Conspiracy?" At least three people said that in unison.

"Come on, man," said someone in the crowd, "get a grip."

"I *have* got a grip," Fielding said hotly. "Someone let that dog out of quarantine."

"I did."

Instant silence fell in the room as everyone's eyes sought the speaker. Jim Knapp, Jillie's mailman, stepped to the front of the room.

"I let the dog out," he said. "It's unnatural to lock a dog up that way, apart from its owner. It's cruel. And Rover's no more got rabies than I do! The dog had his shots and he was only trying to protect a woman from a man who's been pestering her. A man who has been charged with stalking her."

"I haven't stalked anybody," Fielding roared.

"Tell that to the judge," Jim Knapp said. "We all know what we've been seeing."

"Why, you . . . you . . ."

Knapp shook his head. "Protest all you want, Wainwright. The woman divorced you months ago and moved all the way here to get away from you. She hardly gets her feet on the ground here and you show up. Then you sic your mother on her."

"Now, wait one minute!"

Knapp shrugged. "I ain't waiting for nobody, and this hearing is a farce." He faced the council members. "You ain't gonna pass any law that puts every stray dog to death. You know you ain't. You all might have brains the size of peas, but you ain't about to piss off all the voters in Paradise Beach by threatening their little doggies."

Barkdale looked at the others. "He's right, you know."

They nodded—except for Dan Burgess, who looked as if he wanted to strangle somebody.

"You stupid yokels," said Fielding. "Let me tell you how this ought to be done!"

There was little else he could have said that was so likely to arouse wrath. While some, though by no means all, of the local people depended on tourism for their livelihood, they were all sick of outsiders who, after spending a few days or weeks visiting, felt they had a God-given right to tell Floridians how to do things. The room erupted, and depending on who was shouting, the villains were tourists, Yankees, rich folks, or dog haters.

Jillie leaned over to Blaise. "In case you can't guess, the way things ought to be done is Fielding's way."

"I kinda thought so."

"I'm getting out of here. Corky's shivering and I've heard all I want to hear." She turned to Mary to ask if she wanted to leave.

"I'm staying," Mary said. "I haven't enjoyed a brouhaha like this in a long time!"

Outside, the crowd was already beginning to dissipate as word spread that the dog measure had been tabled. People with dogs of all descriptions were trailing away from City Hall in every direction. The police who had come to provide crowd control were leaning against their patrol cars and chatting with each other. Jillie put Corky down and let her sniff around the shrubbery beside the walk.

A few minutes later, Blaise joined her.

"Do you need to call the riot squad?" she asked.

"Nah. I figure I'll wait until we need the coroner."

She laughed and shook her head. "The really amazing thing is that I ever thought Fielding was suave."

"He has an absolute genius for putting his foot in it, doesn't he?"

"It's beginning to look that way."

"Come on." He took her hand. "I'll walk you and Corky home."

Full darkness had fallen and the breeze had shifted, blowing colder air from the mainland. Jillie hunched her shoulders in her light jacket and almost laughed at herself. Up north, temperatures like these in January would be considered balmy, but here she was feeling cold.

"I think we've heard the last of the dog ordinance," Blaise said. "Dan Burgess may try to resurrect it one more time in hopes of getting that campaign contribution, but I don't think the rest of the council will agree."

"It doesn't look like it. And now maybe Fielding and his mother will pack up their tents and go home."

"We can only hope."

The boulevard was crowded with cars, people out looking for a way to spend their evening. Jillie found herself watching license plates, noting all the states and provinces that were represented.

"Would you like to stop somewhere for a drink?" Blaise asked.

"Actually, I've had all I can stand of people for one day. I just want to put my feet up."

"Oh." He didn't say anything for another block. "When are you going to tell Fielding and his mother to go home?"

"I can't do that. They're family."

He looked down at her, his expression inscrutable. "They *were* family, Jill. You divorced them and they're not family any longer."

"A divorce doesn't just automatically end family ties."

"It does between the divorced couple."

He was right, and Jillie found herself wondering why she resisted the notion so much.

"Maybe," he said almost gently, "you need to realize that you don't have to have a family, and most especially not *that* family, in order to matter."

That comment hit her with all the force of a speeding bus. Jillie gasped as her entire self-image was shattered. Unconsciously she quickened her step, wanting to escape this man who saw her more clearly than she wanted to see herself.

"Jill—"

"No. Just stay away from me." She turned on him, facing him on the darkened street, not caring whether others might hear. "You're so damned perfect, so sure of yourself, so . . . so sure you know what other people ought to do! You sit in judgment on all the rest of us, hardly letting life touch you! What the hell do you know about things that hurt?"

Whirling, she hurried away, hoping she'd lose him in the dusk. Instead, his footsteps paced hers, letting her know that he wasn't going away.

"Leave me alone!" she said over her shoulder.

"I will." His answer sounded as if it were coming from between his teeth. "Just as soon as I'm sure you get home safely."

"Damn it, quit being so perfect!"

"I'm not perfect!"

"Yes, you are!"

"The truth of the matter is, *you're* the one trying to be perfect."

Her anger ratcheted up another notch. "I am not!"

"Are too! Jillie, you let people walk over you as if you were dust beneath their feet because you're so afraid they might not like you. Christ, I'm amazed you ever got up the nerve to ditch Fielding! But you probably would have done it years ago if you hadn't been so afraid of being disliked!"

"I'm not afraid of being disliked! I have a big mouth and it makes people mad at me all the time!"

"Your big mouth is not as big as you think, and it's largely directed at people who scare you."

"Where's your degree in psychology, Mr. Know-It-All?"

"I don't need a degree to see what's as plain as the nose on your face, woman. You're letting Harriet and Fielding push you around like you don't matter because you're afraid they might go away and never come back. Is that because your parents went away and never came back? Or is it because you kept getting shifted around from foster home to foster home? What makes you so afraid of losing even the people who are hurting you?"

She whirled around, glaring at him. "Look, Dr. Freud, I don't need any two-bit analysis from a two-bit cop in a two-bit town. Blood is thicker than water."

His expression gentled suddenly, and his voice lowered. "I scare you, don't I, sweetheart? I terrify you."

All of a sudden she wanted to cry. Her anger evaporated as swiftly as if it were a balloon that had been punctured, and she hated him for being able to surmount her defenses that easily. "What the hell are you talking about?"

"Blood may be thicker than water, but the Wainwrights are no more your blood kin than I am . . . and you know it. You usually think more clearly than that, so I guess I have you running scared." He spread his hands. "Sorry. I'm just tired of watching you get beaten up by those two jerks."

"They're not beating me up!" Oh, no? asked one corner of her mind. Then what else do you call it?

"Emotionally, little by little, they're turning you into a bloody pulp."

"Don't be absurd!"

"Then tell me one thing either of them has done that you can point to as proving they love you. Just one thing, Jill."

"They came to Florida!"

He shook his head. "Since the instant she arrived, Harriet has been using every weapon in her arsenal to undermine your self-confidence. She implied you were the reason Fielding cheated. Then she totally redecorated your house right down to the dishes, as good as telling you that you have no taste. Then Fielding bought the house and told you you didn't have to pay rent, implying he didn't think you could stand on your own two feet. Both of them have been engaged in a concerted effort to turn your strength of purpose into pudding so you'd trot tamely back to Massachusetts with them. And remember, Fielding didn't deny he was behind the graffiti that upset you so much. How many times would someone have to scrawl a message on your home or business before you'd become afraid and head back home with them?"

A shudder passed through her, and then another. It wasn't really that cold, but she felt as if she were frozen to the bone. Neither Fielding nor his mother had been treating her any differently than they had before the divorce. Had she simply gotten used to abuse? Or was Blaise exaggerating? Another shiver ran through her.

"Come on," he said. "Let's get you home before you freeze."

This time she didn't try to run from him. When he reached for her arm, she let him tuck it through his and lead her down the street toward her house.

She was feeling suddenly fragile, as if their confrontation had somehow turned her from flesh and bone into delicate glass. Transparent glass, to judge by the things he had been saying. She felt as if a cold wind were blowing through her very center, as if her most private self had been mercilessly exposed to the elements. Worse, she didn't know what she believed about herself anymore.

They rounded the corner and both their houses came into view. Blaise's was dark except for a light in an upstairs window. Jillie's was brightly lit, and when she saw movement at the kitchen window, she stopped dead.

"Oh, hell, Harriet is waiting for me." If ever there was a last straw, this was it. Her ex-mother-in-law was probably waiting to give her a hard time about Fielding's being charged with stalking, or about her opposition to the damn dog ordinance. The world suddenly blurred as tears filled her eyes.

"Come on," Blaise said. "You and Corky can stay with me again tonight. You don't have to go in there and face her right now."

The strong thing to do would be to march in and face Harriet then and there, and Jillie knew it. But she was tired of being tough and independent, and right now all she wanted to do was hide somewhere and lick her wounds before she marched into the next fray. She looked up at Blaise.

He reached out with a tender finger and brushed away a tear that had escaped and was rolling down her cheek. "Come on. Give yourself some time to regroup. You can battle the dragon tomorrow."

Jillie hesitated only a moment before agreeing. Tomorrow was soon enough. Soon enough for everything.

Sixteen

Blaise had left some windows open, and the house felt chilly inside, chilly and damp. After closing the windows, he lit a small fire in the living room fireplace and made them some tea while Jillie sat on the couch and stared broodingly into the flames. Corky curled up on the hearth rug and fell deeply asleep.

"I'm sorry."

The sound of Blaise's voice startled Jillie, dragging her out of the depths of deep thought. She had forgotten where she was, and that she wasn't alone. "Sorry for what?"

"Being so hard on you. It's really none of my business."

"Then why did you make it your business?"

He hesitated, then stepped further into the room. "Because I'm congenitally incapable of minding my own business?"

She looked straight at him then and found herself smiling faintly. "Really?"

He crossed the room and went to sit beside her. Out in the kitchen the teakettle began to whistle. "Actually," he said, "I can't stand to watch them hurt you."

She looked at him then as she had rarely looked at a man before. Yes, she'd noticed before that he was good looking. Heck, he was sexy enough to make her feel weak in the knees. But he was also warm and caring, and he seemed to be genuinely concerned for her. For the first time in forever, she looked at a man as a friend.

Something hard and cold inside her began to thaw and crumble, and she felt terrified. It wasn't safe to care. The one time she'd been foolhardy enough to let herself, she'd wound up with Fielding. Not that Blaise was anything like Fielding, but he might abandon her.

And in a sense, that was what Fielding had done by having affairs. She had told herself it wasn't the same thing at all, and had clung long and hard to her marriage because he would come back to her between affairs, and that was proof he hadn't really abandoned her. But he had. And finally even she couldn't make herself believe otherwise any longer, so she had left.

And she certainly wasn't fool enough to run that risk again, was she? No, of course not.

So what was she doing letting herself fall into Blaise's arms, letting him cradle her close and whisper comforting words into her ear as she battled back more tears?

"It'll be okay," he whispered, tucking her head against his shoulder and stroking her hair gently. "It'll be just fine. You'll see."

And maybe the scariest thing of all was that she couldn't remember when it had ever felt so good to

be held. Or when she had ever felt so safe. A deep
languor had infused her limbs, keeping her where she
was. Leaning against Blaise Corrigan was at once the
hardest and the easiest thing she had ever done.

The teakettle kept whistling insistently, and finally
Blaise laughed softly. "Sorry. I'd better go make that
tea . . . or at the very least turn off that damn kettle."

"Sure." Reluctantly she sat up, freeing him. The loss
of his embrace was almost physically painful to her,
and she had to fight a ridiculous urge to reach out
and cling to him.

But no, she wasn't going to cling to anybody, not
ever again. She knew better than that. The only way
to be safe in this world was to stand on your own two
feet. Alone.

Blaise returned with two steaming mugs of tea. He
placed them on the coffee table, then resumed his seat
beside her. Her impulse was to lean over so that she
rested against his shoulder, but she resisted it. She
was just tired and frustrated, she told herself, and tomorrow she would want to kill herself for her weakness tonight.

Just then Blaise's doorbell rang.

He looked at Jillie and rolled his eyes. "I should
have gotten an unlisted address as well as an unlisted
phone number. I'll be right back."

The foyer was blocked from view by a wall, but
Jillie could hear Rainbow Moonglow's voice.

"I'm so sorry to bother you, Blaise," Rainbow said,
"but I have a message for Jillie."

"Well, I . . . um . . ."

Jillie started to rise, sensing Blaise was hesitating
because he didn't want her to become the subject of
gossip. She didn't particularly want that herself, but
she also didn't want Blaise to feel he had to lie to
protect her.

"It's all right," Rainbow said. "I know she's here." She chuckled. "Being psychic has a few advantages. Not many, but a few."

Jillie was on her feet when Blaise brought Rainbow into the living room. The psychic smiled warmly at her and waved away an offer of tea.

"I won't keep you long," she told them. "It's just that I had the strongest premonition tonight and I felt I had to tell you right away, Jillie."

Jillie sank back on the couch, clasping her hands tightly in response to the sudden nervousness in the pit of her stomach. At some point, she found herself thinking, things in her life had to stop going wrong. Didn't they?

"It's about some people who are pursuing you right now," Rainbow continued. "A man and a woman. I gather you know them. Anyway, I just had this strong feeling—Jillie, don't trust them. They're trying to take something away from you."

Jillie spread her hands. "I don't have anything to take!"

Rainbow closed her eyes a moment, as if looking inward for something, or listening intently to a voice only she could hear. "No," she said finally, "they *do* want to take something from you, but it's something you don't know about. Don't trust them. And that," she added with a smile, "is that. I've said what I needed to."

Jillie didn't quite know how to respond. "Thank you."

"Not necessary. You know these people, don't you? I get the definite feeling you know them. Just be careful."

A few seconds later she was gone.

"Does she do that often?" Jillie asked Blaise.

He shook his head. "I don't think so. But then I

don't know what she does with everyone else. That's the first time she's ever showed up here, though."

"Well, she was obviously talking about Fielding and Harriet."

"Obviously."

"But it's not like the whole town doesn't know who they are."

He smiled. "By now I think the whole county knows who they are. They certainly make a lot of noise, don't they?"

"To say the least. I keep trying to remember if they were always this obnoxious."

He sat beside her again and twisted around so that he faced her. "It doesn't matter, Jillie. Stop second-guessing yourself. Whatever you did in the past you did because it was the best thing to do at the time. Just keep telling yourself that."

"Well, I can't."

"Why not?"

She shrugged a shoulder, aware she was treading very near to something dangerous. "If I could make that big a mistake before, if I could be that blind, then how can I be sure I won't do it again?"

"Oh." He said the word heavily.

"Yeah. *Oh.*" She sighed. "Well, I'll have to think about that one sometime, but right now I'm just plain pooped."

"I'll walk you to bed."

"The dog . . ."

"I'll take care of her." He took her hand as they climbed the stairs to the guest room. In the excitement that morning, she had crept out without making the bed, and it was just as she had left it, the covers flung back, the pillow still dented from the weight of her head.

"Good night." She turned to smile up at him, but

the smile died stillborn before the sudden ferocity of his gaze. "Blaise . . . ?"

He swooped on her like an eagle toward its prey and claimed her mouth in a kiss that left her breathless. When he lifted his head, she sagged back against the door frame and stared dazedly at him.

"I want you." He said it baldly . . . so baldly there was no way she could pretend to misunderstand.

"I . . . no." She shook her head and tried to back into her room. "I . . . don't think that would be wise."

"Why the hell not?"

"Because . . . because everything's a mess right now. Because of Fielding and Harriet and the vandalism and—"

He interrupted ruthlessly. "What does any of that have to do with this?" He stepped toward her, pressing his lower body to her, making her inescapably aware of "this."

Breathing had suddenly become nearly impossible. "Everything . . ." she gasped. "It has everything to do with . . ."

"You're just afraid."

He was right. Blaise Corrigan was always right, and that stirred a spark of irritation in her. "So I'm afraid. I have a right to be afraid!"

"Of course you do." He pressed even closer. "I'm scared, too. Scared witless."

He didn't look like it. Nor did he feel like it . . . oh, heavens, she just wanted to melt into him. Wanted to feel every hard line of him pressed to every soft curve of her. Wanted to do wicked, nasty, delightful things with him. "You're not scared," she argued on a wisp of air. "Why should you be?"

"I *am* scared," he said flatly. "I want you so damn much I think I'll explode if I can't have you. But what if you don't want me, too? What if I can't make you happy? What if I disappoint you? What if—"

She covered his mouth with her hand, silencing him. His admission had a curious effect on her, making her all at once strong and weak. He was as vulnerable as she was, and that somehow made her feel safe. "But . . . my life is such a mess right now. You can't want—"

He shook his head impatiently. "Don't tell me what I can't want. I want you. It's just that simple. If that means I have to deal with Fielding and Harriet and vandalism and all the dogs of Paradise Beach, then by God I will. But not tonight, Jill. Not tonight. Tonight I want it to be just you and me, and to hell with the rest of the world. It seems like I've been patient forever, but I'm not going to be patient any longer. *Now*, Jill. Just you and me. Now."

"But—"

He covered her lips with one finger. "This isn't a good time for a summit conference. Right now all I want is to make love to you. We can figure out the rest of it in the morning."

She opened her mouth, whether to agree with him or to make one last protest she wasn't sure, but before more than a whisper of breath could cross her lips, he slipped an arm around her shoulders and another beneath her knees and lifted her high against his chest. Without another word he carried her down the hallway to his bedroom.

"Blaise . . ."

His eyes burned like blue fire as he kicked open the door of his bedroom and paused on the threshold. "Yes or no, Jill. Nothing else. Just yes or no."

It was as if every yearning she had ever felt suddenly rose in a great tide within her, propelling the single word from her mouth on the merest of sighs. "Yes . . ."

Tomorrow would be soon enough for regrets.

*   *   *

He turned on a small lamp near the door. The only other light was the green glow from the display on the phone by the bed. Jillian stared at it in fascination, noting it was a multiline phone with all kinds of functions. Anything to distract herself from the sounds behind her as Blaise disrobed.

Her heart hammered rapidly, and she wondered wildly what she was doing. But then Blaise was there, standing behind her, wrapping his arms around her, driving all such questions from her mind.

He felt so warm against her back, so big and strong. She felt herself lean backward into him and with that small gesture of surrender all the tension in her slipped away, leaving her soft and compliant.

As if he sensed her surrender, he slipped his hands up beneath her cotton sweater and cupped her breasts. A shudder of delight ran through her and she unconsciously arched her back, pressing herself harder into his hands.

He drew a ragged breath. "You're dynamite," he told her huskily. "TNT."

And suddenly it was all okay. Everything was right, exactly as it was meant to be. She laughed softly and turned in his arms to face him. He was smiling, too, and the sight made her toes curl.

"I'm wearing too many clothes," she told him gravely. He wasn't wearing any at all. The sight should have intimidated her, made her a little nervous. Her knowledge of the male body was entirely limited to Fielding, and he hadn't exactly been prepossessing. But Blaise was . . . Blaise was a marvel of sinew and muscle that made her palms itch to learn his every contour.

The shyness she had expected to feel never materialized, and the nervousness had faded away. With surprising ease, she reached out and ran her hands over his chest, admiring the solidness of his pecs.

With unmistakable fire in his eyes, he reached for her sweater. An instant later it was over her head and flying across the room to vanish into the shadows. His breath escaped explosively as he released the clasp on her bra and her breasts spilled free.

"Oh, my," he said softly. "Oh, my. Tell me these are real . . ."

That startled laugh out of her. "Of course they are!" Nor did she think she was particularly well endowed.

But he was smiling, and when he filled his hands with her, all the breath left her body. "You're perfect," he whispered huskily. "Absolutely perfect . . ."

Then he bent and took one of her nipples in his mouth. If she had a coherent thought left, that scattered it to the four winds. Hot . . . tender . . . hungry . . . all those sensations registered at a place far below conscious thought, at the very center of her cells. Arching her back, she gave herself to him without reservation.

She was hardly aware when he popped the snap of her jeans, but they wound up laughing together when her pants turned inside out and got caught on her shoes.

It was so good to laugh, Jillie found herself thinking, as she lay back on the bed and watched Blaise try to untangle her shoes and jeans. Not once in all the years she had been married had she felt as comfortable with Fielding as she did right now with Blaise.

"Oh, hell," he said finally, and grabbed her heels, pulling off the shoes and pants all at once. "I'll figure it out tomorrow."

She laughed again and he laughed with her, looking at her from where he squatted between her legs . . .

Her breath locked in her throat, driving away all desire to laugh. The humor in his gaze turned into heat and she could almost feel the lick of the flames.

"Jill," he said on a rough breath, then leaned forward until he was kneeling between her legs and bending over her, drawing her face to his for a kiss that touched the very roots of her soul.

At some time in her life she must have imagined a man could make her feel this way, but that had been a fantasy she had come to believe would never be fulfilled—until this very moment, when her every nerve ending sang with awareness and need. This man electrified her as no other, freeing her from every reluctance or inhibition that might have held her back.

Reaching up, she twined her arms around his neck and drew him as close as she could, wanting to feel every inch of him pressed to every inch of her.

He was more than willing to oblige. Nudging her further onto the bed, he came up to lie beside her and draw her into a tight embrace.

No secrets now, she thought, as she felt his arousal against her. No secrets. And that delighted her.

His kiss was consuming, an invasion of his tongue that signaled unmistakably the conquest he intended to make. But then he hurled her to even greater heights by trailing his mouth down her neck and across her shoulders as if he needed to taste every inch of her.

Deep down in her center, an incredible pulsing had begun, a deep, hard ache that demanded satisfaction. Never had she felt this need so intensely, and she gave herself up joyously to the wonderful sensation that her body knew exactly where it was going and all she had to do was tag along for the ride.

"That's the way," he said huskily, as he felt her hips undulate helplessly. "Oh, that's so sweet, darlin'."

He found a nipple and nipped it gently with his teeth, dragging a groan from her. One of her hands flew to his head and grabbed him tightly, pressing him even closer as ever-strengthening waves of passion washed through her.

"Blaise . . ." She whimpered his name, needing more. Needing him.

"Not so fast, honey," he whispered. "I've hardly . . . begun to explore . . ."

Explore. The word caught her attention, seeming as it did to describe perfectly what was happening this very first time. And if he could explore, so could she.

Seized by a sudden courage, she began to run her hands over him, discovering planes and angles, learning where he was ticklish and what could make him groan. She wanted him to feel just as much as he was making her feel. Wanted him to be as helpless before the force of passion as she was.

Wanted him to be *hers*.

"Jill . . . Jillie . . ." He seemed to be incapable of saying anything but her name. With his mouth he latched onto her breast and sent his hand foraging between her thighs, finding damp heat and swollen petals, causing her to groan and arch against him almost desperately. Her hands fell away from him and grabbed at the bedding, giving him a much needed moment to gather his self-control—what little was left. . . .

She was beautiful. She was delightful. She was the kind of lover he had dreamed of—unpracticed and generous, offering whatever she could, wanting to share fully these moments of growing passion. She was, however, in danger of driving him over the pinnacle all too soon.

He wanted to slow down and savor these moments,

to garner memories and take the time to enjoy each new discovery.

But it wasn't going to happen that way. He could feel it in the increasingly hungry movements of her body, and in the increasing demands of his. This first time would not be the luxuriant experience he had hoped for.

And frankly, he was rapidly getting past caring. When Jillie lifted toward him and moaned his name yet again, he gave up and gave them both what they wanted.

Pawing around in his bed table drawer, he found a condom.

She was enjoying it, too, he realized. She enjoyed knowing her power over him, and how maddening her light little touches were to him. She was loving it.

Awareness brought the glimmer of a smile to his lips, but then, staring straight into her eyes, he sank into her, claiming her, filling her with promises that had no words.

Her eyes widened then fluttered closed as a soft smile came to her lips. "Oh, Blaise," she whispered. "So . . . good . . ."

He'd have liked to draw it out for both of them, but he'd been wanting this for too long. Ever since she had glared at him in the headlights of her car and told him she wasn't drunk. He'd believed then that she must be full of fire, and she was . . . she was . . .

He thrust strongly, and she only seemed to gather him closer. "Yesss," she whispered on a gasp. "Yessss . . ."

He didn't hear any more. His body carried him over the precipice, and he dimly realized that she had come with him, leaping over the edge and falling . . . falling . . .

They lay together afterward, cooling down,

wrapped in a warm glow of repletion. Jillie's head rested on Blaise's shoulder and she was wondering why she'd never before noticed just how good skin on skin felt.

"Oh, hell," Blaise said suddenly. "I need to walk the dog."

"Probably." She drew a circle on his chest with her index finger. "I'll do it."

"No, just stay in bed. I'll take care of it."

Jillie twisted, putting her hands on her hips, fully aware that she looked anything but daunting with her hair all tousled and her breasts bobbing free. "Damn it, Corrigan, quit being perfect. I said I'd take care of it."

"Who's the chief of police around here?"

She shrugged exaggeratedly. "In this jurisdiction we're equals."

He smiled crookedly. "I can live with that."

"Yeah?"

"So we'll check on the dog together."

He pulled on a pair of gym shorts and gave her a T-shirt to wear. Together they went downstairs and found the puppy still sound asleep. When she heard them, Corky yawned and stretched, then sat up wagging her tail.

They looked all around but didn't see any sign that she'd messed. Jillie scooped her up and gave her a big hug, telling her what a good girl she was. Corky loved the attention, wagging her tail madly and licking Jillie's chin and cheek with frantic affection.

"I'll take her out back and give her a chance to go," Blaise offered. "Then I'll make us a snack. I don't know about you, but I'm starving, and right now I feel I could eat a whole cow."

"I could make something."

He shook his head, smiled, and touched the tip of

her nose with his index finger. "You already cooked once for us tonight. I'll take care of everything."

She ran upstairs and put on her jeans, then went out onto the deck while he walked the dog down below. Leaning against the railing, she breathed deeply of the sea air and felt goosebumps spring out all over her arms and back. It had gotten decidedly cold out here. Right now, she thought, it didn't feel like Florida at all.

From down below she could hear Blaise talking quietly to the puppy, who seemed to be more interested in sniffing around and chasing bugs than in doing her business.

Listening to Blaise talk gently to Corky, feeling the cool breeze toss her hair, looking up at the stars overhead—something in the combination unlocked something deep inside her, waking dreams she hardly remembered, dreams which had been abandoned long ago.

What she wanted, she realized with trepidation, was the coziness of a family . . . someone with whom she could share her days, someone to come home to, someone who would come home to *her*.

When she had been a child, she sometimes had walked down the darkened streets around whichever home she happened to be living in. Looking into the brightly lighted windows of her neighbors she had felt so sad. She wanted to belong to a home like that, a home with golden light spilling out its windows, a home where people came together on winter evenings and belonged to each other.

Fielding had never made her feel as if she belonged. Maybe no one ever could. Maybe she'd been an outsider for far too long ever to feel she might be an insider.

What struck her as equally sad was that once she

had made up her mind, she'd left Fielding without a backward glance. Not once had she felt she'd lost anything. Not once had she felt any sorrow or guilt. She had felt nothing but relief.

And that was sad. Terribly sad. Maybe she had felt nothing because they had never created a real family. Maybe she was incapable of growing the kind of roots that made someone belong. Maybe that was why Fielding had turned to other women.

"Hey." Blaise spoke from the door behind her. "Come in before you get chilled." Corky stood beside him on the leash, her head cocked inquisitively.

Jillie felt a sudden rush of affection for the two of them and it tightened her throat with yearning. It should be like this all the time, she thought.

In the kitchen, she helped Blaise make hot turkey sandwiches. It kind of surprised her that he had cooked a turkey for himself, but there was the carcass on the refrigerator shelf, along with containers of gravy and stuffing.

"Every now and then," Blaise said, when he saw her looking, "I get a real hankering for turkey and all the trimmings. By the time I get done I have enough food to feed an army for a week, so I wind up eating it for three meals a day. Help me out here."

The stuffing was excellent, as was the gravy. When Jillie complimented him, he grinned and said, "See? I have a few redeeming graces."

"So . . . you'll cook Thanksgiving dinner for me?" She meant it as a joke, but when he looked at her, his blue eyes were as serious as she'd ever seen them.

"Sure," he said. "Gladly."

A warm little glow seemed to settle into the pit of her stomach. One of the things she had most been dreading about her new life was having to spend holidays alone. At least when she'd been married to

Fielding the holidays had been busy. Singlehood promised something she hadn't faced since college: solitude on the days when everyone else was with family.

"You know," she found herself saying to Blaise, "sometimes I think that any family at all is better than none at all."

He nodded. "I gathered that."

"What do you mean?"

"Your refusal to tell the Wainwrights to take a long hike. It's what I was saying earlier."

She shook her head. "Earlier you were saying that I was afraid to be disliked. What I'm saying now is that even family you dislike can be a comfort. An anchor, if you will."

"I guess." He raised a forkful of stuffing, but didn't put it into his mouth. Instead, he looked gravely at her. "I'm at a loss on this one, Jill. I readily admit I don't know where you're coming from. How could I? I've always had some kind of family."

"Tell me about them."

He shrugged. "What's to say? My dad died a couple of years ago, but my mom is still teaching math at UF. She comes to visit during semester breaks. I have two sisters, both living on the West Coast with their husbands and children. They come this way every couple of years to visit. Then there's my brother, Rafe. He retired at the age of thirty to Key West where he bought a business on Duval Street and never has to wear anything but shorts and T-shirts. He keeps telling me I need to come down to watch the sunset, and I keep telling him I see the same sunset over the same body of water from here."

"Maybe he means you need to shake off some of the responsibility."

Blaise laughed and shook his head. "Yeah. He looks

like a beach bum, but there's a hell of a lot of responsibility in running a business. It's all an act."

"Do you ever visit him?"

"Yeah, every now and then. But Key West gives me the heebie-jeebies."

"Why?"

"Do you know how small that island is? And how far from the mainland? I get down there and start thinking what would happen if there was a hurricane with a twelve- or sixteen-foot storm surge. I seriously question whether they could get all those people off the keys in time along that one narrow highway."

She felt a sudden tenderness for him. So Blaise could be afraid, really afraid. "You're thinking like a cop, even on vacation."

"Actually," he said wryly, "I think it's some kind of fear, like claustrophobia. What do you suppose they'd call it? Hurricane-ophobia? Key West–ophobia?"

A smile curved her lips. "Maybe. Some people just don't like islands."

"Maybe. But this is an island, too, and it doesn't bother me. No, I'm pretty sure it has to do with US 1 being so narrow and the distance to the mainland being around a hundred miles."

"But it doesn't bother your brother?"

He shook his head. "He worries about other things, I guess. Anyway, I'm making too much of it. Basically, I go to visit him, but I wouldn't want to live there. It's just not my kind of place. But then, neither is Miami."

They were sitting in the dining room, and now he leaned across the table and took her hands in his. "What do you say we take Saturday for ourselves and go into Tampa? I think you'd like Ybor City, with all its old Cuban flavor. It's the cultural heart of Tampa.

You can even watch someone make cigars by hand, which is practically a lost art. Or we could go to the zoo, or the amusement park . . . whatever you like."

What she liked was that he was asking to spend more time with her. Only in that instant did she realize just how much she'd feared he wouldn't want to see her again. An unacknowledged tension seeped from her body, and suddenly she felt happy, happier than she could remember ever having felt. "Sure," she said, unable to hide her delight.

The doorbell rang, causing them to exchange looks.

"I swear," Blaise said, "this place really *isn't* Grand Central Station. In fact, I don't think I've *ever* had my doorbell ring this late at night."

"It could be important."

"If it was, they'd page or call me. No, it'll turn out to be somebody selling newspaper subscriptions."

Jillie waited in the dining room until she heard Harriet's voice.

"I know she's here, Chief Corrigan," Harriet said sharply. "She couldn't be anyplace else! Besides, the whole town has heard how she came creeping out of your house early this morning!"

Wondering which of her neighbors had gossiped, Jillie leapt up from the table and stormed out to the foyer just in time to hear Blaise say, "She could be at her store, Mrs. Wainwright."

No sooner were the words out of his mouth than Jillie stomped into the foyer to glare at her former mother-in-law. "You know, Harriet, you really take the cake!"

"Actually," said Blaise, "*you* take the cake. When I'm lying for you, you should at least have the decency to stay hidden."

In spite of herself, Jillie almost laughed. He stood there, looking so wryly amused, and not in the least disconcerted by what could have been an embarrassing situation. "I'm sorry," she said, trying to sound contrite.

He waved a hand. "Be my guest. Now I don't have to rack my brains trying to come up with a logical explanation for your disappearance, since you haven't disappeared. You deal with her."

"Deal with her? How am I supposed to do that? She's always been *impossible* to deal with."

His lip twitched.

Harriet objected. "I don't appreciate being discussed as if I'm not here! And just what do you think *you're* doing, young lady, staying at a strange man's house! Look at you! Why . . . that's *his* T-shirt, isn't it?"

"It's none of your business, Harriet."

"It's every bit my business! Fielding is my son! This will wound him! How can you do this to him?"

"What I do is no longer Fielding's business, Harriet. Nor is Fielding any longer my concern. How many times do I have to tell you that?" But she might as well have been talking to herself for all the difference it made.

"Of course it's his business! How can you think a silly piece of paper can make any real difference? My word, Jillian, I never thought you were so dense!"

"Dense?" Jillie felt the last civilized restraints on her behavior beginning to crack. "Harriet, if there's anyone who's dense here, it's you!"

"Me?" Harriet gasped.

"Yes, you! I *divorced* Fielding. I didn't do it because I wanted a couple of months' vacation from him. I didn't do that because I ever intended to go back to him."

"But things have changed—"

"What things? As far as I can see, *nothing* has

changed. He's still trying to have everything his way, and you're still trying to help him get it."

Harriet looked absolutely stunned. "Well, of course I'm helping him! I'm his mother!"

"But you don't get it, Harriet. He doesn't really want me back. I don't know why the hell he's pretending he does, but believe me, he doesn't really want me back."

"You're misunderstanding—"

"It doesn't matter. The bottom line is that I don't care whether he wants me back or not, because *I don't want him back*! Ever. He couldn't possibly change his personality enough to make himself attractive to me. It's over and done with, and the hurts are too deep. And deep down he knows it, Harriet. So quit pushing him and take him home with you."

Harriet's lip curled. "Trust me, I'm not pushing him. I never thought you were suitable for him, and nothing ever changed my mind! You're nothing but a little guttersnipe who married her way out of poverty."

Jillie felt as if the wind had been knocked out of her. Harriet turned sharply and left the house, slamming the door behind her, leaving Jillie gasping for air and holding herself as if she might fly apart.

"That woman," Blaise said harshly, "is pure poison. How did you ever put up with her?"

Jillie couldn't answer. She had loved Harriet. She had even come to believe Harriet loved her. But if Fielding's mother really loved her, she couldn't have said what she'd said, could she?

"Jill . . ." Blaise stepped closer and drew her into his arms. "She was just being spiteful. It was the most hateful thing she could think of. Don't take it to heart. Please."

But how else could she take it? Now Harriet had

abandoned her, too. Everyone she'd ever cared about had abandoned her. She'd be a fool to let herself care ever again.

Wrenching away from Blaise, she began to back up. She needed to keep her distance. It was the only safe way. She had to keep her distance.

"I . . . um . . . I think I'd better go home now." Then she turned and ran for the door.

Blaise had had enough. Or so he told himself. Dealing with all the Wainwrights attached to Jillie was quite enough, but having her run from him that way, as if he were some kind of devil capable of treating her the way Harriet just had, was too damn much.

He let her go and slammed the door after her, telling himself he was better off without that woman and all her scars. Christ. What was he doing getting tangled up with someone who was terrified of caring? What was he doing getting tangled up with someone so recently divorced? Had he forgotten how long it had taken him to get over it?

Wheeling around the corner into the dining room, he came face to face with the puppy. Corky was cowering under a chair, apparently disturbed by the raised voices and the door slamming. Christ, another one, Blaise thought, as he picked up the puppy and petted it reassuringly. The whole world was full of insecure, frightened, wounded hearts.

Well, of course the puppy was insecure. It had been abandoned, after all.

As had Jillie.

The reminder floated up through the layers of his irritation until it had his full attention. The dog in his arms shivered with fear, and that's what Jillie had been doing in her own way when she'd run. She had just been battered by someone whom she thought she loved.

Of course.

Blaise looked down at the puppy in his arms and thought about what had just happened. He hadn't really been giving enough thought to the long term in his pursuit of Jillian. In a very male way, he'd been reacting to his attraction to her without giving any deep thought to where it might lead.

That wasn't fair to Jillie. She was clearly too emotionally fragile to handle a casual relationship of any kind, let alone one such as they'd just embarked upon. She'd been abandoned too many times. And he had been giving only a half-assed consideration to that, being more concerned with his own feelings.

It wasn't fair to him, of course, to have to make up his mind this early in the game about whether his intentions were serious and long-term, but Blaise Corrigan had never been the kind of person who'd expected life to be fair. As his mother had been wont to say to her children when they were small, "Where on your birth certificate does it say that life has to be fair?"

It would have been a lot easier if he could have had more opportunity to know Jillian before deciding on a commitment of this magnitude, but he had also learned a long time ago that life was rarely easy.

But it was early days for a decision like this.

He looked down at the puppy, which was beginning to relax and look sleepy. If only it were that easy to soothe Jill!

A timid knock sounded at the door, and even before he opened it he knew who it was. Jillie regarded him rather timidly. "I left my purse and I thought I ought to get the dog, too."

He stepped back and waved an arm, inviting her

in, but he didn't say anything. He wasn't sure enough of himself.

She hesitated as she started to pass him. "I'm sorry about . . . everything."

He shook his head. "No apologies required."

"The way I left was kind of . . . rude."

She was looking up at him, and her eyes were imploring him for something, but he was damned if he could give it. At this point in this relationship, he wasn't sure what he had to give, and while he was unsure, he didn't dare offer her anything that might eventually cause her to be hurt.

"It's okay," he managed to say finally, as noncommittally as he could. "Don't worry about it." If she thought he was going to put his arms around her as he had just a few minutes ago and act as if she hadn't just run from him like a terrified child, he was forced to disappoint her.

Finally she turned and went to get her things from the guest room—all of them, taking care to leave nothing behind. Then, with a word of thanks, she took the puppy from him and left.

And Blaise discovered that his house was too big, and too empty.

Seventeen

"What's this I hear about a big fight between you and Blaise?" Mary Todd demanded, tapping her cane impatiently.

Jillie, who had been waxing one of the newly delivered tables for her bookstore, straightened and regarded Mary with surprise. "We didn't have a fight."

She had, however, phoned the next day while Blaise was at work, leaving a message on his machine to cancel their Saturday date. Secretly she had half hoped he'd call her and try to change her mind, but here it was Saturday and he hadn't tried to get in touch with her.

"That's what the grapevine says." Mary scowled and eased herself into a reading chair. "Everyone says you went to Blaise's the other night, that the Wainwright woman showed up, and then you came charging out of there like a bat out of hell. You went back but just long enough to get your dog."

339

Jillie sat with a thump, stunned. "Who told you all that?"

"It's what everybody's talking about!"

"But . . ." She trailed off, trying to imagine who could possibly have been interested enough to watch Blaise's house that carefully on Thursday night. And why in the world would anyone care enough to talk about it? "Good God, Mary, don't people around here have anything better to do?"

Mary cackled. "Hee! What's better than a juicy morsel of gossip, especially when it involves a newcomer and the chief of police? We've been watching that young man's antics for several years now, and this is the first time he's come this close to the brass ring."

Jillian felt her cheeks redden. "Don't be silly. We're just—friends."

"Those are some of the most famous last words ever spoken. Don't try it with me, gal. You're crazy about the man."

It was true, Jillie thought. She was crazy about the man. And like everyone else in her life, he was suddenly acting as if he wished she'd fall off the end of the earth—or go back to Massachusetts.

"What I feel doesn't matter," she told Mary finally, and stood up again to resume waxing the table. "It's certainly nobody else's business."

Mary sighed and tapped her cane impatiently on the floor. "A couple of fools, that's what the two of you are. I should probably just wash my hands of you both!"

Jillie pointed to the back of the store. "The bathroom's that way. Help yourself."

Mary's dark eyes looked intently at her, then another cackle escaped her. "You're a woman after my own heart. Blunt and outspoken."

Jillie didn't respond to the compliment, because she

wasn't sure if she was flattered. Oh, hell, who did she think she was kidding? She actually hoped that someday she'd grow up to be like Mary Todd, every bit as feisty and full of joie de vivre.

"Well," Mary continued, "there never was a fool like a fool in love."

"You should know!"

"Are you talking about me and Ted Wannamaker?" Mary cut loose another laugh. "We're not in love! We just like pretending we are."

Jillie stopped rubbing the table, giving her shoulder a brief break, and looked at Mary. "You don't lie very well."

"What do you mean?"

"When you lie your eyes get this look to them. I'm not sure how to describe it."

"How could you? You've never seen me lie!" Mary shook her head and impaled Jillie with a sharp look. "That woman has gone back up north."

"What woman?"

"You know perfectly well what woman. Don't try to fence with me, my dear. I've had a lot more practice. So that woman is gone, which leaves us only her obnoxious son to deal with. What in the world did you ever see in that jerk?"

Jillie almost laughed out loud. "Honestly, Mary, I ask myself that question a dozen times a day. What about you and Ted?"

"I'm not changing the subject, so don't bother trying. We've got to get rid of that jerk. He ruins the otherwise pleasant atmosphere of Paradise Beach. His worst failing is that he doesn't know how to lose. He offered Cal Lepkin five hundred dollars to have that dog put down."

Jillie drew a sharp breath. "You're kidding."

"I don't kid about things like that."

"Cal isn't going to do it, is he?"

"Not likely. But that ex of yours is pond scum. We need to get him out of this town. Unfortunately, we can't do that until this stalking thing is cleared up. He's stuck here until that's settled."

Jillie sat down and looked thoughtfully at Mary. "What makes you think he'd leave even if there were no stalking charges?"

"What I'm thinking, dear child, is that maybe we can get the state attorney to do the dirty work for us. What if they offer to withhold adjudication if Fielding will go away and stay away from you forever?"

"Can they do that?"

"I have a friend who says they can. You'd need to talk to him to get the details, and you'd probably have to talk to the state attorney yourself, because they don't like to go easy on stalkers. It looks bad politically."

Jillie hesitated. "I don't really think he's stalking me, Mary. He never threatened me. Well, except for the graffiti all over everything. He never denied doing it and I guess Blaise is right about it. If Fielding was doing that, then he was hoping to scare me. There couldn't be any other reason."

Mary didn't say anything.

"But I'd still hate to see him convicted of a crime." It was true. Much as she'd come to detest her former husband, she just couldn't feel comfortable about sending him to jail. Particularly for something she really wasn't sure he was doing.

"Well, that's the beauty of this adjudication-withheld thing," Mary told her. "He doesn't get *convicted*. You could kill two birds with one stone."

"How's that?"

"The way my friend explains it, the judge can withhold the conviction but insist that your ex go on probation . . . in this case we'd want his probation to stipulate that he get the hell out of Dodge."

"How?"

"Look, my dear, your ex has been charged with stalking. As part of the plea agreement, the judge can order Wainwright to stay away from you."

"Really?" She had to admit she liked the sound of that. After the last few weeks, she never wanted to see the man again. Or his mother, come to that. "And he wouldn't be convicted?"

"Not as long as he does whatever the judge says."

After the way she hadn't been able to get rid of Fielding, it sounded wonderful. "What do I have to do?"

"I'll have my friend talk to you. His name is Pierce Conlin." Mary looked around. "Do you have a phone in here yet?"

Jillie pointed and watched Mary hobble over to the wall phone that had been installed yesterday so she could handle business while getting her shop into shape. All of the carpentry was done now, and she was awaiting the first shipments of books and business equipment. In the meantime there was plenty of cleaning up and organizing to do.

While Mary waited to speak to her lawyer friend, Jillie went back to waxing the reading tables. She knew she'd probably just have to do it all over again before she finally opened, but making the tabletops gleam was giving her a sense of satisfaction that had been missing from her life for too long.

"Jillie?" Mary covered the mouthpiece of the phone. "Can you meet with Pierce Monday morning at eight-thirty? He'll explain the details then."

Jillie wondered how much this was going to cost. "Sure. I guess so," she said with a worried frown.

"All right," Mary said into the phone. "We'll see

you then, Pierce." After she hung up, she came over and patted Jillie's arm gently. "Don't worry, dear. I helped Pierce get through law school. There won't be any charge."

"Thanks." Jillie gave her a warm smile, then glanced out the window at the bright day and battled back a wave of melancholy. None of this seemed like so much fun anymore, not since she had cut Blaise out of her life.

As of Monday morning she still hadn't seen Blaise. Apparently he was trying to avoid her, because before Thursday she'd run into him all the time, everywhere. She told herself it was good he was staying out of her way, but she didn't really believe it.

Feeling utterly miserable, she climbed into her car and went to pick up Mary Todd for the trip to see the lawyer.

As they were driving over to Saint Petersburg, Mary eyed her sharply. "You look terrible, gal."

"Thank you very much."

Mary tsked. "Don't get smart with me. You *do* look terrible, and it can't be because we're finally going to get this stupid Yankee out of your hair. Did Blaise do something to upset you?"

"No! Not a thing." Nor had he. But his withdrawal, coming so hard on the heels of their lovemaking, had left her feeling raw . . . even if *she* was the one who'd run away.

"Mm." Mary tapped her cane lightly on the floorboard, and appeared to be fascinated by the tall mast of the sailboat that was slipping slowly up the waterway toward them as they crossed the drawbridge. "I guess you ran one time too many."

Jillie's hands tightened on the steering wheel as she battered down sudden annoyance. "Mary . . ."

"Oh, don't bother denying it. You're running scared, but that's hardly surprising. You've been badly hurt by that scumbag you were so ill advised to marry. If you weren't gun-shy I'd have serious qualms about your intelligence."

There didn't seem to be any good answer to that one, so Jillian remained silent. She did, however, wonder how Mary Todd had become so deeply involved in her affairs. She'd met the woman only a few weeks before and was amazed that she couldn't imagine life without her now.

"Turn left at the next light," Mary said suddenly. "It's the easiest way to get to Pierce's office."

"Is Pierce related to you?"

"Well, I suppose you could say that." Mary glanced at her and smiled. "Changing the subject, eh? All right. This time I'll let you! Pierce is actually the grandson of a dear friend of mine. Her life didn't go as well as mine—well, of course not! The poor woman married!—but she *did* manage to have a fine grandson. Anyway, she died when he was halfway through law school. I knew she'd been helping him out, but there was nothing left in her estate, so I just stepped in and took over. It seemed like the least I could do for her."

"That was very nice of you."

Mary laughed. "Pierce thinks so, too. But he may change his mind before too long, when he gets sick of me asking for free legal advice."

"Do you do that often?"

"This is the first time." Her eyes gleamed. "In my experience, the second time is one time too many for most folks. Of course, Pierce may prove to be an exception."

"Just tell me one thing, Mary. If you think marriage

is such a lousy institution, why are you trying to push me at Blaise?"

Mary shook her head as if Jillie had just asked the stupidest question in the history of the world. "My dear, it's not lousy for everyone. Occasionally you find two people who are meant for each other."

Meant for each other . . . the words settled warmly into Jillie's heart, and she found herself wondering if there really was someone meant for her. And if maybe that someone was Blaise.

Conlin's office was on Central Avenue in Saint Petersburg, away from the downtown area, in a shady section populated by other small businesses. He was seeing the woman before the start of his usual business day, and only one of his secretaries was there.

"Go right on in," she said pleasantly. "Mr. Conlin's waiting for you."

The office was pleasant, but not very large, or even very expensively appointed. Pierce Conlin seemed to match his surroundings. He was dressed in khaki slacks, a deep blue shirt, and a necktie. Tall, dark-haired, and athletic looking, he was in his mid-thirties and did not look at all like the lawyers with whom Jillie had dealt regarding her divorce—but this was Florida, after all.

When they entered his office, he was trying to putt a golf ball into a tipped-over coffee cup.

"I know, I know," he said as they entered. "How stereotypical can I get, practicing putts in my office? But I volunteered to play in a charity tournament Saturday, and I don't want to make an ass of myself!"

Grinning, he set the putter aside and came to give Mary a great big hug. "How are you doing, Grammary? You don't call me often enough."

"You know my number," Mary told him tartly. "I'm not the only one who doesn't call often enough."

"I called only three weeks ago," he said. "And you didn't feel like going out with me."

"For hot dogs! I ask you, how can a woman my age be caught eating a hot dog in public?"

But Pierce also didn't take long to come to the point. "So Mary tells me your ex has been arrested for stalking."

Jillie nodded.

"What exactly did he do?"

"Well, he followed me down here from Massachusetts, he won't stay away from me, and he may have painted graffiti on my house and business."

The lawyer steepled his hands. "Okay. Did someone catch him doing it?"

Jillie looked perplexed. "Well, no."

"Then how do they know he did it?"

"He *said* he did it." Although knowing Fielding, he may have just been being difficult.

"I see. Did he threaten you personally in any way?"

"No."

"Are you afraid of him?"

"No. Mr. Conlin—"

"Pierce, please."

"Pierce, I don't want him to go to jail for stalking. I don't think he was really stalking me. Not in a creepy, threatening way."

"Then how did he get arrested?"

Jillie explained the entire scene outside her house that morning, and Pierce nodded.

"So basically what you're telling me is we have a questionable confession, but no other evidence he did it."

"As far as I know," Jillie said.

"And you don't want him to go to jail."

"No, really, I don't. I just want him to go *home*."

Pierce nodded. "Chances are they can't convict him

for anything except trespass after warning—you *did* tell him to leave the property?''

''More than once on other occasions.''

''Okay, so they've got him on that. Well, if you're really not interested in seeing him go to jail, I can probably get the prosecutor to *nolle prosse*—drop the charges. Is that what you want?''

''Only if you can make him go immediately back to Massachusetts,'' Mary said tartly. ''He may be nothing but a public nuisance, but he is definitely a nuisance to everyone he's come into contact with. Jillie deserves to be left alone to get her new life under way, and Fielding Wainwright needs to go home and grow up!''

Pierce smiled fondly at her. ''If the state doesn't prosecute, then there's really no way anyone can make him do anything.''

''Then prosecute him,'' Mary said, tapping her cane sharply for emphasis. ''Put him on some kind of probation and make the jackanapes stay at home!''

''No,'' said Jillie, her voice firm. ''No. I don't want him prosecuted.''

Mary looked at her as if she'd taken leave of her senses. ''Are you telling me you want that man around?''

''No, of course I don't, but I don't want him to be prosecuted, either. What I want is for him to go home.''

Pierce spread his hands. ''Tell the guy you'll go to the state attorney and ask him to forget the whole thing if he'll just leave for good.''

''Will he forget?''

''The state attorney? Yeah, probably. From the sound of it, you'd be his main witness, and if you're not willing to slam the guy, he'll just want to get the case off his desk. He has enough real crime to deal with. Want me to check into it for you?"

Jillie nodded. "Please. And I'll talk to Fielding."

Jillie called Fielding at his hotel that afternoon. "Can you come over? I want to discuss something with you."

"No way, Jillian. No damn way. Not with this stalking thing hanging over my head. My attorney says I need to stay as far from you as this island will let me. I'm not even supposed to talk to you on the phone. Good-bye."

"No, wait! Fielding, I think I can get the charges dropped!"

But he'd already hung up. She slammed the receiver down, sighing with frustration. Wouldn't you know the only time she actually wanted to talk to Fielding he'd refused to talk to her? What now?

Pacing back and forth in her kitchen offered very little relief. Finally, frustrated that she wasn't accomplishing anything useful, she decided to drive over to the hotel and beard Fielding in person. Surely he'd have to listen to her then.

In her annoyance she backed too swiftly out of her driveway. In the rearview mirror she caught a flash of something moving behind her, and she instinctively swerved and hit the brake. As the car came to a stop, she heard a sickening thud.

For an instant she couldn't move a muscle. Oh, God, she had hit someone! Visions of her various neighbors flashed through her head in rapid succession, each one looking progressively worse as he or she lay on the ground behind the car.

Suddenly galvanized, she switched off the ignition, set the parking brake, and hurried around the back of the car to see how bad it was.

It could hardly have been worse.

Rover sat there staring up at her with a big grin, his pink tongue hanging out.

And Blaise Corrigan's mailbox once again lay flat on the ground.

Jillie looked from Rover to the mailbox and back. "You did it on purpose, didn't you?" she said to the dog. She was past caring if she sounded crazy. "You purposely made me run down Blaise's mailbox, didn't you?"

The dog thumped his tail and continued grinning.

"Damn it, he'll never believe it twice. You know, Rover, you really are a demon spawn. *Nobody* would believe you made me run into that mailbox twice!"

Rover merely looked proud as punch, and Jillie didn't have the heart to yell at him anymore. Giving up, she sat down on the bumper of her car and looked from the dog to the mailbox, as if she might discover the answer to a cosmic question.

Blaise was right. This dog was doing this on purpose. From the start Rover had tried to keep Fielding away from her. And now he was trying to keep her away from Fielding, although how he could have known that was where she was heading . . .

She shook her head and looked up into the impossibly blue sky. At this point she was ready to credit this dog with the ability to read minds, and that simply would not do. Thinking like that could get her sent to the funny farm.

Rover whined and squirmed a little, as if trying to get her attention.

"You know," Jillie said, "I thought you were in quarantine. I guess that's over with now, huh?"

The dog cocked his head.

"Yes, it would be," she decided, counting backwards. "It's been more than ten days since you bit Fielding."

Well, what was she supposed to do now? If she moved her car, would she be leaving the scene of an accident? And if Blaise got home before she did and found his mailbox, what would he think?

A note . . . that's what she'd do—tape a note to his door, promising to make good on the damage. That way she wouldn't have to see him. All she had to do was get the note on his door and be gone before he showed up.

Leaving the dog still seated on her driveway, she hurried into the house and hunted up paper and pen. Writing a note was the easy part. Finding tape proved to be a whole lot harder. It wasn't as if she could ever find cellophane tape when she needed it.

Finally she settled on slipping it under his door. She hurried back outside and across the yard toward Blaise's house, note in hand, and saw that the dog was still sitting behind her car. What was the matter with him?

She managed to shove the note halfway under Blaise's door, and on her way back saw that Connie Herrera was standing out front watching. She waved. Connie waved back.

"Did you run over his mailbox again?" Connie called.

Jill spread her hands. "I was trying not to hit the dog."

"What dog?"

Jillie looked and saw that Rover was nowhere in sight. "It was Rover," she told Connie. "He ran behind the car when I was backing out."

"That dog is no good."

"Oh, he's not so bad." Jillie looked around wildly for Rover as it suddenly occurred to her that he might have been sitting behind the car in that strange fashion because she had hit him, too, when she'd hit the

mailbox. And maybe now he had crawled off, injured
. . . her mind was spinning.

Connie said something else, then waved and went
back inside. Jill, meanwhile, kept looking around for
the dog, who, she was suddenly convinced, was seriously injured.

"Rover? Rover, boy, where are you?"

A whimper answered her. Looking around, she still
couldn't see him. "Rover?"

A small bark. From under the car. Oh, no! Getting
down on her knees, she looked under her car and
there was Rover, stretched out in the shade beside one
of the tires.

"Are you hurt?"

The dog thumped his tail. Dogs didn't thump their
tails when they were hurt, did they?

She heard a car engine approaching, then the
crunch of tires behind her.

"Nice view," said an all-too-familiar voice.

Blaise! Jillie froze and felt her cheeks turn red. Considering she was on her knees peering under her car,
she could imagine exactly what view he was talking
about.

"I guess my mailbox got in the way again." The car
door slammed and she heard the crunch of his footsteps as he approached. "Jill? Are you all right?"

"I'm fine," she said, refusing to look at him. "I'm
not so sure about Rover."

"Rover?" At once he knelt beside her and looked
under the car. "What happened?"

"He ran behind the car while I was backing out,
and I'm not sure if I hit him. I was trying to avoid
him when I hit the mailbox. Again." Some nightmares
just kept recurring.

"Rover?" Blaise called gently to the dog. "Come on,
fella. Come out of there so we can see if you're all

right." The dog wagged its tail but didn't move.

"I'm never going to forgive myself if I hurt him. Never."

"You can't blame yourself if he's going to be running in the path of moving vehicles. Sometimes I wonder if that dog has the sense God gave a gnat."

Kneeling side by side, resting on their elbows, they continued to regard Rover. The dog stared steadily back, grinning but not moving.

"He's not hurt," Blaise said finally. "If he was hurt he'd be whimpering, or licking himself somewhere, not sitting there like the damn Sphinx."

"You're probably right."

He nodded; they continued to stare at the dog.

"So," Jillie said finally, "what do you think he's doing?"

"If I didn't know better, I'd say that pooch looks remarkably self-satisfied, wouldn't you?"

Jillie cocked her head, thinking about it. "Maybe. He *does* look rather catlike."

"But what does *he* have to be satisfied about?"

Jillie started to look at Blaise, then thought better of it. She wasn't sure she could look at him without throwing herself into his arms. The longer she was away from him, the more she ached for him. Now he was within grabbing distance, and she was afraid she might grab.

Worse, he looked as if he didn't care one way or another. Her heart squeezed.

"Well," Blaise said finally, "Rover doesn't look like he wants to move in this lifetime. Do you need to go somewhere important?"

"Well . . . sort of. I was going to see Fielding." She wished the words unsaid as soon as they passed her lips. She could feel his gaze on her, and the questions that were going to follow.

"Fielding?" Blaise hesitated perceptibly. "Are you going back to him?"

"Good Lord, no!" Forgetting everything else, Jillie turned to look at him. "I was going to tell him I'll ask the prosecutor to drop the charges against him if he'll leave the state."

"Drop the charges?" Blaise jerked in surprise and his head banged noisily against the bumper of the car. "Shit!"

"Are you all right?" Concerned, she forgot the dog and sat up watching Blaise as he straightened and rubbed the back of his head.

"Shit," Blaise said again. "Yeah. Yeah, I'm okay. Just clumsy. That damn dog can stay there until hell freezes over, for all I care!"

She didn't for a minute believe he meant it. "Did you get a bump?"

He touched his scalp tenderly. "Yep. I must have hit the hardest part of that bumper."

"Let me see." Leaning over, she gently touched his head and felt the burgeoning bump. Touching him made everything inside her quiver with yearning, but she battered the feeling down. "It's not bleeding, though."

"It's not serious. It just hurts like hell." He gave her a crooked grin. "I'll live. And since the dog isn't going to move, why don't I just drive you over to see Fielding?"

She should have hesitated. Warning bells were ringing wildly, reminding her that she'd be a fool to get involved with another man. But, hey, she told herself, she was already involved. It was too late. What harm could another few minutes' exposure do?

"Thanks," she told him. "I appreciate it. But what about Rover?"

"I'm just going to leave him," said Blaise. "I sure

don't want to report him as a stray. Cal is going broke on all these fines and kennel fees."

"Poor guy. He got a real handful with this dog."

"All his dogs have been a real handful. That seems to be the effect Cal has on 'em."

"Maybe we'd better tell him where Rover is."

Blaise nodded. "We can do that. You're a real thoughtful lady, Jill."

She was still blushing pleasantly when they pulled away in his police cruiser.

Behind them they left her car at an odd angle, the downed mailbox, and Rover, who crawled out from beneath the Toyota to stare after them, a wide, pleased-as-punch grin on his face.

Cal answered his door and took one look at Blaise before he started shaking his head. "That dog," he said sorrowfully. "That dadburn dog. He's gonna put me in the poorhouse . . ."

"No," Blaise said quickly. "Rover hasn't been picked up again. "I just wanted to tell you he was over by my place, though. When we left, he was sitting under a car and wasn't in any hurry to come out."

Cal nodded as if he'd heard it all before. "He's up to something. Mark my words, that dadgum dog is up to something."

Blaise cracked a smile. "It wouldn't surprise me, Cal. Anyway, I just wanted you to know where he is. Jill McAllister over there in my car was concerned about that."

Cal nodded in Jillie's direction. "She sure is a fine-looking woman, Chief. When you going to do something about that?"

Blaise didn't even try to answer.

When Blaise got back in the car, he started them

slowly toward the north end of the island. "Actually," he said, "I came looking for you."

"You did?" Her heart skipped a hopeful beat.

"Yeah. My friend the private detective called a little while ago."

She felt crestfallen that his reason for coming to find her hadn't been that he wanted to see her, but she curbed the feeling. "Did he find out something?"

"Do you know any reason a law firm in Waukegan, Illinois, should be looking for you?"

Surprise filled her. "I grew up in Waukegan, but . . . no, I can't imagine any reason anybody'd be looking for me there. I mean, some of my foster parents are still there, I guess, and I suppose one of them could be looking for me. I can't imagine why."

"Did you keep in touch with any of them after you left?"

"No." She hesitated, then decided to be truthful, much as it hurt. "Frankly, I never got the feeling any of them cared if they ever saw me again. I wasn't an easy child."

"Why do I have no trouble believing that?" But the warm smile he suddenly gave her took the sting from his words. "But maybe, just maybe, one of them saw past the mouth and the defenses, Jill. It's not as hard as you might think."

She didn't know how to take that, so she didn't reply.

"Anyway," he said, "I have the firm's name and number. After you talk to Fielding, I think you should call and find out what they want."

"Absolutely. I'm really curious."

"So am I. Can I listen in?"

"Sure." She shrugged as if it didn't matter, but it seemed very important that he wanted to know. As if he might care just a little about her. Besides, it seemed as if he was no longer trying to avoid her.

She wanted that to be true more than she could say.

The hotel was at the far end of the barrier island from Cal's place, but it took only a few minutes to get there. Blaise pulled into a no-parking zone without apology and turned off the ignition.

"I'll go in with you," he said.

"That's really not necessary. I can deal with this myself."

He held up a hand. "Don't get all prickly with me. You don't *want* to deal with this all by yourself because Fielding has been accused of stalking you, and you're the primary witness. In the first place, you don't want to leave yourself open to a countercharge by Fielding that *you're* stalking *him*."

Jillie grimaced. "God, what a thought. As if I would."

"That might not be so obvious to other people. Then, you have to think about him. This could look really bad for him."

"Why? I certainly won't claim he was stalking me."

"But other people could claim it, and use your meeting as evidence."

Jillie let her head fall back against the headrest. "Do people really do stuff like that?"

"Oh, yeah. Take it from a cop. Anyway, if I'm there, it'll keep you both out of trouble."

They went up to Fielding's room without calling first. It just seemed sensible to Jillie. After all, he'd hung up the phone on her, and there was no guarantee he'd open the door to them if he knew they were coming.

Blaise rapped on the door, the heavy-handed pounding that announced to anyone with experience that a law officer stood on the other side. Jillie half expected that Fielding would hear it and not answer.

She was wrong. He opened the door almost immediately. "What do you want?" he asked with a scowl, when he saw Blaise.

"Jill wants to talk to you."

Fielding turned and saw her. His eyes grew huge in his face and he started to slam the door. "No! I can't talk to you!"

"I'm here," Blaise said. "I'll keep it on the up and up."

"Right," Fielding said bitterly, little more than an eye and his nose showing. "You're her *boyfriend*."

"I'm also the chief of police. Come on, just hear her out."

"I've heard all I want to hear!"

"Fielding," Jillie said desperately, "I want to have the prosecutor drop the charges."

"Oh, yeah, right. I'm supposed to believe the two of you are here on a mission of mercy? Hey, that guy's the cop who arrested me in the first place!" He slammed the door.

Jillie leaned her ear against it, knocking. "Fielding? Fielding, I promise you, I'm going to ask them to drop the charges. A lawyer I talked to this morning says they will, since I'm the only witness against you. Fielding?"

Nearly a full minute passed, then Fielding flung open the door, causing Jillie nearly to fall. Blaise caught her elbow and steadied her.

"What do you want?" Fielding demanded suspiciously.

"I told you what I want."

"No, you told me you'll ask them to drop charges. You didn't tell me what you want in return."

"Just go home, Fielding. That's all I want. Just you

and Harriet go home and stay away from me from now on. Just leave me alone."

She expected him to look relieved. Instead, his face darkened even more.

"I can't," he said.

Jillie felt her jaw drop. "Why not? Why can't you just leave me alone? For God's sake, Fielding, you don't love me now—if you ever did. You don't really want me back."

"That doesn't have anything to do with it."

"Then what does?"

Fielding shook his head. "I can't tell you."

Jillie stepped toward him, her hands curling into fists. "You better tell me, or I'll—"

"Uh-uh-uh," Blaise interrupted. "No threats."

Jillie paused, then nodded. "Sorry. It's just that I'm so fed up, Fielding!"

"You think *you're* fed up? How do you think *I* feel?" Fielding put his hands on his hips. "Do you really think I *want* to be stuck in this two-bit backwater tourist trap? Huh? If I wanted to spend time in the tropics I'd pick Bermuda, or Saint Croix. Why on *earth* would I come to this place?"

Before Jillie could reply, he plunged on.

"Because *you're* here," he said. "Beats me why the hell you want to settle here—jeez, even Fort Lauderdale is better—but you're here, and so am I. And you're going to marry me again whether you like it or not!"

"Why? Just tell me why!"

Fielding shook his head. "No," he said, swinging the door shut. "I won't tell you. Get out of here. What's the worst they can do to me? Five years in prison? I can take it."

He closed the door, and the two of them heard the

deadbolt being thrown. Blaise looked at Jillie, expecting her to be upset or angry, but instead she looked thoughtful.

"The law firm," she said suddenly. "I'll bet it has something to do with that law firm! Come on, I've got to get to a phone."

Eighteen

Blaise took Jillie straight home. Her car was sitting precisely where she'd left it, but Rover was nowhere in sight.

"I guess he decamped," Blaise remarked humorously. "Mission accomplished."

Jillie looked at him. "What mission?"

He shook his head, grinning. "You'd never believe me. Am I invited in or do you want me to vanish into the woodwork?"

"No!" The thought of his leaving put butterflies in her stomach and made it sink. "No, come in. Please." *And please don't ever go away.* Although he would. Everyone she cared about went away.

He sat on one end of the couch while she sat on the other and called Barrett, Winslow and Klein, in Waukegan.

Three minutes later she had passed three secretaries and had reached Bruce Klein.

"This is Jillian MacAllister Wainwright?" he asked.

"Yes. Except that I've gone back to my maiden name."

"And that is?"

"Jillian Ruth MacAllister."

"Mm. Would you mind telling me your birthdate? I need to verify a few things before we discuss the matter at hand."

She told him, and answered further questions about the names of her parents, when they had died, and the names of her succession of foster parents.

"Well," he said. "I understood from your husband that you were out of the country and wouldn't be in touch for at least another month."

"My *what*?"

"Fielding Wainwright."

"When did you talk to him?"

"Oh, it was—let me see—approximately five weeks ago. Is that a problem, Ms. MacAllister? I mean, we verified your marriage. He sent us a copy of your marriage certificate."

Jillie considered letting the lawyer have it, but suddenly realized that might be counterproductive. Holding onto her temper, she said, "What have you been discussing with him?"

"Why, your inheritance, of course."

"My what?" Jillie felt stunned.

Klein hesitated. "Um . . . I gather he hasn't mentioned it to you yet?"

"Mr. Klein, Fielding hasn't told me a damn thing about you. It was a private detective who found out you were looking for me."

"Oh." There was a long silence, and Jillie wondered just how Klein was piecing this information together. It probably wasn't a pretty picture. "I don't understand it, Ms. McAllister. I was under the impression he was going to tell you about this as soon as you returned from Nepal."

"Nepal?" Jillie felt as if she had suddenly become caught up in some weird sort of dream. "I was never in Nepal. I moved to Florida."

"Oh, dear, dear, dear! This doesn't sound good at all."

"No," Jillie said sharply, "it doesn't. Now, suppose you tell me what it is you told Fielding."

"Well, as I was saying, you have an inheritance. A rather significant inheritance."

"But from whom? I don't have any family."

"Well, actually, you do. Or you did. Are you sitting down, Ms. McAllister?"

"Yes." Jillie's mind was whirling, feeling as if she was trying to absorb too much too fast.

"Well, your mother had a brother, James McAllister. At the time your parents were killed, James was little more than a boy himself. He was—well, to put it kindly, he was a beach bum. Out in California, living the high life, you see. Not at all suitable to be the guardian of a child."

Jillie felt a pang. "No, I guess not." But better, surely, than a succession of foster parents who didn't really give a damn? How many times had she felt as if she was being clothed and sheltered only because the state paid a stipend to the foster home? And yet, to be fair, there had been a few who'd made her feel like more than a stranger they just happened to be taking care of temporarily. "I—what was he like?"

"A fun-loving sort, from all reports. At least, back then. But later—" Again Klein hesitated. "Please understand, Ms. McAllister, I'm going by what he wrote in his will."

"Okay."

"About the time you were sixteen, Mr. McAllister

had a—well, he describes it as a near-death experience. It apparently changed his view on life."

"I imagine so."

Klein gave a smothered chuckle. "Basically, he nearly got himself killed in a surfing accident. It shook him up badly, so he returned to Waukegan, where he took a job selling pleasure boats at a large local dealership. He used the money from that and some previously unsuspected talent to open a software firm. His company eventually produced one of the most popular and most widely sold educational programs in the country. In fact, I can safely say the company owns the largest market share of software sold to schools for education and tutoring."

"That's wonderful."

"It certainly is for you, since he left it all to you."

Astonishment kept Jillie mute. Surely this was happening to someone else?

"There is no other family, so of course the will won't be contested. There are a number of outstanding offers from other companies for the firm, any of which could make you comfortably well off for life. Mr. Wainwright thought you would prefer to retain ownership, however, and given his business track record, that might be wise. Wainwright Industries could conceivably make this firm worth five times as much in as many years."

And now the entire picture was incredibly clear to Jillian. Fielding had always wanted to get into high tech, and he had seen his chance. Just add little Jillie's company to his conglomerate and watch it grow. She wanted to strangle him.

"Mr. Klein," she said succinctly, "Fielding Wainwright and I have been divorced for the last six months. Don't tell me you've given him any access to this company."

A shocked silence greeted her words. "This is terrible," Klein said finally. "Terrible. He sent us your marriage certificate."

"I'll send you the divorce papers. Just don't tell me that man has gotten his hands on that company."

"No . . . no! Certainly not! The property was bequeathed to you, and it won't be transferred to anyone else. Most assuredly not! But I'm . . . flabbergasted."

"I'm not. You just made some things very clear to me, and answered a whole bunch of questions. I'll get back in touch with you, but first I'm going to deal with that snake Wainwright."

"Don't do anything—rash."

"I wouldn't dream of it." Jillian hung up and looked at Blaise. "I own a software company in Waukegan. An uncle I didn't know I had left it to me."

"Oh." He stared at her, and his expression wasn't pleased. "Does this mean . . . you're going to leave Paradise Beach?"

"Of course not! I love it here. The lawyer said there are buyers, so I'll probably sell it. But I am sure as hell going to deal with Fielding Wainwright once and for all."

She picked up the phone again and dialed the hotel. When Fielding came on the line, she spoke rapidly.

"Fielding, don't you dare hang up on me. If you do, you're going to have bigger legal problems than you ever dreamed of."

"You're stalking me, Jillian."

"No, I am not stalking you. But you'd better listen. I just talked to Bruce Klein at Barrett, Winslow and Klein in Waukegan. Does that ring bell?"

Fielding made a muffled sound.

"I just found out what you've been up to, Fielding. You and Harriet. And I am *furious*. Furious enough to press these stalking charges to the limit."

Fielding squawked.

"Shut up and listen. I have a better plan. I've decided I'll tell the prosecutor to drop the charges. And I won't press any other charges for your duplicity in the matter of my inheritance—and I am sure there are plenty of things you could be charged with, Fielding, I have no doubt of it. But I'm suddenly feeling magnanimous. You and your mother get your butts out of this town within twenty-four hours after I get the charges dropped, and never, ever come within sight or sound of me again, and I won't run you through the wringer. Got it?"

"Jillie—"

"Don't argue. Just promise me you'll be gone within twenty-four hours, and we'll act like this never happened."

"I promise. Shit. I didn't want that stupid company, anyway!" And he slammed down the phone.

Jillie looked at Blaise and grinned.

"Well," she told him, "that was easy. Fielding ought to be gone pretty soon, if I can just get the charges against him dropped."

"Let's talk to the state attorney in the morning. I'll help you convince him. My experience of these things is he'll be happy to get the case off his desk. Especially when he hears you won't testify. Fielding will be free to leave by nightfall, if I have anything to say about it."

"The sooner the better," Jill agreed. "I'll be glad to see the last of him."

And then an awkward silence fell. Jill didn't know exactly where to look. She felt embarrassed and uneasy all at once, uncertain how Blaise must be feeling, especially since their rather uncomfortable separation

Thursday night. He probably just wanted to get out of here as fast as he could.

Her heart squeezed at the thought, but she didn't know what she could do about it. Suddenly desperate for something, anything, that would bridge this awkwardness, she stood up. "I'd better let Corky out of her cage."

"Oh, did you get her a cage?" He was suddenly there, following her into the kitchen where she had placed the cage.

"Kinda big, isn't it?" he remarked, when he saw the size of the gray pet carrier behind the table.

"Well, I figure she'll probably grow into it. The pet shop owner looked at her feet and said she's going to be about fifty pounds."

"That's a safe bet given her parentage. Yeah, she'll grow into it. It's just that she's so small now."

The puppy tumbled out of the carrier in a great rush and slid across the tile until she came to rest against Blaise's shoe. There she went to work happily sniffing all the new odors.

Jillie found herself smiling as she watched. "Are you still going to get a puppy from Doc?"

Blaise nodded. "He's holding one for me. I just need to get around to picking it up." He hesitated, looking from Jillie to the pup. "I don't know, though. How do you feel about more than one dog in a household?"

"But you don't have one right now, do you?"

"No." There was a funny smile around his lips and eyes as he continued. "I was just asking in a general sort of way. Generally, how do you feel about it?"

Her heart skipped into a quicker rhythm, though she didn't know why. "If there's room, I don't see why it would be a problem."

"Do you think my place is big enough?"

"For two dogs? Sure. Heck, you probably even have room for a cat." She meant it to be a humorous comment, but it came out sounding like something else.

"Would you *like* a cat?" he asked immediately.

"Me?" Now her heart was hammering hard. What was he saying?

"I could handle a cat," he continued, looking rather intently at her. "As long as it could get along with the dogs."

"Um . . . yes . . ."

A little smile tugged at the corners of his mouth. "I'd even kind of like a hedgehog, but I hear they need an awful lot of attention. That might not mix real well with people who work all the time. Police work is really time consuming, and of course, with you owning your own business . . ." He shrugged a shoulder. "The dogs would keep each other company, and the cat wouldn't care, but I think a hedgehog would be lonely."

All of a sudden she couldn't stand it anymore. "What are you trying to say?"

He hesitated just long enough to make her heart skip a beat and then gallop even faster. This was no casual conversation; it couldn't be. People didn't talk this way when they were just being casual.

"Well . . ." He looked down at her and pursed his lips. "I'm actually trying to get serious here."

"Serious about what?"

"Us."

"Us?"

"Us."

"Oh." Now her heart was beating so hard it was a roaring in her ears. She ought to be running from this, trying to hide from any possibility of a relationship with a man. Fielding had taught her how awful it could be. Surely she didn't expect better now?

But she did. Somewhere deep inside the optimist in her hadn't given up. Somewhere deep inside she believed that a man could be honorable and faithful. Surely, somewhere in the entire world, there had to be an honest man?

A vision of an old man with an oil lamp suddenly sprang to her mind. "Diogenes never found an honest man."

Looking momentarily confused, Blaise hesitated again, then comprehension dawned. "That's because he never found me."

Jillie drew a deep breath, hardly daring to hope.

"Look, I know I stayed away from you for the last couple of days, but that was because I needed to do some serious thinking."

The reminder of his absence stung her a little. "Thinking about what?"

"About *us*. Damn it, Jillian, it was so crystal clear to me Thursday night that I couldn't keep our relationship casual without hurting you."

She didn't think she liked the sound of this.

"I mean, what with your background and all, you need someone who is prepared to commit to you."

Now she *knew* she didn't like the sound of this. "Blaise . . ." Somehow she had to stop him from saying that he couldn't be the one, from explaining why it was that she just wasn't for him. She'd had too many blows in the last few years to be able to brush it off. Besides, she was crazy about him.

"I'll be perfectly frank," he said, as if she hadn't spoken. "Initially, you were a sex object. I mean—"

A startled laugh escaped her. "A *what*?"

"A sex object." He grinned. "Well, what do you expect? All that beautiful strawberry blond hair is eye-catching enough, but then . . . oh, then, sweetie, there are your legs. The first time I saw you in shorts, I was lost. In fact, I almost crashed my car."

"Really?" Deep down she felt tickled. Nobody had ever thought of her as a sex object before.

"Really. I drooled. I wanted you. And that's all that was on my mind, initially."

It was hard to be crushed by that information, even when she knew he was about to tell her that was all she would ever be. After Fielding, her ego sorely needed someone to think she was sexy.

"But Thursday night I realized that wasn't fair to you. It wouldn't be right to keep on seeing you unless I was serious. The 'let's just keep dating and see what happens' approach was apt to hurt you, especially since we'd become sexually involved. I mean . . . everyone in your life has abandoned you, Jill. I didn't want to be another one who did that to you."

She nodded, touched by his concern. It would have gratified her to be able to deny it, but that would have been untruthful. Rightly or wrongly, she had never had a casual relationship of any kind. Once she got past her walls enough to care, she cared intensely and could be hurt too easily. Oh, hell, she could be hurt too easily by a total stranger. Who was she kidding? Hypersensitivity was her middle name.

"I'm sorry," she said stiffly. "I know I'm difficult."

"Did I say that? I don't recall it," he interrupted. "No, what I recall saying is that I suddenly realized just how grievously I could wound you if I kept seeing you without being prepared to fully commit to you. Now that would be true of anybody, if I'm being honest about it. Anybody. But with you . . . I felt the hurt would be even worse. And I honestly didn't want to do that to you. Most especially not to you."

Her throat was beginning to feel tight, and tears were prickling at the backs of her eyes. This was, she found herself thinking, going to be the kindest rejection anyone had ever been given.

"Aw, Jeez, Jill, don't cry."

Suddenly his arms were around her and she found herself snuggled up to his shoulder while he held her tightly. "I'm not ... crying ..." But she could barely squeeze the words out past the noose that seemed to have wrapped around her throat. All of a sudden she knew she would die if Blaise turned and walked away.

"Jill ... Jill ... oh, sweetheart, I'm making a big mess out of this. I'm trying to tell you that I love you. All I want is to continue seeing you in the hopes that eventually you'll come to love me, too."

She could hardly believe her ears, hardly dare to believe it could be possible. Slowly she tipped her head up and looked at him. "You're kidding, right?"

For an instant he looked nonplussed. Then a huge laugh escaped him. "So tell me, Ms. McAllister, is 'Difficult' your middle name? No, I'm not kidding. I wouldn't kid about something like this!"

He bent to scoop her up and carried her to the bedroom, where he tumbled them down amid the tangled vines and horrendously huge hibiscus.

"I think better lying down," he told her, a wicked gleam in his eye.

Somehow she didn't think thinking was on his mind, not when he insisted on kissing the side of her neck until shivers ran through her entire body and her arms twined of their own accord around him.

"I love it when you shiver like this," he told her huskily, as he began tugging her shirt over her head. "I love it when you sigh, and whimper, and moan, and do all those other sexy little things."

"So I *am* just a sex object?" she asked on a gasp.

"Not just. Never just. I also like your cantankerousness, and I love the way you sometimes look shocked when you realize what you just blurted out. But I fell in love with you when you brought Corky home from Doc's."

He tugged her shirt all the way off, then paused, propped above her on one elbow. "Jill? I really can't put it into words. It just *is*. I love you. I realize you don't feel the same way yet. How could you, with all that's been going on in your life? But . . . will you give me a chance?"

It amazed her that he was asking such an asinine question. Wasn't her answer written all over her face?

"Don't be a jerk, Blaise. I already love you and you damn well know it."

He stared at her in astonishment for a heartbeat or two, then dissolved into a gale of laughter.

"What's so funny?" she demanded.

"Nothing. Not a damn thing. Cripes." He wiped the corners of his eyes with the back of his hand and flopped back onto the bed. "So does this mean rug rats and the whole nine yards?"

"That depends on which nine yards you're talking about."

He turned on his side and smiled at her with so much tenderness that she thought her heart was going to burst. "I mean marriage. Kids. Till death do us part."

All of a sudden she couldn't get her breath. Again? Was she willing to shoot for that again? After all that had happened?

But it was as if there wasn't another answer in the whole universe. Blaise made her heart sing, and without him life would be bleak.

"Yes," she said.

She had found her family.

Epilogue

"Oh, hush, Ted. It all worked out," Mary told her beau sternly.

They sat together on the deck at the beach bar, sipping frozen concoctions that came with parasols and slices of pineapple. The sun was settling in the west, almost ready to touch the Gulf. The water this evening looked spangled in light blue and dark blue, almost like a sea of glittering sequins.

"I still don't think you should have let everyone believe Wainwright was responsible for that graffiti. We should have owned up and taken our licks."

"I couldn't agree more," Hadley Philpott said, as he joined them with his own drink.

"Both of you, stop it. If we start telling everyone what we do, the Hole in the Seawall Gang will become useless. Besides, you're getting all bent about nothing. The charges against the man were dropped for lack of evidence, so no harm was done."

"Except to Jillie, who had both her home and her business vandalized," Hadley said sternly.

As one, they all looked over toward a group of palm trees where Jillie and Blaise, dressed in white, were getting their pictures taken against the sunset. The rest of the wedding party was busy making themselves at home on the deck of the beach bar where the reception was going to be held. The a capella group was singing romantic numbers in the background. Rainbow Moonglow, who had earlier that day predicted that the Corrigans would be parents by this time next year, was giving free readings to all the guests.

"*All's well that ends well*," Mary said. "Those two couldn't be happier, and it wouldn't have happened without us."

"Actually," said the Reverend Archer, who had just joined them, "I think it was the dog."

"The dog?"

He nodded, looking humorous. "Rover. He brought those two together. Did they tell you how many times the dog caused them to meet?" He nodded, rocking back on his heels. "The Lord works in mysterious ways."

"But through a dog?" Mary didn't look as if she appreciated that.

At that moment three dogs joined Blaise and Jillie on the beach. One was Corky, much larger at five months, and another was Corky's sister, Dixie. Between them pranced Rover, looking as proud as punch. The dogs apparently wanted to be in the photos, too.

Ted sighed and looked at the love of his life. "That ought to be us, Mary."

She tossed her head in a girlish way and laughed.

"There's always time," she answered. "Maybe Rover will take a hand."

Hadley rolled his eyes. "Maybe the Hole in the Seawall Gang should take a hand. By the way, who's going to be our new member? You said you'd decided who would replace George Appleby."

"Not me," Ted said swiftly. "I don't want any part of your hijinks."

Mary shook her head. "Not you, Ted. Of course not you. You're too staid, which is why I haven't married you."

"You have a different reason every time the subject comes up."

Mary grinned. "I have to keep you guessing."

"But what about our new member?" Hadley asked impatiently. "What have you decided?"

Mary tossed her head again and looked over at the newlywed couple, who were now laughing and running around with the dogs. "I have to keep you guessing, too," she said.

Then her laughter joined the laughter of the Corrigans, just as the sun set in a blaze of vermilion glory.

Discover Contemporary Romances at Their Sizzling Hot Best from Avon Books

THREE KISSES *by Cait London*
80037-3/$5.99 US/$7.99 Can

MY MAN PENDLETON *by Elizabeth Bevarly*
80019-5/$5.99 US/$7.99 Can

ABSOLUTE TROUBLE *by Michelle Jerott*
80102-7/$5.99 US/$7.99 Can

ANNIE'S WILD RIDE *by Alina Adams*
79472-1/$5.99 US/$7.99 Can

SIMPLY IRRESISTIBLE *by Rachel Gibson*
79007-6/$5.99 US/$7.99 Can

LETTING LOOSE *by Sue Civil-Brown*
72775-7/$5.99 US/$7.99 Can

IF WISHES WERE HORSES *by Curtiss Ann Matlock*
79344-X/$5.99 US/$7.99 Can

IF I CAN'T HAVE YOU *by Patti Berg*
79554-X/$5.99 US/$7.99 Can

We've got love on our minds at
http://www.AvonBooks.com

Vote for your favorite hero in
"HE'S THE ONE."

Take a romance trivia quiz, or just
"GET A LITTLE LOVE."

Look up today's date in
romantic history in "DATEBOOK."

Subscribe to our monthly e-mail
<u>newsletter</u> for all the buzz on
upcoming romances.

Browse through our list of new
and upcoming titles and read
chapter excerpts.